BEAUTIFUL LORELEI

"Oh no, my beautiful Lorelei. You will not get away so easily. Not this time. I shall not let you vanish."

For a moment she stared, mesmerized, into firelit eyes. Then: "None of this is real," he muttered thickly and dragged her down to him.

His mouth closing savagely over hers hurt her, violating the sweet tenderness of her lips. Frightened by his ruthless assault on her innocence, Sabra fought to break away. But with a strength intensified by delirium and unbridled lust, he yanked her back again.

His fingers entangled in her long hair as he forced her to submit to his cruel kiss, to his hand caressing the soft vulnerability of her flesh.

Sabra writhed in his grasp, helpless against the sudden leap of desire. Never had she known that she could burn with need so terrible she feared she must perish from it. His kisses breathed sweet fire into her veins, aroused a conflagration in her secret depths.

Mindlessly she murmured his name over and over as her need grew to an unquenchable ache . . .

Sea Witch

SARA BLAYNE

ZEBRA BOOKS
KENSINGTON PUBLISHING CORP.

ZEBRA BOOKS

are published by

Kensington Publishing Corp.
475 Park Avenue South
New York, NY 10016

First printing: December, 1988

Printed in the United States of America

To Caleb and Katey, who have been so patient while Mamma wrote her book. And to Steve, whose help at home made this all possible.

Special thanks to Joe Van B., whose technical advice on sailing proved invaluable.

Chapter 1

Having come at last to the conclusion that the incessant drum tattoo, which had been nagging at her for some time, was in fact an importunate assault on her door, Sabra Tyree came reluctantly awake and blinked sleepy green eyes at the clock on the mantle. "Good God," she groaned, burying herself under the bedclothes. It was only three hours since she had dragged herself up the stairs to her room and, desiring only to lose herself in oblivion, had flung off her clothing and fallen into bed, clad solely in her silk chemise and knee length drawers. Remorselessly she assigned her irksome caller to perdition, and still the racket continued.

"Miss Sabra? Miss Sabra, is you dead in there?" pursued her relentlessly beneath the eiderdown comforter, followed by the impatient rattling of the latch. "You unlocks this door right now, Miss Sabra, before I has Jubal come an' knock it down."

"Oh, go *away*, Phoebe!" she yelled, emerging from her cozy nest of blankets just long enough to send a pillow flying against the inoffensive oak barrier. "I don't wish to be disturbed."

In the abrupt silence that ensued, Sabra plopped hopefully down upon her single remaining pillow and closed her eyes against the brilliant shaft of sunlight streaming through the window. Vainly she tried as well to shut out the noises of the city already quickening to the business of a new day. The distant rumble of wagons lumbering over the cobblestone pavement of lower Broadway little more than a block away vied with the drunken lyricism of two Redcoats passing beneath her window. Doubtlessly they were making their way back to the barracks from the Holy Ground, she thought

7

ironically, for the unsavory quarters surrounding St. Paul's were the domain of New York's ladies of the evening and thus a favorite haunt of the king's soldiers. Then the injured tones of her maidservant chased away all such trivial considerations.

"Well, if that's what you wants, Miss Sabra, I surely wouldn't *dream* of disturbing you. What do *I* cares if you sees the gentleman who am come a-callin', even if he do say he have word from Mistuh Wesley? Ain't no skin off my nose. I'll jest go right down and tell him you doesn't want to be disturbed."

With a shriek Sabra cast aside the bedclothes and flew from the bed.

"Phoebe, don't you dare!" she cried, her fingers all thumbs as she struggled to turn the key in the lock. Then at last the door was open to reveal the Negro maidservant, waiting with arms folded across her generous bosom and a self-satisfied smile on the round, comely face. "Quick, tell me who he is. Does he come from the frigate *Warren?* How is it that he can move through the British lines? Phoebe, for God's sake, don't just stand there. Come in and help me dress. I must see this gentleman at once."

"Now, now, Miss Sabra," Phoebe remonstrated, drawing her mistress into the room and closing the door firmly behind her, "there's no sense in gettin' all het up. I put the gentleman in the parlor and set him to samplin' one of my mince-meat pies. He'll be occupied for a spell, don't you worry none."

"But who is he? He must have given you his name," Sabra insisted, in a quake of impatience. But the old servant of long standing was obviously in no hurry to answer. Inwardly Sabra groaned as Phoebe propped her hands on plump hips and gazed about her in scandalized reproach.

"Laws a mercy, Miss Sabra, what has you done to this room? I knows I taught you better than to throw good clothes down." Then suddenly the keen brown eyes sharpened to shrewd points as they came to rest on a curious anomaly among the welter of silk petticoats and satin gowns strewn with careless abandon about the chamber.

Silently Sabra cursed her heedlessness. Little wishing to

undergo the inevitable lecture from her dear, but over-inquisitive, former nanny, she had had every intention of concealing that bit of damning evidence along with the other things that had lain buried beneath her gowns in the bottom of her trunk. She had simply been too tired to think of everything, which was small consolation as she watched the old Negress stoop with a low grunt and pluck from the floor the man's *habit á la française,* complete with coat, waistcoat, and small clothes, done all in black. Rising then, Phoebe turned to gaze upon her mistress with an ominously cocked brow.

"Now, I *knows* you ain't had no man in your bed," she declared, peering at Sabra out of the tops of her eyes, "so maybe you'd like to tell old Phoebe what these be doin' here on the floor."

"They're mine," Sabra said boldly as she snatched them to her bosom, then, crossing haughtily to a walnut highboy, stuffed them in a drawer.

"I *knows that.* What I doesn't know is what you be doin' with 'em."

"And it's best that you don't know," snapped Sabra, coming about with eyes flashing dangerously and her chin up. "So for both our sakes, let's please just drop it."

Instantly the old nanny relented, her aspect filled with sympathetic understanding as she gazed sorrowfully at her fiery young mistress.

"Laws, chile, you think I doesn't know how hard it be for you with Mistuh Wesley gone an' you trapped here like a lamb among thieves?" she said. "But, honey, you ain't got no business doin' what I knows you be doin'. Sneakin' off for days an' weeks at a time on some pore excuse and comin' home lookin' wore to the bone. You was never at Mrs. Featherstone's for no houseparty, now was you. You doesn't have to say it. Her girl Jesse tole me you wasn't."

Sabra went suddenly still, the familiar clamp of fear clutching at her innards.

"So I didn't go to Mrs. Featherstone's," she shrugged, feigning an indifference she was far from feeling. "What of it? I've a right to change my mind, haven't I? But I suppose you and Jesse had a deal to say about it. Well, I won't have you gossiping about me, Phoebe, do you understand? It's bad enough that I have to tolerate the malicious slander of those fine, upstanding ladies whose husbands line their pockets with British sterling and then turn around and sell contraband to the outlying colonies. Damn them for the self-serving hypocrites that they are! Just what did you tell Jesse? That your mistress must be off on one of her questionable jaunts? That she makes a practice of disappearing for weeks at a time, and Lord only knows what she's about?"

"Now, you knows I ain't no fool, Miss Sabra," retorted the shrewd, old nanny, refusing to be baited. "Old Phoebe covered for you. But what if it'd been somebody else askin' after you? Like that army colonel or one of them navy men who be always swarmin' around you like bees about a fresh pot of honey?"

"Then you would do just as you did with Jesse," Sabra answered carelessly, though she felt sickened with herself. Good God, had she, in truth, sunk so low as to doubt those whose loyalty did not deserve to be questioned? It was only that she was tired, she told herself. And Phoebe *could* be such a dreadful nag at times. "You would make up some cock and bull story about how I was staying with friends in another part of the city," she continued, "or that I had departed to my father's estate on Long Island. You would think of something, I'm certain. But, meantime, you must try not to worry about me. I know what I'm doing, believe me."

Phoebe, however, was not so easily persuaded.

"You jest thinks you does, Miss Sabra," she said, slowly shaking her head. "But we both knows if Mistuh Wesley learn how you be takin' chances with yourself, ain't no way he gonna like it. You be playin' with fire, chile, and if you doesn't mend your ways, you is goin' to be burned."

At that, Sabra uttered a short little laugh and turned to find herself face to face with her own reflection in the looking glass. For the barest instant she paused, startled at the subtle signs of strain written on her face.

"You're wrong, Phoebe. I'm *not* a child anymore," she declared, but with a curious hint of sadness lurking in the sea-green depths of her eyes. Then she blinked and, tossing her head with something of defiance, moved away again. "Nor have I been for quite some time. Indeed, I am a woman of one and twenty and well able to manage my own affairs. So now if you can bring yourself to fetch me a pitcher of hot water, I should be very grateful. I have a visitor waiting below, in case you had forgotten."

"Whatever you says, Miss Sabra," returned the Negress in tight-lipped resignation. "I reckon you has to learn things for your own self. Don't do no good talkin' when a body jest won't listen."

Still shaking her head, Phoebe sighed and strode heavily from the room. Laws, what was to become of the chile? she pondered as she made her way down the stairs to the kitchen to carry out her mistress's orders.

Left to herself at last, Sabra felt the hard knot in the pit of her stomach slowly give way, and with it, the false spurt of energy that had sent her flying from her bed moments earlier. Phoebe was right about one thing: She felt worn to the nub after her six weeks from home, and she would have liked nothing better than to sleep around the clock. But the game she played was too important for her to give in now to fatigue. That very day she must begin the accustomed round of morning calls in order to catch up on the latest gossip and at the same time let it be known that she was back in circulation again. Then the invitations would start to roll in and she would have to make her appearances as if nothing had happened. Doubtless she should plan a ball for the middle of next month as well and, of course, the usual suppers and smaller entertainments for which she had become renowned among the ruling elite of the occupied city. A "turtle feast" in the garden would not be amiss. The young naval officers particularly enjoyed those "quaint" gatherings peculiar to New Yorkers, and if lobster or crab could not be found for the al fresco supper, she would have Jubal roast a pig over an open pit. A pity the house on the East River had been commandeered by the Redcoats. It was so much more pleasant this time of year on the outskirts of the city.

Damn! she thought, suddenly flinging herself down on the

11

bed. She was sick of such endless details and, if she were to be perfectly honest with herself, she was sick of her assumed role as New York's reigning beauty as well.

How ironic that it had taken a war to force Elizabeth Tyree's rebellious offspring into the very role for which she had sought to prepare her, mused Sabra wryly. Still, she could only be grateful that her mother had never lived to see the distinction paid her daughter, not only as a leading New York hostess, but as one who was much sought after as well, both for her gracious accomplishments and her undeniably breathtaking beauty.

And, indeed, at one and twenty, Sabra Tyree possessed the same sea-green eyes and glorious mass of red-gold hair, which, at seventeen, had crowned her youthful fire and innocence. Only now her willowy height and girlish slenderness had ripened into soft, alluring curves and a woman's graceful loveliness. While the deceptively cool, green eyes, luxuriously framed in thick, dusky lashes, concealed a strong will and a fiercely independent spirit, there was that about the full lips, enticingly pursed over a slight overbite, that seemed to promise a fiery depth of passion. The combination of a keen intelligence and a penetrating wit, in addition to her other attributes, rendered her particularly well suited to the dangerous roles she played, and yet peculiarly vulnerable as well, if she had only known it.

Sabra had never cared for subterfuge and, what was more, she was finding it harder and harder to play the part of the infinitely alluring, but ever unattainable, Sabra Tyree, to whom men must be irresistibly drawn, like moths to the candle flame. Beneath their fine clothes and powdered wigs, most were pompous fools or greedy, drunken louts — harmless enough, and useful to her on occasion. But there were others who made her skin crawl. They were the ones who desired her as some rare and lovely thing to be possessed and used. Still, she had never been deluded into thinking that her allure would have lasted beyond the discovery that she could either be intimidated or won. She was safe with them only so long as she kept them at a distance. These were the profiteers who took advantage of the sufferings of others to fatten their purses and whose secret dealings touched every aspect of the war. She despised them all with every fiber of her being and felt neither regret nor remorse for exploiting their greed to her own purposes.

No, it was the remaining few who worked upon her conscience, the handful of brave, unassuming men who were there out of loyalty to king and country. They were drawn to her out of loneliness and out of the mistaken belief that she was like the women and young girls they had left at home. How she detested herself for wooing them with sweet smiles and ready sympathy! They talked so freely, so trustingly, and even as she listened, storing up every useful tidbit of information for future reference, she saw in each some semblance of the gallant young men, the sons of her father's former acquaintances, who had befriended and courted her long ago in England and whom she now was betraying.

But she must not think of that, she told herself. What she had done, she had done for Wesley, and for her country. And she must go on doing it for them. She would simply try to take things one step at a time, and right now she must see to the gentleman caller who claimed to have news of Wesley, she reminded herself.

Some little time later, Sabra, attired simply, but becomingly, in a yellow silk caraco and skirt with a wide, pale blue flounce and matching edging, paused briefly on the parlor threshold to view her visitor within.

The middle-aged gentleman stood with his shoulder turned toward her, the other arm propped on the carved oak mantle as he gazed with apparent preoccupation at a Dutch fleet tapestry panel screen ranged next to the fireplace. Not above average height, he was yet sturdily built, his fingers thickened by physical labor—a farmer or a fisherman, perhaps, for his face and the backs of his hands were weathered to a deep bronze. How odd that she had not guessed he would be one of the Society of Friends, she thought, taking in at a glance the plain cut of her visitor's attire and the Holland hat set uncompromisingly on lightish hair beginning to show gray. Naturally, as an avowed neutral, he would be allowed the freedom to come and go as he pleased.

Suddenly filled with a vague sense of foreboding, Sabra stepped quietly into the room.

"I have always been particularly fond of that piece," she remarked, smiling and graciously extending her hand as the gentleman turned to observe her with frank blue eyes. "Mr. Pattison, I believe? I am Miss Tyree. I was told you might have word for me of a friend of mine—Mr. Wesley Locke?"

"I do, indeed, mistress," he answered, his expression grave, but kind, "though perhaps before I begin, it were better if we sat down."

"Why, yes, of course, by all means I pray you will be seated," she said and gestured toward a walnut sofa facing the fireplace and bounded on either side by matching tapestry armchairs turned partially to face one another.

It was to be ill-tidings then, she thought as she settled, outwardly composed, on the sofa and gazed expectantly across at her visitor perched, rather uneasily it seemed, on the edge of one of the chairs. Steeling herself for the worst, she smiled and said calmly, "I should be grateful, Mr. Pattison, if you would relate what you have to say without round-aboutation. You see, I have known Mr. Locke since childhood, and though—circumstances—have made it impossible for us to continue our acquaintanceship, I have never ceased to entertain a great fondness for him. Thus to speak plainly would in the long run be kinder, I think."

"Aye, perhaps it would at that," nodded the gentleman, seeming to relax somewhat. "But first, I would have thee know that I have never met or spoken with thy friend, Mr. Locke. What I have to impart comes from a British naval officer, who wishes to remain unknown."

"Very well, Mr. Pattison, I understand—for the moment. Now if you would, I am most anxious to hear whatever you can tell me of Wesley—Mr. Locke. You see, I have had no word of him since the twenty-eighth of July. News reached us then that a Continental fleet was making for Fort Bragaduce in Penobscot Bay. His frigate, the *Warren*, was among them. The last I knew, the British under Commodore Collier were preparing to sail on the third of August, but because of my own absence from the city, I have heard nothing concerning the outcome of the affair."

"I fear, Miss Tyree, thy friend and his compatriots have fared badly in this venture," Pattison responded all too soberly. "Mr. Locke, it would seem, was taken prisoner the seventeenth of August and hath since been impressed into service aboard a British man-of-war. It was the captain of this vessel who desired this news to be imparted unto thee. He further wished me to assure thee that Mr. Locke presently abides in good health. That, Miss Tyree, is the extent of my knowledge concerning thy friend's welfare."

For the barest instant Sabra felt the room tilt.

"He's alive. Thank God," she breathed. Then, as she squeezed her eyes shut against the sudden dizzy sensation, she heard her name uttered as from a great distance and with an effort rallied her senses. Drawing a deep breath, she opened her eyes to Mr. Pattison bending solicitously over her.

"Mr. Pattison, forgive me," she murmured, a rueful smile trembling on her lips. "I-I had thought you were come to inform me of my half-brother's death. I fear I was momentarily overcome with relief at hearing rather more joyful tidings."

A look of sudden consternation swept the man's honest features.

"Indeed, Miss Tyree, I was given no inkling thy feelings were so closely involved in this matter!" he exclaimed. "If I broke the news ungently, I beg they forgiveness."

"No, of course you could not have known," she rejoined instantly, vexed with herself for having made such a slip. Under the circumstances she had deemed it wise never to reveal that her nearest living relative was a naval officer in the Continental Navy. Indeed, in her precarious position she could not afford the slightest suspicion that she was even remotely connected to anyone or anything involving the rebel forces. There was nothing for it now, however, but to redeem her mistake as best she could.

"I-I'm afraid, Mr. Pattison, that my brother and I do not see eye to eye on this matter of American independence. We

15

have neither met nor spoken with one another for over three years now." Suddenly she averted her face. "Still, he is my brother," she managed with only the slightest catch in her voice. "I have tried to follow his career as best I could, hoping that one day . . ." She did not finish, but pressed the back of her hand convulsively to her mouth and mutely shook her head as if she could not possibly go on.

For an instant the gentleman appeared to hesitate, discomfited no doubt at having been the one to occasion such heartfelt grief. But at last he straightened and gazed upon his hostess's bent head with kindly compassion.

"I think perhaps I should leave thee now," he quietly suggested. "But before I go, would thou have me summon thy servant to thee?"

"Oh, no," said Sabra, glancing quickly up. "I'm fine now, truly. Please, won't you stay a while longer?"

Again he hesitated, but compelled by the eloquence of her silent pleading, he relented.

"Well, perhaps — if I can be of some comfort . . ." Slowly he returned to his chair and deliberately seated himself. "In what manner may I serve thee?"

"There is so much I would know," said Sabra, one hand fluttering in the air as she appeared to gather her thoughts. "Can you, perhaps, tell me how Mr. Locke was taken?"

He shook his head.

"I fear I know very little about it. I have heard only that, while attempting to take the fort on Bragaduce, the rebels were driven up the bay by the British fleet. Most of them escaped overland to Boston after destroying their own vessels to keep them from falling to the British. Unfortunately for the rebels, however, two ships had already been taken at the outset. Apparently thy Mr. Locke was aboard one of these — a privateer, I believe, called the *Hampden.*"

"The *Hampden?*" Sabra exclaimed, considerably taken aback at this startling piece of information. "But Wesley's ship was the frigate *Warren.* I'm afraid I don't understand."

"I fear I cannot tell thee why it should be so," Mr. Pattison returned, shaking his head. "The *Warren,* however, was most certainly one of the vessels destroyed by the rebels."

Sabra glanced suddenly away, her throat working as the full implications of Wesley's plight began to sink in.

"I suppose it matters little in the long run," she said, unable to keep the bitterness from her voice. "He is nonetheless a prisoner and must suffer a prisoner's lot."

It was obvious, thought Sabra, having seen the pity in his eyes, that Mr. Pattison knew as well as she just how desperate *was* a prisoner's lot under the British. Thanks to the colonists' practice of releasing more prisoners than they kept, the exchange of American captives for British occurred but rarely. But even had there been sufficient numbers to warrant an exchange, the likelihood of such an event would have been no less remote. The king was hardly likely, after all, to suddenly relent in his steadfast refusal to acknowledge captured Americans as prisoners of war, for to have done so would have meant to recognize, as well, the independence and sovereignty of the rebelling colonies; with the result that all American prisoners were considered rebels and traitors and most often were treated with extreme harshness, even gross inhumanity. Indeed, it was possible that if he did not perish from the effects of such cruelty as was daily reported of the British jails and prison ships, Wesley might languish for years in captivity, either here or in England, without the slightest hope of release.

Oh, God, it did not bear thinking on! And yet she knew that she *must* think of it, and with greater deliberation than she had ever pondered anything before. Indeed, she must find out where Wesley was being held, and then somehow she must effect his escape. Knowing full well that what she proposed doing was a desperate, almost impossible undertaking, Sabra nearly gave into despair. Then suddenly she got hold of herself. If escape was all the hope Wesley had, then she would do everything in her power to bring it about, and the first order of business quite clearly was to uncover the identity of the mysterious naval officer in whose keeping he resided.

Sabra turned her huge, lovely eyes, shimmering with unshed tears, full on her unsuspecting visitor.

"It was good of you to come so far out of your way, sir," she

17

said with only the slightest tremor in her voice. "And yet there is one other to whom I must consider myself indebted for having commissioned your compliance in this matter. Can you not tell me to whom I owe this kindness, that I might express my gratitude in some small way?"

Mr. Pattison, though clearly not immune to the touching picture of fragile womanhood she presented, was yet one of a society who practiced what they professed to believe.

"I am truly sorry," he answered in honest sincerity, "but even if I knew his name—and I do not—I could not tell thee it. The gentleman was most insistent that thou should know nothing of him."

"I see," Sabra conceded. Obviously her task was not to be an easy one, she thought. Her Quaker visitor was an honorable man. In token of her acceptance, she demurely lowered those disturbing orbs. "Then perhaps you could tell me how he came to entrust you with this mission. Are you and he well acquainted?"

"I have had the pleasure of his company only once," replied the gentleman, settling more easily into his chair. "I own a small farm near East Hampton, where it is not unusual to encounter the officers of the king's navy. Their ships often lie at anchor off Gardiner's Island. One evening, no more than a week past, the captain of whom we speak came to my farm, having learned from someone in the village of my intent to deliver produce to Vlie Market. It being the custom of the Friends to deny no one hospitality, I invited him into my house to sup with my family. Though at first he expressed some reluctance, he did finally accept of my invitation, saying that it was some time since he had sat at table with gentlefolk and that he had no wish to cause my wife undue inconvenience."

The Quaker looked at her then with the barest hint of irony in his expression.

"This I judged to be most uncommon in such times when men are ordered by the king to quarter his soldiers and Hessian mercenaries," he said, "indeed, when a man's horses and wagons may be commandeered in the midst of harvest, and Negroes, whether freemen or slaves, taken by force from the fields to be sold elsewhere into slavery. Still, I believe him to have been sincere in his regard for our comfort, for I soon found him to be a man of discernment, who dealt kindly with my children and with fine respect to myself and my wife. After we had broken bread, we spoke at some length, and it was then that he made known his wish that I seek thee out. After much consideration, I agreed, and that is all that I can tell thee."

Having listened to this account with mounting interest, Sabra had to bite her tongue to keep from crying out in vexation at the abrupt curtailment of it. Thus far she had learned nothing that would help her identify her man.

"But surely you can describe him?" she said, hard put to conceal her impatience at her caller's unshakable integrity. "Was he tall or short? Stocky or slim? Was he old or young? Please, it would comfort me so to know something of the man in whose hands rests the fate of my — my friend."

Breathlessly Sabra waited as Pattison appeared to weigh conscience against a strongly sympathetic nature. Then her heart nearly faltered as he met her look squarely, his plain, honest face peculiarly compelling.

"He is young, I would say, though hardly a youth any longer, and he is both tall and well made; perhaps — but I am a poor judge of such things — even fair to look upon. His face was stern for his years, as if he had seen and known much of violence, and yet he did not strike me as being of nature violent. Despite the fact that he was soft-spoken and displayed a gentleness of manner unusual in one of his calling, I would hardly say he is a godly man. Indeed, I think that I would fear for his soul if he were my son, for I sensed the recklessness in him, the hardness. He has the temper to fight. And I think he must always do so with both fearlessness and resolution. Such a man is a dangerous enemy." He paused then, before pointedly adding, "And that is why, Miss Tyree, I believe thou may draw courage from my presence here today."

"I-I beg your pardon?" faltered Sabra. "I'm afraid I don't understand you."

"Truly, mistress? And yet does thou not think it passing

strange that this man has troubled himself for a sworn enemy of both king and country? One who must of necessity be *his* enemy, too?"

The curious intensity with which this last was pronounced was not lost upon Sabra. Suddenly her head came up and for a long moment their glances locked and held.

"You believe that I know him," she said wonderingly, but the man's face was closed to her at last. Deliberately he rose from the chair and stood for a moment looking down at her.

"I believe him to be a just man, Miss Tyree," he said quietly. "He will deal fairly with thy friend in so far as it is in his power to do so."

"And that is all you will tell me?" she queried, coming gracefully to her feet. Then, when he did not answer, she smiled and moved with him toward the door. "Very well, I understand. It will be comforting for me to know that Wesley is so near as Gardiner's Island and in the safekeeping of one who might very well be a friend. I thank you for coming, Mr. Pattison."

"I am glad if I have been of some comfort to thee," he answered, but Sabra did not fail to note that he seemed suddenly troubled.

"What is it, sir? Is there something more — something which you have perhaps only just recalled?"

For an instant he appeared to hesitate. Then he turned to her as if he had just come to some difficult decision.

"I never meant to give thee to believe that thy Mr. Locke was yet nearby," he said slowly. "The captain's ship was to make sail with the tide the very night that he came to me. They are many leagues from Gardiner's Island by now, on their way to the West Indies. I am truly sorry."

In a somewhat convulsive gesture, Sabra averted her face to hide the sudden fierce leap of excitement in her eyes. At last, the clue she had been hoping for, she thought, then quickly schooled her features to a semblance of stoic acceptance.

"How foolish of me not to have expected that such might be the case," she said, putting up a courageous front. The warmth, however, with which she once more expressed her gratitude to the gentleman for his many kindnesses and bade him Godspeed was not feigned, but issued from a sincere regard for the man's kind and gentle goodness. It was only then that she bethought herself of the risk involved if any of what had passed between them that morning should become known.

"Oh, and Mr. Pattison," she began, lifting troubled eyes to his, "if anyone should ask . . . If there should be some inquiry as to why you have come here today—"

"Thou need have no fear, mistress," he interrupted, grasping her hand firmly. "I shall speak of it to no one. May the Lord look kindly on thy brother, and on thee."

Then he had gone, leaving Sabra prey to her own disquieting thoughts.

"Dear God, let Wes be all right," she murmured, summoning a vision of her brother as she had seen him the last time, a little over three years ago. How it hurt to picture his laughing blue eyes beneath the shock of sun-bleached hair and the wide, full mouth quirked most often in a careless grin! Five years her senior, he had always figured as something of a hero to her, and yet he had been a boon companion, too. Unlike her friends' elder brothers, Wes had seldom taken exception to having his kid sister tag along behind him. He had been the first to take her out in a boat and the first to set her hand to the helm. He had taught her how to fish and swim and all sorts of other marvelous things thought improper for a young girl of good breeding. And when her aristocratic father had died, he had served as both parent and mentor to the young girl, hardly in her teens. Doubtless those living memories of her brother as much as anything had driven her to come to New York and open her father's former townhouse, for Wesley had soon left after the war broke out to join the fight for independence.

The evening that he had taken her for a walk along the Marblehead pier in order to break the news that he was going away was indelibly etched in her memory. She herself was only just returned home from England, having gone in fulfillment of a pledge Wes had made their mother on her deathbed that Sabra should seek out her father's family.

21

The night had been brisk with the first chill of autumn and the breeze blew inland off the sea, but she had hardly noticed as they strolled down the old familiar streets to the wharf. The warehouse with its weathered sign, Tyree & Locke, Import and Export, which had been financed by her father and built by Wes's, was sprawled along the waterfront, a reminder of the early days in which the younger son of nobility had joined in partnership with an ambitious New Englander to the ultimate prosperity of both. The usual fishing boats lined the harbor, and in the distance the steeple of St. Michael's glinted in the moonlight. The bay, the shipyards, the fort perched on a rocky promontory—nothing had changed, and yet somehow nothing had seemed the same either. Or maybe she was different, her outlook altered by her long absence and all that she had seen and done in her father's native land.

She remembered she had been going on about Sir James, her Aunt Caroline, and her grandfather, the Earl of Dearing, when at last they had stopped to look out over Washington's newly formed Massachusetts fleet, which was moored in the bay.

Suddenly Wes had cut in on her, his long arm sweeping up to point at one of the sleek new frigates lying at anchor.

"There, Sabra, do you see it?" he said, the excitement in his voice striking a sudden alarm in her. "The neatest little lady ever to fight in the cause of independence. She's the *Warren*, of thirty-two guns, and I've signed on to sail with her."

Hurt and a little angry that he could think of leaving her so easily, she had listened in stony silence as he described the frigate, his fellow officers, and his duties as third lieutenant on a ship of war with an eagerness she had never seen in him before. At last she had turned away, unable to keep the misery from showing in her eyes, for it had come to her with bitter clarity that in her absence things had changed between them. He was glad to go, relieved, no doubt, to be free of the irksome responsibilities of the family business and a bothersome younger sister, she thought, catching her bottom lip between her teeth.

Then suddenly he drew near and she realized he had

ceased to speak some moments earlier.

"I know this is a rotten homecoming, but, Sabra, you must try and understand," he said quietly. "I have to go. It won't be so bad, you'll see. You'll have Phoebe and Will Skyler to look after you. And Robert Wayne will still be on hand if you need help with the business. This war can't last forever, and then things will be just like they used to be."

Deliberately he had turned her round to face him, and her heart had ached at sight of his lips quirked in the old, familiar grin that had ever seemed reserved somehow just for her.

"I'll always come back to you, Sabra, I swear it. No matter where I am or what happens, I'll find my way back to you."

She had shivered, listening to the waves as they broke against the rocks and thinking of the long, desolate winter that lay ahead for her in the old house at the top of the bluff, with only her memories to keep her company. It had seemed empty enough with her mother gone, but now Wesley, her playmate from earliest childhood, would leave her, too, and she had not known how she would bear it. For in spite of all the malicious rumors, half-truths and lies, in spite of the bitter knowledge that while Josiah Locke's only son was scorned by her mother's family, Phillip Tyree's daughter was pampered and loved, yes, in spite of the fact that Elizabeth's father had disinherited both his daughter and his only grandson in favor of Sabra herself, Wes had ever remained her staunchest ally and friend.

Less than a week later he was gone, and with the coming of spring, she, too, had packed her trunks and headed for New York. She simply could not stay longer in Marblehead, prey to her fears and, worse, to her memories. Especially not when events were moving with such rapidity, and New York, more than any other city, had seemed destined to be the hotbed of contention. The rest had just followed naturally, for she had attracted a deal of flattering notice almost from the moment she stepped down from the carriage in Nassau Street before the five-story brick house, which, along with a sizeable income from his former shipping interests, had been her father's legacy to her.

From the first she had been troubled that Wesley would

never understand why she had remained, even when it was certain that General Howe would defeat the rebel forces and take over the city. How much less would he have understood her apparent traitorous collaboration with the enemy! Still, she had seen almost immediately how unique was her position as a daughter of English nobility in a city occupied by the British and, more importantly, how she might use it to the benefit of the American cause.

Thus with some trepidation as to how her actions might be viewed by her brother were he ever to learn of them, but with little or no uncertainty as to whether she either would or should undertake to do them, she had set herself up as one of New York's most celebrated hostesses and, consequently, as a very valuable source of information to the rebels. How glad she was now that she had done it, for she had every intention of employing her not inconsiderable resources in winning Wesley's freedom!

Calling for Jubal Henry and her carriage, Sabra donned her hat and gloves and set out to make the first of her many morning calls, not the least of which would be a lengthy chat with a particular lady friend of a certain officer high up in the navy echelons.

Chapter 2

"But it's been more than two months. Surely we should have heard something by now!" exclaimed Sabra, turning fitfully from the bay window overlooking Nassau Street to address the young man seated in an attitude of dejection near the fireplace.

For some time she had been staring bleakly out at the huge flakes of snow drifting lazily earthward. Once she would have experienced a childish delight upon awakening to the first storm of winter as it dressed the city in pristine loveliness, but not today, or any other day so long as Wes remained in captivity. While the fresh blanket of snow might hide New York's hideous scars — the charred remains of the two great fires that had swept the city since its occupation by the British — it must inevitably add to the hardships of those in the British prisons. She could not bear to think of Wesley, somewhere nearby perhaps, yet beyond her reach, suffering cold and hunger and possibly even illness. Faith! She could not remember when she had felt so dreadfully helpless.

"It seems incredible to me that we can learn nothing other than that he was impressed into service aboard a nameless frigate. One, moreover, which set sail for the West Indies, only to vanish, 'twould seem, in the mists." Frowning in vexation, she began to prowl aimlessly about her father's study lined with bookshelves and made cozy, despite the chill, with overstuffed chairs and oriental rugs. "Who *is* her captain, Robert? Why is everything concerning this ship so enshrouded in secrecy? Surely *someone* must know *something!*"

Robert Wayne spread wide his hands.

"If they do, they're not talking," he answered shortly and, shoving himself out of the chair, made his way to the fireplace, his labored, uneven gait more pronounced than usual.

Instantly Sabra suffered a swift stab of conscience at sight of his worn appearance. Indeed, there were fine lines about his eyes and mouth that she had not noticed before, and the lean, rather aesthetic cast of his face, with its prominent cheekbones, long, straight nose, and narrow chin, appeared drawn, the thin, transparent skin unnaturally pallid.

She had known Robert Wayne since the old days in Marblehead when his father had served as the local schoolmaster. He and Wesley, closer than most brothers, had sworn to sail together one day to the South Sea Islands and beyond. It had been perhaps harder on him than anyone to be left behind while his oldest friend went off to fight for the cause in which they both ardently believed. But his crippled limb, the result of a break that had been improperly set and thus poorly mended in his youth, had precluded his active participation in the war. As he had stood beside Sabra on the pier, watching the frigate *Warren* make her curtsey to the breeze then sail majestically out of the bay into the open sea, she had seen the torment and self-loathing in his eyes.

On impulse Sabra had asked him to serve as her secretary and adviser in purely business matters, and he had gratefully accepted, even agreeing, albeit somewhat reluctantly, to accompany her to New York. It was thus inevitable perhaps that he should have become a part of her other, surreptitious concerns as well. Indeed, she had come to rely on him a great deal, and in times such as these she feared she asked too much of him.

"I've questioned everyone I could think of," he said, jabbing almost savagely at a smoldering log with a poker. "Anyone who might have even the remotest knowledge either of Wes's whereabouts or of this phantom ship. It was the merest chance that I discovered the only naval vessel to weigh anchor from Gardiner's Island within two weeks previous to Pattison's visit was a frigate that stole from the channel under cover of dark. And no sooner do I make inquiries about such a vessel than everyone clams up tighter than a drum." Deliberately he replaced the fire iron and straightened. "Someone with a deal of influence has put a lid on this for reasons about which I can only speculate," he continued, turning at last to give his employer a long, pointed look. "I'd be very careful about how you pursue this matter, Sabra. I don't like the feel of it."

"Who, Robert?" demanded Sabra, her gaze searching. "Murdoch, Giles, Fisk—the governor himself? Who would have that much power?"

Wayne shrugged thin shoulders.

"Doubtless you would know that better than I. Who would be likely to have high-placed connections in London and the money to purchase favors? Remember that it is no small matter to procure the services of a man-of-war when the British fleet is already stretched thin."

Suddenly Sabra's eyes shone with a hard glitter.

"Sir Wilfred Channing," she said without hesitation. "I should have known. It's hardly a secret that he has friends in high places. He's wealthy enough to buy an audience with the king himself if he wanted, and a large part of that fortune was earned in bribes and fees paid him as a vice-admiralty judge. I should know. He pocketed a tidy enough sum from the fabricated charges brought against Tyree and Locke. And what was his reward when the publicity of such racketeering forced London to put an end to it? Faith, he was made a baronet, of course."

Wayne's sensitive brow furrowed in concern as Sabra uttered a short, brittle laugh.

"I hope you are not thinking of doing something brash," he murmured significantly. "Channing's a dangerous man to cross."

"Is he?" countered Sabra, tossing her red-gold curls with something of disdain. "And yet he, no less than the others of my cortege, comes readily enough if I do but bat an eyelash. Did I tell you he offered me a priceless emerald brooch if only I would grant him the favor of my company for a single evening? —*dans l'intimité, naturellement.* The slithery reptile! I would sooner spend an evening alone with a polecat. Still, if it meant I could learn something of where they are keeping Wes, it might be worth the sacrifice."

"Don't be a fool, Sabra! Wes would not have his freedom at

such a price!"

"And who would tell him?" Sabra demanded ringingly. "You, Robert? Is his life not worth a single night out of mine?"

"Enough. You know that I would give my own life for Wes. But what you propose is—is . . ."

"Indecent? Wicked, even loathsome and vile? Once accomplished, should I then be the harlot others already paint me?" she queried bitterly. "Why is virtue accounted so less worthy a sacrifice than a life, Robert? Especially when either yours or mine, no matter how nobly offered, would avail Wes nothing."

"That's wild talk, you insane girl!" he cried, limping heavily across the room to grasp her urgently by the shoulders. "Listen to me. Allowing a man like that even to touch you would destroy whatever chance at happiness you and Wes might have after all this is over. Don't you understand? I wouldn't have to tell him. He'd see it in your eyes, sense it in your manner toward him. You just can't hide something like that. In the end it would be the same as if you had taken a knife and plunged it in Wes's heart."

"Can you be so sure, Robert? Can you truly be so sure?"

For a long moment he stared speechlessly into the shadowed depths of a sea-green eyes that had the power to bewitch and mesmerize, and suddenly he felt a hard knot of fear tighten in his belly at what he saw in them.

"Yes, I'm sure, you headstrong little innocent," he growled, shaking her a little as if by that he might get through to her. "We'll find another way, I swear it. Only promise me that you won't do anything foolish."

A reluctant laugh seemed forced from her.

"How can I promise what I cannot keep?" she said, pulling away. "But for the present, I will do nothing more than watch and listen, beginning tonight with the Governor's Ball. Everyone who is accounted someone will attend, so you need have no fear for me. My virtue shall be safe enough among so many, surely."

Wayne was far less certain. Even among a multitude, a woman as spirited and lovely as Sabra Tyree would ever be at risk, especially without a man to protect her, not only from the treachery of her wholly unconscionable enemies, but from the consequences of her own dauntless will.

"Very well," he murmured, resigned to the fact that he would win no further concessions from her, and though he could not help loving Sabra as some rare and exquisite creature, he was suddenly very glad that he had not the taming of her. Indeed, there were times when he thought it might have been better for all concerned had the fiery young beauty chosen to remain in England. Doubtless in time and with an ocean between them, Wes would have gotten on with his life, unfettered by his volatile, green-eyed half-sister. Eventually he might even have formed an attachment for some uncomplicated female and settled down to raising a family. As it was, there wasn't a chance in hell that Wes would not find out about his sister's exploits since her arrival in New York, and then the fat would be in the fire for certain. He hated to think of the hurt and misunderstanding that might attend his friend's return. But that was neither here nor there. Long ago he had learned that life was seldom kind or just.

As for Sabra Tyree, there was no one with a nobler or more generous heart. He, perhaps better than anyone, knew the price she paid for the dangerous work she did. Thus far she had conducted her secret campaign with an almost unnerving coolness, as if somehow she sought to detach herself from some lingering feelings of ambivalence. But if it developed that Wesley Locke was dead, indeed, had suffered cruelly at the hands of the enemy, might that not be the spark that would ignite the fiery depths of passion within her? He shuddered to think what might be the consequences of such an event.

He gave Sabra a final, lingering glance as she stood silhouette against the window and staring out at the drifting snow. Becoming arrayed in a green *robe à la française,* the lavish folds of brocade falling from Watteau pleats at the back, she presented a deceptively fragile appearance. Indeed, he was suddenly reminded how very young she was, and how alone she must feel at times. For an instant he hesitated, wishing there were something he could say or do to banish the somber look

29

of brooding from her face. But at last, well aware that she had forgotten him, he merely turned and left her to her thoughts.

The strains of a spirited country dance greeted Sabra as she paused at the top of the marble stairs that descended into the governor's pillared ballroom and waited for a liveried footman to announce her. In keeping with her reputation for the dramatic, she had chosen a ruched polonaise dress of black velvet for the evening. The cutaway skirt, draped over a hooped petticoat of purest ivory, accentuated her willowy slenderness, while the tight-fitting bodice with the daring decolletage revealed a creamy expanse of bare shoulders and shapely bosom. Her hair, adorned with ostrich feathers dyed to match her dress, was powdered and arranged *à la pompadour* with a single, white curl allowed to fall intriguingly over the soft swell of her breast. Behind her stood Jubal Henry, Phoebe's stalwart son, contrastingly attired in white velvet, complete with a snowy turban bearing a magnificent black opal at the center front.

For an instant a hush seemed to descend over the great hall and a sea of faces to turn toward the striking vision of feminine loveliness for which the towering Negro with his noble physique served most admirably as the foil. Sabra dropped into a low curtsey, upon which she was immediately surrounded by a swarm of gentlemen eager to offer her a hand in rising. Choosing the scarlet sleeve of an army officer, Sabra came gracefully to her feet.

"Why, Colonel Ridgley, what a pleasant surprise," she said with sincere warmth as she gazed over the top of her black lace folding fan at the distinguished-looking man in his early forties. "I had not thought to see you here tonight. Indeed, it was my understanding that your regiment had been ordered south to Charleston in the Carolinas. I am relieved that the rumor was apparently greatly exaggerated."

"Miss Tyree, the pleasure must be accounted all mine," rejoined the colonel with graceful gallantry. "As for the rumor of my imminent departure, it is only too true. Now that the French fleet under Count d'Estaing has finally sailed for home, General Clinton intends to lay siege to the rebel stronghold. We shall take Charleston before spring, God willing."

"But of course you will," agreed Sabra, smiling and nodding at acquaintances as she allowed him to lead her through the throng. "No doubt we shall have you back again in time for the promenades along the Green Walk. You will take me to the very first concert there, and we shall pretend we are at Vauxhall Gardens in London instead of the ruins of Trinity Church in New York. It will be pleasant to remember happier times, will it not?"

The colonel could not fail to note the wistful tone in which this last was uttered or the determined manner in which she sought to hide her fleeting lapse into melancholy.

" 'Pon my faith, Miss Tyree," he softly exclaimed, his hand going to hers resting lightly on his arm, "you sound positively blue-deviled. Is something troubling you, my dear?"

Immediately the exquisite fan fluttered delicately before her face as the lady averted her eyes in apparent confusion.

"Am I truly so transparent?" she murmured, her laughter just a trifle too bright. "I assure you 'tis nothing. Doubtless I am a little offset by the change in the weather. Pay it no heed, I pray you."

Ridgley guided her into an alcove fronted on either side by large potted plants. At a glance from Sabra, Jubal Henry bowed from the waist and quietly withdrew to a discreet distance. For the moment she and the colonel were relatively alone.

Sabra, glancing quizzically up at her companion, experienced a small twinge of conscience at having to use him so. She liked and respected Ridgley. He was a relatively uncomplicated man, a soldier who had served in several campaigns and who had little to show for it but an untarnished reputation and the unflagging loyalty of his men. Still, she had no choice in the matter but to try every avenue open to her, and Colonel Ridgley was an aide-de-camp to General Clinton himself.

"It is of course my wish to obey your slightest command,"

he said slowly, as if feeling for the words. "Nor should I like to seem to pry, and yet I cannot but think you are in some sort of difficulty. Can you not bring yourself to confide in me?"

"You are most discerning, sir, and very kind," she answered, smiling ruefully up at him. "But truly I should never forgive myself did I choose to burden you with my insignificant concerns. This is an evening for gaiety, perhaps the last for you for a very long time. Come, let us dance and forget my thoughtless lapse."

Almost she wished he would take the out she had given him, but she knew he would not let it drop there. He was a gentleman in the truest sense of the word.

"But nothing could give me greater pleasure than to be of some small service to you," he urged. "Come, I insist. Tell me how I may help you."

Catching her bottom lip between her teeth, Sabra turned away from him.

"Now you have truly put me to the blush," she uttered in a muffled voice, and for a moment longer stood with her back to him before taking a deep breath and coming about to face him with self-accusing eyes. "How can I confess to you that my heart is uneasy over the uncertain fate of a man who has been your enemy? Oh, how it hurts for me to say it, and yet it is true. He is a rebel and a traitor to the king. Indeed, I should seek to wipe all memory of him from my mind, not as if he were dead to me, but as if he had never lived. But I cannot. I am naught but a female, after all, and he is my brother. In my woman's heart I cannot but love him in spite of everything. But how can I possibly expect you to understand? It is only that you have asked me. And because I value your friendship, I have answered in the hope that you will not turn from me in disgust."

"My dear girl," exclaimed Ridgley, clasping her hand in quick concern, "you could never do anything to earn my disgust. Quite the contrary, I assure you I am prepared to listen to anything you might wish to tell me and to help you if it is at all in my power."

"How good are you," she murmured, her smile tremulous. For a moment longer she appeared to hesitate. Then, apparently giving in at last to the prompting of her heart, she lifted a countenance striking for its unearthly calm. "Perhaps you have heard that the American privateer *Hampden* fell to Admiral Collier some time ago. What you could not know is that my brother—my *half*-brother—was taken captive. For nearly three months I have made repeated inquiries at the admiralty, the hospitals, even the prisons. But no one could tell me anything." Suddenly her brittle composure snapped. "Faith, I have been driven half mad with not knowing if Wesley is alive or dead—haunted by the thought that he might be close by and in need of me!"

"But how should you not in such singular circumstances," agreed the colonel, greatly moved by her distress.

Sabra gave him a wry smile.

"Even worse, perhaps, is that I find myself at my wit's end. I know not what I should do next or to whom I might turn. I have never in my life felt so utterly helpless."

For an instant he appeared to hesitate. "Would you, I wonder, allow me to make a few discreet inquiries of my own in your behalf? I cannot promise to turn up anything, but occasionally there are some advantages to being a general's aide."

"Oh, but I should be eternally grateful if you tried, sir," Sabra exclaimed, awarding him a look that nearly took his breath away.

"Nonsense, my dear," he said dismissingly. "I shall be only too glad to do whatever I can."

Her lips parted as if she would say something more, but then suddenly their secluded nook was invaded by a bevy of young men chiding Ridgely for trying to keep Miss Tyree to himself and demanding her presence on the dance floor. She could do no more than murmur her thanks one last time before she was swept, laughing and protesting, from the colonel's presence.

For a long moment he stood watching her. What a marvel she was! Had he not just been privileged to glimpse behind the charming facade, he would never guess her heart was so heavily burdened. She appeared, as ever, dazzling. Her eyes sparkled with gaiety. Her smile flashed roguishly, and he

33

knew each of those dancing in attendance felt she smiled for him alone—the poor, besotted puppies. A whimsical expression played briefly about his lips. Who was he trying to fool? Though nearly twenty years their senior and a hardened soldier, he was not one whit less intoxicated by the incomparable Sabra.

Stifling a sigh, he left the alcove to make his way through the boisterous melee in search of Colonel Cathcart, the provost marshal.

"You cannot mean the churl actually had the effrontery to hold you up at your own front gate?" indignantly exclaimed a young infantry officer of the enchanting Miss Tyree. "Ecod, the entire lot of riffraff should be run out of the city."

It was the supper dance, and the young beauty was surrounded by her usual host of admirers. Indeed, after having been beguiled with a plateload of dainties, she had laughingly agreed to relate the particulars of a rumored confrontation between herself and a brigand.

"Now, now, lieutenant," Sabra dimpled, " 'twas not the *front* gate, but the back. Nor was it I the fellow would hold up, but only the gate itself, as he himself informed me with all due respect. Indeed, despite his disreputable appearance he behaved quite the gentleman. Not all the poor souls of Canvas Town are riffraff, 'twould seem, but simply men who have lost everything."

"But what happened to the fellow?" demanded another of the gentlemen. "Surely you did not let him off scot-free?"

"Oh, indeed no," she answered artlessly. "Though he was exceedingly reluctant, I quite *insisted* he come in for tea and biscuits."

"Tea and biscuits? Good God. One does not invite a felon into the house. He might just as well have robbed ye blind as do the niceties."

"But what would you have had me do? I admit to a certain fondness for my gate. I simply could not bring myself to let him cart it off. And, besides, even if firewood is accounted more precious than gold these days, I feel quite certain he earned every billet he took with him. Phoebe would see to that, for she can be the very devil of a taskmaster, I assure you."

An appreciative outburst of merriment greeted this sally, for there was not a soul among them who was not acquainted with the redoubtable Phoebe Henry. But then, as the laughter died down, a new voice intruded, which served immediately to put a damper on the group.

"No doubt a beautiful woman may be excused an overly soft heart. Still, you are far too generous, my dear Miss Tyree. Had I been present, the lout would have found himself strapped to the gatepost and flogged for such impertinence."

Sabra experienced a ripple of revulsion at the man's arrogant insensitivity. Schooling her features to reveal nothing of her dislike, she lifted cool green eyes to observe the newcomer.

Of average height, he was elegantly slim, his graceful figure artfully arrayed in red silk, fine lace, and exquisite jewels. Drooping eyelids and delicately arched eyebrows conveyed the indolent air of one used to having his presence felt; an arrogance, which was heightened, in fact, by the sculptured perfection of a face remarkable for blue, metallic eyes, luxuriously lashed and accentuated by a black beauty patch placed artfully at the top of a rouged cheek. A powdered bagwig, the black silk *solitaire* tied fashionably about the neck over a white linen stock, seemed particularly suited to the overall impression of studied refinement. And yet there was that about the unnaturally pale complexion and the sardonic curl of sculpted lips which rendered the whole peculiarly sinister. He was, she knew, totally without scruples, a man who accumulated wealth and power solely for the pleasure of manipulating and coercing others to do his will.

Sabra smiled with disarming sweetness as Sir Wilfred Channing made his bow.

"Then, sir, 'tis perhaps fortunate that you were *not* present," she murmured, waving her fan ever so gently back and forth. "For 'pon my faith I have never been fond of the sight of blood. Why, doubtless I should have swooned, like the veriest

35

feeble-hearted female."

"*Mais naturellement*, mademoiselle. Such matters are better left to those whose duty it is to guide and protect the weaker sex," he drawled, insufferably sure of himself.

" 'T's all a hubble-bubble, I tell ye," came the slurred accents of one who had obviously imbibed rather too freely. "Not the type to fall into a distempered freak. I'll wager she's never swooned a day in her life."

A distinct snort issued from one of the gentlemen. A peculiarly unpleasant glint flared briefly in Sir Wilfred's eye. Then visibly he relaxed. The thin lips stretched in a smile intended to be charming.

"Well, Miss Tyree? *Have* you ever once in your life succumbed to a fainting spell?" he queried in velvet tones.

"No, never," Sabra serenely admitted. "Perhaps 'tis a flaw in my character, do you think?"

A subtle ripple of amusement swept the group at Sir Wilfred's expense. Flushing slightly, the gentleman inclined his head and ironically murmured, "Touché, my dear," in acknowledgement of an artful set down.

"I'm quite sure I haven't the least idea of what you mean, sir," she replied, her aspect guilelessly demure. "But then there is so much that escapes me. This matter of privateers, for instance. Why, Captain Briggs was only just telling me that not three months past another of your coasters fell victim to one of those dreadful vessels. The one which has created such a stir, I believe. Oh, dear, I fear I've quite forgot its name."

"Undoubtedly you are referring to the *Nemesis*," responded Sir Wilfred Channing, never once taking his eyes off her as, negligently, he trailed an exquisite lace handkerchief beneath his nose and sniffed its perfumed fragrance. "She's made quite a name for herself at my expense. But I think you will find her days are numbered. Indeed, I am sure of it."

Sabra's lips curved with the faintest hint of irony.

"Then you have devised a plan to rid us of the brigand. But how marvelous! Still, 'tis a clever rogue who can elude Admiral Collier and these other brave gentlemen. Come, sir, will you not tell us how you intend to accomplish what the entire

British fleet has failed to do?"

The baronet appeared not the least put out by such a notion. Indeed, if anything, Sabra judged him to be rather amused at her show of naivete.

"I fear I am not at liberty to divulge how the thing will be accomplished," he condescended to inform her, "but I pride myself on my word. The master of this privateer will most certainly find himself trussed in irons soon enough, and his crew confined in prison."

"Ah, but 'tis boldly spoken, sir," murmured Sabra, gazing at him out of the corners of magnificent eyes, shimmering like emeralds above the black lace of her fan. "Doubtless we shall all breathe easier just knowing Sir Wilfred Channing has sworn to bring the rogue to justice. Alas! Were it up to me, I fear I should be tempted to cease all shipping till the safe resolution of this matter."

"You surprise me, my dear. I should have expected *you* to agree that 'tis unwise ever to give in to the intimidation of rascals and thieves. My coaster *Meridian* is even now well on her way to Nova Scotia and shall return within two weeks' time, or I shall know the reason why. But now, if you will excuse me," he ended, presenting an elegant leg in a manner no less ironic for its graceful execution, "I perceive the governor entreats my presence. Mademoiselle, as always, sight of your beauty has been an inspiration."

Graciously Sabra inclined her head.

"*À bientôt, monsieur,*" she murmured, watching the baronet's retreat. Behind her fan the hint of a smile played briefly about the lovely lips. "*À bientôt y merci bien!*"

The next morning found Sabra closeted once again with Robert Wayne in her father's study. Outside, the storm had fled, leaving the hope of fairer weather, and it was all she could do to attend to matters of mundane business when she wished only to be safely on her way.

"Yes, yes, if you feel such measures are necessary, then you have my approval. I'm sure you know better than I what Wesley would have wished done," she said distractedly when

37

Wayne had finished his rather lengthy financial report.

Wayne looked up, his glance speculative. Obviously his employer was preoccupied with something, but somehow he doubted it had the least thing to do with the fluctuating European market. A slight flush becomingly tinged her averted cheek, and there was a sort of feverish intensity about the way she kept glancing out the window. Wayne suddenly frowned.

"You're going out again, aren't you," he said accusingly.

Wishing to avoid a lengthy debate, Sabra hesitated the fraction of a second before turning to look at him. Her intent, however, must have been written on her face.

"I thought we had agreed to wait till spring before *Nemesis* made her next foray," he blurted before she could either affirm or deny his earlier assertion. Botheration, she fretted, irritated at this new delay, but annoyed even more at her failure to keep the matter from Wayne.

"Obviously I've changed my mind," she answered shortly, and heartlessly wished him to the devil.

"But why? What happened last night that you haven't told me?"

"Nothing happened. I'm simply tired of sitting around waiting for word of Wes. Sometimes I think I shall go stark raving mad if I am forced to endure one more evening of playing the charming lady. Besides, I happened to learn that Channing has sent a coaster north. It would seem he wants to demonstrate his contempt of 'rascals' and 'thieves.' Indeed, I took it as something of a challenge. It would be a shame not to oblige him, don't you think?"

"Good God, Sabra, you'll be taking an awful chance. For one thing, you're sure to be missed. How do you propose to explain your absence at the height of the winter season?"

Sabra shrugged indifferently.

"I've already taken care of that. You see, after having just received word of a bereavement in my family, I have chosen to go into seclusion. Indeed, I am departing for my estate on Long Island this very morning for an indeterminate length of time. That should do nicely," she ended with a hint of bitterness. "After all, 'tis not so far from the truth."

Wayne's heart sank. How well he knew that look of hers!

"I don't like it," he said. "It's too soon. I wish you would reconsider. What if there's news of Wes while you're gone? Or suppose Channing puts two and two together and comes up with Sabra Tyree, who just happened to be conveniently absent when his ship was attacked?"

"Oh, I don't *know!* I don't know! And I *wish* you would stop flinging obstacles in my way!" she cried, turning her back on him.

Wayne's lips clamped shut, and after a moment's hesitation, he limped angrily to the fireplace.

Sabra drew in a shuddering breath.

"I'm sorry," she said. "I know you're only worried about me. Still, right or wrong, I'm going."

He did not look up as she crossed to the door. For the barest instant she hesitated, her hand on the brass handle. Then, in something like anger, she thrust open the door and left him.

Chapter 3

The day had promised fair, with only a thin haze of clouds and the breeze steady out of the southwest. What was more, they had discovered the coastal brig *Meridian* sailing as expected, close-hauled to the wind on a nearly true course south toward Nantucket from Yarmouth at Nova Scotia. At first sign of the armed schooner bearing down on her, the brig had fallen off, reaching broad on the starboard bow for the safety of the coastal harbors—too late, for the *Nemesis,* anticipating such a move, jibed to port seconds ahead of her and, crossing abaft, raked her stern with grapeshot, leaving black gaping holes where the stern windows had been.

Her rudder lines having been severed in the assault, the *Meridian* lugged drunkenly to starboard, an easy prey to the armed schooner coming about for the kill. Even as the excited cry that the brig had lost steerage swept the decks of the *Nemesis,* the *Meridian* had struck to her attacker.

And that should have been that, thought Sabra Tyree, as the *Nemesis* clawed once more to the windward before paying off on the port tack. But instead their luck had apparently played out.

"She's wore ship," called out William Skyler, who had served as master on coasters belonging to Tyree and Locke for as long as Sabra could remember. Just then he wore a worried frown on his seamed, weathered face, and his eyes never left the British frigate that had been matching them maneuver for maneuver for the past four hours, never falling farther than eight cable lengths away as she held steady to a parallel course off the schooner's starboard. "She's pulling up, or I'm shark bait," Skyler bit out, jetting a stream of tobacco juice over the side.

40

"A little, perhaps," Sabra answered. Concealing her own misgivings behind the lovely mask of her face, she glanced up at the mainsail holding taut with the wind. "It'll be dark soon now, and then we'll slip away."

"I wouldn't count on it, Miss Sabra. Not the way that devil's been comin' after us. It's like he knows what we'll do long afore we knows ourselves."

Sabra offered no comment, but she, too, had begun to chafe under the unknown captain's uncanny ability to antici-pate their every move. No sooner had the *Meridian* struck to them than the frigate had seemed to appear out of nowhere, bearing down upon them under full sails. Only a sudden shift of wind had bought the *Nemesis* time to slip away. Then, as the British ship had made certain the stricken brig was not in danger of going under, the schooner had seized the chance to put some distance between them. They had been beating a zigzag course back to Long Island ever since with the blasted frigate hot on their heels.

After the first two hours, Sabra had ceased to vary the pattern of their flight, but instead had set herself to making as much headway as was possible. That had been the obvious reason for her choice of strategy. She hoped the other would be much less discernible as the minutes crept by like hours until at last it was time to tack again.

Again, like some distant shadow, the British frigate moved with them, shaving off a little more of the distance separating the two vessels. Damn! thought Sabra, torn between a mounting hatred of the implacable frigate and a reluctant admiration for its captain's seamanship. Given enough time, the British captain could bring his ship to within range of his port guns, and then the little schooner would not stand a chance. It was up to Sabra to pull a miracle out of her bag of tricks, and if she had guessed wrong, the extraordinary suc-cesses thus far attributable to the *Nemesis* would come to an exceedingly swift and better end.

Thus it was that two hours after nightfall, the *Nemesis* altered course. Wearing ship to sail with the wind, she back-tracked for close on to two hours before once more coming about. Then, through the long night of beating to windward, making for the Long Island Sound with as much sail as the little schooner could bear, Sabra waited, tortured by uncertainty and yet conscious of a strange sort of exhilaration as well.

From her first slow mastery of the little catboat her father had given her on her tenth birthday, Sabra Tyree had discovered a mounting passion for the sea. Only when her hand was at the tiller and her face turned toward the open water had she seemed to come truly alive or to feel gloriously free, for on land she had been fettered by convention and by all the restrictions imposed on females in general, but most in particular upon herself as the only daughter of a prominent New England family. How she had chafed at her mother's insistence that she be schooled in all the accomplishments of a proper English lady! Indeed, not once since her mama's death shortly before Sabra's seventeenth birthday had she felt the slightest urge to take up either her embroidery or the detested sketch pad and charcoal. While grieving over the loss of her parent, she had yet been conscious of an overwhelming relief that nothing should ever again bar her from the sea.

Once she had thought nothing could compare with the sheer excitement of running free across a stiff breeze, a seemingly limitless expanse of blue water before her, but that was before she had undertaken to launch her own, private fight against New York's unscrupulous war profiteers.

She had seen the ragtag band of prisoners brought in after Washington's retreat across the Delaware. Poorly clothed and ill fed, they had roused in her both pity for them and a slow-burning rage at those who had grown wealthy at their expense. It was then that she had determined, not only to remain in New York following its occupation by the British, but to make herself useful to the rebel cause.

Garnering information from those who attended her extremely popular entertainments had required only that she be charming and well to look upon. Pitting the *Nemesis* against both the British navy and those coasters involved in war profiteering had demanded considerably more of her. Still, the test of wit and courage had seemed only to whet her appetite for ever more such adventures, and it was not long before word of the exploits of the armed schooner, having the figurehead of a winged woman with the sword of vengeance in her hand, had spread up and down the coast. For two years, now, she and her small band had wreaked havoc on coastal shipping of a nefarious nature, and up till now no one had come even close to catching them.

Never, before the British frigate had taken up the chase, had she faced a great challenge and, while reason and instinct acknowledged the very real peril, something deeper and more elemental gloried in it. There was something compelling about the forbidding vessel, with its figurehead of a black swan, wings unfurled in an attitude of fiercely anticipated battle, she thought with a shiver, something which was separate and distinct from the obvious threat it posed. Indeed, it had more to do with the man who commanded the ship than with the ship itself.

At first sight of the enemy vessel bearing down on them, she had known with unreasoning certainty that the British captain must have been waiting for the *Nemesis* to make an appearance. Nor had subsequent events lessened that apprehension. Indeed, she had become more convinced than ever that it was herself he was after, or, to be more precise, the one in command of the schooner, which had become a thorn in the side of Sir Wilfred Channing.

She no longer need puzzle over the baronet's scheme to ensnare the master of the *Nemesis*. She had sailed straight into his trap, and now it behooved her to find a way out again!

Thus what in different circumstances might have been a not unusual occurrence between vessels of opposing factions, had instead assumed the proportions of a personal duel between herself and the British naval captain. It was the mettle of her skill and cunning pitted against his, and therein lay the source of her ambivalence as she waited for the coming of the dawn both with dread and a certain breathless anticipation.

The stars, fading before the first pale light of the slowly rising sun, found Sabra and her crew of forty men straining for the sight of the enemy sail. By her reckoning, the *Nemesis* should be somewhere off the northern reach of Cape Cod

43

and, if the wind continued steady, perhaps a day's sailing from Long Island Sound. If the British captain had fallen for her ruse and kept all night to the course she had so carefully established the day before, he should be well around the point by now, perhaps even as far as the southern shores of Nantucket Island. Then, with any luck, having discovered no sign of his quarry and knowing himself to be in such close proximity to the fleet lying off Sandy Hook, he would realize the futility of further pursuit and continue on to New York, leaving *Nemesis* the field.

That, at any rate, was Sabra's fervent hope, as she braced herself against the steady pitching of the schooner and squinted against the half-light of dawn.

The distant bulge of land assuming solidity out of the rapidly paling dark confirmed the first of her expectations. There was no mistaking the curved arm of the cape jutting, clawlike, into Massachusetts Bay. Then, as she waited for the sun, oozing like a great, gelatinous ball into the sky, to clear the horizon, the cry of "sail off the starboard bow" sent her scrambling to the windward, her heart hammering in her breast.

For an eternity, it seemed, Sabra struggled to bring her glass to bear on the phantom sail, but whether from her own fatigue or from the sudden clamp of bitter certainty upon her vitals, she searched the heaving ocean in vain. She could feel the men watching her, waiting to see what she would do, and absurdly she felt like lashing out at them. They had always known she would fail; indeed, they had been waiting for it. After all, having either a woman or a parson on board was unlucky and, given a choice, they doubtless would have preferred the latter over her, she thought in unreasoning anger. What did it matter that it had been her brains and daring that had carried them this far or that because of her they had taken better than a dozen prize vessels in the past two years? She was a woman, and that was all that mattered.

At last, little caring that the men closest to her heard, she let go an explosive "Damn!" Hardly a second passed before strong hands closed on the spy glass, steadying it.

"She be yonder, Miss Sabra," said a deep voice.

Feeling the breath hard in her throat, Sabra looked up into the remote gaze of Jubal Henry. The black face was as impassive as usual, the expression of a man whose mama and papa had been slaves until her father had freed them. Still, it came to her suddenly that he had not always worn that look, not when they were children playing children's games together. She and Jubal and Wesley — they had been practically inseparable. When had things changed? she wondered with a swift pang. Why had she never noticed before?

Then something in the man's unswerving regard broached the hard knot of her anger and doubt. As if compelled, she glanced around her at the men, seeing them as if for the first time. They were all Americans, every one of them — men who had remained loyal to Wesley and her father, even in the bad times after the customs officers had seized three of their ships in quick succession on purely trumped-up charges. With the ships and cargoes condemned by the admiralty board, her father's reserves had been stretched dangerously thin and the confidence of his creditors and correspondents severely shaken. Indeed, it had seemed inevitable that many of those who had always shipped on vessels owned by Tyree and Locke would have to be let go. Still, they had stayed on, content to weather the storm till things changed for the better.

In a sudden rush of shame, it occurred to Sabra that not one of them had ever questioned either her ability or her right to be master of the schooner she herself had commissioned to be built and fitted out. Indeed, they had signed on willingly, not only out of loyalty to Wesley and her father, but out of loyalty to her.

She was not just some woman who might bring them bad luck; she was Sabra Tyree, who had grown to womanhood on the vessels they sailed. She was master of the *Nemesis*. It was that simple. And they were waiting for her to give them their orders.

All at once both self-doubt and the last dregs of weariness melted away before a sudden, swift surge of humility and pride. With such men as these to believe in her, could she not dare anything, or, indeed, any*one?*

Impatiently she brushed a stray lock of hair the color of burnished gold from her face. Then, looking once more to Jubal Henry, she softly murmured, "Still pulling me out of my scrapes, Jubal? After all these years? One of these days the bill is going to become too great for me ever to repay it."

"You jest gets us out of this alive, Miss Sabra," he retorted with a slow wink. "Now that I got more money'n I knows what to do with, I ain't lookin' to die rich."

With Jubal guiding the barrel of the scope, it was not long before the fierce figurehead of the swan leaped into focus — jet-black and shimmering in the strengthening sunlight. Never would she have guessed a creature lauded for its majestic grace could appear so ferocious, came briefly to Sabra's mind, and swift upon that, the sudden prickling of her scalp. It was like feeling spying eyes on the back of her neck, she thought with an instinctive spark of resentment. Knowing what she would find, she swept the length of the frigate deliberately with the glass till she came at last to the quarter-deck.

The short, ironic bark of laughter seemed forced from her at sight of the British captain, a spy glass held to one eye as he stared coolly back at her. Silently she cursed the man's cunning, even as she acknowledged a wry respect for his astute seamanship. Standing a discreet distance off the Cape, the enemy vessel was yet effectively placed to cut off any possible retreat into Boston Harbor.

"Damn him for his arrogance!" she muttered savagely, seeing him touch fingertips to his cocked hat in a salute, deliberately mocking in its execution. Slamming the telescope shut, she pivoted on her heel to face the waiting crew with hands on hips and her green eyes glittering dangerously.

"It's the king's frigate all right," she said with a chilling smile, "bold as brass and her captain twice as sure of himself."

Coolly gauging the mettle of their mood, she let the sudden rumble of voices die down before she swept the sea of faces with a piercing glance.

"I don't have to tell you that this Gentleman Jack of the

46

British navy outguessed me last night. But what he doesn't know is that he hasn't even begun to take our measure. These are our waters, and there's not a man Jack among 'em who knows this coastline as well as we do. I say, let's show 'em what American sailors are made of. What say you, lads?"

A suspicious stinging came to her eyes as the decks erupted in a savage cheer. Swallowing hard, she turned away to stare blindly out to sea. No matter what, she told herself, she must not let them down. Then, feeling someone draw near, she turned to find William Skyler studying her with curious intensity.

"Well?" she said, softly quizzing.

Skyler shrugged.

" 'Twas bravely spoke," he answered and leaned his hands casually against the rail beside her. Still, something in his dry tone brought Sabra's eyes up, searching.

"You don't approve," she said, watching him squint against the sun and salt spray, his gaze, going beyond her shoulder, unreadable. "Why?"

"Any one of us would walk on water, if you asked it," he said with marked deliberation, "or die trying. But that don't make it right to ask."

"Meaning, I suppose, that we've as much chance of outrunning that blasted frigate as we'd have trying to walk on water," she retorted cuttingly.

"I reckon that's about the size of it."

Abruptly Sabra turned toward the rail, her arms clasped across her breast against the sudden chill. Of all those on board, William Skyler was the last person she would have expected to find pitted against her. He had always stood her friend; indeed, he had taught her everything she knew about sailing ships.

"I see," she murmured, struggling to make sense of it. Skyler was no coward. She had seen him handle a ship in hurricanes with a cooler nerve than most possessed. No, there was more to this than met the eye. "So what would you have me do?" she asked quietly after a moment, bracing herself for whatever he might say. Still, she was hardly prepared for what came next.

"There's worse things than strikin' your colors when the odds is all against you," he answered in the same inflectionless voice. "I reckon there's no shame in knowin' when you've been licked."

For a moment she stared at the man, too stunned to reply. Then the memory of the British captain, coolly mocking, rose up to strike fire from her eyes.

"Are there worse things than rotting in a stinking prison?" she demanded incredulously. "Personally I'd rather die cleanly than to be beaten and starved to it in one of those British hell holes."

Still the first mate remained unruffable. Looking her squarely in the eye, he chilled her to the bone.

"There ain't no need for you to do either," he retorted carelessly — too carelessly, thought Sabra, watching him with a dazed sense of unreality. "We've talked it over, me and the lads. If you was locked below when the British come aboard, it'd be natural for them to think you was here against your will. Especially was you to have on one of them fancy gowns you keep in your trunk instead of them breeches you're so fond of. We'd say you was a prisoner that we'd took for ransom, like. Ain't no reason for them to suspicion a thing, you bein' a well-known lady an' all. All you'd have to do is tell 'em about your grandpappy bein' an earl. I reckon the rest'd be easy."

As the full import of what he proposed sank in, Sabra felt a hard lump rise to her throat.

"I see. You have it all worked out, haven't you? And while you and the rest of these crazy fools are in chains, I suppose I'm to be content making eyes at that — that damned conceited jackanapes of a British naval captain. Well, it won't wash, William Skyler."

"Dammit, Sabra!" he said, his reserve broken at last. "You and I both know we ain't got a chance in hell of makin' it through this."

"And even if we don't, can you still look me in the eye and tell me that if things were different — if you were in charge without having me to worry about — you'd follow your own advice to give up without a fight? If you can, I swear I'll haul

48

down the colors with my own hands."

"What I would or wouldn't do don't count a groat, and you know it, Sabra Tyree. I owe it to your pa to make sure you get through this without harm. But more important, how'd I ever face Wes if you was found out to be master of the *Nemesis?* Think, girl, what it'd do to him if you was taken or killed out here. Seems to me it was time you started carin' a little less about this damned crazy notion of yours to sail a privateer and more about what you owe your brother."

Had he tried, the old sailor could not have struck Sabra a more telling blow. Uttering a sharp gasp, she paled to the color of fine ivory, and for the barest instant it seemed that Skyler had won the round.

"Damn you, Skyler," she breathed. "You push friendship too far."

"Then I'm sorry for it. All these years I've watched you grow to a woman with more courage and just plain recklessness than any female had ought to've had, and no one to put a curb on it. You're just so damned fine and lovely, no one could refuse you anything once they got a look in those eyes of yours. Your pa never could when he was alive, and while I reckon Wes done his best by you, he was always too moonstruck to see just where you was headin'. Your mama seen it, and that's why she wrung that promise from you to go to England, in the hopes you'd find the man strong enough to tame the wildness in you. *She* wasn't never strong enough to stand up against you. I reckon it ain't your fault you was born a woman with more brains and nerve than most men have, but that's the way it is. Now you gotta learn to make the best of it, for Wes's sake. And that's all I got to say."

"Indeed, that's quite enough," said Sabra, coming about to face him with her magnificent eyes ablaze.

"Do you truly believe I haven't lain awake at nights thinking about what might happen?" she demanded passionately. "Haunted by the thought that Wes would find out and despise me for all I've done? Well, maybe he does deserve better from me, but, as you pointed out, I am what I am, and I can't change for him or you or any man. So if you're finished, Mr. Skyler, I suggest you return to your post, for I'd as soon ram this schooner down that British captain's throat if need be, than to play the simpering female. Have I made myself perfectly clear?"

For a long moment Skyler said nothing, but only gazed at Sabra standing straight-backed and unflinching before him, the very picture of glorious womanhood with the sun glinting sparks in her hair. Then suddenly he shook his head, a hint of bafflement tinged with reluctant admiration on his grizzled face.

"I reckon the man ain't alive who could resist you for long, Sabra Tyree," he drawled, relenting to her youthful fire. "Least of all William Skyler. Howsoever, ramming the *Nemesis* down the British captain's throat ain't exactly the best notion you've had up till now. My guess is you've got something else up your sleeve. Might be you should let me in on it if I'm to be any help to you."

It soon developed, however, that the first mate was to remain in even greater doubt concerning his employer's alternate strategy, for in spite of having instantly forgiven him the liberties he had presumed, she nevertheless stubbornly refused to enlighten him as to exactly what she intended doing. For the present they would content themselves with running a course as far ahead of their pursuers as they could possibly maintain, while ever bearing south-southwest, with any luck eventually to reach the vicinity of Long Island.

The second day of flight taxed the endurance of all on board the *Nemesis*, but perhaps Sabra's most of all. For the greatest part of the day she kept to herself in her cabin poring over Skyler's charts and her own painstakingly gathered data on currents and tides, till at last the germ of an idea, which had come to her as she stared aft at the frigate glinting like some ill omen in the early morning sunrise, began at last to assume definite shape in her mind.

For some time Sabra had been puzzled at the British captain's tactics. Even acknowledging that the *Nemesis* was an excellent sailor, designed to move light and swift through the water, the frigate had made no all-out effort to overtake her.

Indeed, the captain seemed odiously content merely to bar her from any possibility of making a safe harbor. It was as if he were deliberately driving them south, forcing them to lead him to their hidden port on Long Island Sound. Such a notion was fraught with dire implications, for it could mean that Sir Wilfred had guessed that the privateer's uncanny success was due to the leakage of inside information and, further, that that information was garnered in the major center of British occupation — either Long Island or the city of New York itself. In short, it could mean the *Nemesis* was only a pawn in the larger scheme of uncovering an entire network of American spies, and that possibility was far too close to the reality for Sabra's comfort.

If such were the case, then she doubted not that the hitherto unshakable frigate would conveniently fall back as they approached the Sound, leaving the way open for the *Nemesis* to make her escape. Were she to enter the Sound, that would be evidence enough to prove what had previously been suspicions only. But if she were to appear to be attempting to flee past Long Island, it could be assumed her intended anchorage had been Boston Bay or some other northern port friendly to the rebel cause. Then nothing would hold the British captain back. Indeed, he would be forced to close with them.

Therein lay the kernel of Sabra's burgeoning plan, for she intended not only to make good their escape, but to throw a cloud of uncertainty over the entire matter of their port of origin, even going so far as to stage the final disappearance of her beloved schooner. What she contemplated doing was both desperate and risky in the extreme, for what was meant as a ruse might very well become in point of fact the death run of the privateer *Nemesis*.

Having made her decision, Sabra felt a sudden calm descend over her. In just a matter of hours she and the detestably arrogant captain would play out their final moves in the game of strategy. Thus far, he had demonstrated little difficulty in reading her mind. She could not help wondering if he would see through her last desperate ploy as well.

Inevitably she found herself trying to formulate a mental image of the man. That morning she had been able to make out very little of his actual physical appearance; the frigate had been too far away. Hopefully he had been frustrated as well in gaining a clear image of herself.

Up close, there could have been no mistaking her true gender, despite the fact that when on shipboard she wore a man's coat and breeches and kept her hair bound in a queue at the nape of her neck. At that distance, however, it would surely have taken a discerning eye indeed to see other than a slender male perhaps a little above average height.

As for the captain, she placed him somewhere in his late twenties or early thirties, perhaps. It was, after all, only reasonable to assume that an older man with his obvious ability would surely have rated a ship of the line instead of a mere frigate. Still, if she were to be honest with herself, it was not reason that made her so sure, but something she felt about the man. Indeed, almost from the first he had seemed to loom in her mind as being young and reckless, which befitted the dashing captain of a frigate, but also tall and having strong, probably handsome features. After this morning she had given them an arrogant cast as well, with thin lips curved in a cynical smile.

She felt the blood rush to her cheeks all over again at memory of the man's insolence. Damn the coxcomb! She had met his ilk before, in the fashionable salons of London. World-weary gentlemen of wealth and breeding, who whiled away their time and fortunes at prize fights, races, and gambling halls; she had felt a natural antipathy for the indolent, well-dressed paragons of fashion. Doubtlessly the arrogant captain was unfortunate enough to have been born a younger son forced to make his way in the navy, else he, too, would have been lounging in one of the elite men's clubs in London instead of pursuing her down the length of the Atlantic coast.

Sudden misgivings drew her stomach muscles into a hard knot. Thus far he had outguessed and outmaneuvered her at every turn. Perhaps she was a fool to tempt fate one last time. Inevitably she thought of Skyler and Jubal Henry, and all the

52

others who had implicitly placed their faith in her ability to bring them safely through. Her courage almost gave way. Who was she, after all, to think she stood a chance against the seasoned crew of a British man-of-war and a captain of obviously superior command experience? Probably he was enjoying himself immensely at her expense. He had certainly made his contempt of her and her crew blatantly apparent with his last, mocking gesture.

Suddenly furious with herself for having conjured up the disquieting memory, Sabra abruptly stood, nearly braining herself on one of the low-lying beams overhead. Oddly enough the sharp pain served somehow to clear her mind and steady her nerves so that she immediately saw how irrationally she was behaving. Indeed, she was reacting just as he had intended that she should.

"Damn him!" she uttered aloud and sent a wine decanter crashing against the bulkhead. As if by this she might banish once and for all the specter of the tall figure on the quarterdeck, his arm sweeping up in an elaborate salute endlessly mocking, she reflected bitterly as she viewed the shattered remains of fine crystal strewn about the cabin.

Hastily Sabra caught up her boat cloak and left her cabin as if pursued.

"Have you utterly lost your mind?" demanded William Skyler of his employer some hours later as they watched the fading light of day glint off Montauk Point to the south and west of them. "By the grace of God, we've finally managed to put some distance between us and that blasted frigate, and there's Block Island Sound just waitin' for us."

"Nevertheless, you will continue on this heading," Sabra insisted, refusing to back an inch before her highly incensed first mate. "You must trust that I know what I'm doing."

"I'd like to have one good reason why I should. Sabra Tyree, if I hadn't had the trainin' of you myself, I'd say you was talkin' like some ignorant landlubber that didn't know no better. You and I both know that if we keep to this heading, we'll find ourselves run aground on the shoals off Fire Island.

53

Then God Himself couldn't help us."

"But that's exactly what I intend," said Sabra, a devil of laughter in her eyes. "Or at least that's what I intend that it should appear to our British captain."

"Hang it, girl," thundered Skyler, thrusting his sizeable nose within six inches of Sabra's, "either you talk plain sense, or I take over command of this vessel right here and now. Is that understood?"

"Well, if it's to be mutiny, I suppose I've no choice in the matter," she reflected aloud, instantly sobering. "Tell me, Mr. Skyler, in the norm, just how much water lies over the sandbar off the south shore of Long Island?"

"No more than eight feet at its deepest, and that's why—"

"And what depth of draft does the *Nemesis* carry?" Sabra interjected before he could finish.

"Ten feet when we ain't heavy loaded."

He was beginning to calm down, she noticed, trying to figure just where her questions were leading.

"And what," she said coolly, "if I were to tell you that I can practically guarantee at least eleven feet of water over the bar no later than seventeen hundred hours?"

"I'd say you'd something up your sleeve and, just guessin', I reckon it'd have to be the spring tide. But what's the point, girl? Once in, it ain't likely we'd ever sail out again. Why in hell would you want to take such a risk for?"

"Because for the past two days we've been playing cat and mouse with a British frigate, and we, my friend, have been the mouse. Why else would our wily captain fall back all of a sudden, just as we arrive at the Sound? In fact, why hasn't he made any effort to close on us, or even to get near enough for a shot from his bow chaser? Surely you don't suppose that he is intimidated by our puny nine-pounders?"

"He was lettin' us lead him to home, the scurvy son of a lubber," pronounced Skyler with a dangerous glint in his pale eyes.

After that it had taken only moments to bring the first mate to a thorough understanding of what exactly was at stake and, consequently, to reluctant agreement that the stakes far outweighed the risks in what Sabra proposed doing. She had left it to Skyler to similarly convince the crew, and he had been ably assisted by the reappearance of the British frigate coming at them with its bow-chaser belching fire.

It wanted less than ten minutes of being five in the evening when the *Nemesis* was driven to the sandbar, which, a quarter of a mile off shore, spanned the length of Long Island from Montauk Point to Fire Island. Forced to sheer off, the British frigate hove to, its guns silenced as the schooner was carried out of range and vanished with the last light of dusk.

The officers aboard His Majesty's frigate *Black Swan* were equally divided between the opposing theories that the thunderous explosion, which occurred some twenty minutes later, had been either deliberate or the result of an accidental spark in the schooner's magazine. The proponents of the first explanation cited the inevitability of the vessel's being trapped in the narrow channel between the sandbar and the beach, for it was impossible that she could have gained the open sea with the wind to inland. Likely they had destroyed their own vessel rather than let it fall as a prize to the British, God rot the bloody Yanks.

Whatever the explanation for the explosion, however, everyone was in vociferous agreement on one thing: that the vessel had most certainly been blown to kingdom come. After all, other than the figurehead of a winged woman bearing a raised sword, and in addition to various and other scattered debris, little else had been discovered of the American privateer *Nemesis*. Everyone was in perfect accord, that is, with the exception of the captain, who, offering neither opinion nor agreement, remained for a considerable time on the quarterdeck in inapproachable solitude.

Matthais Bolt, the *Swan*'s sailing master, stood at the helm, his eyes carefully averted from the tall figure pacing endlessly to-and-fro, when abruptly he was startled out of his stoic front by the low-voiced exclamation of his superior.

"The portholes above the gun ports, of course!" muttered the captain, bringing his hands down hard on the quarterdeck rail. "The Yanks used sweeps to reach the nearest gap in the bar. Probably Fire Island or Moriches. Then, once back through, they simply slipped away with no one the wiser."

The sudden gleam of a smile shone whitely against his face.

"My respects to the Master of the *Nemesis*," he murmured, ironically saluting the vanished schooner. " 'Twould seem the first round goes to you. But never doubt that there shall come another!"

Chapter 4

"They was horse racing 'round Bowling Green, if you can imagine that. Them with their fancy women and high-falutin' ways. Officers, too, they was. Why, 'twere a disgrace!" exclaimed Mrs. Harding in righteous indignation.

Sabra, to whom the garrulous draper's wife had attached herself with daunting pertinacity when first they had boarded Brooklyn's ferry, smiled woodenly and murmured some appropriate phrase before turning her gaze once more to the vessels plying the harbor. Vaguely she was aware that her fellow passenger continued her diatribe on the licentious practices of the occupying forces, the rampant spread of crime in the streets, and the exorbitant costs in housing, food, and services in the city, but she had long since ceased to pay her any heed beyond an occasional nod or monosyllabic utterance. Sabra had far more pressing matters to contemplate; indeed, there was the distinct possibility that her welcome home would be attended by a warrant for her arrest.

Faith! she thought, feeling the perspiration suddenly cold against her skin. It had been a near thing this time. She, better than anyone, knew they had been luckier than they had any right to be. If the wind had not shifted or if the channel had changed in the weeks since Skyler last updated the charts, there would have been a less happy ending for them all. In truth, the captain of the British frigate had nearly done them in, and only she knew how desperate had been her decision to chance an escape through the treacherous inlet.

Who the devil was he? she wondered, as she had never ceased to do since the chase had first begun down the New England coast. Obviously his ship was new to these waters, for it was a peculiarity of sailors that they never forgot a vessel they had seen before, and none of the crew had recognized this one. Had he in truth been summoned solely to hunt down and either capture or destroy the *Nemesis?* Whoever he was, he was no novice. Indeed, if she lived to be a hundred, Sabra would never forget the way the British captain had anticipated her every move with uncanny precision *or* how her skin had prickled as she peered through the smoke-filled distance at the indistinct figure on the quarterdeck just before the light had utterly failed.

Sabra shivered. It had been rather like sensing one's own doom, she mused grimly, then mentally shook herself. It would hardly do to allow herself to begin thinking like that. Not now, when her nerves were already stretched thin with the uncertainty of what might be awaiting her arrival in the house on Nassau Street. And besides, close call or not, they had made it to her father's old shipyards with the *Nemesis* intact, except for the jettisoned guns, some spare timber, and the figurehead — all of which had been sacrificed to make it appear the schooner had been blown asunder. She regretted the figurehead most of all, for Skyler had assured her the rest could be replaced in time, and time was all she had for the present — providing, of course, that it had not run out the moment she was stupid enough to swallow Sir Wilfred's carefully planted bait.

A hard glitter came to her eyes at thought of the ease with which the baronet had played her. Good God, what a naive little fool she had been! A child should have sensed something untoward in his unguarded manner, and *she,* after all, had been forewarned. Nor would it matter one whit if it developed that he had not been casting his hook for Sabra Tyree. Obviously he had been using her for his own purposes. It remained only to see what those purposes were.

What a damnable toil she had woven for herself! she bitterly reflected. Why had she not listened to Robert when he cautioned her to be wary of Sir Wilfred Channing, and again when he entreated her to forego the plump coaster that seemed so ripe for the plucking? Inevitably she suffered a sharp pang of remorse, recalling how unforgivably she had behaved toward her old friend and advisor on the morning of her departure. Robert had been right that time, too, after all. In her position of prominence, she hazarded a deal of unwelcome speculation with *any* prolonged absence from the city. But how much more had she risked with this foolhardy venture!

"Ah, here we are at last," said Mrs. Harding, beginning to gather up her various possessions. "Will you be stopping here at the Vlie, my dear? The market looks to be doing a fair amount of trade today."

Sabra, jarred from her unrewarding ruminations, glanced up to find the Negro oarsmen laboring to bring their clumsy vessel into Vlie Slip.

"What? Oh. No, I have a house in the city," she answered with a distracted air.

Curiously Mrs. Harding turned her glance in the same direction as her companion's rather fixed stare.

" 'Tis enough to give ye the shivers, ain't it," she remarked, observing the wretched hulk anchored a little way off Tolmie's wharf near the bustling Vlie Market. "It's the *Jersey*, I'm told, that used to be a hospital ship. But now they've turned it into a prison."

"Good God," breathed Sabra, feeling the bile rise to her throat as she looked with renewed horror at the grisly thing. Stripped of ornament, figurehead, sails and rigging, and with only the bowsprit, a hoisting apparatus, and a flagstaff at the stern for spars, the once proud ship crouched ignominiously at its moorings. The portholes had been sealed so that the only avenues for air and light to reach the interior were in the form of small squares, perhaps ten feet apart, which had been cut through the ship's sides. Sabra shivered at sight of the iron bars, wedged like gruesome semblances of crosses into each aperture. They, no less than the grimy, blackened hull, were grim reminders of the human suffering they contained within.

"God have mercy on the poor souls," Sabra murmured in a voice hardly above a whisper. Then dragging her eyes from the gruesome sight, she left the ferry and made her way up the stone steps to Vlie Market in search of Jubal Henry, who was supposed to be waiting with the carriage.

"I be tellin' it jest like Mistuh Robert done tole it to me," Phoebe insisted some time later as she helped her mistress out of her ermine-lined pelisse. "He say there be hell to pay an' for you to sit tight an' do nothin' till he come back. What'd he mean by that, Miss Sabra? Has you gone an' got yourself into some kinda trouble?"

Playing for time till her heart might cease its fearful pounding, Sabra frowned and tugged at her tan kid gloves one finger at a time.

"I haven't the least notion what he could mean," she managed with a semblance of indifference as she handed the gloves to the anxious nanny. "Did he mention where he was going or when he would return?"

"He didn't say nothin' more. Jest lit outta here like his coattails was on fire. It was right after Jubal come in with that look on his black face that say he ain't talkin' to no one nohow, so I knows you been up to no good, Miss Sabra. All that was last evenin', and I ain't seen hide nor hair of Mistuh Robert since."

Sabra crossed, outwardly calm, to the gilt-framed looking glass hung in the receiving hall. Undoing the silk ribbons beneath her chin with an absorbed air, she slipped the accordion-like calash off her head before turning back to her agitated servant.

"I shouldn't worry if I were you, Phoebe," she dissembled, wishing only to be rid of the well-meaning nanny. "Doubtless it is something to do with finances. You know how Robert takes these things to heart. Now, if there are no more messages for me, I intend to retire to the study until dinner. You may have Jubal carry up my trunk when he comes in, if you please."

"Laws a mercy, Miss Sabra! In all the goin's on I done nearly forgot," exclaimed Phoebe, retrieving a sealed letter from a voluminous pocket of her apron. "This come for you this mornin'. That Colonel Ridgley brung it by. Tole me to give it straight in your hand the instant you walked in the door. An' that's jest what I be doin'."

Sabra's heart gave a little leap.

"Thank you, Phoebe," she murmured, careful to let none of her excitement show before the old nanny's keen-eyed scrutiny. "Please send Mr. Wayne directly to the study if he comes in, will you?"

"Yes, Miss Sabra," muttered the disgruntled Negress, flinging up her hands in disgust at her mistress's failure to confide in her. "Whatever you says, Miss Sabra. Don't nobody listen to old Phoebe nohow."

It was all Sabra could do to keep from flying up the stairs. As soon as she reached the privacy of the book room, she tore open Ridgley's letter with fingers that slightly shook. Hastily she scanned the brief message. Then for a moment she stood staring vacantly into space before sinking at last onto a stool as if her limbs could no longer bear her.

"Good God," she said aloud, then nearly jumped at the sudden, urgent rap on the study door. Hurriedly she concealed the letter in the folds of her gown and came to her feet as Robert Wayne burst into the room without waiting for permission to enter. His aspect exceedingly pale, he crossed swiftly to her.

"Sabra, thank God you're safe!" he declared, clasping her by the shoulders and surveying her from head to foot as though still not convinced she was there in the flesh. "I've been at my wit's end with worry since we heard the *Nemesis* had been sunk. Until Jubal arrived, I was tortured with all sorts of dire imaginings."

"Oh, dear, I was afraid that would be the case," Sabra answered with a rueful smile. "I'm glad I thought to send Jubal ahead to relieve your mind."

"No less than am I. What in blue blazes happened out there?"

"It was a trap," she said simply, moving out from beneath his hands still resting on her shoulders. "There was a British frigate waiting for us when we came upon Channing's coaster." Without roundaboutation, she quickly filled him in on all that had happened since last she had seen him. "I was almost certain there would be a warrant out for me when I returned," she added, coming to the end of the tale. "Nor was I the least comforted to learn you had bolted from the house yesterday, raving something about there being the hell to pay. I came home to find Phoebe near to a fit of the spasms, I promise you. Whatever were you thinking of?"

Wayne grinned a trifle sheepishly.

"That was rather lack-witted of me, I'm afraid." Immediately he sobered, however. "Channing was here yesterday. He claimed he had only just heard you had suffered some sort of bereavement and thought he would drop by to offer whatever comfort he could."

"The devil he did," uttered Sabra with a chilling little laugh. "And what did you reply to his kind offer?"

"I told him that rumor had greatly exaggerated your indisposition and intimated—in the most delicate of terms, I assure you—that what was presumed to have been a bereavement was in actuality nothing more than an unsettling disappointment. Indeed, though you felt the need to withdraw from the public eye for a brief period of time, I was quite certain you would soon come to grips with your blighted expectations. He left with my assurances that doubtless you would be back in circulation quite soon again."

"Robert Wayne, you rogue!" exclaimed Sabra, her eyes shimmering with mirth. "How dare you imply that I was suffering from a broken heart. By now it must be all over the city that the incomparable Miss Tyree has been jilted!"

"I shouldn't doubt it for a moment," Wayne agreed without a flicker of remorse. "After due consideration, you see, it occurred to me that the necessity of affecting black gloves upon your return might prove somewhat inconvenient."

"Faith, I never thought of that. Still, there might have been some advantages in being forced to remain in relative seclusion for six months of mourning," she reflected wryly. "I could hardly get into much trouble confined at home. I suppose you might as well learn the rest of it," she added, handing him the message she had received from Colonel Ridgley.

My dear Miss Tyree, (began the letter)

I deeply regret that I shall be unable to take my leave of you in person. Even as I write, the regiment is preparing to embark on shipboard, and I have little time left. I wish only to say that you have made an old soldier feel less lonely during his stay in your city and more at home than he has felt at times in his own London Town. Perhaps the news that I have to impart will in some way repay you for your ever gracious hospitality.

I have been able to learn very little concerning your brother's fate, except that he was apparently impressed into service aboard H.M.S. *Black Swan* shortly after his capture. As to the identity of the ship's captain or his mission in American waters, I can only tell you that they have been placed under an unbreakable ban of silence. I am sorry.

> With sincerest regards,
> Your servant,
> P.R.

"Dear Ridgley," murmured Sabra when Wayne had finished reading. "He must have known after making his own inquiries that a deal more was at stake than the mere fate of a captive rebel, but he has nevertheless done just as he had promised. He has discovered the name of the ship on which Wes is being held. And more than that, he has even gone so far as to communicate an oblique warning for us to proceed with caution. Indeed, he must have thought long and hard before deciding to reveal that the matter is being treated in the strictest confidence by his superiors. I pray he will suffer no harm for it," she added, feeling distinctly uneasy about the manner in which she had taken advantage of his kindness.

But then all thoughts of the gallant colonel fled as Wayne reminded her of the dire possibilities inherent in the news Ridgley had imparted.

"Good God," he ejaculated, his look grim indeed. "This must be the same frigate that almost did you and the *Nemesis* in!"

"It would seem so," mused Sabra. "But what are we to

make of it?"

Retrieving Ridgley's letter, she deliberately dropped it into the fire crackling in the fireplace before turning to cross with a preoccupied air to the window. Carried on a draught, the sheet of paper lifted and fluttered to the back, its corners curling as the flames caught.

"I should think it is obvious. Channing must have known, or at least suspected, that you have been involved in gathering information about his smuggling activities. My guess is that he set up this whole thing just to lure you out into the open."

A log collapsed in the fireplace, sending sparks flying. Kneeling down with the poker to shove a glowing ember back in the grate, Wayne uttered an ironic bark of laughter.

"Egad, but he was mostly damnably clever about it, too. Knowing your curiosity would be piqued — to say the very least — by the mystery surrounding Wes's disappearance, he made certain that you heard of his capture. It was practically inevitable that eventually you would be led to conclude Channing was behind all this secrecy. He had most to gain from exposing you. He knew you would be forced to try to milk him for more information, and then, by God, he had you exactly where he wanted you. Dammit, Sabra! We played right into his hands."

"Indeed we did if all you have speculated is true," Sabra said, troubled by the vague feeling that some important piece of the puzzle was still missing. "And yet to accept your theory is to presume Channing must clearly have been aware not only of Wes's capture, but of his relationship to me as well. But how could he have known? Until I was forced to try to find Wes, I'm sure I never told anyone about him. Maybe it is only coincidence that my brother became involved in all of this. I cannot help but wonder if there might not be some other explanation for everything that's happened. Something we have overlooked."

"You won't anymore, however. Not after I tell you what else I've learned about Sir Wilfred Channing," Wayne predicted with a peculiar glint in his eye. "You see, I've spent the last twenty-four hours trying to track down the source of the rather exaggerated report of your demise. You'll never guess who let the information out."

"Not Sir Wilfred?" she hazarded and felt the hairs rise at the nape of her neck at Wayne's nod in the affirmative. "You're quite sure?"

"There's no possibility of doubt. The admiralty denied any knowledge that one of their ships had met with and caused the destruction of an American privateer in these waters. Indeed, they seemed as startled as I was to hear of it. But most damning of all is the fact that it was Channing himself who informed *me* of it."

"When he came to inquire about my absence!" concluded Sabra with utter certainty. "Good God, Robert. How could I have been such a fool?"

Shrugging, Wayne let his glance slide away from hers.

"I don't know," he said, reaching out with his foot to shove an ember, smoldering on the hearth, back into the fire. "Maybe it was inevitable that we'd be discovered. We've been confoundedly lucky up till now. I expect we were bound to slip up sooner or later. The curious thing is that apparently a dozen or so others in the West Indies were not so lucky as the *Nemesis*. They not only fell for the bait. They swallowed it hook, line and sinker."

"Faith, a dozen, Robert? Not one escaped?" She did not need Wayne's dire shake of the head to confirm it. They now knew, after all, that the *Swan* had been cruising the islands, and none was better acquainted than she with the deadly efficiency of the frigate's captain. Suddenly her head came up. "But would not so many seem to defy the element of chance?" she queried with a curious glint in her eyes.

Wayne went abruptly still.

"Aye, now that you mention it," he said grimly, "it would appear to suggest the dice were somehow weighted against our people. Sabra, if someone's working both sides of the fence, don't you think it's time we got out—while we still can?"

Sabra did not answer at first. The taste of failure was bitter in her mouth, but a smoldering rage was slowly building up inside her. Channing had to be the snake in the grass. She'd wager her life on it. And she was damned if she would turn tail and run before she had the evidence to prove it.

"I won't quit yet," she said at last, her chin up and defiant. "Sir Wilfred cannot prove anything, and with the *Nemesis* apparently blown to kingdom come, he has only one ace left in his hand. He still holds Wes, and we can do nothing more until we know where Channing is keeping him."

Wayne's eyebrows shot together in sudden alarm.

"Sabra, I little like that look," he uttered in accents of dire speculation. "What folly are you plotting now?"

Sabra met him glance for glance.

"One last mission before we get out of here for good," she answered, dangerously calm. " 'Tis time, I think, that I paid Sir Wilfred a little visit."

Sabra, a copy of Henry Fielding's *Amelia* tucked under her arm and Phoebe parading a few steps behind, strolled unhurriedly along the rows of bookshelves toward the lending-library's front exit. The rustle of her silk skirts, draped *à la polonaise* over three panniers, and the soft click of her Italian heels set well under the soles of dainty silk brocade shoes attracted the attention of more than one of the gentlemen who sat reading the latest papers to reach New York from England. Not the least of these was Sir Wilfred Channing, who, glancing up from the *London Times*, arched his arrogantly drawn eyebrows with something of surprise. Leisurely laying his paper aside, he rose languidly from his seat to accost the lady.

"Ah, Miss Tyree. How delightful to see you out and about again," he murmured, sweeping her trim figure with a heavy-lidded glance.

"Sir Wilfred!" exclaimed Sabra, artfully surprised. "Faith, you quite startled me."

"Then naturally I must beg your pardon for it," he returned with studied grace.

Still, Sabra was quick to note the ironic curve of his lip. Obviously he was not fooled by her display of innocence. Nor, if she was any judge, did he believe for a moment that

66

theirs was a chance encounter. But then that was just as she had intended it to be. Channing, after all, had thrown down the gauntlet. She would make certain he knew before she left him that she had come to accept his challenge. Everything depended on it.

"Not at all, sir," she laughed, becomingly flustered at her unseemly outburst. " 'Tis only that somehow I never expected to see you here, of all places. Do you make it a practice to come often?"

"As a matter of fact, I do. A habit I developed in my youth as a valuable means of keeping abreast of worldly events. Not having been born to position or wealth, I was ever ambitious of making up the deficit."

"Indeed, and you have been wondrously successful at it. Why, you have even brought an end to the maraudings of that rascally privateer, have you not? But then you did say you were as good as your word. I remember it quite distinctly."

"I am gratified to have made so great an impression, mademoiselle," Channing murmured, inclining his head in acknowledgment of the supposed honor she did him. "As for the privateer, I fear the matter is not yet finished, since I still have not the master and his crew in irons."

"Oh, but I assumed they must have perished with their vessel," Sabra rejoined in wide-eyed innocence. "Why, surely we have seen the last of them?"

Channing's lips curved in a cold glimmer of a smile.

"I intend to make certain of it, Miss Tyree. After all, as you have already pointed out, I have pledged my word on it."

"Well, then," shrugged the lady prettily, "I suppose the thing is satisfactorily settled, is it not?"

"If not, then it shall be directly," he countered suavely. "And may I infer from your appearance here today that you are fully recovered from your unfortunate *maladie de coeur?*"

"But of course, monsieur. I have never been one to pine over what cannot be helped. Henceforth I shall know better than to entrust my sensibilities to a blue-coated will-o'-the-wisp—here today, gone tomorrow."

"Am I to understand," he queried, lifting an arrogant eyebrow, "that our incomparable Miss Tyree has fallen victim to a uniform? But how *drôle*. You must tell me sometime how the rogue managed anything quite so extraordinary."

Sabra awarded the gentleman a haughty glance.

"I fear your point escapes me, sir. I hardly consider it 'extraordinary' that a young, unmarried female should yearn for masculine companionship. Someone to ease her solitary existence, as it were, and to satisfy — shall we say — her 'natural inclination to be affectionate'?"

"Shall we indeed?" said the gentleman with a sudden glimmer of interest. " 'Pon my faith, you intrigue me. Dare I suggest, I wonder, that a single gentleman suffers dispositions of a similar nature?"

"You may suggest it if you like," Sabra retorted with cool disdain, "but I fear you must excuse me if I confess not to believe you. It has been my observation that while gentlemen may be pleased to profess an undying affection for a lady, once presented with a fait accompli, they are most apt thereafter to display a preference for purely masculine company. A man's greatest loyalty is to his fellows, while a woman's is to the man who wins her heart."

"My poor Miss Tyree, if you would not suffer such disillusionment, you must avoid losing your heart to sailors. Such men may be expected to succumb to the demands of duty and the pursuit of glory. You require someone who would value your exquisite charms as a connoisseur values a rare and lovely masterpiece of art. Someone, indeed, such as this, your humble servant."

"Are you by any chance making me a proposal, sir?" the lady demanded with a distinct air of incredulity.

"Rather say a 'proposition,' mademoiselle," amended the baronet, smoothly bowing.

Sabra gritted her teeth to keep from delivering him a stinging report. What an insufferable coxcomb he was, to be sure. Her smile, as he indolently straightened, was openly contemptuous.

"But of course," she murmured, "I should have known. Now, if you will excuse me?" Deliberately she summoned Phoebe with a glance and, nodding faintly to the baronet, started to move past him. Channing's hand came to rest lightly on her arm.

"You have not heard my proposition yet," he reminded her in tones of velvet-covered steel. "It occurs to me that I should enjoy the pleasure of your company this evening in my private suite. For dinner, shall we say? Believe me when I tell you that it would be to your own best interests if you accepted my invitation. Indeed, should you be so foolhardy as to refuse, rest assured that my next would be of a far less amiable nature."

"But I would not dream of refusing," Sabra said, her green eyes faintly mocking. "I shall be there no later than ten."

A flicker of surprise passed briefly across the pallid visage. Then the indolent mask dropped instantly in place again.

"I shall look forward to it, mademoiselle." His eyes never left hers as he carried her hand to his lips. "You will come unattended by your disapproving duenna, *vous savez*," he added, nodding significantly toward the frowning maid servant.

"Mais certainement," Sabra flung airily over her shoulder as she turned to go. "Phoebe, after all, would be decidedly *de trop*, would she not?"

Her mood swiftly altered, however, as she left the rather gloomy environs of the library and stepped out into the bright sunlight of a chill December day.

"Miss Sabra, has you done lost your mind?" Phoebe exploded as soon as the door closed behind them. "You ain't goin' to no man's room, less'n it be over this black woman's dead body. Does you hear me?"

"Yes, I hear you," Sabra snapped. "Doubtless the whole world will hear you unless you instantly cease to yammer."

A steely glint hardened her eyes to a cold sheen. She had achieved her purpose in waylaying the baronet, but she would need a deal of luck and a woman's wiles to see her safely through the final phase. Suddenly she was impatient to be home, to think and plan.

"Enough," she said, cutting short whatever else Phoebe had been about to say. "I'm in no mood for a curtain lecture, I warn you, Phoebe. No matter how well intentioned it is meant to be. Please, just get into the carriage."

One look at her mistress's unyielding aspect effectively silenced any further remonstrances from Phoebe. Muttering direly beneath her breath, she did as she was bidden.

Chapter 5

The city's streets that night were occupied by the usual diverse smatterings of people. Drunken brawlers, garish women, and the ragtag who managed a miserable existence in "Canvas Town," the shambles of wretched hovels that had sprung up amid the charred ruins of the two great fires, formed by far the largest segment of those present. Still, an ample number of Redcoats stood out in sharp relief among the nondescript of the other passersby, for the king's soldiers were the favored customers of the taverns and houses of ill repute with which the city abounded. Only slightly less prevalent were the conveyances of the rich, bearing their elegantly attired occupants to and from the various nightly entertainments reserved for them alone. Sabra, however, took notice of none of them. Huddled in the shadowy interior of her carriage, she was preoccupied with disquieting thoughts of what awaited her at the end of the brief journey.

The carriage, turning off Maiden Lane on to Queen Street, came at last to the Royal Arms Hotel overlooking Vlie Market and the East River, and suddenly she shivered from more than the chill air. In spite of anything she may have said to the contrary, she knew she would sacrifice a deal more than her virtue if Channing had his way with her. Indeed, she shuddered to the depths of her soul at the thought of having to endure his touch, his eyes on her.

"Oh, God. How shall I bear to face Wes after 'tis over and done?" she groaned, clenching shut her eyes. As though she could block out the dreadful realization of what she meant to do, she thought bitterly, or the tormenting uncertainty that Wes would ever forgive her for paying the price for his freedom. The memory of her half-brother, his grin awry as he

71

chucked her under the chin and warned her to behave herself while he was gone, came to haunt her. For a moment she thought she could not bear the terrible rending of her heart. But at last her head came up to reveal eyes that glittered with a fierce flame.

She must dare anything, she told herself, *do* anything that was necessary to discover where they were keeping Wes. Whatever else happened in the next few hours, she must keep on telling herself that that was all that mattered. Concealing the upper half of her face behind a black mask, Sabra gathered her silk domino about her and stepped down into the street. Then for the briefest instant she paused, struck by a sudden thought.

Once a long time ago, she had sworn no man would lay a hand on her unless he first won her heart, and now she was about to break that vow. All at once her lips curled in a wry grimace. But then she had yet to meet the man to whom she would willingly give her heart. Perhaps he did not even exist.

"Wait for me, no matter how long it takes," she said over her shoulder to Jubal and crossed without further hesitation to the hotel's entrance.

The foyer smelled of cigar smoke, old wood, and lemon oil, and the single globed lantern suspended from the ceiling did little to relieve the gloom, but at least she seemed to be the only one about, thought Sabra with a faint sigh of relief. Then her breath caught in her throat as, out of the corner of her eye, she glimpsed a dark figure detach itself from the shadows.

"How dare you sneak up on me like that!" she exclaimed more sharply than she had intended, for she had perceived almost immediately that he wore the crimson and silver livery of one of Channing's servants.

"I beg your pardon, miss," he said, bowing unctuously. "If you will please follow me, I have been instructed to take you directly to the gentleman's rooms."

Little trusting his looks, but wishing even less to attract more attention than was necessary, Sabra reluctantly complied with his suggestion that they proceed immediately to the back stairs, which were reserved for the use of the servants.

Narrow and poorly lit, the servants' passage offered little in the way of inducement *beyond* the obvious advantage of being unfrequented by the hotel guests. After enduring for a seemingly endless climb the smell of refuse and the appalling scutter of mice from beneath her feet, even her dread of the assignation with Sir Wilfred began to pale before her eagerness to escape the loathsome stairwell. She had only just congratulated herself on managing to accomplish the thing unremarked, when, approaching the end of the third flight, the muffled sound of voices issued from directly ahead.

"He wouldn' fight, I tell you. An' you weren' 'n any shape to know what 'as happ'n'in'. I only did what the ge'lman tol' me t'do," echoed sullenly down the stairwell.

"You are a liar, Mr. Inness, and if I had a shred of solid evidence that you have been dealing under the table, I'd have you court-martialed so fast it'd make your head spin. Henceforth you will take your orders from me and no one else. Is that understood?"

Sabra faltered and nearly stumbled on the steps. Faith! she thought, what was it about that voice to make her stomach knot and her knees to turn suddenly to water? She must have made a sound as well, for the heated exchange was cut abruptly short and she could see the two on the landing turn to stare down the stairwell. Angry with herself for having ruined any chance of remaining unseen until the gentlemen had left, she gathered up her skirts once more and started up the remaining steps to the landing.

In the dim light, Sabra could make out little of the men, save only that, while both were attired in the blue coat and white breeches worn by naval officers, one was fully a head taller than the other and pleasingly broad-shouldered. Wordlessly they parted to allow the footman to pass, then Sabra, turning sideways to allow for the fullness of her hooped petticoat, started to ease past the taller man.

Without warning her heart began to pound alarmingly as she drew abreast of him. Indeed, the narrow confines of the passage seemed suddenly stifling, and it was all she could do to fill her lungs with air. Unexpectedly, she brushed against

73

him. Like the veriest fool, she blushed with embarrassment and, succumbing to instinct, blurted, *"Pardon,"* in her distinctively throaty French.

Inexplicably, she felt him stiffen. Then to her mounting confusion she found herself suddenly and acutely aware of the lean, masculine body strung like a whipcord scant inches from her. With something akin to panic, she squeezed past him. Conscious then only of an overwhelming desire to get as far and as quickly away as was possible, she did not see the other man lurch unsteadily into her path until it was too late. Sabra gasped, finding herself suddenly pinioned against a hard chest.

"What'sh hurry, li'l ladybird?" slurred her captor, giving forth a convulsive hiccup. Inwardly Sabra groaned. Ecod, the oaf was clearly three sheets to the wind. Instantly she ceased to struggle.

"I fear you are mistaken, sir," she retorted imperiously. "But if you unhand me this instant, I shall contrive to forget the matter."

"Why, shert'nly. A lady's wish ish command. Only give ush a kiss firsht. Ain't too much t'ashk. One li'l kiss t' let li'l ladybird free," he leered and lunged drunkenly for her lips.

Instinctively Sabra twisted her head aside then cursed as her hood slipped to her shoulders, leaving her red-gold curls bared to the world. Without the least twinge of remorse, she brought her heel down hard against the officer's unprotected instep.

"Hellshfire!" he grunted and precipitously released her. In a flash, Sabra gathered up her skirts and fled up the stairs, driving the befuddled footman before her.

Fleetingly she heard the thud of footsteps starting in pursuit. Then a deep voice rang out.

"Have done, Inness. Leave her be."

"Leave 'er *be?* The bitch demmed near broke m' foot," drifted faintly to her. Then she heard no more as the footman, directing her along the fifth-floor corridor, halted before a set of carved oak doors.

"No, wait," she panted, seeing him grasp the door handles. "A moment to catch my breath, if you please."

Hastily, Sabra adjusted her rumpled domino. Faith, 'twas a wonder the clumsy lout had not dislodged her mask, she fretted, more shaken by her misadventure than she would have thought possible. After all, 'twas not the first time she had had to discourage the advances of a gentleman who was under the influence. But then it was not the drunken oaf who had upset her equilibrium, she knew, but the other one, the tall officer who had rather belatedly come to her assistance.

Indeed, she seemed still to feel him standing over her, his muscles tensed as if with some powerful emotion. And his voice — she had heard that voice somewhere before, she was quite certain of it. Indeed, when one thought of it, there had been something distinctly familiar about the broad-shouldered, slim-hipped figure glimpsed but briefly against the dim light of a hall lamp. Irritably she berated herself for not having stolen a glimpse of the man's face as she slipped by him, whereupon it came immediately to her to wonder at herself. Faith, what did it matter one way or the other who the man was? He might have been any one of a number of officers whose chance acquaintance she had made in the past two years, and she had more serious business before her.

Dismissing both the man and the incident from her thoughts, Sabra drew in a deep breath and nodded to the disgruntled footman.

"You may open the door now, if you please," she said with at least the semblance of her usual composure. "Doubtless in the circumstances, I am as ready as can be expected."

Obviously Sir Wilfred was used to intimate entertainments, Sabra mused ironically as she found herself ushered into the gentleman's spacious sitting room. A Jacobean sofa and matching armchairs, all upholstered in turkey work and ranged about a hexagonal walnut tea table, occupied the center of the room, while a tapestried wing chair, fronted by a long stool in the style of a duchesse, was placed all too cozily before an intricately carved fireplace. Situated to offer a stunning view of the harbor through a large bay window was an oval dining table, elaborately laid out for two. Sir

Wilfred's parlor boasted, in addition, a spinet and a standing harp, plush cushions and oriental rugs, numerous urns, mirrors, and incense burners, and a veritable fortune in objets d'art displayed about the room on ornate laquered tables, pedestals, and in glassed cupboards.

The overall effect was something of a cross between a French salon and an eastern potentate's harem, she decided, though she little doubted it exuded a certain seductive charm for one so inclined. She, however, most emphatically was not — so long as she could avoid it.

Suddenly her gaze alighted on a worn oak desk box. Set out of the way atop a lovely, contoured maple lowboy just beyond the dining table, it seemed peculiarly out of place among all the finer pieces. Obviously it must have seen a deal of service in the company of its owner; indeed, it was just the sort of thing in which a gentleman might keep valuable documents, especially if he anticipated the possibility of having one day to make a hurried departure. Instantly she experienced an overwhelming curiosity to know what was inside the box.

The sudden prickle of nerve endings warned her that she was not alone, and she turned to discover her host studying her from the doorway of an adjoining room in which could be glimpsed a great poster bed draped in damask.

"You are, if anything, punctual, Miss Tyree," drawled Sir Wilfred, closing the door gently behind him. "I find that particularly refreshing in one of your gender. Waiting, even for a woman as beautiful as you, can be so very irksome, *vous savez.*"

Faith, the evening promised to be far worse than she had imagined, reflected Sabra with a sinking heart, as she observed the baronet attired *en déshabillé* in an elegantly cut, striped silk banyon, which reached to the ankles. Even more revealing, however, was his departure from the customary, elaborately dressed wig in favor of his own hair, which was lighter in color than her own and worn in a queue at the nape of the neck. In lieu of a folded stock, he sported a white linen cravat flowing with fine lace and tied loosely about the throat, and his face was only lightly rouged and painted.

Obviously he had determined on an informal evening, interspersed, no doubt, with his own brand of parlor games, thought Sabra grimly.

"Doubtless I am gratified to have spared you any such inconvenience," she answered dryly as she sank into a curtsey.

In revulsion she felt his hand, soft as a woman's, bidding her to rise. Then, coming gracefully erect, she found him scrutinizing her with heavy-lidded insolence, and suddenly it came to her that he wanted her defiant; indeed, had counted on it. But then she had always known he desired her only for the amusement of seeing her submit to him against her will. Nor did she doubt for a moment that he would glory in breaking her as another might exult in crushing the pride of a spirited animal. Refusing to give him the satisfaction of knowing how totally he revolted her, Sabra returned his look with a disdainful arch of the eyebrow. Still, it was all she could do to remain coolly indifferent as he drew insinuatingly nearer.

"On the contrary," he murmured, holding her with those soulless eyes as he lifted her hood back and let it drop about her shoulders, then deliberately removed her mask. "You are not in the least gratified, you know." In spite of herself, Sabra flinched ever so slightly at the brush of his fingertips against her throat. A chilling smile touched his lips. "But, indeed, you should be, my dear," he continued in those same insidiously languorous tones, his fingers working leisurely down the front of her domino, undoing the fastenings, one by one. "I am lamentably lacking in the more divine virtues of compassion and forgiveness, having long since discovered they are but poor excuses for weakness." Moving back a step, he drew the domino open. Slowly he exhaled before raising gloating eyes once more to hers. "You will soon learn, however, that should it prove necessary in achieving a desired object, I can be infinitely patient."

With an effort Sabra quelled the nausea rising to her throat. His every look, his every word and deed had been a calculated assault on her sensibilities. He was worse than despicable. He was sadistic, cruel and vile, and any pleasure he might take in bedding her would derive solely from the sense of power it gave him.

Strangely enough, the knowledge, instead of filling her with dismay, served rather to steady her nerves and strengthen her resolve to defeat him at his own perverted game.

"Am I to infer that you allude to my presence here?" she queried, slipping the domino off her shoulders and draping it casually over the back of the sofa. Her cream silk robe *battante* shimmered in the light of the crystal chandelier as coolly she came about to face the baronet.

An appreciative gleam shone briefly between Channing's slitted eyelids.

"What do *you* think, mademoiselle?" he said, allowing his gaze to linger insinuatingly on the bare expanse of milk-white skin above the daring decollete of her gown.

"I think you are playing very deep, monsieur," she shrugged, and began to stroll provocatively across the room, pausing here and there to trail her fingers negligently over some priceless oddity.

Channing, drawing forth an exquisite enameled snuffbox, never took his eyes off her slow progress.

"I, on the other hand, have not the slightest notion of what you mean," he said, flipping open the lid with the flick of a thumbnail and taking out a pinch.

"Oh, but I believe you do." Suddenly she halted in her apparently aimless wandering to pick up a delicately wrought Marseilles faience ewer. "Indeed, it occurs to me that you are quite French in your tastes, are you not? I should have thought someone in your position would prefer Wedgewood, or at the very least, Staffordshire."

"You surprise me, Miss Tyree," he replied imperturbably. "I was not aware you were a connoisseur of fine porcelain."

Shrugging, Sabra replaced the ewer and moved on to the oval dining table.

"I am not totally unversed in the finer things. But you still have not answered my question, Sir Wilfred."

She had to will herself not to look as she listened to his indolent steps approaching at her back. His touch, like the insidious caress of a viper, made her flesh crawl. Indeed, she thought she must scream as she endured his hands trailing with calculated deliberation up her arms till at last they came to rest on the bare slope of her shoulders above the neck of her gown.

"Suffice it to say that I am a man of the world," he murmured insufferably. "One with resources great enough to pick and choose whatever I desire."

Sabra stared rigidly before her as she felt his breath, loathsomely warm and moist against her skin. Sublimely confident in his ultimate victory, he was toying with her, she knew, and yet she sensed that she had taken him by surprise. As his lips brushed the tender flesh below her ear, she slipped smoothly from beneath his hands and stepped to the window.

"And what is it that you want from me?" she asked casually, as if it were a matter of little import. "I am not easily bought, I promise you."

Letting his hands drop to his sides, Channing shrugged.

"I would not have you if you were, mademoiselle. But in this case, I am confident we shall reach an equitable agreement—once you are acquainted with the terms." The last was uttered with a chilling significance that was not lost on her.

"Shall we indeed?" she rejoined, coolly appraising. "My bondage to you—in exchange for what, I wonder. Only the life of one very dear to me could be worth so much, for I swear to you I would rather die by my own hand than submit to an extortionist for less."

"Ah, I see you are as quick as ever to grasp my meaning," he said, savoring her proud loveliness. "I confess to finding you a never-ending delight, Miss Tyree. But you, on the other hand, must think me a very poor host. May I offer you some refreshment? A glass of champagne, perhaps, before we dine."

Sabra hesitated the barest instant before ironically inclining her head.

"Indeed, why not? 'Tis the civilized thing, after all."

Faith! He was as cold-blooded as a reptile, she thought, watching him fill two crystal wineglasses from a bottle on the table then turn indolently to offer her one of them. Raising his glass with the arrogance of one celebrating what he already considered to be a fait accompli, he saluted her before sipping the wine with delicate refinement.

"Well, monsieur?" she murmured, slowly twirling the stem of the glass between her fingers. "Now that we have observed the amenities, perhaps you would see fit to relieve my curiosity. What are these 'terms' you would offer?"

"Very well, since you insist on business before pleasure. Perhaps you would humor me by taking in the view from the window. There—do you see it? The vessel moored a short distance from the slip?"

Suddenly an icy hand clutched her heart. Carefully Sabra swallowed before answering.

"It is the British prison ship. What of it?" With an indifferent shrug, she raised her glass to her lips and pretended to drink.

"Quite simply stated," he said, "it was recently brought to my attention that a certain young American, perhaps dear to you, has been confined in that ship, which, I might add, is fast earning a reputation for—shall we say—extreme conditions?"

"You may say whatever you wish, I am sure. And still I do not see what it could possibly have to do with me. Or perhaps you have forgotten that I am the granddaughter of an English earl? I can hardly be concerned over the suffering of some misguided rebel with whom I might once have been acquainted. Or perhaps you are questioning my loyalty? If so, I fear I must demand to know what evidence you hold against me."

"Come now, Miss Tyree. We both know whatever proofs I might have offered were destroyed with the *Nemesis*. In truth, I must admire your accomplice for his audacity. You have both been very clever and have, as a result, caused me a deal of trouble and money. But now it is finished."

A faint, ironic smile touched Sabra's lips. So, *he* was not quite so clever as he believed himself to be, she thought with a certain grim satisfaction. He had yet to figure out that she, and not some mythical accomplice, was the privateer he wished to see in irons.

"I'm sure I haven't the least notion of what you are talking about, Sir Wilfred," she said aloud, playing the game out to the very end, all the while her mind working with lightning speed.

She little doubted that with the crew of the *Nemesis* to help her, they must surely find a way to break Wes out of the prison ship, but it would take time, and time was at a premium so long as Sir Wilfred had the power to do as he wished with his hostage. If only she could find the means of neutralizing the baronet's influence among those in high places, she thought, her eyes drawn as if of their own volition to the oak box a tantalizing two or three feet away.

It seemed, however, that Channing had anticipated her thoughts — at least in part.

"You will never get him out alive, you know," he said, taking the bottle of champagne in his free hand and moving languidly to join his guest before the window. "You will observe that a guard ship patrols the area night and day, and there, do you see the vessel moored a few yards to inland? That, my dear, is a hospital ship, to which the prisoners are taken — to die, for the most part, of their many ailments. It also has a guard. And there, the line of small fires extending east on the banks of the cove toward Hurl-Gate. Those are sentinels, regularly spaced for some three and a half miles. And that is only the beginning."

Deliberately he paused to refill her glass before continuing to catalogue the obstacles that faced anyone attempting to breach the defenses of the floating prison.

"I should warn you that the ship itself is well guarded. Except for the burial detail, no more than two prisoners are allowed at any one time above deck, and the gun ports of the lower deck are barred strongly with iron bolted to the sides of the ship. So you see there is only one escape possible for those poor unfortunates. If you wish it, I shall take you to view for yourself where the tides daily uncover their partially decomposed bodies."

Never would she have thought it possible to subdue the flood of bitter loathing that swept her then. But somehow she did. Nevertheless, she judged that she had learned enough. It

81

was time to make good her own escape, if she still could.

Vaguely surprised to find her nerves rock steady, Sabra raised the glass to the baronet in a salute deliberately contemptuous.

"I offer you my congratulations, Sir Wilfred. You have just demonstrated that you are far more depraved than even I had imagined you to be. And now, since I am quite lacking in appetite, I really think I shall be going."

Calmly setting down her drink, Sabra crossed with cool disdain toward the sofa on which she had left her cloak. The slow, measured clap of his hands in mocking applause brought her to a halt, her fingers curling into fists at her sides.

"Bravo, mademoiselle, bravo. A masterful performance. But we both know 'tis only a bluff. If you walk out that door, I promise your brother will be dead before the dawn breaks."

So, the game was truly over, came fleetingly to Sabra, the need for pretense at an end.

"I see," she murmured, without turning around. "And if I stay?"

She could sense his careless shrug.

"I am not without influence. It is possible an exchange might be arranged, if I could but be persuaded to drop a well-placed word here and there. You see, 'tis wholly up to you whether or not you would see your brother again — alive."

A moment longer she stood rigidly unmoving. Then visibly she relaxed. Channing's thinly drawn eyebrows lifted as, coming gracefully about to face him, she smiled with beguiling artlessness.

"How foolish of me to believe myself up to your weight in a duel of wits," she sighed. "You have bested me at every turn, have you not? Ah, well, *qu'est-ce qu'on peut dire?* Naturally, I will do whatever I must to save my brother."

Tantalizingly she tugged at the ends of the first of the bows that held her gown together in front.

"You see I can be most compliant when necessity demands," she said. Then, teasing him with her eyes, she undid the second bow and provocatively slipped the gown from one creamy shoulder.

"Ah, I can see you are not displeased with your latest acquisition. Tell me, how can I be sure you will keep your part of the bargain?"

"But I thought you had already agreed I am a man who is as good as his word," he answered, coming toward her at last.

"Did I?" she murmured, the palms of her hands suddenly clammy with sweat. And all at once she knew she could not go through with it. Apparently he saw it, too.

"You poor, naive little fool," he sneered, and without warning, wrenched the fabric of her bodice down to her waist. For an instant a cold gleam came to his eyes at sight of the fullness of her breasts swelling against the top of her lace corset. "Ah, you are lovely," he gloated and grasping her cruelly by the arms, he slowly lowered his head toward her.

He seemed to revel in her stifled gasp of pain as, deliberately ruthless, he bruised her soft flesh with his lips, assaulted her innocence with his touch. From somewhere Sabra found the strength not to resist him. Divorcing herself as well as she could from her own feelings of horror and revulsion, she concentrated on working her hand through the placket slit in her petticoat to the small gun concealed in the pocket beneath. She thought she must give in to the rising tide of panic before at last her fingers found and curled about the grip.

At the cold caress of tempered steel against his ribs, Channing stiffened.

"Softly, monsieur," murmured Sabra in chilling tones. "Your life hangs by the merest thread."

Carefully he straightened and drew away, his eyes riveted on the small, but deadly looking pistol trained unerringly on his chest. Running his tongue over suddenly dry lips, he looked at Sabra's face and held.

"Don't be a fool," he said. "We both know you don't intend to shoot. They'd hang you for it."

"Would they? Are you so sure? Look at me. Obviously I am only a woman forced to protect herself. Now, if you would be so kind as to give me the key to that box, I might be persuaded to let you live just a while longer."

Instantly she knew she had not guessed wrongly. Indeed, she could not mistake the sudden leap of fear in his eyes.

"Quickly!" she prodded. "I am in no mood to be patient."

A glimmer of cold rage twisted across his face. Then all at once he shrugged with all his former arrogance and drew forth a ring of keys from a sidepocket.

"Here, take them," he sneered, dangling the ring from limp fingers.

Sabra's lips curved in a humorless smile.

"Oh, I think not, Sir Wilfred. Indeed, I should prefer to have you do the honors."

"But of course. How very wise of you," he murmured acidly. Walking over to the box, he inserted the key and turned it in the lock. "There, 'tis done, though what you could possibly find to interest you among my personal effects utterly escapes me."

At her fierce gesture with the gun, he shrugged once more and obligingly retreated a few steps toward the window.

"How odd it never occurred to me you might be a thief as well as a traitor," he mused, settling carelessly on the edge of the dining table, his legs propped out before him. " 'Tis too bad, actually. I might have found a use for your peculiar talents beyond the usual employments of a mere paramour. Indeed, in time you might even have come to an appreciation of all that I was prepared to offer you."

"Somehow I doubt that very much," Sabra retorted, cautiously circling round to the lowboy. With icy deliberation, she leveled the gun at his heart. "If you value your life, Sir Wilfred, you will not move a muscle. I seldom miss a target, *vous-savez?*"

The baronet's thin-lipped smile was anything but pleasant.

"You would be well advised to reconsider while there is still time," he said in velvet-soft tones. "If you lay down the weapon now, I promise I shall forget this small infraction. Otherwise, you may be sure your brother will pay the bill for it in full, and I shall still have you — one way or another."

"In hell, perhaps, Sir Wilfred," Sabra answered coldly and spilled the contents of the box onto the surface of the lowboy. A small journal bound with a ribbon to a slender packet tumbled out, along with several obviously expensive pieces of jewelry, a large bundle of British currency, and a purse, apparently plump with silver. Ignoring the other things, Sabra picked up the journal and packet.

"As I don't wish to take up any more of your time, I fear I shall just have to take these with me to read at my leisure," she said, slipping the small bundle into the pocket beneath her petticoat. "And now I really must be going. If you would be so good as to withdraw to your boudoir? . . ."

His easy compliance should have warned her, but she was only relieved when, sardonically inclining his head toward her, he straightened and began to move past her toward the closed door of the adjoining room. Too late she glimpsed the glass of champagne in his hand, ironically the one with which she had toasted him earlier. Flinging its contents in her face, he lunged for the gun.

Blinded, Sabra gasped at the cruel clamp of his fingers about her wrist. Grimly she hung on, fighting him with silent desperation, until at last her grip loosened and the gun dropped from nerveless fingers. Channing's face swam before her eyes, the rouged lips twisted in a hideous grin.

"I did try to warn you," he said. "A pity I must teach you a lesson you will not soon forget."

Pain was a white-hot flame searing her arm and wrist as deliberately he bent her hand back, forcing her to her knees before him. When at last he released her, she groaned and clutched the hand to her breast. Then, swaying drunkenly, she remained with her head down, her glorious hair a disheveled mass of curls about her face and shoulders.

As from a distance, she heard Channing gloating over her.

"Ah, yes, that is more like it. 'Tis time you learned what it is to kneel before your betters. To grovel as I have had to do. But you would know nothing of that, would you, or how often I've dreamed of having you and all the others like you just as you are now. But this is only the beginning. Before I'm through teaching you the lessons of humility, your fine name and noble heritage will mean nothing. You will be no better than a rag, not fit to wipe my feet on."

Pride and a fiercely burning hatred brought her head up.

"Damn you to hell," she uttered, searing him with her contempt.

Viciously he struck her with his fist, snapping her head around and knocking her nearly senseless to the floor. Suddenly he was on top of her, his fingers closing painfully in her hair. Holding her head fast, he kissed her brutally, savagely tore at her clothing, and when she resisted, he hit her again and again with his open hand. Desperately Sabra fought him till her senses reeled and a terrible darkness threatened her mind. Then she felt something cold and hard against her side and with a sudden, fierce joy, knew it was the gun.

Blindly she clutched at the pearl handle and with the strength of utter despair, pressed the barrel-mouth against Channing's side and fired. She felt him stiffen, heard him utter a blood-chilling curse as he lurched to one side, his hand clutching at the wound. Then she was dragging herself up, her breath coming in painful gasps as she struggled to her feet.

A voice inside her head nagged at her to flee, to escape while there was still time. Weaving dizzily on her feet, she made her way across the room to her cloak draped across the back of the sofa. Somehow she got it on and with a final glance at Channing, lying groaning on the floor behind her, started for the door.

With a bitter sense of defeat, she heard footsteps beyond the oak barrier and the rattle of the door handle. Knowing it was useless, she raised the empty gun anyhow and waited with the vague thought that she might yet bluff her way out. Then the door was flung open and a tall figure burst into the room.

For a single, breathless moment, Sabra stared into piercing gray eyes. Then suddenly she uttered a short, painful laugh.

"Good God, it's you," she gasped and fainted dead away.

Chapter 6

It had been nearly a week since the disastrous encounter with Sir Wilfred Channing, and though Sabra had left her sickbed some three days past, she had yet to venture from her room, a circumstance which had not gone unnoticed by those of the household. Indeed, from the cook, who, undeterred by the trays returned untouched, continued to try to tempt her with specially prepared delicacies, to the stableboy, who came round to the house one day with an offering of a basketful of week-old kittens for the mistress, the entire staff was aware that Miss Sabra was in some sort of difficulty. But more significantly, Jubal Henry, more close-mouthed and unapproachable than ever, had suddenly taken to standing guard in the hall outside Sabra's door each night until dawn.

Phoebe, continuously popping into the room on one pretext or another, had given up trying to browbeat her mistress out of her brooding. New York's reigning beauty could neither be persuaded to put off her silk nightdress and wrapper for one of the fashionable gowns hanging in her wardrobe nor cajoled into allowing Phoebe to do more than brush her hair and leave it falling, undressed, down her back in a luxurious mass of red-gold waves. Sometimes she languished for hours staring listlessly into space, which was enough to give anyone the jitters, but especially her former nanny. In all the years she had looked over the spirited girl as if she were her own, Phoebe had never known Miss Sabra to behave as if the heart had been taken out of her. Not even when her parents had passed on, she declared one day to Mrs. Kirkpatrick, the housekeeper.

Worse than seeing Miss Sabra so despondent, though, was to listen to the monotonous tread of her footsteps creaking

87

overhead in the wee hours, as she wore herself and the carpet thin with her endless pacing, back and forth, back and forth. It was during those times that Phoebe wished most fervently that Mr. Robert were there to try and talk some sense into the child. Wayne, however, upon being assured by the attending physician that Sabra had suffered no permanent ill effects from her alleged run-in with a brigand, had immediately departed on some pressing business matter. That had been four days ago, and he had not yet returned.

That morning, which had dawned chill and bleak, with huge snowflakes drifting out of a thick mantle of gray, promised to be no different from all the rest. Sabra, bundled in a fur rug, sat curled up in the windowseat looking out, her brow furrowed in thoughts as dreary as the weather.

For three days and nights after she had been carried, swooning and suffering from shock, to her bed, she had lain in the grips of a fever that had left her curiously listless and weak, the result, according to Dr. Ashbury, who had taken her to task for burning the candle at both ends, of her generally run-down condition. But even more disturbing, she had awakened to discover her memories of that fateful night were hauntingly disjointed and confused. Indeed, it was almost as if something inside her did not want to remember, she thought distractedly, as, endlessly mulling everything over and over in her mind, she tried to piece all the fragments together.

She remembered with terrifying vividness Channing's saying her brother would be dead by morning and then his grappling with her for the gun. She had relived a hundred times in her dreams his fist striking her, his weight pressing her to the floor, then his hands, hitting her over and over, tearing at her clothes, touching her—Oh, God, how she wished she could wipe that much at least from her mind! Time and again she clutched the gun in her hand, squeezed the trigger, felt him stiffen as the shot rang out, but the rest remained a shadowy distortion of images and half-remembered phrases echoing through her brain.

In her dreams she was visited with horrid visions of dead and mutilated bodies rising from shallow graves of sand to torment her with vacant, staring eyes. She saw Wes being borne away from her on a shroudless ghost ship into darkness and heard herself crying over and over again, "I have killed him. I have killed him!" But whether she meant Channing or her brother, she did not know. And through it all moved a tall figure from her past, his hair black as ravens' wings and his eyes piercing gray.

She saw him in a shadow-laden tunnel, his face obscured in darkness, and again, riding with her in a carriage, his inimitable smile derisive as he offered her a treasure chest filled with gold and precious jewels. When she reached out to take the proffered chest, he held it tantalizingly out of reach. " 'Tis not for whores and traitors," he mocked her and, slamming the lid shut, caused the chest to vanish into thin air.

"Damn him! Damn him," she groaned, dropping her head on her bent knees, clutched to her chest. "I must be mad. What in God's name does *he* have to do with this?"

Suddenly, as if in answer, a loud commotion erupted in the hall outside her door.

"Stop, does you hear me? You ain't got no right shovin' your way in here. I done tole you Miss Sabra ain't receivin' no callers."

"Fallen into a fit of the sullens, has she?" grimly commented a dry, masculine voice. "You have my sympathies, ma'am. And now, as I have no intention of similarly indulging Miss Tyree, you will please move aside."

The door was thrust open to reveal Phoebe standing with her back stolidly to the room and her front bristling before a tall naval officer, his impressive figure draped in a greatcoat with a single shoulder cape.

"Don't take another step. I is warnin' you," Phoebe pronounced in no uncertain terms.

The officer, insufferably cool, strode past her into the room.

"No doubt your loyalty is to be admired, my good woman," he drawled, "but I assure you I mean your mistress no harm. Miss Tyree will ring, if she requires your further attendance." Closing the door firmly on the outraged nanny, he turned the key in the lock. Then straightening, he came about to face

89

Sabra with a flinty smile.

"And now, Miss Tyree," he said, "you will kindly explain what you think to accomplish by this childish display of the vapors."

Sabra, having observed this intrusion with her lips parted in astonishment, stared speechlessly at the man's lean, handsome countenance.

At first she was unable to believe her eyes. Indeed, for the barest instant she thought she might actually be suffering some sort of relapse of her former delirium, for there could be no mistaking that high, intelligent forehead or the strong, stubborn chin, let alone the startling combination of black hair and steel-gray eyes, the likes of which had returned to haunt her in her dreams the past few nights. Good God, how well she knew that face! The bold slash of dark, arrogant eyebrows hinted at a strong, reckless nature, which, she had learned to her sorrow, was tempered by a cool nerve and an iron will. Though the long, straight nose and prominent cheekbones might give the impression of sensitivity, the thin, sensual lips were cynically stern. Faith, it seemed like yesterday since last she had seen him, she thought grimly, so little had he changed.

"Commander Trevor Myles," she pronounced in accents of bitter loathing.

"*Captain* Myles, if you please," he corrected coolly, having observed with sardonic amusement the interesting panoply of emotions play across the lovely face.

"Naturally you will forgive my ignorance, sir," she retorted in honeyed accents. "But then, with your connections, I suppose I should have known you would make captain rather sooner than most."

"Even so," drawled the captain, the sudden, humorous curl of his lips creating an odiously fascinating indentation at either corner of his mouth.

Sabra drew in a sharp breath, the memories of Myles and her single season in London unpleasantly crowding her mind.

"How dare you force your way into my home?" she demanded, suddenly all fire encased in glittering ice.

90

Slinging off the greatcoat and dropping it negligently over a straight-backed chair, Myles made his way leisurely across the room. The sword slung at his side, which, along with his uniform, had seemed ever an integral part of him, glinted in the lamplight. It was like a symbol, she thought, noticing in spite of herself, the lean, hard frame, devoid of any excess flesh, of the man himself—finely tempered steel honed to a fighting edge.

"For that I most humbly beg your pardon," he offered without a glimmer of remorse. "I'm afraid, however, the redoubtable Phoebe gave me little choice in the matter. I really could not be put off another day, and she, after all, refused to be persuaded you would not dream of turning away so memorable an acquaintance from England."

Sabra choked on bitter gall, like bile, rising to her throat. He was as arrogant as ever she remembered him. Nor had the years lessened his devastating masculinity. God, how she hated herself for the involuntary quickening of her pulse as she watched him come toward her with unconscious, sinuous grace.

His every movement, like the man himself, suggested controlled, supple strength. And, indeed, his shoulders were broad and muscular, tapering to a narrow waist and well-molded, sinewy thighs. Unaccountably she was recalled to a hated memory of the firm chest and long, lean torso, rippling with muscle and bronzed by the sun, and suddenly she paled with anger.

She had been forced to flee England in disgrace because of Trevor Myles, but she would see him in hell first before ever she let him touch her again!

"Good God," she breathed in unutterable contempt, "you've a nerve showing your face here."

"You disappoint me, Miss Tyree," he rejoined casually, the gray eyes beneath the drooping lids, mocking. "Indeed, I was sure you would be glad to see me."

Perilously close to betraying herself, Sabra quelled the urge to give way to her mounting fury. Faith, it would never do to lose her wits now, she thought, suddenly wary. Not with Trevor Myles. Indeed, there was a time when she would rather have cut out her tongue than give him the satisfaction of knowing how easily he pierced her defenses.

Suddenly she flung back her head and laughed. God, it was funny, the tricks fate had a way of playing on one.

"Captain Myles," she gurgled, assuming her old role of the pampered beauty, "you cannot possibly know how glad I *am* to see you."

Trevor Myles arched a single, bemused eyebrow.

"I find that singularly intriguing," he commented, observing the lady's animated visage with profound interest. "Unaccountably, I had the impression you had not changed your mind about me in the least."

Sabra glanced up at him and quickly away again.

"No, how could I?" she said, then shrugged a silk-clad shoulder. "We are meant to be enemies, you and I, are we not?"

"Oh, indubitably," he concurred without the flicker of an eyelid.

Sabra caught her lip between even, white teeth. There had been a time when she believed she was something quite different to him, she recalled, experiencing an odd sort of wrench at old wounds. Deliberately she chided herself for a fool. It was only that he had caught her when she felt hopeless and sickened with grief. Long ago he had killed whatever affection she might once have had for him. Myles meant nothing to her now, nor ever could again.

"Yes, well, incomprehensible as it may seem," she continued, rallying with an effort, "I *am* nevertheless relieved to see you, despite our — our many — well . . ."

"Past differences?" Myles supplied with an insufferably amused quirk of the eyebrows.

"To put it mildly, yes," she retorted, wishing him to the devil. Suddenly her head came up, her delightfully pointed chin jutting in unconscious defiance. "What I have been trying to tell you is that I have been uncommonly distraught of late. As a matter of fact, until you so rudely invaded my privacy, I was uncertain as to whether I had actually encountered you earlier, or if I had only dreamt it. But seeing you today has helped me to remember certain things. Indeed, I have only just realized I have you to thank for bringing me home that dreadful night."

"On the contrary," he drawled at his most maddening. "You need thank me for nothing."

Sabra gave him a small toss of her red-gold curls.

"Nevertheless, I do," she said. "And now that I see you are not simply a figment of my delirium, perhaps I can begin to make sense of . . . well, of other things."

At the end her voice faltered and died away, her lovely face assuming a peculiarly lost and haunted look.

The officer's eyes narrowed to glittering points.

"Is it your usual practice to treat callers to long periods of meditation, Miss Tyree?" he queried significantly after several moments of silence had ensued.

Sabra, returned to a sudden, acute awareness of Myles's disturbing presence, felt the blood rush to her cheeks.

"I beg your pardon if you find me less than scintillating company, Captain Myles," she replied with icy formality. "On the other hand, I did not request your presence here. Perhaps you would care to postpone your visit for another time? I assure you I should not feel in any way offended if you chose simply to withdraw."

"Leave you alone to suffer the mopes on such a day? I should never be so disobliging," he assured her, his blithe tone belied by the hint of steel in his manner.

Sabra's lips curved in cool disdain.

"How very kind, I am sure. I, however, have not the least desire to be either charming or charmed, and you, sir, have no business dallying in my boudoir."

"Come now, this from a woman of your worldly experience," Myles returned in mock incredulity, "a liberated female who thinks nothing of entertaining a gentleman in his private lodgings? You surprise me, Miss Tyree."

"How dare you?" she exclaimed, abandoning all pretense at indifference. Thrusting aside the fur, she came unsteadily to her feet. "I want you out of here. Or as God is my witness, I'll have you thrown out!"

A sudden flame leaped in his eyes at sight of her loveliness clad revealingly in shimmering silk. The thin lips curved mockingly.

"So, you've some spirit left," he said. His smile deepened, the sensuously curved creases flashing in the tanned cheeks. "For a while I was afraid there was nothing of the spitfire left in you."

Sabra inhaled sharply, her green eyes sparks of icy rage. Then deliberately she threw back her head and shouted, *"Phoebe!* Phoebe, come here at—"

Strong arms clasped her ruthlessly to a hard chest. Sabra gasped, the air forced from her lungs. For an instant she froze, paralyzed with inexplicable fear.

Slowly the smile faded from Myles's lips. The gray eyes narrowed to glittering pinpoints, and suddenly Sabra found the strength to struggle. Too late. Myles's grip tightened.

Her glorious hair flew wildly about her face and shoulders as Sabra fought with silent fury. Writhing from side to side, she shoved hard against his chest with her hands, her supple length straining backward over the arm clasped about her waist. Still, she was no match for him. Inexorably he bent her to his will. His mouth closed over hers in a brutal kiss.

Sabra froze as waves of shock radiated upward through her belly. God, this was not happening, she groaned inwardly. Knowing she could do nothing to quell her awakening desire, she yet willed herself not to give in to the molten flames he had ever the power to rouse in her. At last, mercifully, he released her.

For a moment she stood, too stunned to do more than stare at Myles in speechless outrage, when all at once at least one piece of the puzzle fell suddenly in place.

"Good God!" she exclaimed in a husky voice. "All the time, it was you on the stairs!"

A cold glimmer of amusement flickered in the gray, smoldering eyes.

"A rather bizarre twist of fate, that," he drawled reflectively. "I confess I was not at all prepared to hear the incomparable Sabra's voice in such unprepossessing surrounds. As a matter of fact, I was telling myself that it could not possibly be she in the stairwell, when you obliged me by losing your hood. I might point out, Miss Tyree, that if you wish to remain incognito on these clandestine excursions of yours, you really ought to affect a powdered wig. And learn to keep your lovely mouth shut."

"No doubt I shall take your advice into consideration," Sabra acidly retorted. Then, realizing she was still clutched firmly in the captain's arms, she jerked angrily away. For an instant the world seemed suddenly to lurch and spin around her, and with a groan she pressed a trembling hand to her forehead.

Myles swore softly.

"Apparently your precious baronet does not scruple to use his fists," he remarked grimly, brushing the hair back with an oddly gentle hand to reveal a large, purplish bruise at her temple. "You damned little idiot. Did you think Channing would deal kindly with you?"

Sabra uttered a reluctant laugh. "Doubtless it is only what I deserve," she retorted bitterly. Proudly disdaining his help, she made her own way back to the window and sank gratefully down on the cushioned seat. "Indeed, you don't have to tell me that I must consider myself exceedingly lucky to have escaped with only a few lumps and bruises."

Casually leaning a shoulder against the wall, Myles shot her a speculative look.

"You, my darling Sabra, are a deal luckier than you know," he said. "Unless, of course, you were already aware that Sir Wilfred's wound was not desperate *before* you thought to flee the scene of your crime."

Her crime? thought Sabra bitterly. God, she might have known he would blame *her* for what had happened. But then, what else could she expect? To be a spinster, caught in a man's rooms would be enough to condemn any woman, but to be Sabra Tyree so placed was to be doubly damned, was it not?

Suddenly she felt immensely tired. What did it matter, after all, what he, or anyone, thought? She had failed miserably in everything she had set out to do. Wes was dead, and she had no one to blame but herself.

"No," she answered, turning her head away to hide the despair in her eyes, "I didn't know. But how very fortunate for Sir Wilfred that he shall apparently recover."

"No doubt your sympathy does you credit," Myles observed acidly. "And are you not the least concerned as to the probable consequences to yourself for that evening's folly?"

"I shall likely be brought up on charges." She shrugged, feeling rather ill and strangely remote from everything that had happened. "It hardly signifies."

The cruel clamp of fingers on her wrist brought her head sharply around.

"How dare you!" she gasped in spite of herself. Then suddenly she paled before the steely glint of gray eyes boring into her own.

"Perhaps I should have spared myself the bother of pointing out to Sir Wilfred how little a public airing of his dirty linen would profit him. You, no doubt, would prefer to hang for attempting to murder one of the king's trusted agents."

"I fail to see why you should be concerned one way or the other," she flung back at him, stung out of her lethargy by his biting sarcasm. "Rather than number yourself among my admirers, you have never failed to make your low opinion of me abundantly clear. On the event of our first unfortunate encounter you tried to charm me into your bed. And on the last, as I recall, you were kind enough to refer to me as 'a scheming American adventuress out to snare a fortune.' By the way, how is Ferdy? Safely wed to some simpering little milk toast, I trust?"

A singularly hard gleam flickered briefly in his eyes.

"My cousin is safely removed from the ploys of conniving females desirous of wedding either his money or his title. But you, 'twould seem, are still up to your lovely neck in artifice and intrigue. Perhaps you would care to tell me what you hoped to gain from this latest endeavor — a proposal of marriage or the distinction of becoming Channing's newest mistress?"

Sabra drew in a sharp breath. Good God, four years had not altered Myles in the slightest. He was still the same insufferably arrogant swell who had deliberately ruined her name among the fashionable elite of London, and all because he had believed her to be a fortune hunter with neither breeding nor conscience. How perfectly ironic that after all these years he should suddenly materialize on the event of her one and only lapse in moral judgment. But no matter. Even had she dared reveal to him her true purpose for meeting with Channing, she would have scorned to disabuse him of the notion that she was anything but the conniving female he thought her.

"Actually," she retorted with the careless shrug of a shoulder, "it was a simple business proposition. Unfortunately, Sir Wilfred and I failed to come to terms. I had only agreed, after all, to a single night of intimacy in exchange for a certain favor. He, on the other hand, preferred to drive a harder bargain. When I decided it was time to leave, he proved rather ugly, I fear. It's a shame really, the way things turned out, for undoubtedly I shall only have it all to do over again."

Deliberately Myles leaned over her, a strange glitter in his eyes.

"You, Miss Tyree, are an unconscionable liar," he stated flatly.

"Am I?" she countered bitterly, consigning him without remorse to the devil. "And wherein lies the falsehood? Surely you cannot doubt that I am exactly what you have always believed me—a common whore for sale to the highest bidder? God knows you did your best to convince the world of it."

Suddenly overcome with weariness and the incessant pounding at her temple, she sighed and, leaning her head back, closed her eyes.

"But what can it possibly matter now?" she murmured, little caring what he thought or did. "Indeed, why do you not do us both a favor and simply vanish from my life once and for all?

"Don't think for a moment that I shouldn't like to, but unfortunately I have gone out on a limb for you. You, my darling Sabra, owe me, and I intend to collect. One of Sheridan's comedies is opening at the John Street Theater tomorrow night. I shall call for you at nine. Wear something in silk—red, I think. That color has always seemed particularly well suited to you."

Sabra's eyes fluttered open in furious disbelief.

"You break into my house, openly assault my person, and end by accusing me of all manner of willful wrongdoing. And now—never mind what happened four years ago in London—you have the gall to propose that, not only am I somehow in your debt, but that I should lower myself to go out with you? Faith, captain, you are not lacking in nerve."

The devastatingly masculine dimples flared disarmingly.

"So I've been told on more than one occasion," Myles said with unaffected humor, which might have taken her off her guard had she not known him better. "However, be that as it may, you will still do as I have requested."

"Indeed, sir?" she queried dangerously. "And why, pray tell, should I?"

"Because, madam, if you refuse, you are very likely to find yourself locked up in the stockade for the attempted murder of a very influential man. It would seem that you and I are promised to one another, or at least that is what I led Sir Wilfred to believe. In the circumstances, he was more than willing to agree to drop the entire matter."

"I, on the other hand, am not!" declared the bride-to-be in tones of unutterable loathing. "Indeed, I should prefer the stockade rather than to have my name linked with yours even for a single moment."

Myles shrugged broad shoulders.

"Then so be it. It little matters to me one way or the other. However, I should warn you that in the event you are convicted of treason, this house and any other properties presently in your possession are subject to confiscation by the crown. Of course, it can little signify if you have no near relatives who might be thus deprived. And no doubt those employed in your service will have little difficulty in finding other positions, things being what they are. Providing, that is, that they can satisfactorily demonstrate they had no part in the conspiracy to do away with one of His Majesty's trusted agents."

Sabra went deathly white with rage and bitter frustration. There was little doubt what sort of treatment would be meted out to those who were closest to her; indeed, to anyone even remotely associated with someone of prominence who had been pronounced a traitor. She felt ill, recalling the fate of four men who had been rumored responsible for plotting to set fire to the city some months after its occupation by the British. She had little wish to see Phoebe or Jubal similarly in the hands of a hate-maddened lynch mob. And what of Wayne? He had tried to stop her from going to Channing and, as always, he had been right. She could not bear to think that he should be made to pay for her stupidity.

Resolutely Sabra lifted her head. Fixing her gaze on a point directly before her, she proudly disdained to look at Myles.

"Very well, since I apparently have no choice," she uttered coldly, "I shall grant you an evening of my company."

The captain's sardonic chuckle set her teeth on edge.

"You, my darling Sabra," he drawled acerbically, "will be seen frequently on my arm for the next few weeks. You might as well accept that fact with grace. For in truth you have no viable alternative."

Involuntarily she stiffened, her eyes flying as if of their own accord to his odiously handsome face.

"Why?" she demanded in a harsh voice hardly above a whisper. "What do you want from me?"

"Nothing, Miss Tyree, I assure you. Nothing, that is, save for your mutual assistance in saving your pretty neck."

Suddenly he gave her a long, pointed look that, in spite of all her loathing of him, somehow took her breath away.

"There is no need for this to be an untenable arrangement. You are right about one thing after all," he added, his tone strangely altered. "Whatever our past differences, all that formerly passed between us was finished a long time ago. I see no reason why we should not try to put it behind us and start afresh. We might even discover we get on quite well together. Either way, the die is cast, and whether we proceed as enemies or as friends is wholly up to you."

Good God, he could not be serious, she thought, regarding with open suspicion the strong, supple hand he held out to her. It was a ploy; it had to be. He was Trevor Myles, after all, and she knew him so well. But what could he possibly be after?

All at once their glances met and held, and suddenly Sabra's heart seemed to stop. Indeed, as the clock on the mantle ticked the seconds away, it struck her that the room had grown inexplicably warm, the air stifling and difficult to breathe. Somewhere in the back of her mind, a small voice clamored a warning, but for some reason she could not summon the will to heed it. Indeed, she was on the brink of meeting his hand halfway, when the sound of a fist hammering at the door shattered the silence.

"Sabra!" shouted a frantic voice. "Sabra! Are you all right? Sabra, for God's sake, answer me!"

Sabra blinked, and the moment was gone.

"A moment, Robert," she called, then turned with cool deliberation back to Trevor Myles.

"Friends, captain?" she queried frostily. "I'm afraid that is quite impossible. Now, if you will please unlock the door, I believe you have overstayed your welcome."

Myles's hand clenched and dropped to his side.

"Very well, Miss Tyree," he murmured coldly. "Perhaps I was a fool to think you might unwittingly have landed yourself in deep waters." Deliberately he walked to the door, then, pausing, turned back as if he had just made up his mind to something. "Channing and I go back a long way. If he is blackmailing you, as I suspect he is, you could do worse than to trust me. But try to play it alone, and you will soon find a rope around that lovely neck of yours, never doubt it for a moment."

Startled and confused by his persistence, Sabra glanced quickly away.

"It is *my* neck, nonetheless," she answered. "You, sir, need involve yourself no further."

"On the contrary, I am already involved, and distasteful as it may be, I am thus forced to see the matter to a satisfactory conclusion—one way or the other. Do I make clear?"

For an instant she hesitated, tempted to tell him to go to the devil. But then Wayne, anxiously rattling the door handle, brought home to her how neatly she was trapped.

"Oh, yes," she said bitterly, "I see it all perfectly now."

"I thought perhaps you might," he drawled and turned the key in the lock.

"Don't be absurd, Robert," Sabra admonished moments later, "I'm fine. Really I am." Gently she released her hands from Wayne's anxious clasp. "I'm sorry if I alarmed you. Myles and I had a simple misunderstanding, that's all. But it's over now, and he was just leaving, weren't you, captain."

Trevor Myles, observing the affecting reunion with a sardonic twist of the lips, inclined his head ironically.

"Just so," he agreed. Them, apparently unmoved by Wayne's slow, appraising glance, he strolled easily across the room to retrieve his cloak. "No need to show me out," he added, slinging the handsome garment over magnificent shoulders. "No doubt the two of you have a great deal to talk over."

"So very thoughtful, as ever," murmured Sabra in honeyed tones.

"Kind of you to notice," Myles countered, his expression insufferably bland. "Oh, by the way, I almost forgot," he added, pausing at the door. One hand delved into a pocket of his greatcoat to retrieve a velvet-covered box. "A small token of our mutual understanding. I'll just set it here for you to open at your convenience. Until tomorrow then, my love. Mr. Wayne, your servant, sir."

"Captain," murmured Wayne, hard-pressed to conceal his bewilderment at the undercurrents of tension running rife in the room.

Hardly had the tall officer departed than Sabra had crossed swiftly to the door and fairly slammed it shut.

"God help me, I swear I shall kill him ere I am through," she uttered, white-faced with rage. Then, disregarding Wayne, she snatched up the box off her dressing table and opened the lid.

"Bloody hell," she swore bitterly as she took out the pearl-handled gun which had nearly killed Channing.

Sabra's fingers tightened on the grip, and for a long moment she stared with cold, glittering eyes into space. But then she appeared to shudder.

"Faith," she murmured, sinking slowly down on to the dainty gilt chair before the dressing table, "I remember now. The book and the packet I took from the box. They were still in my petticoat when I fainted."

Suddenly her glance flew to Wayne, who was watching her with worried eyes.

"Robert, you must summon Phoebe at once!" she exclaimed. "And God grant that it is not too late!"

Chapter 7

Nodding curtly, Myles strode past Phoebe, out the door and into the spitting snow. The clouds were thickening, and the air was about as chill as the look in the old nanny's eyes, he noted, pausing briefly to draw his greatcoat more firmly about him. A faint, sardonic smile touched his lips at the sound of the door pulled emphatically shut behind him.

Sabra Tyree's formidable duenna had not changed a whit in the four years since he had seen her last, he reflected wryly. Obviously she thought as little of him now as she did then. Of course, there was a time when she had seemed to favor him over the score or so of other bloods in pursuit of her darling. That sentiment, however, quite naturally in the light of subsequent events, had undergone a drastic transformation. She was as fiercely protective now of her charge as she had been then. And apparently she had need to be.

Recalling the image of Sabra Tyree's face, the delicate bone structure pronounced beneath the pearly translucence of her skin, Myles swore softly to himself. Damn the chit! Why had she to be so cursed pale and listless? It was bad enough to have encountered her, battered, stripped half naked, and on the point of swooning, but then to find her brooding and despondent when he had expected something quite different had given him a decidedly unpleasant jolt.

Setting off abruptly down the street, he cursed himself for a bloody fool. After all, it suited his purposes very well, did it not, to have the scheming little wretch vulnerable, her instincts for self-preservation lulled by whatever the bloody hell was eating at her. It was not as if she were deserving of his pity. It had been some time since he had had any illusions as to what she was. Why, then, should he suddenly have found himself struggling against the desire to see her eyes sparkle with all their former defiance? Indeed, what, in the name of God, had possessed him to kiss her?

Not that there was any doubt that he had aroused her fighting mettle. Considering the female in question, no other reaction had been possible. But equally certain had it been that he himself would be made to foot the bill. Savagely he cursed the fate that had thrown her in his path again — her silken beauty, her glorious hair scintillating sparks, the damnably sweet scent of her. In spite of everything, the years spent doggedly putting her from his mind, the knowledge of what she was and what she had become, still he had wanted her, wanted her now with an intensity that was bitter gall to him. Damn the chit! Even cold and unyielding, she was infinitely more desirable than any other woman he had ever known. For him to have kissed her had inevitably to be an act of utter madness!

He had been singularly naive to think it might be otherwise, he told himself, his aspect exceedingly grim. Even as a green girl of seventeen Sabra Tyree had possessed the power to make men fools with naught but the sight of her bewitching loveliness. Or, he grimly appended, a single glimpse into sea-green eyes that could entice a man to forget everything, even who and what he was.

Indubitably she had changed, of course. In fact, it was with an odd sort of regret that he had noted the difference four years had wrought in the intriguing beauty who more than once had dared to cross swords with him. It had been evident from the first moment he stepped into the room and, seeing her, apparently on the road to recovery, had experienced an unexpectedly intense feeling of relief. Relief, however, which had quickly given way to an involuntary wrench at the sight of her wan appearance.

Sabra Tyree was no longer the fiery young girl who had taken London by storm, but a woman, whose promise had blossomed into something exquisitely lovely, yet remote somehow, and inaccessible. It was a pity, really, that the years had taught her to keep a tight rein on that gloriously hasty temper of hers, he reflected with a wry twist of the lips. For what had once been quicksilver seemed now a deep pool shrouded in mystery; the cool green eyes, which had used to scintillate emerald sparks at the drop of a hat, guarded now and shadowed with secrets. Whimsically he wondered if somewhere beneath the frozen exterior lay the smoldering embers of that youthful fire, a passion awaiting a flaming ember to set it off again.

Realizing where his thoughts had taken him, he drew up short, unmindful of the curious stares of the passersby. Careful, he mused cynically. He had fallen for the deceitful little baggage once. He'd be a damned fool to let it happen again. With a shrug, Myles started off again, but his thoughts returned as of their own accord to their former ruminations.

Inevitably his lips narrowed to a grim line at the memory of the purplish discoloration only partially concealed by the luxurious mass of hair, and the tell tale marks of lesser bruises still faint against the pallor of her skin.

The little fool, he thought savagely. What had she hoped to gain by risking so much? The Sabra Tyree he had known in London was both headstrong and fearless, showing a reckless disregard for herself and the proprieties, but she had never been slow-witted. She must have known what Channing was when she agreed to a clandestine meeting with him, and still she had gone. His lips curled in a hard, cynical smile. But then he had always known she would stop at nothing when once she set her mind to a thing, he mused. In that and certain other respects, they, two, were appallingly alike.

Thus occupied with his thoughts, Myles made his way to Broadway and then northeast along the wide cobblestone street past Canvas Town and the blackened rubble left by the great fire, till eventually he reached Barclay Street, bordering King's College. Turning into the narrow lane, he came at last to a modest brick house fronted in the Italian style, and knocked briskly at the door. Moments later his summons was answered by a Negro maidservant, who gave his long, lithe form an appraising glance.

"Handsome, was you wantin' to see someone in particular?" she queried with a provocative tilt of her sloe black eyes.

The glimmer of a smile twitched at the corners of his lips.

"Please inform Captain Ellsworth, Captain Myles is here to see him," he answered, amused at the chit's impertinence.

"Why, honey, you come right on in. Captain Ellsworth been expectin' *you*."

Myles was quickly ushered into a spacious parlor, made sumptuous with plush sofas, flock wallhangings, and a thick Aubusson carpet.

"You jest takes off that coat and makes yourself at home," said the maid. "I'll tell the cap'n you is here."

Left alone, Myles crossed leisurely to the fireplace and knelt to warm his hands over the low-burning flames. Allowing his gaze to roam casually about the rich setting, complete with gilt-edged woodwork and red-velvet drapes, he came at last to a reasonably accurate rendition of Titian's nude *Venus and the Lute Player*, garishly framed and hanging in a position of prominence over the mantelpiece. A bemused smile touched his lips. Obviously he would have to reassess his previous conception of William Ellsworth. Despite the proximity of the house to the Holy Ground, somehow he had not expected to find the admiral's liaison ensconced in what gave every indication of being a bordello.

Rising to shrug off his overcoat, he heard a quick, light step and the faint rustle of silken skirts. A lilting cry brought him around just in time to receive the rapturous embrace of a well-endowed female. Instinctively he clasped his arms about the sumptuously curved waist as his assailant kissed him full on the lips.

"Trevor Myles! It *is* you," exclaimed the lady moments later. "I couldn't believe my ears when Mayella told me. However did you find me?"

"By purest chance, I assure you," confessed Myles, recovering with aplomb. "I was instructed to meet Ellsworth at this address. You, my dearest Lily, are a delightfully unexpected surprise."

"Then 'tis business that brings you to this quaint little love nest. Faith, I might have known," she uttered, her brow puckering suddenly in a frown of displeasure. "Ellsworth said only to expect an officer. How like him to neglect to mention it might be you."

Myles retained a bland expression, belied somewhat by the gleam of humor in his eye. A full-blown beauty with silvery blond hair and china-blue eyes, Lily Barrett was every bit of five and thirty. Yet she had retained the smooth skin and creamy complexion of a woman half her age. Nor had her generously proportioned figure, draped rather revealingly in a rose silk dressing gown, suffered with the passing of time. She was as seductively winsome as when he had first met her, a reasonably successful actress, not averse to sharing her bed with a man she liked and who could afford to entertain her in the manner to which she had grown accustomed. That had been five years ago, when he was naught but a young lieutenant cooling his heels in London till he should receive new orders, and when *she* had yet to meet and fall in love with William Ellsworth.

"Come now, is it not possible you are being a trifle hasty?" he murmured, sweeping with an appreciative glance her lissome form clad *en déshabillé*. "Doubtless Will only learned of it this morning, as did I. It occurs to me that even I should be reluctant to disturb your beauty rest for anything quite so trivial."

The enticing mouth pursed enchantingly as Lily paused to reconsider.

"Tis true that I have yet to see him this morning," she mused, placing a dainty finger against her lips. "I arrived home late last night and have only just got out of bed. But how did you—" Suddenly she halted, her glance winging to his face. "Oh," she choked, perceiving the devil of amusement in his eyes, "in all the excitement I quite forgot I was not presentable. Perhaps 'tis true, think you, that old habits die hard?"

"Oh, indubitably." Myles grinned in unaffected delight at her simple candor. "I, for one, however, should be devastated to find you any other way," he hastened to assure her.

"Faith," she breathed, her gaze decidedly bemused, "I had almost forgot how charmingly you can smile. 'Tis enough to turn a lady's head, even an old married lady like me."

"Then obviously you are suffering delusions. Lily Barrett could never be old. You are, if anything, more ravishingly lovely than ever before."

"Flatterer," she scoffed, pleased nonetheless. "It comes to you far too easily, this devastating effect you have on women. Methinks 'tis time some enterprising female took you down a peg or two."

"But one has," he instantly rejoined. "When Lily Barrett threw me over for the likes of William Ellsworth."

"Now you are being absurd," she said, laughing delightfully. "And here's Mayella to take you in to Will."

Slipping her arm beneath his, she turned to walk with him to the door.

"By the way, my dearest Trevor, I'm to be your excuse for calling in the neighborhood. With Lily Barrett as your inamorata, no one should be suspicious at your frequent visits. That's why you find us in this wonderfully indecent house. The story is that I've decided to make a comeback on the stage. In fact I am giving my premiere performance tomorrow night as Sheridan's Lady Teazle. I shall expect you afterwards in my dressing room, to offer your congratulations, shall I not?"

"But naturally," drawled Myles, raising her ivory hand to his lips. "I shall be looking forward to it. And with a deal more pleasure than I had previously thought possible."

"Go on with you now," chuckled Lily, giving him a playful shove. "I'm sure Ellsworth will be as glad as I to see you. And tell him I shan't soon forgive him for keeping you a secret," she called after his retreating back. "It'll serve him right if I'm a smashing success tomorrow night!"

Scant moments later Myles found himself in a handsome book room, his hand clasped in a bearish handshake.

"Trevor, by heaven it's been a long time since the *Antioch*," boomed William Ellsworth, rigorously pumping Myles's arm.

"Softly, man, I've still use for a good right upon occasion," Myles complained with a wry twist of the lips.

Ellsworth gave a hearty chuckle and thwacked Myles ungently on the back.

"You've seen Lily, I take it. I heard her laugh. The stubborn wench couldn't be persuaded to stay in London like a dutiful wife. Followed me here, and now she's taken the damned fool notion of playing the spy. Bloody females. They play the very devil with a man's peace of mind."

"How very true," drawled Myles ironically, reminded of another mettlesome female. But then a gleam of humor flickered in his eyes. "Still," he added helpfully, "you need only say the word, and I shall be only too glad to take the charming Lily off your hands."

A look of perfect understanding passed between them.

"Never, this side of hell," Ellsworth flatly stated.

"Quite so," Myles murmured, upon which, a grin tugged at the older man's lips.

"Damn if you ain't a sight for sore eyes," he said, deliberately changing the subject. "I suppose you heard they retired Dekker after you left us? Never doubt for a moment that we weren't grateful to you, lad, every mother's son of us. Likely I'd still be first officer on that stinking tub if you hadn't shown him up for what he was."

Myles's expression remained impassive. A big man with a powerful frame beginning to thicken around the middle, Ellsworth gave the appearance of bluff amiability, but he was nobody's fool. As second lieutenant on the old *Antioch* and Ellsworth one rung above him on the ladder of advancement, Myles had come to know him well. Indeed, there was no one he would rather have had at his side in a tight corner than William Ellsworth. Still, he was vaguely nettled with his old shipmate for such plain speaking.

"Dekker was a hard man, but he was a seasoned veteran with a good record in battle," he quietly rejoined. "It was unfortunate we were attacked at a time that he was feeling less than himself. Indeed, if my actions were in some measure responsible for his losing command of his ship, then I am sorry for it."

"Hellsfire!" Ellsworth sputtered, eyeing his friend in disbelief. "The man was flat on his back and stinking drunk. If you hadn't taken command, he'd have lost his ship anyway — to Barbary pirates. God knows I'd have done it myself, if I hadn't taken a cursed musket ball at the first wave of attack." Seeing the handsome lips thin to a stern line, Ellsworth relented. "Ah, well, like as not we'll never see eye to eye on the subject of Dekker. Pull up a chair, my lad," he added and returned to his seat behind a littered oak desk.

Taking up a crystal decanter that sat on the desk, Ellsworth filled two glasses with brandy and handed one across to the other man. "We can at least drink to better days, what?"

Myles's rare smile eased the coldness from his eyes.

"Indeed, to better days," he said, lifting the glass. "And may we live to see them."

"Here, here," murmured Ellsworth, and downed a liberal portion. Setting down the glass with a gusty sigh, he turned keen blue eyes on Myles. "And now, I suppose we must attend to more serious matters."

Myles gazed thoughtfully at the lamplight glancing through the amber liquid in his glass.

"How *is* the admiral?" he said quietly.

Ellsworth shrugged beefy shoulders.

"Weary. Harrassed by the need to blockade the entire coast with too few ships. Worried that the French fleet will finally decide to fight." The creak of leather as Ellsworth leaned heavily back sounded loud in the quiet of the book room. "Dammit, Trevor! This is no war for the likes of us. Everywhere you look you see men growing fat off the bloody spoils, and the army goes short of supplies more often than not. Hell, good British sailors are giving their lives, and you'd hardly know it from all the fancy dress balls. You can't tell who's a bloody Yank and who's playing both sides against the middle. And here we are, pussyfooting in dark alleys when we should be standing on the quarterdeck with the guns rolled out and the colors flying. It don't make sense, I tell you."

Deliberately Myles raised the glass to his lips and emptied it. With cynical detachment he felt the brandy, like fire, explore his empty belly. When at last he spoke, his voice was peculiarly expressionless.

"I've made contact with the girl," he said, leaning forward to set the glass on the desk. "And for the time being she has no choice but to accept me in her circle of admirers. As a matter of fact, it is about to be made public that she and I

110

have reached an understanding."

"An understanding? You and Sabra Tyree?" sputtered Ellsworth, suddenly leaning forward. "Good God, man. However did you manage it? After London I should have thought she would sooner skewer you than wed you."

Myles's lip curled sardonically.

"I gave her little choice in the matter. It was either pose as my betrothed or go to the gallows. Actually, I believe she would have preferred the latter, had I not pointed out how exceedingly unlikely it was that she would hang alone. In the end she was made to see the wisdom of submitting to my demands."

Ellsworth appeared anything but amused by his friend's cryptic utterances.

"Perhaps you'd like to start over at the beginning, old man," he said, leaning back in his chair again. "And leave nothing out. The admiral is not an overly patient man these days."

Myles shrugged.

"Suffice it to say that Miss Tyree was induced to meet with Sir Wilfred Channing in his rooms at the Royal Arms. They had a disagreement, and apparently Channing proved something less than a gentleman. The lady was forced to shoot him."

"Good God. So someone finally had the nerve to give the rotter back some of his own. Dead, is he?"

"No, fortunately for Channing, the bullet scraped the ribs and came out clean. I left him to the ministrations of his valet while I transported the swooning Miss Tyree to her home. By the time I got back to him, he was awake and exceedingly put out with the lady."

Ellsworth laughed shortly.

"Little wonder," he said meaningfully. "If the story gets out, he'll be the laughingstock of the town."

"Indeed, I was at some pains to point that out to him. Oddly enough, he didn't seem to give a tinker's damn what anyone thought."

"Not give a damn? Channing? Why the man's as vain as a bloody woman!" scoffed Ellsworth, his contempt for the baronet unmistakable.

"Quite so, and that's why I'm convinced there's a deal more involved than first appears on the surface. It occurs to me that the lady may have gotten away with more than her somewhat dubious virtue intact. When I came into the room that night, there was a wooden box lying open on a table, its contents spilled out. When I next came there, the box was gone, and Sir Wilfred claimed no knowledge of it. I think she took something from Channing. Something that he very much wants back. Enough, in fact, that I think he would not hesitate to kill for it."

"I don't know, lad," said Ellsworth, sobering. "The man's a bloody bastard, but I find it hard to believe he would stoop to murder, even if the baggage did steal from him. The man's rich as Croesus. He can afford the loss of a trinket or two."

Myles's eyes took on a frosty glint.

"If you think that, you sadly mistake the lady," he said, his voice velvet-edged steel. "The devious Miss Tyree is a great many things, but she is not a thief, not in the sense you mean. It was not gold she was after, but something far more important."

All at once he stood, and propping his hands on the edge of the desk, leaned over it to peer at Ellsworth with gimlet eyes.

"Does it not occur to you to wonder *why* she was there? Consider all that she risked if she were discovered—reputation, position, the certainty of being ostracized by those who are most valuable to her. Had I not intervened on her behalf, her usefulness to whatever cause she serves would have been instantly at an end. Why, then, was she there?"

"Channing had something on her," stated Ellsworth flatly. "And evidently, she managed to wrest it away from him. Am I right?"

"Not exactly," rejoined Myles, smiling oddly.

Suddenly he straightened and began to pace thoughtfully before the desk.

"Some months ago, an American naval officer was taken prisoner," he said in the manner of one merely rehearsing his thoughts aloud. "He was impressed into service aboard a

British man-of-war, where he remained until Channing used his influence to have him moved. For a time it seemed that he had simply dropped off the face of the earth. But I have since learned that he was transferred to the prison ship *Jersey*."

"A beastly fate, even for a bloody Yank, from all I've heard," observed Ellsworth guardedly. "I suppose this story has some point to it?"

"Indubitably. You see, the naval officer is Wesley Locke, Miss Tyree's half-brother."

Ellsworth let of a low whistle.

"Quite so," drawled Myles, his face unreadable. "Obviously Miss Tyree was willing to risk everything for him. But something happened. Maybe she got cold feet. Or maybe she discovered something that would enable her to put Channing in check."

"Something in the wooden box," Ellsworth speculated. "But what?"

"I don't know," Myles said, "—yet. But rest assured, I intend to find out."

The older man frowned.

"Channing is an influential man," he pointed out. "Privy to a great deal of information concerning military operations. It hardly seems wise to allow a suspected rebel spy the opportunity to make use of him."

Myles gestured impatiently.

" 'Tis true there is risk involved. But on the other hand, everything thus far has been the purest speculation. We haven't a shred of evidence to prove that Miss Tyree is guilty of anything more damning than having committed a rather foolish indiscretion."

"Then we'll haul her in. She'll soon be made to talk."

"No." Myles swung sharply around to face Ellsworth with glittering eyes. Then, seeming to recollect himself, he drew in a deep breath, his lips thinning to a controlled line.

"That, old friend, is exactly what we must not do," he said, deadly calm. "Sabra Tyree is the only link we have. Tip our hand now and we might never uncover the traitor in our midst. That is what we're here for, is it not? To discover why a French ship of the line should have known my mission in

113

the Caribbean down to the last detail?"

"Dammit, man!" said Ellsworth testily. "I know my orders as well as you. But this would seem to put a new light on the matter. The admiral at least must be informed of it."

Myles shrugged coldly, a shutter seeming to descend over the stern features.

"You will, of course, do as you think fit," he murmured dispassionately.

"Meaning, I suppose, that I can go to the devil."

"Did I say so?" Myles queried, his lips curling cynically. "But then 'twould seem we all shall, sooner or later."

Ellsworth uttered a short, explosive oath. "And what do you intend doing, I wonder. Oh, no need to answer that. You'll go after the bastards in your own way, no matter what it costs you. Just give me one reason why I shouldn't advise the admiral to reassign you now, before your bloody career goes the way of Dekker's?"

Myles's eyes glinted icy sparks.

"*You* ask me that? You, Will?" Myles countered, his voice edged in steel. "Putting aside the damage done to my ship, is not a bill of twenty dead and twice that number wounded sufficient to warrant my displeasure? The bloody bastard set me up, and Waincourt paid the price. Can you wonder that I should want his head?"

"And what if it's the girl behind it?" demanded Ellsworth. "What then? Will you be as keen to see her hang for treason?"

"I would place the noose about her neck with my own hand, if I found proof of it. Never doubt it for a moment."

Ellsworth felt a cold shudder touch his spine at the look in Myles's eyes. Suddenly he sighed.

"Very well," he said, resigned, "I shall keep my own counsel for the time being so far as Sir Wilfred is concerned. What would you have me report to the admiral? I'll have to tell him something."

"Tell him that after tomorrow the pawns will all be in place, the play ready to commence. I expect very shortly to depart with my enticing future wife on a brief excursion into the country. One needs time alone with the object of one's devotion, you would agree, if one hopes to achieve a certain desired intimacy. Besides which, I'm told her father's estate on the East River is well worth seeing."

"Good God, Trev," growled Ellsworth, observing his companion in dumbfounded amazement. "You're not lacking in nerve. Miss Tyree is hardly likely to be overjoyed at such a prospect."

Myles smiled, a hard glint in his eye.

"You are right of course," he admitted. "I doubt not, however, that in the end she will be persuaded, one way or another." After all, he added grimly to himself, her only alternative was to find herself one morning floating facedown in the East River.

Ellsworth gazed speculatively at the stern, unreadable features. For a moment it seemed he would speak, but then his lips clamped grimly shut. Finally he nodded.

"I'll tell him," he said gruffly. "Is there anything else I can do for you?"

Myles stood up and walked to the door. A hand on the knob, he turned to look back at the other man, still seated at the desk.

"Keep an eye on my first officer. He's in this up to his bloody neck. And I should be grateful if you could speed the refitting of my ship. I want her ready to sail when this cursed business is finished."

"It wont' be easy, but God knows you've earned that much at least. I'll see what I can do. And, Trevor, old man, guard your back well. This is a devilish game. If the rotters find out what you're up to, they'll not hesitate to put you out of the way."

Myles smiled coldly.

"They may try, of course," he murmured, the gray eyes silvery in the lamplight. "But then, you forget. I am in command of their queen. I think they will be cautious about making any rash moves."

Myles spent most of the following day trying to bribe, bully, or threaten harbor officials to fill his requisition orders for spare cordage and spars, which had become as rare as hen's teeth, limes and salt pork to last a complement of two hundred fifty for three month at sea, fresh water to be sent to his ship in lighters, and rum for the men's daily allotment — in short, everything a king's man-of-war required to be ready to put to sea. By late afternoon, weary and short of temper, he returned to his rooms at the Royal Arms. There, a message from Sir Wilfred awaited him, inviting Myles to call on the baronet at his earliest possible convenience to discuss certain matters pertaining to his betrothed and her rather questionable activities.

"Bloody hell," he swore out loud, crumpling the missive in a clenched fist.

"Trouble, cap'n?" queried Ezra Leeks, his homely face carefully impassive.

Myles glared at the big coxswain.

"Perhaps you'd care to read it and make up your own mind," he suggested pointedly.

"I'm afraid that's not possible, sir, me not knowin' my letters 'n' all. But if you was to tell me what was in it, belike I could give you the benefit of my vast worldly experience."

Myles uttered a blistering oath.

"You are impertinent, Leeks," he stated flatly and without thinking, thrust the crumpled piece of paper into the pocket of his greatcoat before peevishly slinging out of the heavy garment.

"Aye, sir," rejoined the coxswain, focusing studiously on a point beyond his captain's shoulder as he moved to retrieve the greatcoat, which had been discarded with no less distemper on the floor, to be followed in swift succession by coat, small clothes, and wilted neck cloth. "Your bath is ready, sir. Shall I order your meal sent up now?"

Myles regarded the man's bland expression in telling silence. He would have to do something about Leeks someday, he mused darkly. Then suddenly his mouth twisted in a wry grin. Without the stubborn loyalty of his coxswain, he would not be standing here today.

"Very well, Leeks, you may carry on," he said, his ill humor giving way to resignation, no doubt just as Leeks had intended that it should, he realized with dry amusement.

Leeks, however, appeared not to have heard. Indeed, Myles, shrugging out of his soiled linen shirt, emerged to find his coxswain standing stubbornly as before.

"Er—was there something else, Leeks?" suggested Myles, pointedly.

The big coxswain nervously shifted his feet.

"Well, sir, you know I ain't commonly one to meddle in the cap'n's affairs. Only beggin' your pardon, sir, I just happened to've stumbled into something that you had ought to know about."

Myles suppressed the temptation to wish his coxswain to the devil.

"I shall withhold comment, Leeks," he temporized, in exceedingly dry tones, "on your first, demonstrably erroneous, supposition. As for the second, I suppose I shall have to hear what you have to say before deciding whether to thank you or, more possibly, to have you flogged for causing me needless delay. You will, I trust, keep it short?"

Leeks, who had served under Myles since the battle with Barbary pirates that had won't he young second lieutenant his first command, never blinked an eye. In all the time he'd been with him, he'd never known the captain to order a flogging save only once, and then he was given no choice but to have done it. With obvious effort, Leeks maintained a suitably grave expression.

"Aye, sir," he said, perceptibly relaxing. "I'll try my best, but there's some things that jest naturally can't be told without some roundaboutation. Take me, for example. All my life I been a subject for undue speculation, and never no more so than since I been here. 'Course me bein' the new lad about, so to speak, an' one, moreover, that ain't exactly hard to spot, well, naturally I tend to draw what some might consider more'n my share of attention. Not that I mind, o' course. But at times it can lead to a fair amount of trouble."

Myles gave an audible sigh.

"If you are trying to inform me," he said with studied patience, "that you have incurred the probably justified wrath of a jealous husband, I think I should warn you, Leeks. I entertain a decidedly dim view of becoming embroiled in domestic disputes. Particularly those not of my own making."

Leeks's sudden grin was hugely appreciative of his superior's keen-witted grasp of the situation.

"Naturally, sir, I'd never dream of bringin' you into what ain't like to amount to nothin'. I'd not've been brought to mention it all if the wench wasn't wed to a certain baronet's gentleman's gentleman."

Myles settled with marked deliberation on the edge of the marquetry commode, his long legs stretched out before him.

"At last, Leeks," he drawled, "you begin to intrigue me."

The coxswain's grin grew even wider.

"Aye, sir," he said. "I thought as how I might."

It was soon to develop that Leeks, who had a certain knack with females of the serving class, had drawn the interest of a pert young chambermaid with the dubious distinction of being wife to Mr. Titus Quinby, Sir Wilfred Channing's personal valet of long-standing. Leeks, never one to look a gift horse in the mouth, was not averse to allowing himself to be lured one afternoon into the linen closet, where, amid other, more pleasurable, pursuits, he managed to learn a great deal about Mr. Quinby's employer.

"I ain't exactly certain, cap'n, what any of it means, but the wench seemed right curious about you and the lady that shot Sir Wilfred. Well, sir, I figured you wouldn't mind if I just sort of strung her along like. Not that I let slip anything that you wouldn't mind Sir Wilfred Channing himself knowin', but just enough to kinda egg her along, if you know what I mean."

"No doubt I could venture a fairly accurate guess," replied Myles acerbically. "On the other hand, it does not seem at all likely that it would profit either of us very greatly. Perhaps, Leeks, it would not be too much to ask that you come directly to the point?"

"Aye, sir, I was just about to. Maybe you was already in the way of knowin' Sir Wilfred and the lady go back a long way."

"I am not unaware that, while serving as vice-admiralty judge, Channing came very near to ruining her father, if that is what you are driving at," said Myles, with every appearance of fast succumbing to an advanced state of ennui.

"No, sir, not exactly. That would've been before all the trouble in Boston back in '70. I reckon Miss Tyree couldn't have been much more'n a slip of a girl in them days. I'm figurin' it to be more like four, maybe five, years ago. It was then that Miss Tyree was about gettin' herself launched in polite society. Back home it was, cap'n, in London Town, and the talk was that she was turned up sweet on one of the bloods payin' her marked attention."

"Yes, I recall the event," remarked Myles with sudden, steely composure. "What of it?"

"Well, sir, nothin'—maybe," the coxswain admitted, giving a doubtful shake of the head. "Only Kitty swears Channing wasn't none too pleased with the rumors. Said he meant to have her for himself—along with her father's shipping interests. Sort of in the way of settling a long outstanding debt against Tyree. She says he swore he would make sure of it."

"Indeed?" commented Myles, his expression betraying little beyond a casual interest. Leisurely he straightened and, turning, reached dispassionately for a decanter of port on the commode behind him. "Somehow I find that singularly odd," he continued, pulled out the stopper. "A threat, after all, coming from a man separated by the entire Atlantic Ocean from the lady in question, would seem a rather empty one, would it not?"

"Aye, sir, I suppose it would," agreed Leeks, seemingly disappointed in Myles's reaction or, rather, his lack of one. "Except, of course," he added, brightening, "that by then Channing had been recalled home." For a bare second, Myles's hand, holding the decanter, went still over the wineglass. "To accept the king's reward of a baronetcy," Leeks expanded. "He was in England, cap'n, when he made that threat. Though what it's got to do with nothin', I'm sure I couldn't guess. Nor it ain't likely I'll be learnin' much more, leastwise not from Kitty. Right then was when Quinby found us."

Myles, who had a very good idea what pertinence it might have, deliberately finished pouring his drink and set the decanter down. For a moment he stood, the decanter lid in

119

his other hand apparently forgotten as he stared with curious fixity at his reflection in the shaving mirror above the commode.

"Are you quite certain, Leeks?" he queried softly then.

The big coxswain shifted uneasily, sensing, no doubt, the tautness in his captain's unnerving stillness.

"Aye, sir," he said. "Kitty's not like to've got it wrong. It was then that she was wed to Quinby."

Myles's slender fingers closed hard about the cut-glass stopper.

"I see," he murmured with a chilling lack of inflection and slowly unclenched his fingers. For a moment he stared at the droplets of blood welling from his hand where the points of the fine-cut glass had bitten into the palm. Odd that he should have felt nothing, he reflected absently. Then deliberately he dropped the lid in the mouth of the decanter and, picking up a towel, wiped the blood from his hand.

"There's more, cap'n," warned Leeks. Averting his gaze as Myles came about, he said, "Quinby was fair out of his head at findin' us in what might be considered suspicious circumstances. When he got Kitty alone, he worked her over pretty good. I expect it wasn't the first time neither," he added, clenching his big hands into fists.

"I'm sorry, Leeks," Myles said, surprised a little at the depth of his coxswain's feelings. "It would seem Quinby was acting within his rights. I'm afraid in the circumstances there isn't much I can do for your Kitty, except, perhaps, to try and discover how she goes on."

Leeks nodded.

"I'm obliged, cap'n," he uttered shortly. "But that's not what I'm here for. I'll be takin' care of Quinby when the time's ripe. What's more to the point right now is that Kitty, bless her soul, has managed to sneak a message out to me by one of the serving maids. Cap'n, Channing's hired some riffraff to make off with your lady."

A hard little glitter came to Myles's eyes.

"How very odd of Sir Wilfred," he murmured tonelessly. "And did Mrs. Quinby by any chance give some indication as to when this abduction was to occur?"

"There wasn't no more to the message," Leeks said unhappily. "I'm sorry, sir."

"You needn't be." Myles smiled grimly. "Indeed, I am indebted to you and your Mrs. Quinby for having shed light on certain particulars which have puzzled me for some time. At the very least one must presume that not a few of Sir Wilfred's dealings would not bear scrutiny. And as for my lady love, *she*, it would appear, has a great deal to answer to. It is time, I think, that I had a long talk with Miss Sabra Tyree. I doubt not that she could reveal the solutions to many unanswered questions, could she but be persuaded — and she is about to discover just how determined I am that she shall be."

"I beg your pardon, sir?" queried Leeks, misliking the reckless glint in his superior's eye.

Myles, as if recalled to an awareness of his subordinate's presence, clapped a hand briskly to the coxswain's shoulder.

"Never mind, Leeks," he said. "It is nothing to concern you. You have other duties to perform, not the least of which is to carry a message to a certain house in Barclay Street near the King's College. I shall depend on you to be back here by the time I have returned from my interview with Sir Wilfred. I should, after all, be sunk beneath reproach if I arrived at my lady's doorstep past the designated hour."

Chapter 8

"The Tyree diamonds ain't been wore more'n once since your mama—God rest her soul—done passed away," grumbled Phoebe, struggling to fasten the clasp of a magnificent diamond necklace at the nape of her mistress's neck. "What's got into you to bring 'em out now, chile? You be askin' for trouble, mark my words. There's no-good trash that'll knock a body alongside the head for a whole lot less temptation."

Sabra gritted her teeth in order to keep from uttering a sharp retort. Faith, she fretted, was it not enough that she was already strained and on edge at the prospect of the coming evening, without having Phoebe's incessant nagging to endure as well? Resolutely she drew a deep breath and let it out again.

"You really must try to stop worrying," she said, affixing her mother's earrings to her earlobes. "After all, I shall be in the carriage with Captain Myles, and Jubal will be riding guard. And if that is not enough, I shall have my pocket gun. Now will you please do as I ask and fetch me my enameled patch box? Captain Myles is due to arrive within the hour, and I have still to speak with Robert before I go."

"Humph!" snorted Phoebe in disgust.

Watching her cross ponderously to the highboy with the air of a misunderstood martyr, Sabra steeled herself for the worst. It was not long in coming.

"You and that no-good man," she said, yanking open one of the drawers and rummaging through its contents. "Lawd, I never thought I'd see the day. Has you forgot all his low-down tricks? Draggin' you off to that house in the country, the way he done. Makin' folks b'lieve you had done gone an' eloped with him jest when that nice young duke be fixin' to

122

ask you to marry him. You doesn't have to get all gussied up like the king hisself be comin'. You jest say the word, an' ol' Phoebe'll slam the door smack dab in the man's smilin' face."

"Oh, no, Phoebe," Sabra murmured in such a way as to make Phoebe's hair stand on end. "I have other plans for the captain." Her lovely eyes glinted green sparks at the thought of all that Channing's papers had revealed. Oh, yes, Captain Myles should prove very useful in the next few days.

Suddenly she was in a fever of impatience to learn what else Wayne had been able to discover. "Phoebe, what's taking you so long? Have you not found it yet?"

Phoebe, uttering a low grunt, dragged a dressing case out of the bottom drawer.

"Laws o' mercy, you doesn't need t' bite my head off. I is hurryin' as fast as I can." Setting the piece on the vanity table and opening the lid, she glanced sidelong at her mistress. "What's got you all het up, chile? You is skittery as a fly on a griddle. If I didn't know no better, I'd think you was plumb moonstruck. Honey, you ain't fallin' for that lowdown cap'n again, is you?"

"Falling for him!" echoed Sabra, in open amazement. "Good God, Myles forced his way into my home and then insulted and used me in the most despicable manner possible. He is overbearing, arrogant and insufferably rude. What could I possibly see in the man to make me 'fall' for him?"

"Well, he am a handsome devil," Phoebe mused sagely as she held out a dainty enamel patch box. "But a devil nonetheless, and best you doesn't forget it."

"Oh, *enough*, Phoebe!" cried Sabra, fairly snatching the box from her old nanny's hands. "I am more likely to become enamored of Sir Wilfred Channing than I am to succumb to the wiles of Captain Myles."

"Don't you b'lieve it, chile," muttered Phoebe, noting her mistress's flushed cheeks and flashing eyes. "That man got his ways." All at once she sighed. Almost anything was better than having Miss Sabra in the grip of the blue devils. Yet to think that 'that *man*' should have come in answer to all

Phoebe's prayers! Mercy, but the Lord moved in mysterious ways.

"There, that should do it," said Sabra, giving a final pat to a heart-shaped beauty patch at the corner of her mouth. Scooting back the vanity chair, she stood up and shook out her skirts. "Well, what do you think? Will the odious captain find me in the least attractive?"

Phoebe slowly shook her head.

"If the man got eyes, you be goin' to knock 'im over," she muttered, her eyes misty. "Chile, you is fire, ice, an' honey, all rolled up in one."

Sabra, slowly pirouetting before the full-length mirror, was not herself displeased with her reflection. The dress of carmine silk worn open over an ivory-colored hoop skirt embroidered in sprig was everything she had hoped it would be. The disarming femininity of the delicately ruched over-dress and skirt, along with pagoda sleeves, trailing graceful *engageantes* below the elbows, was perfectly offset by the daring neckline, which was cut low off the shoulders to reveal an enticing expanse of milk-white bosom. On her feet she had white lace hose and silk brocade shoes, which shone to advantage below the ankle-length hemline. Her mother's diamonds sparkled at her neck and ears, and her hair was dressed in a cadogan style, with horizontal curls about the face and the queue at the nape of the neck caught up in a silk bow. She was both tastefully elegant and bewitchingly lovely. Indeed, though she was certain Myles had meant it as an aspersion on her character, it was nevertheless true that red silk did suit her quite admirably, she decided with a dangerous gleam in her eye.

"You need not wait up for me, Phoebe," she said, gathering up her ermine pelisse and muff and heading for the door. "I can undress myself tonight."

"You jest makes sure you does it without no man's help," Phoebe retorted repressively and bent to the task of returning her mistress's dressing room to its former neatness.

Painfully aware of the clock ticking away the seconds till Myles's arrival, Sabra hurried along the hall to the stairs.

She had hoped for at least fifteen minutes with Robert, who, having returned to the house after she had already entered her bath, was now waiting for her in his study on the ground floor. But time had seemed maddeningly to slip away. Indeed, it had been all she could do to sit still while Phoebe dressed her hair, not once, but twice before the former nanny was satisfied with her handiwork. *Then* what must she do but discover the slight rent in the hem of the gown, which Phoebe had insisted must be repaired before she would allow her mistress to put it on. God grant that she had just a few seconds left to speak with Wayne, she fervently prayed. She must know if he had been able to reach Jackson, the go-between for the Continental forces. So very much depended on it.

Midway down the curved stairway that descended into the entry hall, Sabra faltered as the clock struck nine. Faith, it could not be *so* late, surely, she thought, upon which, the brass knocker sounded in mocking reply.

"Damn!" she breathed as Robert Wayne crossed the floor below her and answered the door. All at once her heart began to hammer beneath her breast. She had been so preoccupied with other matters that she had momentarily forgot her dread of seeing Myles again, and now, when everything depended on her keeping her wits about her, she suddenly felt her mouth go dry and her knees turn to water.

"Captain Myles," said Wayne, stepping back, "won't you come in please. Miss Tyree will be down directly."

For an instant Sabra felt frozen to the spot as she saw Myles enter, his tall figure seeming to dwarf the other man. Indistinctly she heard him murmur something in reply. Then, inevitably, he turned and beheld her standing there.

Even across the intervening distance, she could see the fiery glitter of his eyes. His lips curved, ever so slightly, and suddenly her breath caught hard in her throat. Gracefully he bowed.

Damn, she thought, why had he to be so cursedly handsome? Inexplicably, she experienced a wild impulse to turn and flee up the stairs. Then she got a grip on herself. Myles might be able to coerce her into participating in his charade, but she would be damned if she would allow him to get the better of her. Gathering her courage about her like a cloak, Sabra walked regally down the stairs to greet him.

"Captain Myles," she said simply, dropping into her curtsey.

A tingling of nerve endings shot up Sabra's arm as Myles lifted her to her feet and, bowing over her hand, lightly brushed his lips against her knuckles. Then carelessly he straightened, and taking her mantle from her, made as if to place it around her shoulders.

"Shall we go?" he drawled, his gaze opaque and cynically bored.

For a moment she stared at him in outraged disbelief. How dare he behave as if he had not even seen her, she fumed, thinking of the time she had spent in planning and executing her appearance. The dress, her hair, her mother's diamonds — they had all been wasted on him. Faith, she might have known!

"Am I to understand, then, that I pass inspection, captain?" she queried acerbically. Her head high she stood before him, a breathtaking vision of proud womanhood.

Incredulously she saw him raise a hand to his chin and study her with marked deliberation. As though it were necessary to give the matter careful consideration! she thought, her eyes blazing with indignation.

"Yes, I fancy you will be quite the rage," he drawled, leaving little doubt that he was less than impressed with what he saw, "although I question the advisability of a patch *d'amour* at the corner of the mouth. A lady unwise enough to advertise a propensity for flirtatiousness is asking to be insulted after all, and duels at dawn are so very tedious. If you insist on keeping the patch, I suggest you move it to your left cheek. At least that would be in keeping with the theme of this evening's charade — the revelation to the world of our betrothal."

126

It was on her tongue to tell him he could go to the devil when she glimpsed the slight twitch at the corner of his lips. Instantly she lowered her eyes and drew a breath. Good God, she thought furiously, he was baiting her. The abominable wretch to believe for a moment that she would fall for anything so flagrant! It was, after all, an old ploy, one she herself had employed often enough since she had learned its rules the hard way—with Myles as her teacher.

Suddenly her nerves steadied to a steely calm. This time the play would be quite different, for she was hardly the trusting innocent she once had been. In fact, it had been some time since she could be accounted a novice in the art of allurement. Raising the thick veil of her eyelashes, she gave him a brief, tantalizing glimpse of the discerning woman beneath the facade of the pampered beauty. Myles's gaze narrowed sharply.

"But of course, captain," she said, coolly removing the beauty patch and placing it at the top of her left cheek. "I am, after all, yours to command, am I not?"

Myles grinned, the sensuous crescent at each corner of his mouth appearing like twin flags before the bull. "You exaggerate surely, Miss Tyree," he drawled mockingly as he draped the pelisse over her shoulders. "It must ever be a gentleman's desire, after all, to accommodate himself to the lady in such matters. However, you did ask my opinion."

"But how generous of you, to be sure, captain," she retorted in tones oozing honey. "As to the matter of the patch, it was meant only to conceal the last, lingering reminder of my recent misfortune. But doubtless 'twill not be remarked. The lighting in the theater *is* rather less than perfect."

In grim satisfaction she saw his lips thin at the sight of the faint scar left by the baronet's signet ring at the corner of her mouth. Then, with a toss of her head, she turned haughtily toward Wayne, who thus far had remained an interested observer. Immediately she sobered, perceiving the unmistakable signs of strain in his eyes. He had been bitterly opposed to the idea of using Myles in this new ploy of hers, and she knew he was worried.

"Robert, I am sorry," she said with sincere remorse. "I am unforgivably late, and now I fear our business will just have to wait. Would tomorrow morning be convenient?"

"As a matter of fact, I was going to suggest that very thing," he answered, his ease of manner belied by the piercing quality of the look he gave her. "Indeed, I'll make it a point to be on hand early."

Sabra felt the hairs at the nape of her neck prickle with sudden foreboding. It was to be bad news then, was her fleeting thought.

"Yes. Very well then. I shall be expecting you." Reluctantly she turned to go. But after a step or two, she stopped and looked fleetingly back again. "Good night, Robert," she said softly. "And do try to get some rest. You've been pushing yourself far too hard these past few weeks."

"Now you're being absurd. If anyone should be made to have a care, 'tis you," he scoffed and shooed her brusquely toward the door. "Keep a close watch on her, will you, Myles?" he added, giving the other man a pointed look. "I fear Miss Tyree may have made a dangerous enemy in Sir Wilfred Channing."

"Oh, you may count on me," drawled Myles, his gaze, going to Sabra, distinctly ironic. "Indeed, I shall take most particular care never to take my eyes off her."

Clenching her fingers in her muff, Sabra stepped past him and out on to the stoop. So, she thought, he intends to play the watchdog. Well, we shall just see about that, *Captain* Myles.

She forced herself to relax as she felt Myles slip his hand beneath her elbow.

"Your solicitude for each other is most touching, *ma mie*," he said, amused, as he led her across the walk toward the carriage waiting at the curb.

Sabra's chin came up.

"Robert is a good friend," she answered coldly. "I could hardly have gotten along without him these past few years."

"I see, another of your hopeless victims, as it were. Content somehow to serve but never touch?"

Sabra gave him a withering look.

"We have known one another since we were children. His interest, I assure you, has never been other than fraternal."

"I stand corrected then," he countered smoothly, a tremor of laughter in his voice.

It was only then, as a hulk of a man dressed in seaman's garb stepped down from the perch in back to open the door for them, that Sabra drew up short.

"But you are not Jubal!" she exclaimed before she thought. "And *this* is not my carriage!"

"No," Myles said affably. "It is *my* carriage, and this is Leeks, my cox'n."

"Your *cox'n?*" she repeated incredulously.

Myles drew a patient breath.

"I believe 'tis customary for the captain of a naval vessel to have a barge at his disposal, and the cox'n that goes with it."

Sabra awarded him a fulminating glance.

"This, sir, is hardly your barge. What have you done with Jubal and my carriage?"

"Oh, them. Well, naturally, since I saw no purpose to having two conveyances, I dismissed Jubal and instructed your driver to return yours to the stable. Have you some objection to riding in mine?" he queried blandly.

Sabra gritted her teeth and glanced away. Of course she objected to it. It meant that she would have no one near whom she could trust. Indeed, it meant she would not have Jubal Henry's stalwart presence to rely on, as Myles must very well have known. Still there seemed little she could do to alter the situation without playing the utter fool, and Myles was waiting to hand her into the carriage.

Shrugging with elegant indifference, she gathered up her skirts.

"No, why should I?" she said, her cool smile curiously at odds with the glitter of her eyes. " 'Tis only that you took me by surprise. After all, one hardly expects a naval captain to have his own conveyance. Indeed, I must compliment you on your resourcefulness. An Italian chaise of this quality is rather difficult to come by these days."

"Indeed?" murmured Myles, helping her to step in. "I'm afraid I wouldn't know. As it happens, this one was placed at my disposal by an old and very dear friend—a Miss Lily Barrett. Perhaps you've heard of her. She is an actress of some acclaim."

"I'm afraid I have not the pleasure, captain," answered Sabra, inexplicably annoyed. How dared he bring up the subject of a female—an *actress*—with whom he was obviously on intimate terms!

Myles, stifling a grin, entered after her and seated himself in the corner. Though his face was nearly obscured in shadows, Sabra could feel his eyes on her as the carriage gave a slight lurch and started down the street. Folding her hands in her muff, she stared rigidly before her.

For a time neither made any attempt to speak, and gradually Sabra's resentment changed to a disturbing awareness of the man sitting next to her and of the silence fraught with all that was left unsaid and unresolved between them.

Faith, what was it about Myles that his mere presence was enough to render her peculiarly lack-witted? No other man had such an effect on her. But then few others smelled tantalizingly of fresh linen and shaving soap, untainted by heavy perfumes, she thought wryly, uncomfortably mindful that the clean, subtle scent of him was playing havoc with her senses, arousing disquietingly familiar yearnings. And, truth to tell, it had been no different in London, even after she had come utterly to despise him. The simplest things one normally took for granted—the gesture of a strong, shapely hand, a lock of raven hair falling rebelliously over the forehead, the pulse throbbing in the muscular column of his neck—any one of these, or any number of others, might catch her suddenly unawares, causing a strange, queasy sensation in the pit of her stomach.

Inevitably another memory sprang to mind, the memory of Myles in naught but his breeches and boots, his bare torso rippling with muscle. A hard pang, like a knife thrust to her vitals, was quickly followed by bitter anger. It was at that moment, as he had opened the door of the hunting box to his cousin and the duke, that she suddenly had realized how despicably she had been used. For an instant she felt sickened with all the old horror and shame.

Damn him, she thought, gripping her hands tightly together as she fought her nausea. The pain helped steady her, and suddenly she recalled the reason she had refused to flee the city as Robert had wanted her to do. Wes was dead, and she had yet to avenge him. In the face of that, Trevor Myles was as nothing to her—nothing but the instrument of her revenge!

"Tell me about your ship, captain," she said, her nerves rock steady and her heart as cold and unrelenting as her resolve.

It had been meant as a polite inquiry only, a natural topic for conversation under the circumstances, but she sensed a subtle change in him, a tautening of the lean, muscular body, which, faint though it was, yet piqued her curiosity. Then the fleeting impression faded, leaving her uncertain as to whether or not she had only imagined the whole thing.

"Ah, my ship," he said with an odd sort of mockery in his voice. "The driving obsession of every naval officer worth his salt. My *ship* resides presently in wet dock receiving long-overdue repairs. And there she is likely to remain till hell freezes over—or until the naval yard chooses to fill my requisition orders, either one of which is about as likely as the other. Which is why you are privileged to enjoy my company. That, and the fact that I have been temporarily assigned shore duty in order to recuperate from a slight indisposition."

"Indeed? Something of a morbid nature?" she queried, vaguely surprised. Thus far she had seen scant evidence that he was the least debilitated.

"Only in the mind of the fellow who shot me." His smile was cynically hard. "A sharpshooter," he added, noting the startled parting of her lips, "on a French man-of-war. If Leeks hadn't shoved me aside, no doubt he'd have done for me."

Sabra gave Myles a searching glance from beneath the

luxurious veil of her eyelashes.

"Leeks, 'twould seem, is a handy man to have around," she observed, well aware that Myles's "indisposition" could hardly have been so insignificant as he made it out to be. "How fortunate for you that you command such loyalty. Have you a large complement of such men?"

"Large enough," he smoothly evaded. "Despite the loss of not a few who were less fortunate than I."

Sabra shivered at the hint of steel in his voice. The bill must have been high indeed, she reflected, experiencing an unwitting pang of sympathy at all that he had left unsaid. No stranger herself to the burden of command, she knew well enough what it was to take men into the heat of battle, men who dared to face death out of loyalty and blind trust in the one who gave the orders. One never really got over it, and judging from the rigid line of the captain's mouth, the encounter with the French man-of-war had cost him plenty.

"I am sorry," she murmured, momentarily forgetting their differences. "I had no idea."

"But of course you had not." His amused laugh somehow stung her. "Indeed, how should you? 'Tis hardly the sort of *on-dit* one picks up in ladies' drawing rooms or at fancy dress balls, is it?"

The sympathy she had momentarily felt for him underwent an instant eclipse. Indeed, it was on her tongue to tell him that not all females were empty-headed chit-chats with naught to do but sit around and gossip, but she caught herself in time.

"No, I don't suppose it is," she said instead and lapsed once more into stony silence.

The carriage drew near then to the theater and was caught up in the squeeze of vehicles arriving for the evening's performance. Sabra, smiling and nodding to acquaintances as she and Myles awaited their turn to pull up in front and disembark, steeled herself for the coming ordeal.

By himself, Myles would have attracted a deal of attention for his striking physical appearance alone, but in the company of Sabra Tyree, he commanded the instant notice of everyone present. No sooner had they entered Sabra's reserved box than a murmur went up and a sea of ogling faces turned openly to survey them. Myles, displaying a cool disregard for the stir they were causing, came up leisurely behind Sabra to help her off with her mantle.

"Twould seem that nothing has changed, *ma mie*," he murmured, the featherlike brush of his hands against her shoulders creating a disturbing tingling sensation. "You still command an audience whenever you make an appearance, do you not?"

"Perhaps," she answered, nodding graciously to the governor and his wife in the box next to them. "But tonight all eyes are turned on you. Indeed, I suspect that from this time forward you may expect to be something of a celebrity, Captain Myles."

For an instant he seemed to consider.

"Then let us give them something more tangible to contemplate, shall we," he said. Her heart leaped as his head bent suddenly near. Before she guessed what he intended, his lips found the soft vulnerability of her neck where it met the shoulder, and in a gesture, provocatively intimate, he kissed her.

Sabra, swept by the sickening realization of what he had done, only just managed to stifle a gasp of stunned outrage. In that single gesture he had as good as declared her to be either his intended or his mistress. Not that it mattered which, she thought bitterly, for whatever the interpretation of his action, Myles had irrevocably compromised her jealously guarded reputation. By the morrow everyone who was anyone would have heard that the enticing, but hitherto unassailable, Tyree had taken herself a lover. It was all she could do to keep from turning on Myles in a cold fury.

"Damn you!" she breathed.

"Gently, my love," Myles cynically cautioned as, languorously, he took the seat at her left. "Remember, all the world is watching."

Forcing a smile, Sabra acknowledged the sanctimonious

133

stare of a hatchet-faced matron in the gallery opposite them.

"Good God," she exclaimed under her breath, "you might just as well advertise that you intend to cohabit with me."

"As a matter of fact, that is exactly what I've done," he murmured complacently back to her.

"How dare you," she began, only to be rendered speechless with anger as, a finger to his lips, he enjoined her to silence.

"Not now, *ma mie*," he drawled at his most maddening. "The play is ready to begin."

And, indeed, the candles had mercifully been dimmed, and the strains of the voluntary were issuing forth from the pit. Sabra, vexed at having to hold her tongue, clamped her lips shut. Still seething at the manner in which he had tricked her, she settled back in her chair, prepared to await the intermission and the inevitable onslaught of those who would come swarming to satisfy their curiosity about Sabra and her intriguing new escort.

Thus it was some time before she found herself paying attention to the performance going forth on stage, and in particular to the delightfully portrayed Mrs. Teazle.

Understandably, Sabra had been in no frame of mind to pursue the printed dramatis personae before the play began, and now that there was insufficient light, she found herself piqued with curiosity about the actress. Obviously she was a talented veteran of the stage, and yet she was not familiar to Sabra, who herself was hardly a stranger to the theater. Briefly she toyed with the idea of asking Myles about her, but then mentally she shrugged. There would be time enough during the intermission to check her program, after all, and she would rather remain in ignorance than be forced to address the odious captain for any reason whatsoever.

In spite of herself, Sabra became immersed in the unfolding web of interwoven plots; so much so, in fact, that she jumped when, close to the end of the second act, Myles's hand closed over hers as it rested on the curved end of the armrest. Before she knew what he was about, she felt him slip something on her finger. At that moment the curtain came down and the house lights were lit, catching the brilliance of interwoven diamonds and emeralds sparkling magnificently on her hand. Going rigid with surprise, she turned her head to stare at Myles.

"Good God, what mockery is this?" she demanded in a flinty voice.

"I should have thought it was obvious," he drawled, observing her heightened color with interest. "A betrothal ring would seem a necessary property in the charade we play, would it not? Merely to lend credence to the farce, you understand."

"Oh, indeed," she bitterly rejoined. "I understand perfectly. And yet I wonder that you would risk anything so precious as this. It seems something of a sacrilege, after all, to perpetrate a lie with the ring that once graced your mother's hand, and your grandmother's and great-grandmother's before her, ad infinitum."

The dark eyebrows rose inquisitively.

"You intrigue me, *ma mie*. Indeed how, I must ask myself, could you possibly be aware of that particular? But then you always did your homework so well, did you not? Indeed, did I not know better, I should suspect you might once have had designs on someone other than Waincourt's heir apparent. His ne'er-do-well cousin perhaps, the next in line to the title?"

"I fear you overrate your dubious charms, captain," she countered with a certain air of sardonic triumph. " 'Twas Lady Anne herself who told me the history of the Myles betrothal ring, even going so far as to suggest that in me she saw a worthy match for her errant son, did I but choose to set my cap for him. In retrospect I cannot but wonder at her lack of perspicuity in that instance, for in all other respects I found your mother wondrously acute in her perceptions." Suddenly she met his look squarely. "Indeed," she added pointedly, "I felt her loss most keenly when I learned of it, for in spite of everything, she, at least, seemed never to waver in her affection for me. Nor did I in mine for her."

Had she been anything but sincere in her final statement, Sabra might have enjoyed the satisfaction of beholding Myles momentarily deprived of his usual sangfroid. As it was, she was granted a brief glimpse of the handsome brow creased in a forbidding frown before their privacy was invaded by Colonel Cathcart and his lady wife.

The intermission was every bit as trying as Sabra had known it would be. No sooner had the first of their inquisitors presented themselves than the box seemed to fill with chattering females who cast envious glances at Myles's tall, manly figure and chided her for having kept the existence of so delectable a creature to herself. With stoic calm Sabra endured the chorus of exclamations over the ring sparkling conspicuously on her finger, answered the barrage of prying questions concerning the most intimate details of her betrothed's history, family connections, and future prospects, and feigned ignorance of the frequent exchange of sly, knowing looks over the tops of fluttering fans. She was, nevertheless, exceedingly grateful when the orchestra signaled the play was about to resume.

Myles, who had been similarly grilled by the male contingent, bowed to Colonel Cathcart, the last to depart. Then, turning, he met Sabra's wry glance and grinned in such a way as to make her heart lurch.

"You may relax now," he said, taking his seat beside her. " 'Twould seem the worst is over."

"Would it?" she retorted acidly. "Indeed, I wonder."

"But how not, *ma mie?*" Stretching his legs out before him, he crossed them at the ankles and leaned comfortably back in his chair. "By tomorrow we shall be an accepted *on dit.* And the day after that, decidedly *demodé.* There is nothing so dreary, after all, as stale news, would you not agree?"

Sabra, who had been thinking of a potential for unpleasantness of an entirely different sort, made no reply as the curtain went up on the third act of Sheridan's *School for Scandal.* She must simply be prepared for any and all contingencies, she told herself grimly, for she little doubted that everything Myles had done thus far had been done with a definite object in mind. Nor did she have any difficulty guessing what that object was. He had, after all, as good as declared it, had he not? Damn him for his bloody arrogance!

Suddenly her lips curved ever so slightly. But then he had tried to bed her once before and failed, she thought in cold amusement, and she had only to put him off for a week or two. After that, her plans would be complete, and she would be long gone from the city and safely out of reach of Trevor Myles.

Resolutely she put all such matters from her mind. It might be some time before she had the pleasure of attending a theater again, and she would be foolish in the extreme if she let Myles spoil it for her, she told herself, settling back to enjoy the unraveling of Sheridan's tale. Nor was she to be the least disappointed, either with the plot or the performance, save only that they had perforce to come to an end after five exceedingly humorous acts.

The rest of the audience, equally pleased, gave a thunderous applause as the curtain fell on the final scene. Moments later the curtain went up again, and as one by one the actors presented themselves for the curtain call, the applause continued, crescendoing to an uproar as Lady Teazle came forward to take her bow.

At that moment a footman bearing a magnificent bouquet of hothouse roses crossed the stage and, presenting it to the actress, whispered something in her ear. Instantly her eyes lifted to Sabra's box nearly directly above her and to Myles standing at the fore.

All at once Sabra's smile froze on her face. In a sort of nightmarish dream, she beheld the seductively beautiful Lady Teazle, the flowers clasped to her shapely bosom, drop into a deep curtsey, then, rising, pluck a single red rose from the bouquet. In a gesture that left little doubt as to its meaning, she pressed the blossom to her lips and then with a flourish of a shapely arm, flung it from her. For an instant the world seemed to recede, leaving only Sabra and Myles and the actress smiling up at them as the rose lifted and sailed in a perfect arc. At last Myles, leaning easily forward, plucked it from the air. Her cheeks hot with humiliation, Sabra could do naught but watch in tight-lipped fury as the man who had announced himself to the world as her promised husband, raised the rose to his lips and bowed to Lady Teazle.

Nor was that to be the final, or even the worst, humiliation of the night, she was soon to discover, as Myles, helping her on with her pelisse, inquired how she had enjoyed the entertainment.

"Which entertainment had you in mind, captain?" she countered acidly. "Mr. Sheridan's delightful comedy of manners or the little farce just now enacted for—whose benefit, I cannot but wonder."

Incredibly, he had the gall to pretend innocence.

"Farce, *ma mie?*" Sabra's disdainful arch of a haughty, disbelieving eyebrow apparantly jogged his memory. "But can you possibly be referring to the simple exchange of compliments between old acquaintances?" His amused laughter set her blood to boiling. "I did tell you Miss Lily Barrett was a particular friend of mind, did I not?"

Sabra's head came up in startled disbelief.

"Oh, indeed," she said bitterly. "What you failed to mention, however, was that she would be playing the part of Lady Teazle. Oh, how cleverly you set me up. And now, I suppose, you intend to rush to her dressing room in order that you may congratulate one another on your triumph. Well, don't let me keep you from it, captain. I can find my own way home, I assure you."

Angrily she turned to leave, determined to hire a hackney, or, failing that, to walk home should it prove necessary. Myles's fingers, closing with a steely grip about her arm, brought her hard about.

"You blasted little idiot," he growled through teeth clenched in a smile for the benefit of any curious onlookers. "Surely you must be aware that if you walk out of here alone, you throw yourself to the wolves."

"Can you possibly mean you would wash your hands of me?" queried Sabra, gazing up at him with exaggerated innocence. "Captain, if I believe that, nothing could keep me from it. Indeed, I should vastly prefer the wolves outside to the snake in the grass within."

"No doubt," he drawled acerbically. "I, however, have every intention of keeping to my end of the bargain, in return for which, I intend to hold you to yours."

"Keep to your end of the bargain?" Sabra uttered an incredulous laugh. "Faith, do you take me for an utter fool? Or perhaps you thought I should find it amusing to be made sport of in public by you and Miss Lily Barrett, your 'very dear friend'?"

"On the contrary, I believed you a woman of the world. But you, *ma mie*, are behaving perilously like a jealous female. Now if you are through enacting a Cheltenham tragedy, Miss Barrett is graciously waiting to receive us in her dressing room."

Sabra stared at him in stunned disbelief. Surely even Myles could not be so low as to present her openly to his mistress. Good God, they would both be sunk beneath reproach!

"Then I fear you and she have presumed too much," she said in withering accents. "Indeed, I cannot but find the notion of consorting with your—with an *actress*—distasteful in the extreme. But then you cannot but be aware that no decent woman could feel otherwise. The truth is you intend, do you not, utterly to humiliate and ruin me, just as you did in London."

For an instant their glances clashed, leaving no doubt in Sabra's mind that she had at last penetrated Myles's formidable defenses. Indeed, she almost quailed before his eyes, boring through her like glittering points of steel.

"You, *ma mie*, will not only attend Miss Barrett in her dressing room, but you will do so with every appearance of good grace."

"No, captain, I shall not. Indeed, I can think of no earthly

139

reason why I should."

His smile was anything but pleasant.

"Can you not?" he murmured. All at once Sabra shivered. "Then perhaps I misjudged your motives for attending Sir Wilfred in his private quarters. I had believed, you see, that you were interested in saving your brother's life. Apparently I was mistaken."

Sabra's face paled suddenly to a pearly white.

"Damn you!" she uttered in scathing accents. "How dare you think to use him against me as did Channing before you. Wes is dead. Did you truly believe I should not be aware of that?"

A flicker of surprise shone briefly in his eyes, and for an instant it seemed that the stern face softened with something akin to enlightenment. Instinctively Sabra backed up a step, one hand rising unconsciously to her throat.

"I cannot pretend to know on what you have based so erroneous a judgment," drawled Myles, his gaze never once wavering from hers. "But I assure you, Miss Tyree, that Wesley Locke is very much alive."

For the space of a single heartbeat, Sabra felt her senses reel. Then instantly she had herself in command again.

"It's a lie," she stated flatly. "You are trying to use me, just as you have always done. But it won't work. I have been haunted by Channing's voice from that dreadful night, bragging that my half-brother would be dead by morning, and I can conceive of no reason why he should have altered his plans. Or perhaps you would have me to believe the baronet could be swayed by pity, captain?" she queried in a voice, hard with bitter mockery. "Pity for the woman who did her best to put a period to his existence?"

"That would be stretching the bounds of reason, I quite agree," Myles rejoined with infuriating imperturbability. "No, Locke is alive because Channing believes you are about to be aligned with a noble house second only to royalty itself. To wit, the house whose head is Waincourt. And only so long as he believes it will your half-brother continue to live. Of that you may be certain."

At last Sabra could not deny that he was telling the truth. While Myles by himself might not have been enough to give Channing pause for thought, Waincourt was a name to be reckoned with. In the game he played, Channing would be a fool to incur the wrath of a nobleman whose wealth and titular influence reached even so far as the throne of France!

"Faith, 'tis a perilous toil you weave, is it not?" she uttered, turning suddenly away. "Indeed, I begin to wonder what I have gained in the bargaining. Sir Wilfred, after all, would have been content merely to defile my womanhood and break me to his will." Deliberately she came about again. "With what will you be satisfied, captain?" she demanded, her gaze upon his lean, handsome face singularly devoid of emotion.

Myles's lips curled in a slow, cynical smile.

"But surely you must know the answer to that, Miss Tyree," he drawled, hatefully cool. "You, who have made it a point to dangle yourself before the interested parties, rather like the prize in a *concours des armes*. I shall not rest satisfied, *ma mie*, until the game and the spoils are mine."

Chapter 9

Feeling as though the world had suddenly turned topsy-turvy, Sabra allowed herself to be led through a maze of backstage paraphernalia, interspersed with machinists, actors, and a goodly number of visitors. That she was truly about to find herself outside Lily Barrett's dressing room door seemed almost too ludicrous to contemplate. As a matter of fact, she was still too stunned by the news that Wes was alive to have given much consideration to what might lie in store for her beyond that, as yet nebulous, wooden barrier. Her single, overriding concern thus far had been simply to get through the remainder of the evening with as much dignity as was possible, then, hopefully, to find herself finally at home—alone and in the privacy of her own boudoir.

She must have time to think. A plan had immediately to be devised for getting her brother out of the prison ship *Jersey.* Of that much, at least, she was quite certain, for though Myles had managed to stay Channing's hand for the present, it would have been foolish in the extreme to rely on the baronet's indefinite forbearance. No, eventually he would act. Indeed, she could not see that he had any other choice so long as she retained possession of evidence that damned him as a traitor, not only to England, but to France and the colonials as well. And while Channing's private journal and the dispatch she had inadvertently intercepted might very well prove to be the key to obtaining Wes's freedom, they were also a warrant for her own death. She had to be very careful indeed as to how she proceeded from this moment on.

These, however, were not the only, or even the most troubling, of her concerns, she mused darkly as she lifted her eyes to the stern, unreadable features of the man at her side. There was Myles himself to be considered, and his motives. From the moment he had barged into her bedroom and revealed his unexpected involvement in her affairs, she had been cudgeling her brain to discover some reason for his interference in matters that could not possibly concern him. That his sole interest was to save her from the hangman, she had dismissed offhand as being too farfetched in the extreme. His more recent avowal, however, was hardly more believable. Truly she could not decide what was more incredible: that he should consider her the prize in whatever bizarre game he was playing or that he should exert himself to become the victor.

Good God, none of it made sense, and least of all did the fact that he should have deemed it necessary for her to become personally acquainted with his light of love, she fumed upon finding herself at last on the threshold of Lily Barrett's dressing room. Certainly, she reflected as Myles gave a brief rap at the door, in the face of all that lay before her, the next hour or so could not possibly be considered in any other light than a rather bizarre and, quite probably, irksome inconvenience.

Then Lily Barrett's voice called out to them to enter. Myles obliged by opening the door, and instantly it became apparent that Sabra had grossly misjudged the entire matter. Certainly she was not at all prepared for the sudden feminine shriek of delight with which Myles was greeted or for Lily Barrett herself, who, her shapely figure all but revealed beneath the shimmering silk of a mauve peignoir, launched herself at Myles.

"Trev, darling!" cried Lily. "I thought you would never come."

Sabra's mouth clamped shut as Myles, catching his mistress about the waist, swung her high off her feet, then set her lightly down again. Good God, she thought, she had actually hoped to get through this with dignity? All at once she was struck by the utter absurdity of it all. Faith, who but Myles would have the audacity to bring his intended and joie de vivre together in a single room? Clearly he was flirting with disaster!

"Did you hear them? I can hardly believe it yet," his mistress chortled, nearly beside herself with glee. "Whatever will Ellsworth say when he finds out I am the object of so much adoration?"

Yes, what will he say, Trevor, darling? thought Sabra sardonically, wondering who the deuce Ellsworth was and what it could possibly matter what he thought or said—a rival lover, perhaps? An unsuspecting husband? To her disappointment, Myles remained unruffled.

"But what should he say?" he answered with insufferable charm. "Has Lily Barrett ever been anything but adored?"

Sabra rolled her eyes ceilingward. Good Lord, she thought.

"On occasion, yes," replied Lily ruefully. "And I have been away so long, you know. One could not be sure how I would be received." Laughing, she hugged his neck ecstatically. "Faith, I thought I should never escape the crowd. It was marvelous, truly it was."

Suddenly the incredibly blue eyes lifted to encounter Sabra's, regarding her with sublime interest from the doorway. Lily blinked and looked again.

Little knowing what else to do, Sabra grinned and waved hello with a dainty flutter of the fingertips. Uncertainly, Lily fluttered back before disappearing from view in front of Myles.

"Faith, Trevor," carried in an aghast whisper to Sabra's appreciative ear, "why did you not say you had someone with you? And, from the looks of her—" the blond head peeped furtively round the broad, masculine shoulder then hastily was withdrawn. "A lady. What in heaven's name can you be about? She would hardly appear to be in your usual style."

A delicious bubble of laughter rose to Sabra's throat. Then Myles replied, and suddenly she was anything but amused.

"No, not in my usual style," he agreed, perfectly aware, no doubt, that she could hear everything, thought Sabra. "But

144

then, a man's promised wife seldom is. A pity, really. Still, one hopes that, given enough time, the lady might eventually learn to measure up, even to Lily Barrett."

Lily, audibly choking on a startled giggle, must soon after have experienced a most sudden revelation.

"Good God," she gasped. " 'Tis *she!* Myles, you *rogue,* how *could* you have brought her *here* of all places?"

"But what would you have had me do?" he drawled maddeningly. "I could hardly abandon my future wife to find her own way home, now could I?"

Sabra could almost feel Lily glower back at him.

"You could have warned me what to expect," she pointed out, clearly annoyed with him for having placed her in so untenable a position. "But now 'tis done, you might introduce us, you know."

"That was my intention, I assure you." Stepping languidly to one side, Myles drew Lily in plain sight of the doorway. "Lily Barrett," he said, "Miss Sabra Tyree."

"Miss Barrett," pronounced Sabra, her eyes fixed on Myles with chilling intensity.

Giving Myles a brief, searching glance, Lily let her arm slip with apparent reluctance from around his waist.

"Miss Tyree," she said, and after only the slightest of hesitations, extended her hand. "Please, do come in. I cannot imagine what Myles must be thinking of to leave you standing there."

Wondering herself what the devious captain could be contemplating behind those sleepy, hooded eyes, Sabra allowed his mistress to draw her into the room. Experiencing a sudden shiver down her spine, she had the oddest feeling that she had just committed some terrible blunder. Then she became aware that her hostess, having closed the door, was looking her over with sympathetic curiosity.

"You are not very happy at being here, are you, my dear?" said the older woman with a disconcertingly knowing look. "And who can blame you? Backstage dressing rooms, after all, can hardly be to your taste. It was unforgivable of Myles to bring you."

Startled at such unexpected frankness, Sabra regarded

145

Myles's joie de vivre with renewed interest. The actress had removed her stage makeup, and in lieu of Mrs. Teazle's powdered wig, she wore her own silvery blond hair swept high off the forehead in a less than immaculate pompadour. Indeed, trailing wisps of hair floated in abandon about the alabaster perfection of her face, which could not but add to the compelling sensuality of large, heavily lashed china-blue eyes. Her nose was short and delicately *retroussé* above a small mouth, which appeared tailored for a wide range of lively expression. With her cheeks becomingly flushed and her skin as smooth as a young girl's, Lily Barrett was even more tantalizingly lovely than she had appeared on stage. She was, in fact, everything one would expect in Myles's inamorata, Sabra decided, and was inexplicably annoyed at the thought.

"Not at all, Miss Barrett," she said at last, and summoning a faint, ironic smile, let her gaze swing deliberately to Myles. "No doubt I am pleased at having been granted the opportunity to tell you how greatly I enjoyed your performance. The play was marvelously entertaining. Indeed, I find it wonderful that these sordid little intrigues can be rendered quite laughable in the hands of a comic genius. And you, Miss Barrett, play the part to perfection. I consider myself quite indebted to Captain Myles for so illuminating an experience."

Myles, keenly appreciative of the double-edged barb contained in those final remarks, inclined his head with every appearance of gracious civility. But only someone rendered totally insensate could have missed the invisible sparks which flew between the flint-eyed captain and the slender girl.

"Yes, well. How very kind, I am sure," murmured Lily, who, still trying to sort out just exactly *what* Miss Tyree had intended in her somewhat pointed comments, was feeling suddenly quite *de trop*. "I'm afraid that since my maid is not here at the moment we must simply try and make do without her. Perhaps you would allow *me* to take your pelisse, Miss Tyree. Uh . . . Miss Tyree?"

"What?" faltered Sabra, seeming to wrench her eyes from

Myles's. "Oh, my pelisse, yes. Yes, of course. Thank you."

Letting the mantle slip off her shoulders, Sabra glanced curiously about the chamber, perhaps more accurately described as a closet, which, in addition to a fine oriental carpet, contained more the elements of a snug sitting room than those which might be expected of a theatre dressing room. From this she quickly decided that a door, partially concealed behind a tapestried panel screen, must lead into a wardrobe, which in turn must serve both as a clothespress and *cabinet de toilette*.

"I've never visited backstage before. It would appear surprisingly comfortable," she noted, her gaze lingering on a walnut daybed of rather unique design, for it was not only plump with cushions, but it gave the appearance of most unusual capaciousness. Indeed, she doubted not that it would hold two quite conveniently. "But then naturally," she generously suggested, "you must be required to spend a deal of time here in order to perform Sheridan so brilliantly."

Lily, who could hardly have missed either the object of her visitor's curiosity or the subtle irony in her tone, glanced fleetingly at Myles.

"Indeed you are *too* kind, Miss Tyree," she demurred, giving forth a little ripple of laughter as she sidled closer to Myles's tall, masculine figure. "In truth I am astonished at how rusty I have become. It seems I rehearse hours and hours to get the simplest thing right. But it was not always so, was it, *mon chou?*" she queried, walking coy fingers up Myles's coat sleeve. "In the old days we used to have such marvelous times, did we not?"

The sensuous quirk of Myles's lips was nothing if not efficacious.

"Oh, indubitably," he agreed, sublimely oblivious to his intended's frigid-eyed scrutiny. Prompted by some demon of perversity and the glimmer of unholy amusement behind his alleged mistress's smile, he blithely continued. "But then in those days your performance on stage would seem to have mattered far less to you than the frivolities off it. As I recall, you were not at all averse to relying on a prompter."

Lily's mirth went suddenly awry.

147

"Then your memory, my dearest Trevor," she murmured through her teeth, "is either faulty or far too keen for comfort." Giving his chest a less than gentle shove, she turned vivaciously to Sabra. "At any rate, Miss Tyree, you would do well to believe nothing Myles says of me. He is a notorious rakeshame without an ounce of scruples."

Sabra, who had already witnessed Miss Lily Barrett's eccentric proclivity for receiving while in an extreme state of dishabille, was ready to believe anything of her. Indeed, she had no trouble at all in discerning the hidden message in each intimate flutter of her eyelashes. In short, she appeared to be exactly what Sabra had supposed her to be: a woman of rather loose moral character, to put it kindly. Still, there was something vaguely puzzling about Myles's joie de vivre, something that somehow did not ring true. To her discomfort, Sabra found herself struggling not to like the flamboyant Lily.

"I shall endeavor to keep that in mind, Miss Barrett," she murmured dryly.

"Good," said Lily. "And now I pray you both excuse me while I rid myself of the last of Mrs. Teazle." Waving airily toward the only seating accommodations in the less than commodious chamber, the walnut daybed and a pair of straight-backed chairs crowded about a small folding table, she headed for the tall, paneled screen.

"Oh, by the way, Trevor, darling," she called over her shoulder, apparently as an afterthought, "you will find there is a decanter of reasonably good Madeira in the cabinet, should you be so inclined." Adding, "I shall be only a moment, I promise," she disappeared behind the screen.

Sabra, left to wander curiously among the memorabilia of a younger Lily, which cluttered the walls, table, cherry-wood cabinet, and even the wood-framed looking glass, was vaguely surprised to find nothing of a more recent date than nearly five years previous. Apparently Miss Barrett's retirement had been lengthy indeed, she mused, wondering how the actress had passed those unaccounted-for years. Despite her preoccupation with Lily, however, Sabra did not fail to note the easy familiarity with which Myles availed himself of the decanter and three long-stemmed wineglasses.

Pouring himself a generous portion, he glanced inquiringly at Sabra.

"Thank you, no," she said, her eyes cool and very green. "I fear I've little liking for strong spirits on a queasy stomach. But you go ahead. Somehow I feel certain you and Miss Barrett will want to drink to your—or, pardon me, rather *her*—succès fou."

Despite his facade of languorous indifference, there was all at once something singularly intimidating about Myles.

"In which case," he suggested pointedly, "you would naturally wish to join us." Filling the glass, he held it out to her.

For an instant their glances locked. Then, well aware she had no choice but to acquiesce, Sabra furiously showed him the back of her head. Thus she missed seeing Myles, setting the drink on the folding table near at hand, slip something in the wine.

"Perhaps, Miss Tyree, you would care to be seated," he drawled, all cool affability again. "From past experience I can assure you that time means very little to Lily. With her, a moment is far more likely to exceed an hour."

Sabra, in no mood to be generous, could not have cared less about Lily's peculiarities.

"I should prefer to stand, thank you," she declared. "Unless, of course, you have some objection?"

For the barest instant it seemed he would object, tellingly. Then surprisingly he shrugged.

"You must, of course, suit yourself," he said, reaching up, unbelievably, to loosen his neckcloth. Glass in hand, he walked casually to the chaise longue. "I, however, have had an interminably long day."

Speechless with outrage, Sabra stood by and watched as Myles stretched out on his mistress's daybed. Good God, he could not have made his contempt of her any more plain, she thought in a cold fury. But then her gaze narrowed on the handsome, suspiciously bland countenance, and suddenly it came to her that he was being deliberately provoking.

"Faith, you are enjoying this immensely at my expense,

149

are you not?" she bitterly observed. "How I detest you," she added, making an about-face of utter contempt.

Imperturbably, Myles hooked an arm comfortably behind his head.

"So you've said before, Miss Tyree," he murmured, without discernible interest, and lifted the glass to the light, presumably to study the color of Lily Barrett's vintage Maderia.

Stung by his indifference, Sabra came quickly back again.

"Yes, countless times," she said scathingly. "And doubtless I shall be moved to say it again ere I can finally wash my hands of you."

Manifestly unmoved at such an eventuality, Myles lowered the glass without answering and, apparently satisfied with both clarity and brilliance, began gently to swirl the purplish-red liquid about the sides of the vessel.

Sabra quirked a cynical eyebrow.

"But then, since you hold my brother hostage, it would be exceedingly unwise of me to feel anything which did not suit you, would it not?" she prodded, wanting desperately to dash the cursed glass out of his hand.

"But on the contrary, my love. You are naturally free to feel anything you like," he drawled. "so long as you remember to behave yourself."

Impossible to mistake his unspoken threat, Sabra went deathly pale. The miserable cad! One day she would make him pay for his insolence! But not until she had purchased Wes's freedom, she forced herself to remember, and certainly not before she had what she wanted from the detestable captain. With the greatest effort, she managed to clamp a lid on her temper.

"You did promise," she mentioned after a time, with exaggerated politeness, "there was to be some sort of purpose to this visit, did you not? Other than pleasure, of course."

"I did," he agreed affably and, raising the glass, inhaled deeply of the wine's subtle fragrance.

"Well?" demanded Sabra.

"Hm-m," Myles replied, his brow furrowed deeply in thought. "Rich, but not too much so," he ventured, consideringly. "Let us say piquant, rather, perhaps even racy. Yes, most definitely racy. This begins to show some promise, I believe."

"The devil!" rejoined Sabra acidly.

"I beg your pardon?" Myles turned his head to regard her with polite curiosity, and though a keen observer might have detected an almost imperceptible twitch at the corners of his lips, Sabra saw only the hatefully cool facade of the arrogant tyrant. "Did you say something?"

For an instant Sabra stared at him in speechless wonder. Good God, the man was clearly impossible! Still, she was not averse to giving as good as she got.

"Who, me?" she replied, as, wide-eyed with innocence, she raised an elaborate hand to her breast. "Indeed, captain, you must be mistaken."

"Ah," he remarked, giving a brief nod before settling contentedly against the cushions once more.

Wholly sensible by now that the wretch was irrevocably set on playing the fool, Sabra forced herself to hold her tongue as he took a sip of wine and, with elbaborate care, rolled it interminably around and around in his mouth. At long last, he swallowed.

"M-m-m, excellent," he pronounced, perfectly aware of Sabra, standing over him. Deliberately he smiled, glancing up at her. "You really should try it, you know. Lily has a rare gift for turning up trumps."

Sabra's eyebrows shot toward her hairline.

"Oh, I shouldn't doubt it for a moment," she granted. "After all, she turned up you, did she not." With an angry swirl of silk skirts, she flounced down in the chair farthest away, furious both with him and herself. Even though in the end she had managed to have the last word, she could not but be acutely cognizant of the fact that Trevor Myles, irrefutably, had won the first round.

Myles stifled a grin and, settling more comfortably against the cushions, sipped thoughtfully at his wine. That should hold her for a spell, he reflected with amused satisfaction. At least until Lily chose finally to stage her reentrance. By then, Leeks should have had time to carry out his orders and come back with the carriage. Things were progressing rather more smoothly than anticipated, he decided, especially after the contretemps in the box following the show.

The lady, he mused with a wry twist of the lips, was proving to be a much better player than he remembered her to be. Indeed, it was distinctly possible that in the impetuous Tyree, he had come very nearly to meeting his match, for he was quite ruefully aware that despite his ace-high suit, she had yet managed to force his trump. He had much preferred, after all, that she go on believing he knew nothing of her real reason for being in Channing's rooms. Things would have been so much simpler that way. Still, it could not be helped, and in the long run, perhaps everything had turned out for the better. Wesley Locke, it seemed, was likely to prove a far more effective tool for keeping the little spitfire in line than fear of Sir Wilfred Channing had done. In fact, her unexpected rebellion had come close to ruining all his carefully laid plans.

As if compelled, his gaze went to the proudly aloof figure perched in the chair across from him.

She would seem to be on the edge of collapse, he noted, wryly observing the pinched look about the eyes and mouth. And despite her outward appearance of icy calm, he could not fail to see the slender hands clasped tightly in her lap, the knuckles white beneath the smooth skin.

Uneasily he wondered if he had been right to decide on the sleeping draught. The last thing he wanted, after all, was to have her rendered seriously indisposed. It would, in fact, be a devil of a nuisance, he reflected, almost giving in to the impulse to resort to other, less drastic, means of achieving his object. Then silently he cursed. He had already covered that ground, over and over, in his mind. Had there been any other reasonable alternative, he would not have hesitated to take it. As it was, Sabra herself had tied his hands, and with any luck at all, she would come through it just as she always had: on her feet and fighting mad.

Damn the little vixen, he mused, the cynical glint in his eyes altering to an odd sort of bafflement. How ironic that the one woman who never palled on him should be an unprincipled hoyden who was very likely up to her pretty neck in treason. Nor did it help in the least to reflect that the whole thing might easily have been averted four years ago in London. The truth was he had allowed himself to be played like the worst possible fool.

All at once his eyes hardened to a steely sheen. But then, tonight would see the incomparable Sabra repaid in full for at least one of the accounts left unsettled, and after that, he would be free to see to the other.

"Ah, here we are," said Lily Barrett, appearing suddenly to float into their presence bearing with her the fragrance of roses. She had changed from the indecently revealing peignoir into a *saque* gown of *eau de nil,* the decollete of which was so daring as to hardly restrain her voluptuous charms. "I cannot tell you how marvelous it is to be backstage again celebrating an opening night." Becoming aware of the strained attitude of at least one of her guests, she faltered ever so slightly. But immediately she covered the momentary lapse with her lilting laugh. "And how charming," she added, "that I have you both to share it with me."

Myles, rising gallantly to the occasion, came smoothly to his feet.

"To Miss Lily Barrett," he said, lifting the glass, "and her undeniable triumph."

Sabra, who had been looking forward to this moment with anything but pleasure, visibly stiffened. Indeed, to Lily, observing her out of the corner of her eye, it seemed that she would refuse the toast. Then all at once her head came up, and her glance brushed over Myles with cool disdain. Reaching deliberately for the glass, conveniently placed on the table, she rose gracefully from her seat.

"To Miss Barrett," she said, turning unfathomable eyes on her hostess, "a most charming Lady Teazle."

Lily, meeting the full force of those green eyes, felt a sudden twinge of conscience. Oh, dear, she could not help but like the girl's spirit, in spite of the fact that circumstance had placed them on opposite sides. What was a little talebearing after all? Everyone did it, in one form or another.

And besides, if all Ellsworth had told her about the girl and her father were true, Sabra Tyree had little reason to love British rule. It would be a pity, of course, were it to develop that the impetuous young fool actually was to blame for betraying Trevor to the French. For, except for that dire possibility, she was everything Lily could have wished for Myles.

Ah, well, she reflected philosphically. Mercifully 'twas not for her to decide, one way or the other. Dismissing such depressing thoughts from her mind, Lily accepted a glass of wine from Myles and laughingly allowed him to pull her down beside him on the lounge.

Having drunk to her intended's mistress against her will, only then to be forced to witness the two romping merrily on the daybed, Sabra sank wearily onto the rather less than inviting straight-backed chair. The subtle taste of burnt sugar beneath the mellow richness of the fermented grape she found surprisingly pleasant to her palate. Thinking that in the circumstances another swallow or two might serve to steady her jaded nerves, Sabra experimentally took a second sip. A faint sigh breathed through her lips. Relaxing imperceptibly against the chair back, she took yet another, and finally another. And that was the last that she remembered.

Chapter 10

Sabra came reluctantly to the edge of awareness, prodded by the persistence of hands, dragging her up, holding her, tugging her this way and that. Why must she be bothered now with anything so insignificant as undressing, she fretted, when all she really wanted was to burrow deep into the thick cushion of pillows beneath her and sleep? Fed up at last, she roused herself sufficiently to register a protest.

"Go to *bed*, Phoebe," she grumbled, trying to throw off the hands. "Can undress myself."

"Easy, love," crooned a feminine voice, syrupy sweet. "We shan't be much longer." Sabra frowned. Something was wrong, but for the life of her, she could not quite put her finger on what it was.

"There, now. Put your arm through here and we're done," she was told and, still struggling to puzzle things out, Sabra allowed herself to be maneuvered into something cool and silky. Indeed, it was not until she was made the recipient of a condescending pat on the shoulder, accompanied by an equally patronizing, "There's a good girl," that at last all the pieces seemed to fall suddenly into place.

"*Not* Phoebe!" she muttered emphatically and struggled to sit up. The effort, however, soon proved too much for her. With a groan she fell back and sank once more into the paralyzing arms of deep lassitude. Having momentarily exhausted her strength and the will to drag herself out again, she lay, quiescent, and yet languidly aware of voices issuing from somewhere near.

"Is this really necessary, Trevor?" demanded one of them. It was the woman again. She could not mistake that full-bodied lilt despite the fact that the mellifluous overtones had

155

eroded to a distinctly caustic edge. "I mean, dosing her wine with a sleeping draught—it all seems terribly base somehow. Surely you might simply have charmed her into your bed."

"Had I wished to bed her, my dearest Lily, you may be sure I would have done so," drawled an amused voice, loathsomely familiar—indeed, the voice of Trevor Myles.

Sabra muttered an incoherent oath, which, fortunately, was drowned out by *dearest Lily's* startled rejoinder.

"But then, why—"

"Because," Myles cut in, "it occurs to me that Miss Tyree's health would profit from a brief sojourn in the country. Unfortunately, it is far more likely my loving bride would choose to spit in my eye than to agree to such a proposal, coming, as it were, from me. As for the rest, I'm afraid you will simply have to trust that I know what I'm doing, Lily."

"That is all very well for you to say," insisted Lily crossly. "I still think, nonetheless, that you might have warned me in advance what you intended. I take scant enjoyment in having my guests, even uninvited ones, collapse without warning to the floor. And then to discover the cause of her swoon! I feel positively Machiavellian, Trevor, and it isn't the least bit comfortable, I assure you."

"Then I suggest, in order to ease your mind," said Myles, with steely composure, "that the alternatives to our present course would have been far more distasteful to Miss Tyree. And now, if it is not too much to ask, you would do well to apply yourself to finishing your toilette in something less than your usual time. Regrettably, from what I was able to glean from my ship's surgeon, we can expect Miss Tyree to be insensitive no more than a mere four or five hours."

"Well," sniffed Lily, "you needn't be sarcastic. After all, you've only yourself to blame that I have not Mayella to assist me with the fastenings, or need I remind you that it was at your request that she has been given the evening off. But there, 'tis done." A doubtful sigh carried clearly across the room. "One might have wished, of course, that Miss Tyree and I were more nearly of a size. Still, I suppose in the dark the ill-fit will not be noticed."

An importunate rap at the door startled a gasp from Lily. Fitfully Sabra stirred, nagged by the thought that somehow she must get to her feet and find her way out of the trap she felt closing in about her. Instinctively she froze at the sound of footsteps coming toward her. Her heart in her throat, she heard them pause and felt a hand, oddly gentle, brush her cheek, before they continued past her to the door. Myles! she thought with loathing as she heard him call out softly, "Yes, who is it?" A name, uttered in a masculine voice, struck her oddly—Ellsworth! Damn, who the *hell* was Ellsworth?

"Oh, Will, thank God," Lily murmured with an audible sigh as the door opened and then was quickly closed again. "I was certain either Miss Tyree's friends or her enemies had found us out. Neither one of which would be at all welcome in the circumstances."

"Miss Tyree? Good heavens, is she here?" A mental image of a big, bluff man, formed itself in Sabra's consciousness. A man to fit the deep, resonant voice.

"Over there, on the daybed, sleeping like a lamb. If you've come, thinking to take me home, Will, I fear I cannot oblige you. I'm to act the part of decoy while Myles makes his getaway. With any luck, I shall be home long before daybreak."

There was a sudden exclamatory silence as the newcomer digested this unexpected tidbit. Then Sabra heard him draw a breath.

"This, I must assume, is your doing, Myles. I suppose it would be asking too much to expect some sort of explanation for what is going on here? Your message, I must say, left a deal to be desired."

"No doubt," Myles imperturbably agreed. "It seemed advisable, in the circumstances, not to be too explicit, since there was every possibility Leeks might be intercepted. I have been aware for some time that someone is keeping tabs on my activities. And I now suspect that someone to be the gentleman who formed the major topic of our last discussion, Will."

"The devil you say," Ellsworth muttered with obvious feeling. "But why should he when you are here due to his influence?"

"Curious, is it not?" rejoined Myles in a flinty voice. "Indeed, it recently occurred to me that it was time we shook things up a bit in certain quarters, simply to see what birds might be flushed from the bush, as it were. A little pressure applied in the right places very often goads an uneasy conscience to brashness, and somehow I feel quite confident that Miss Tyree's sudden, unexplained disappearance should produce just the desired effect."

Sabra suffered a sharp stab of fear. Wayne, she thought, and Jubal and the others. It must be. In the event that she turned up missing, who but they, after all, could possibly be at risk in trying to discover what had happened to her?

"Which is why, Lily, *I* invited Will to join us tonight," Myles continued. "With Lily in the guise of Miss Tyree, the two of you are about to take the carriage on a very leisurely jaunt through the city. Leisurely enough, in fact, to draw off anyone who might be watching, while I assay to spirit Miss Tyree out of the city. It's that simple."

"Simple," said Ellsworth grimly, "if we're not held up and Lily carried off by mistake in the process, you mean. I don't like it, Trevor. It's far too risky. If it were just m'self, it'd be different, but I have Lily to think of."

There was an uneasy silence, but Sabra knew her adversary too well to allow herself to hope the plot would be aborted before it went any farther. Myles, she doubted not, would find a way to circumvent any obstacles put in his way by Ellsworth or anyone else, should he choose to. The captain, however, was to prove as unpredictable as ever.

"You do, of course, have every right to object," he said at last, his well-modulated tone noticeably devoid of its customary irony. "I myself confess to having entertained certain reservations concerning Lily's involvement, but there wasn't time to make other arrangements. If it is your wish, you must simply take her home, Will. Doubtless I shall manage well enough without her."

Lily, less than pleased with the outcome, did not hesitate to make her opinion known.

"You, Trevor Myles, will do no such thing," she declared. "How dare the two of you discuss me as though I were incapable of making my own decisions! Admittedly, I was not in favor of using Miss Tyree in so reprehensible a manner, but if Trevor believes it is necessary to ferret out the traitors in our midst, I daresay I am as able as either of you to carry the thing off. I'm going through with it, Will Ellsworth, and that's final."

"Damn *fool*, blasted woman!" ejaculated Ellsworth, an assessment with which Sabra was in heartfelt agreement. "You haven't the least idea of what you're up against. This is not a theatrical production, Lily. These are hardened men who would think nothing of wringing your pretty neck."

"And I am no green girl," Lily retorted frostily. "Or had you forgot I spent my salad days in the less than tender environs of traveling theater companies. Believe me, I know my way around desperate men."

It was all Sabra could do to keep her eyes closed as she waited for Ellsworth's response. Nevertheless, she was hardly surprised when a heavy sigh permeated the taut silence.

"Oh, very well," conceded Ellsworth, albeit grudgingly. "I suppose with Leeks along, we can handle whatever comes our way. But, Trevor, old man, you had better see to it that I hear from you soon. Neither the admiral nor I take kindly to being left in the dark."

The chilling response, coming as it did in Myles's calm, dispassionate drawl, sent a shiver slicing through Sabra.

"I shall, of course, make the endeavor. However, if you have heard nothing in the next forty-eight hours, I suggest you begin looking over the roster for my replacement. Now, if everything's settled, I think we should be going. I'll come with you as far as the outer door to make certain there are no unwelcome surprises. Be sure to keep your head covered, Lily. A single glimpse of Lily Barrett's incomparable silken curls would be a dead giveaway."

"Myles," gurgled Lily, her laughter receding into the distance. "How ever so charming!"

At the sound of the door closing, followed by the rattle of the key in the lock, Sabra struggled to sit up.

"Oh, Lord," she groaned, feeling her head was about to split open. Clenching her teeth, she shoved herself upright. For a moment she waited for the room to quit spinning before she dragged her legs over the side of the lounge. With a last valiant effort, she made it to her feet, to stand, swaying drunkenly.

All at once she uttered a blistering oath.

"*Damn* Myles!" she breathed, having come to the lowering realization that she was clothed in little more than her mother's priceless diamonds and Lily Barrett's absurdly indecent peignoir. Instantly she felt her cheeks grow hot with the memory of those unseen hands disrobing her. Good God, she would have Myles horsewhipped for that if ever she got out of this alive, she vowed, and stumbled toward Lily's wardrobe.

Quickly she discarded the notion of trying to make do with her hostess's gown, which was designed for a female four inches shorter and very likely that much larger in the bust. Faith, it would be a wonder if the woman did not burst the seams of the purloined carmine silk, mused Sabra in wry amusement. Suddenly her heart leaped at the sight of an ivory hoop skirt embroidered in sprig, which lay in a heap at the bottom of the wardrobe. Lily, it seemed, had decided to substitute an underskirt of her own rather than attempt the impossibility of shortening the hem of Sabra's.

Afraid to hope for too much, Sabra knelt and thrust her hand through the placket slit in the skirt. Unbelievably, her fingers met the marvelous touch of cold, tempered steel. Drawing forth her hand, she sank down on her heels. For a moment she could summon the strength to do nothing more than count her blessings and stare at the pocket gun, clutched in her hand. Then suddenly she shook herself.

Faith, what was she about to tarry when Myles would return at any moment? Dragging herself up, she struggled out of the peignoir and into her own panniered skirt and a rather hideous puce velvet jacket left hanging in the wardrobe. Heaven forbid that anyone should see her thus, she thought with scant humor. Her reputation would never survive it. Finally, taking down Lily's fur-lined pelisse, Sabra closed the wardrobe. At the sound of footsteps approaching, she wheeled—too sharply, it seemed.

All at once she staggered, a hand going to her forehead as the room started to pitch and turn. In something of a panic, she heard the ominous click of the bolt sliding free. Her heart started to pound madly. She was still struggling to make the world stand still when the door opened to reveal Myles framed in the doorway.

For a moment, neither moved. Then Myles, folding his arms across his chest, let his gaze trail deliberately over Sabra. An arrogant eyebrow quirked in sardonic amusement.

"I confess I rather prefer the mauve peignoir," he observed insufferably, his glance playing but briefly on the gun. "It possessed a certain—shall we say—*je ne sais quois*, somewhat lacking in your present ensemble."

For the barest instant Sabra gritted her teeth as she felt herself weave.

"Shall we indeed," she uttered scathingly, willing the dizziness to pass. "And you, naturally, intended to drag me through the city clad in nothing but finespun silk. I am sorry to disappoint you, Captain Myles."

Myles waved a negligent hand in the air. His eyes, however, never left her face.

"Think nothing of it. You are right, of course. The peignoir was totally impracticable for traveling."

Good God, thought Sabra distractedly, how could he be so unfeeling? She had meant something to him once, if only fleetingly. But then he had changed. Why? she wondered, surprised she had never thought of it in exactly that way before. But then 'twas likely only the drug, twisting things up inside; that made it so difficult to think at all rationally. She doubted not that he had not a single nerve in his body.

"And where had you intended to take me this time?" she demanded, struggling with the bewildering mixture of hurt and anger. "You will pardon me if I find it hard to believe you have a hunting box tucked conveniently away outside

161

the city."

Myles casually propped a muscular shoulder against the door frame.

"I'm afraid I had not reached that point yet in my reckoning," he admitted, his lips twisting in a curiously wry smile. "Things moved rather too quickly, and as it happens, I know relatively little about the immediate vicinity. Perhaps I thought you might be able to suggest something suitable."

"Perhaps *I* might—" Astonished at anything so patently absurd, Sabra broke off sharply. "You cannot be serious!"

"On the contrary, I have seldom been more serious. Indeed, who better than you? Somewhere not too far removed from the city, I should think, and yet relatively isolated. You probably could name a dozen such places."

For a moment Sabra stared at him speechlessly. He appeared totally at ease, the still, gray eyes unclouded either by conscience or drink. Further than that, she could read nothing in his face or manner that gave her a clue as to what game he was playing.

"Either you are mad, captain," she declared, suddenly quite weary, "or up to something. Personally, I am inclined toward the latter. But whichever it is, I have no intention of remaining to sort it all out." Sabra tightened her grip on the gun. "Kindly step away from the door, if you please."

Myles, to her vexation, displayed no perceptible inclination to comply with her demand.

"But I'm afraid I do not please," he said, appearing to waver and blur in her sight. Shifting the gun, Sabra brushed a hand across her eyes. "As a matter of fact," he continued, the unswerving steadiness of his regard, dangerously at odds with his relaxed, slightly bored demeanor, "doubtless I should regret it exceedingly."

"You shall regret it a deal more if you don't!" snapped Sabra. Faith, she was distracted beyond bearing by the fog clouding her vision and by Myles, coolly waiting for his chance at her. Indeed, her nerves felt stretched perilously near the breaking point, and the gun, moreover, had become a leaden weight dragging at her arm. Clearly she could not hold out much longer. With an effort she got a grip on herself.

"That, sir, will be quite enough," she stated with deadly calm. Deliberately she clasped the gun with both hands to hold it steady. "You are stalling, captain. Move out of the way!"

For an instant, Myles appeared to hesitate, then leisurely he straightened.

"Very well. It appears I have no choice in the matter." Holding his hands in plain sight, out from his sides, he moved easily away from the doorway.

Absurdly, Sabra felt suddenly like laughing. It was happening all over again—the gun in her hand, Myles, like Channing, coming toward her. It was all too damned easy, just as before.

"Stop. Don't come any closer," she warned, edging warily to one side. "I'm not afraid to shoot."

"I never supposed that you were," said Myles and took another step toward her.

Willing him to give it up, Sabra falteringly shook her head.

"Don't be a fool, captain." She was pleading with him and hating herself for it; and, worse, she knew with utter certainty that she would pull the trigger if he forced her. "I have every reason to kill you. God knows, I've never kept my feelings a secret. I despise you utterly!" she flung at him, and backed a step.

Myles moved with her.

"Do you? Are you quite sure?" he murmured, his eyes steely in the lamplight.

Another step brought him almost within reach of the gun.

"Yes!" she answered, and knew instantly it was a lie. "Yes. Oh, Myles, don't!"

His hand shot out, and Sabra fired.

Myles staggered back.

Feeling suddenly dizzy and weak, Sabra stood, swaying slightly, an odd sort of roaring in her ears. Slowly she let the gun drop from nerveless fingers to the floor as she struggled not to give into the sickness pressing at her throat.

"Oh, God," she choked, staring in horrified fascination at the splotch of red that had appeared magically on Myles's coat sleeve above the elbow. Suddenly her limbs started to tremble, and to her abject horror, she knew she was going to cry. *"Damn!"* she gasped. "You insane, mule-headed, impossible fool. *See* what you've made me do. I told you I would fire. Did you truly think I wouldn't? 'Twould have served you right if I hadn't jerked the gun aside. Indeed, 'tis only by the grace of God—or the devil—that you're alive."

She saw Myles look at her strangely as, never once letting up in her blistering diatribe against his unstable character, she went distractedly about helping him out of his coat. And no wonder, she thought, biting her lip at the sight of his shirt sleeve soaked in blood. She was carrying on like an absurd, hysterical female, but somehow she did not care. Nor could she stop herself. Furiously, she ripped the sleeve open to the shoulder and then free of the seam.

"Only look at you! Very likely you will bleed to death," she fumed, hastily fashioning a tourniquet out of the length of ruined sleeve. "And I'm sure I don't care in the least." With hands that were surprisingly steady, she placed her ivory folding fan in the loop and twisted the tourniquet tight. Then brusquely ordering a pale, but bemused, Myles to hold it in place with his free hand, she set about tearing a long strip from the hem of her petticoat. "Indeed, why should I?" she continued, securing the fan with the second strip. "You—you are arrogant and—and scheming, and you care for no one but yourself. You drugged me! Good *God!*" she exclaimed, suddenly reminded of the full extent of the outrage to which she had been subjected. "I could kill you gladly for that alone. But then what must you do but force me to shoot you. *Damn* your insufferable pride!"

Feeling her knees go suddenly rubbery beneath her, Sabra groaned and pressed a quivering hand to her temple. As from a distance she heard her name uttered sharply, then a steely arm closed about her as she sagged toward the floor. Becoming aware of her cheek pressed against a hard chest, she struggled ineffectually to free herself.

"Bloody hell!" she gasped and, giving into a tumult of

emotions welling up inside, weakly beat the side of her fist against that offending chest.

"Anyone with an ounce of sense would have stopped," she choked. "But not you. Not Trevor Myles. You'd rather stop a bullet than give Sabra Tyree a bloody inch. Well, you got just what you deserve, do you hear? Oh, God, how I hate you. I do, you know. I should be glad to see you dead if 'twas by any other hand but mine."

"Hush!" he growled. "If ever there was a woman who talked too much, 'tis you, Sabra Tyree."

Furious, Sabra drew back, but before she could give utterance to a suitably scathing reply, he crushed her mercilessly to him. "Enough," he uttered thickly and silenced her with his lips.

For an instant Sabra's single-most thought was how very like Myles it was to take advantage of her in her exceedingly vulnerable state. Then without warning, a kindling heat pervaded her belly and swept upward like molten fire through her veins. As of their own volition, her arms lifted to entwine about his neck, and suddenly she forgot everything but Myles's insatiable lips, demanding more and more of her. Her own awakening hunger was like a hot wind fanning the flames of a passion she had thought long since dead, and with a fierce, wild abandon, she pulled him to her, answering him, kiss for kiss.

"Sabra," Myles groaned as he released her lips at last. Devouring her eyes and cheeks, he fumbled with the fastenings at the front of the puce jacket and at last bared the tumultuous swell of her bosom to his caress. His hand cupped one of the soft mounds of flesh, while his thumb stroked the pink thrust of her nipple. Murmuring her name, he lowered his head.

She thought she must die of the swift surge of pleasure coursing in waves through her body as he molded his lips to the hardened nipple and sucked at her breast. Then his hands were trailing silken flames over and down her bare back beneath the jacket till at last, his fingers, finding the drawstring at the waist of her underskirt, gave a quick tug. The petticoat slid down over her slender hips and legs to the floor, and she gasped as his hands, shaping themselves to the rounded curve of her buttocks, drew her hard against him. As if the fire consuming her had burned away the last barriers of bitterness and restraint, she strained unashamedly against him, her leg lifting and curling about the back of his sinewy thigh, as she enfolded him hungrily into the warm cradle of her deepest desire.

Instinctively her palm sought the hard bulge of his manhood. "Myles," she moaned, wanting him, needing to feel his flesh against hers. Feverish and hardly aware of what she was doing, she pressed her lips to the vein throbbing along the muscular column of his neck. "I've waited so long," she breathed, little thinking what she had said. "Wondered what it would be like to touch you, *be* touched by you. Oh, God, Trevor! I am afire with wanting you."

Sabra felt a shudder course through the hard, muscular body, then icy fingers clutched her heart as Myles abruptly put her from him.

His breath came hard and fast, and his eyes smoldered with the flames that had swept them both. Yet for an interminably long moment he stared at her, his expression rock-hard and unreadable, and suddenly she had the oddest sensation that he was looking through her, or past her, to another time, another place. Then it came to her that her foolish maunderings must have reminded him that she was naught but a whore unworthy of his touch.

Her cheeks flaming crimson with bitter understanding, she turned hastily away, dragged the jacket over the white swell of her breasts with fingers that trembled and bent to retrieve her petticoat from the floor. Wordlessly she covered her nakedness. Then aghast at how easily she had forgotten the past, how near she had come to giving in to the wild surge of passion that had ever lain buried beneath the surface, waiting for Myles to release it, she came hard about, her eyes flashing dangerously.

"Why, Trevor?" she demanded, her voice harsh with bitter accusation. "Good God, how could you have done anything so dreadfully cruel? Have you any notion of the nights I have lain awake, tormented with trying to piece it all together, wondering what I said those many years ago, what I did to earn your contempt? In your heart you must have known Ferdy was never in any danger from me. Dear, sweet, Ferdy, who at nineteen seemed ages younger than I. Why do you not answer me? Damn it, you *must* have known I could never take advantage of a mere, lovesick boy, heir to the dukedom or not!"

Finally Myles appeared to shake himself, and her blood went cold at the sudden, cynical twist of his lips.

"Quite so," he drawled, strangely mocking. But whether he mocked himself or her, she was not sure. Her breath caught painfully in her throat as all at once he appeared to loom over her. Holding her captive with eyes that glittered like gray points of steel between slitted eyelids, he ran the back of his hand slowly down her cheek. "That much at least I've learned to my regret." Then his arm closed around her and pulled her close.

Shaken to the core by something she felt but did not fully understand, she overlooked the fact that in the end he had not really answered her question. Instead she clung to him, till her heart should cease its fierce pounding, and she knew only an odd sort of easement, the kind of relief one feels in the sudden calm between storms.

"*Damn* you," she uttered weakly after a while. "Had I the sense I was born with, I would have made certain of my aim."

An unwitting thrill pierced her through at the sound of his startled chuckle, deep-throated and oddly husky.

"No doubt your aim was sufficient to give me my due," he drawled ruefully. "It feels like a thousand toothaches coming awake in my arm."

Sabra's heart gave a convulsive little leap.

"Oh, God. Myles, how could I have forgotten? Your wound, it must be cleansed and bound at once!"

"My 'wound,' " he refuted, pulling her firmly back into the circle of his arms, "is not so serious that it cannot wait a moment or two longer. Though 'tis true that by morning I shall have a devil of a time just buttoning my waistcoat, let alone giving you the beating you deserve for putting a hole in my best uniform."

Sabra's laughter was more than a trifle shaky.

"I am all atremble at the prospect, I assure you," she retorted and gave him a wry grimace. Then suddenly her heart skipped a beat at the unwonted warmth in his look. Hastily lowering her eyes, she tried ineffectually to pull away. "Now kindly unhand me," she protested as his clasp perceptibly tightened about her waist, "so I may finish tending your arm, captain. Humanity alone, after all, would seem to demand it."

Unfairly, he bent his head to nibble maddeningly at her ear.

"You are all heart, madam, but I pray you will not be unduly concerned. I am not likely to die," he assured her, but the words sounded thick and a trifle slurred, rather as if he were experiencing some difficulty in uttering them.

With an effort Sabra rallied her flagging defenses.

"No, of course you are not. Trevor Myles allowing himself to succumb to a wound inflicted by a female, and this female at that? Why, 'tis not to be thought of," she retorted with false brightness. "Nevertheless, you will allow me to cleanse and wrap it. And then, I think," she added firmly, noting the unnatural glitter in the disturbing eyes, "a physician should be summoned. There is always the danger of inflammation. Indeed, I should be greatly surprised if you are not in a fever before morning."

"I consider it not at all improbable," he agreed, his smile curiously awry as he watched the interesting play of emotions cross her face. "However, I'm afraid I shall have to make do with naught but your solicitude and perhaps a hastily contrived bandage of some sort."

Sabra looked up at him in alarm.

"Myles, don't be a fool—" she began, only to be interrupted by a finger placed firmly to her lips.

"Not now, *ma mie*," he murmured in a voice which would brook no argument.

Sabra stared at him, feeling helpless in the face of what seemed naught but stupid, blind arrogance on his part. But then her gaze narrowed sharply as she glimpsed the subtle signs of strain about his mouth and eyes. Surmising at once that he was in a great deal more discomfort than he let on, she instantly subsided. Biting her lip to keep from giving utterance to her exasperation, she wordlessly set about gathering what she would need to care for his injury.

Chapter 11

Sabra maintained a stony silence as she bound Myles's arm in clean linen. Without stitches, it seemed all too likely that a bandage would prove only a temporary stop-gap against further bleeding, and there was always the danger of infection. At least they could be grateful it was no worse than it was, she mused tiredly, for though the bullet had gouged deeply for several inches along the inside of his arm before passing through the top of the bicep and out the other side, it had, so far as she could tell, missed the bone entirely. She shuddered to think what she would have done had the bullet lodged. In her present state, it was extremely doubtful she could have achieved its surgical removal. Indeed, it was all she could do to finish a less than tidy knot with fingers that uncontrollably shook. But then, Myles, rather than give her time to do the thing properly, would have been content, no doubt, to rough it out with the bullet yet in him. More the fool, he, she thought, giving the ends of the knot a final, emphatic yank.

At his involuntary wince, she glanced up.

"Oh, dear, I am sorry. Does it hurt dreadfully?" she queried, all kind solicitude.

"Not so much as hot tar or finger screws might have done, perhaps," he admitted acerbically, "but enough, I assure you."

For a moment it seemed he would say something more as his gaze grew suddenly probing on her face.

Sabra forced herself not to fidget as the silence lengthened. She felt weary and cross and more than a little flustered at the sudden turn of events. Indeed, she did not see how it was possible that Sabra Tyree, who had always prided herself on being a woman of keen wits and level-headed reason, should suddenly discover herself caught in such a damnable toil.

The fact was that she did not know herself at all. For when Myles had kissed her, it was as if all the lies and conceits, the carefully constructed illusions about herself and her feelings for him, had disappeared in the resulting torrent of desire. She had been left with naught but some pitiful, amorphous creature whose sole concept of self was a bewildering turmoil of emotions and a single, dreadful, and, as yet, only partially glimpsed, truth. She very much feared that what her mind had sought to conceal with such dogged determination, her body had, in that single moment of unbridled passion, irrevocably revealed, and that was that she loved Trevor Myles with every fiber of her being. Even yet she could not fathom how it should have come about, but nor could she deny that it had.

"What *is* it, captain?" she prodded at last, her unrewarding thoughts and Myles's protracted stare having stretched her nerves nearly to the breaking point.

Myles, displaying something less than his usual urbanity, collected himself. For an instant she had seemed to glimpse something in his eyes—a hint of bafflement or uncertainty, perhaps. She wasn't sure. Then the shutter dropped in place again, and the sternly chiseled features appeared as impenetrable as ever. "Nothing," he said, and reached for his bloodstained coat.

"Then why did you look at me that way?" she demanded.

"No doubt I was struck anew at how lovely you are," he rejoined. His smile was enigmatic and cynically mocking. Then unwisely he stood. A grimace of pain lanced across his face at his heedlessness.

Sabra clenched her teeth in annoyance. The stubborn fool would have the wound bleeding again if he were not careful. Heaving a sigh, she rose and, taking the coat from him, helped ease him into it.

"Wait. That arm shall rest easier in a sling," she said,

171

crossing with firm steps to the wardrobe. Taking perverse pleasure in the necessity of wrecking another of Lily Barrett's expensive linen skirts, Sabra removed the finest of the lot from its hangar and savagely ripped a generous portion from the hem. Then returning to her flint-eyed patient, she quickly fashioned the piece into a sling and slipped it carefully over his head.

"If you have the least care for yourself, that should do for the time being," she pronounced with scant satisfaction when his arm had been safely lodged in its makeshift support. What he really needed was a physician's attention and several days of rest, she mused acidly as she studied the ominously rigid line of his jaw. His color was unnaturally pale, his lips, thinly drawn and tinged with gray. And, indeed, how should they not when he had lost a deal more blood than was good for him? she concluded, and looked away lest he glimpse the worry that must be writ plain on her face.

Then she felt his eyes on her once more with disquieting intentness, and suddenly her patience snapped.

"Spare me your silence, captain, I beg you. If you have something to say, pray say it and be done. I doubt at this point that anything could surprise me."

Very well. Since you ask it, I shall not insult you by tendering anything less than the plain, unvarnished truth. 'Tis highly likely my little ploy has been uncovered by now. And since my present state puts in some doubt my ability to protect you from those certain to come after us, I'm afraid I must insist on a speedy departure."

Feeling as if she had been struck, Sabra recoiled.

"You cannot mean to go through with this—this insane scheme of yours?" she demanded, her glorious eyes, wide and probing, on his face.

"Sabra—" Myles began on a note of exasperation, when all at once a shutter seemed to descend over her lovely features.

"Oh, no, captain," she interrupted, feeling sick and frozen inside. "You do not have to say it. I can see it in your eyes that you do." Suddenly she wheeled away. "Good God, what a fool I was to believe anything had changed between us!"

Myles's lips thinned to a grim line. "Sabra, listen to me."

Her taut, slender figure appeared momentarily to vibrate, then draw very still.

"You, captain," she enunciated clearly, "can go to the devil!"

A flame leaped in the gimlet eyes. Then Myles's hand shot out. Dragging her hard about by the wrist, he yanked her roughly to him.

"Quite so," he murmured in a voice that cut like finely honed steel, "and sooner than late, if Sir Wilfred's little plot for this evening bears fruition."

Sabra's breath caught hard in her throat, and instantly she ceased to struggle.

"Channing!" she uttered, suddenly afraid. "But you promised that Wes—"

" 'Tis not your brother," Myles broke in. "Not this time. It's you he wants, and not for an evening of quiet pleasure."

Sabra's face went pearly white.

"The purpose of this evening's fiasco, my impetuous love," he continued, "was to thwart the baronet's planned entertainment. Indeed, had you been any other female, I should have had you already bundled in the wagon waiting outside. With an ounce of luck, we should have been well on our way out of the city long before Channing's paid ruffians tumbled to our little stratagem. As it is, we shall instead be fortunate to escape before they arrive here looking for us."

Sabra stared into the cynically stern face, her eyes hard with suspicion.

"If what you say is true," she countered, "then why go to the lengths of rendering me insensible? Why did you not simply tell me the truth?"

"Because, *ma mie*, you had already made it plain that you

173

could not bring yourself to trust me and, quite frankly, I found the notion of attempting to drive unnoticed through the streets of New York with you as an unwilling companion doubtful in the extreme. You were, I judged, quite capable of bringing an entire regiment down on us, if you chose."

Sabra's glance flickered. Damn! He made it all sound so plausible—too plausible perhaps.

"I don't believe you," she said, unable to hide the uncertainty in her voice. "It's a trick of some sort."

His handsome lips curled ironically.

"You know it is not," he drawled. "We are both aware, after all, that you have something that belongs to Channing. Oh, you needn't bother to deny it. Indeed, it is time, I think, that you told me exactly what it is that the baronet would dare anything, even abduction and quite possibly murder, to have returned to him."

Sabra's eyes widened in alarm. Slowly she shook her head. How could he possibly have known? she thought, trying desperately to gather her wits. Indeed, how much of it was pure speculation and how much cold, hard facts? She knew just exactly how devious Myles could be, how skilled at manipulating people and events to his own ends. In the light of past experience, she would be a fool to believe he would go to such lengths for Sabra Tyree, the woman whose innocence he once before had betrayed with singular cold-bloodedness.

And yet she knew that she longed to believe it; indeed, did believe it, in her heart, that traitorous organ from which she now realized she had never totally succeeded in banishing him. She had had almost to kill him to find it out, but it had been there all along, waiting for this night, waiting for his kiss to bring it to light. She loved him, had never ceased to love him. Indeed, she doubted not that she would die loving him. Oh, God, what was she to do?

Myles, seeing her wavering, drew near and, hampered by the sling, yet clasped her lightly by the arms. Sabra

174

winced. Then his hand beneath her chin impelled her to look at him, and as her eyes met his, she went deathly still.

"Sabra, trust me," he murmured more gently than she had yet heard him speak, and more compellingly. "I shall do everything in my power to help you. But you must tell me what Channing wants from you."

Sabra hesitated, his closeness playing havoc with her senses, making it difficult to think. Indeed, she was tempted beyond bearing to tell him, to have someone with whom to share the burden of knowing what Channing was and what he intended. After all, she reasoned, there was nothing in it to link her to the *Nemesis* or any of her other secret activities; and, besides, had she not meant to use Myles all along to bring Channing to justice? But then that was before she had learned Wes was alive, she reminded herself. If Myles knew the truth too soon, might not any chance she had of forcing the baronet to arrange her brother's release be lost forever?

Suddenly she knew that even though her heart might indeed urge her to trust Myles, she dared tell him nothing.

Steeling herself against the softening influence of feelings she had only just begun to realize and as yet but imperfectly understood, she made herself gaze limpidly up into his face.

"I am sorry, captain," she said, "but I have already told you. Sir Wilfred mistakenly believed I could be persuaded to a liaison with him. He refused to accept no for an answer. You know the rest. Indeed, I'm afraid there is nothing more that I can tell you."

All at once it was as if they had been thrust backward to that other time in London, for, indeed, just so had he looked at her then, with a chilling blankness as if suddenly a door had been closed, shutting her out. She shivered when he let his hands drop, the muscles leaping along the lean line of his jaw as he was recalled to a painful awareness of his wound. Clasping the arm with his other hand, he turned coldly away and, crossing to one of the chairs,

175

retrieved a parcel from the seat.

"Here," he said with unnerving dispassion and tossed the bundle unceremoniously at her feet. "Unless you entertain a fondness for your present ensemble, I suggest you exchange it for what you will find therein. It is time we were going."

"Going?" she echoed, like a mindless idiot.

Myles glanced briefly over his shoulder at her.

"Did you think I would be persuaded to leave you here, *ma mie?*" he queried. His laugh was harsh in the uneasy quiet. Unwittingly she flinched beneath its lash, then stood, mesmerized by the hard glitter of his smile. "No doubt that would be the course of a wiser man. I, however, find myself committed to extricating you from whatever toil you have wrought for yourself. Irrational of me, I admit, in light of the fact that you very likely deserve whatever punishment fate has meted out for you. But then, it is quite true that prudence has seldom been accounted one of my virtues. I suggest, my dear, that you waste little time in making ready to depart."

All at once she was acutely aware of her slender form clad disreputably in the hideous puce jacket and her once lovely skirt, now torn and stained with blood. Blushing, she bent distractedly to retrieve the bundle and Myles's greatcoat, which had slipped from the back of the daybed to the floor.

"You are aware, I suppose, that in your present state you have no business undertaking to drive a team," she observed ill-humoredly as she shook out the heavy folds of the coat. "Very likely you will end up contracting a fatal inflammation of the lungs, and then where shall we be?"

"In hell, no doubt," rejoined Myles with grim humor, "which is, in any case, only what you would wish. Or so you have informed me on more than one occasion. Whereas, you, my love," he added, turning away to pour himself a libation of Lily Barrett's fine Madeira, "with any luck at all, will find yourself far enough away from Channing's men to effect your own escape. Of course, we might both still have a better than even chance of getting through this alive, were you to come up with a temporary haven suitable for our needs."

"The devil!" muttered Sabra, but whether in response to Myles's suggestion or to the fact that the greatcoat had fallen from suddenly nerveless fingers to the floor was not certain. Impatiently she deposited the parcel of clothes in one of the chairs and gathered up the fallen garment. Brushing crossly at the bits of dust and lint clinging to the fabric, she bitterly cursed Myles's obstinacy.

Her hand encountered an unseemly bulge in the pocket, and without conscious thought, she reached in to remove the cause, which she soon discovered to be a single crumpled sheet of paper. Suddenly her pulse leaped at the sight of the remnants of sealing wax on the outside, which yet held the imprint of an official seal. For a moment she hesitated, her sense of duty at war with her sense of propriety. Then, stealing a furtive glance over her shoulder to ascertain that Myles was not watching, she hastily unfolded the missive and read its contents.

The invitation, for so it proved to be, seemed more in the nature of a command. Indeed, Captain Myles was summoned to report any progress in his investigation of recent events involving Miss Sabra Tyree and the possibility of criminal charges resulting therefrom. The boldly scrawled signature at the bottom of the script appeared to leap off the page at her. Sir Wilfred Phillip Channing, Baronet! she read and felt suddenly ill.

Good God, all of it, from the very beginning, had been a lie! she thought, returned to an awful awareness of how close she had come to confiding in Myles. The captain was in league with her most dangerous enemy, and everything he had done, he had done in the hopes either of winning her confidence or of tricking her into inadvertently revealing enough to damn her in a court of law. Suddenly, so much that had been puzzling before, seemed dreadfully clear: Myles's unsatisfactorily explained motives in coming to her aid; his insistence that she appear to acknowledge him as her intended in order to force her into an intimacy she would never have accepted otherwise; the purpose behind his own attempt to drug and abduct her, which, contrary to his hastily contrived excuses, was and always had been to entrap her and her alleged accomplices in espionage. Indeed, in light of what she now knew, everything made perfect sense—everything, that is, except that damnably earth-shattering kiss and her own overwhelming reaction to it.

And, indeed, in the past half hour, she had forgotten everything: her half-brother, Channing, the cursed war. It had seemed all the animosity and ill will, even the loneliness she had never recognized within herself till now, had been broached in those fleeting moments of madness. But then, she should have known better than to trust in her feelings where Myles was concerned. Whereas moments before she had been embued with the knowledge that her unreasoning love had somehow, in spite of everything, survived intact within her secret-most self, she now knew only a terrible coldness and the need to pay Myles back in full for his unconscionable treachery.

"Very well," she said, having come to a decision. "I know of a house on the East River. At present it is occupied by the military, but there is a cottage as well, some distance from the main house. To my knowledge it is not in use." Slipping the damning piece of evidence back in the pocket of his coat, Sabra turned to look squarely at Myles.

"It was my father's," she added without a flicker of emotion as, casually draping the coat over the back of the chair, she picked up the bundle of clothes. "If you wish, we can go there."

Myles paused with the glass halfway to his lips. For the barest instant his gaze flicked to her face and held there, as if he could sense the change in her, and she forced herself to hold steady beneath his scrutiny. At last, flinging back

178

his dark head, Myles tossed off the remainder of his wine and set the glass down.

"Then I suggest we leave as soon as you have changed," he said brusquely and reached for the bottle. His hand froze at the sound of a voice from the doorway.

"I'm real sorry, cap'n," jeered the newcomer, "but *you* ain't goin' nowhere."

Sabra, seeing Myles tense as if to spring, wheeled sharply to be confronted with the less than pleasing aspect of a ruffian, unkempt and obviously filthy, his yellowed teeth bared in a sneer.

"*Easy*, cap'n." Thumbing back the hammer of a Highland "cutthroat" clutched in one beefy fist, he aimed the brass barrel deliberately at Myles's chest. "I'd hate to put another hole in that fancy uniform of yours."

Mistrusting Myles's reputation for sheer cold-blooded nerve, Sabra stepped coolly between them.

"How dare you intrude on something which cannot possibly concern you," she uttered at her haughtiest. "Just who are you and what do you want?"

The small eyes, sunken between a bulging forehead and fleshy cheeks bristling with whiskers, raked her over. A gleam ignited as he took in her slender loveliness, fearlessly defiant. In crude imitation of his betters, he assayed a bow.

"Jake Tanner, ma'am, at your service. I reckon you be everything His Lordship tole us you was." His heated glance lingered on the glitter of diamonds against the soft swell of her breasts. "Generous of 'im to allow as how we might enjoy the tamin' of a real, blooded lady. 'Do as you wants with 'er,' says he, 'so long as she's got breath enough to talk when you've finished.' "

"I see," murmured Sabra, her mind working with lightning speed. "And what do you intend to do about Myles? Surely Sir Wilfred must know he cannot get away with this."

"I reckon you ain't well acquainted with His Lordship, ma'am. It looks to me like the cap'n's stuck his nose in

179

where it ain't wanted," confessed Tanner, grinning. "I've me orders to cut it off—at the neck, if you takes my meanin'." Sabra felt a cold chill invade her spine. Indeed, the graphic gesture of a hand across the throat left little doubt as to the letter of Tanner's orders.

Then all at once her pulse quickened. Good God, if Channing wanted Myles dead, then it suddenly made no sense to assume the two of them were working hand and glove. On the contrary, Sir Wilfred must see Myles as a threat, and a very dangerous one at that. But why? What was the real significance of the crumpled missive in Myles's pocket? The answer came with blinding clarity. Myles was working as an agent for the admiralty, and somehow he had come to have suspicions of Channing. No wonder he had been so interested in learning what she had taken from Channing's rooms! And why he was so anxious to keep her safe from the baronet's cutthroats! But more than that, she suddenly realized he had been telling her the truth about his own reasons for trying to abduct her!

She could almost feel Myles behind her, tensed and waiting, willing her to move out of the way. With calculated insult she cocked her chin at the villain and allowed a small, contemptuous smile to play about her lips.

" 'Twould seem that Sir Wilfred is hardly like to get his money's worth," she declared recklessly. "I daresay it shall take more than a fat dolt with the stench of a swineherd to break me."

She waited only long enough to see the leap of rage in the brutish eyes before she rammed the bundle hard against the barrel of his gun. The pistol went off, and the ball, lodging in the ceiling, showered them with dust and bits of plaster. Nearly deafened by the pistol's discharge, Sabra delivered a punishing kick to the lout's unprotected groin. Then as Tanner let out a tortured bellow and doubled up, Myles thrust her aside and handily finished the job with the hilt of his sword.

"Remind me, my love," he said, panting a little from his

exertions, "never to engage you in hand-to-hand combat. Undoubtedly I should find the experience both humiliating and painful."

Unaccountably Sabra's cheeks grew warm at the look in his eyes. Her lips parted to deliver a pert retort to his teasing, but before she could utter it, Myles lifted a hand in sudden warning.

"Sh-h! Listen!" he hissed, his head cocked toward the open doorway. Sabra stiffened. Then a muffled shout penetrated the taut stillness.

"Quick, lads, this way! It were a shot, I tell ye."

Without waiting to ascertain the identities of the newcomers, Myles drew forth a long-nosed pistol from the pocket of his greatcoat. Jamming the weapon into his belt, he flung the garment at Sabra.

"Quick. Put it on. Perhaps with any luck we can still make it to the rear exit," he said grimly and moved quickly to douse the lamps.

"No, wait!" called Sabra softly. Slinging the coat around her shoulders, she hurriedly bent to gather up the bundle of clothes and Tanner's pistol. Then, giving the room a last, sweeping glance, she stepped lightly to Myles's side.

"Now," she said, reaching out to extinguish the lamp, "I'm ready, captain, if you are."

The room plunged into darkness and, together, Sabra and Myles slipped out of Lily's dressing room into the theater's nether regions contiguous with the fourth belowstage. After that initial shout, which had seemed to issue from the hall beyond the pit, they had heard nothing more, but Sabra never doubted for a moment that somewhere in the gloom there were men stalking them. At least the villains must remain as hampered by the darkness as she and Myles, she thought grimly, for it would have been foolhardy in the extreme for either party to render themselves vulnerable to attack by lighting the lamps. And while Channing's cutthroats would be forced to grope their way somehow through the confusion of backstage paraphernalia

181

to the stairs descending to the bottommost level, Myles appeared to know exactly where he was going.

His fingers clasped firmly about Sabra's hand, the captain guided her unerringly past the deserted dressing rooms and from there along a corridor to a rather steeply ascending brick ramp. Briefly it came to her that it must be used for loading and unloading large props and the sort, a theory that was to be quickly borne out as they drew near a pale shaft of moonlight cutting a swath through the gloom and she was able to make out double doors, one of which had been left partially ajar.

All at once Myles halted with a muttered curse.

"What is it?" whispered Sabra, acutely aware of the warmth of his body close to hers, the muscles, strung like whipcord beneath the fabric of his uniform.

"Someone has been here before us," he answered grimly. Suddenly he turned to her. "Very likely it was only Tanner, but we cannot overlook the possibility that the villains left someone to guard the exit. I fear I really must have a look, *ma mie*. I want you to wait for me here. If I don't return in a reasonable length of time, try and reach number thirty-six Barclay. Ellsworth and Lily will know what to do."

"Oh, no doubt," she retorted ironically. "I, however, am not some poor defenseless female to be left behind at the first sign of danger. If there's someone waiting for us out there, then I'm coming with you."

"At the risk of offending your tender sensibilities, I suggest that high heels and a hooped petticoat render you unsuited for stalking desperate criminals. You, my girl, shall for once in your life do as you are told. Do I make myself clear?"

For a moment it seemed she would not answer. Then because there was no gainsaying that he was right, she grudgingly acceded to his demands.

"Oh, very well, just this once. But don't think for a moment that I shall be bullied or ordered about. I daresay that even in petticoats, I am more than a match for any brigand."

But Myles, motioning her to silence, had already left her, his tall form seeming to melt into the gloom so that for an interminably long moment she lost sight of him. Suddenly her breath caught hard in her throat as a shadow darted across the swath of moonlight. Then the glint of a gun barrel caught her eye, and at last she could see him, standing with his back to the door that was closed, the gun raised above his head as he peered through the gap left by the other. All at once she stiffened as she saw him lower the pistol and slip quietly out of sight into the alley beyond.

Damn his pigheadedness! she fumed, annoyed beyond bearing at being left to cool her heels while he plunged recklessly into danger. But then it was just like Myles never to give the smallest consideration as to how she might feel about all this unsolicited meddling in her affairs. In point of fact, she would gladly have taken on the entirety of Channing's paid cutthroats single-handedly than feel herself the least bit in debt to Trevor Myles. Faith, but the man was impossible, *and* utterly incomprehensible.

Suddenly she gave a wry grimace and, settling with her back to the wall, prepared to wait.

Actually, when one came right down to it, she mused, Myles's erratic behavior could hardly be considered less bizarre than her own. Indeed, she could not imagine by what perversity of fate she should find herself in love with a man who had caused her nothing but turmoil and grief almost from the moment she had met him.

With a sigh she leaned her head back and thought of the first time she had ever laid eyes on Myles. With those lovely orbs closed, she could picture him quite clearly; indeed, almost as if it had been only yesterday, she saw him coming towards her, making his way with careless ease through Almacks' crowded ballroom. His uniform, the single stripe of gold braid on the sleeve denoting the rank of commander, had seemed molded to magnificent shoulders, and she grew disturbingly warm all over again recalling the smooth ripple of muscular thighs beneath skin-tight white breeches.

She had been only seventeen, but, having lived all her life around men, she had recognized at once that aura of leashed power in his every movement. Here was a man to whom other men would look in a crisis, and one to whom women would all too readily yield, she remembered thinking and smiled a little to herself. Indeed, she thought she had never seen anyone so abominably cocksure of himself.

Still, her heart had given a little flutter as she saw him stop before Mrs. Fitzroy, one of the foundresses of Almacks', and had known somehow with utter certainty that he was soliciting an introduction with herself. Pretending a sublime indifference, she watched him out of the corner of her eye as he came toward her, Mrs. Fitzroy on his arm, and decided that she must inevitably dislike him for his arrogance alone. Indeed, she determined to display naught but a cool aloofness. But that was before she had glanced up into steel-gray eyes, the kind that mesmerized without even trying, or, worse, had beheld the sensuous leap of masculine dimples as he smiled that cursedly devastating smile.

That, no doubt, had been the moment of her downfall, she reflected dryly, though his subsequent behavior had hardly been of the sort calculated to enamor her of him. It had taken scant moments after Mrs. Fitzroy left them for Sabra to realize that, despite all appearances to the contrary, Commander Trevor Myles was extremely well to live—quite drunk as a fiddler, in fact. Hardly before the final strains of the minuet were dying out, he had the gall to propose that she give solace to a lonely sailor—between the bedsheets, as it were, and she had come within an inch of slapping his face before the whole world. It was sometime later that she learned he had only just come home from a harrowing battle with Barbary pirates, which, while it had made him something of a hero, had yet seen his ship badly damaged, the cost in lives staggeringly high.

184

Suddenly unable to bear more of her memories, Sabra opened her eyes to the dismal reality of her surroundings. What a silly, blind fool she was in those days, she thought, having suddenly perceived quite clearly just how very unlike himself Myles had been that night. For though afterward she was to see him imbibe freely on more than one occasion, she had never since known him to be more than a trifle bright in the eye. In a way, he had been vastly more likeable that first evening at Almacks' than at any other time in their tumultuous acquaintanceship; indeed, at no other time had he seemed so fallibly human.

Sabra's throat constricted. How odd to think that all those years of hating Myles had been naught but a sham to hide her true feelings, a barrier, in fact, erected to shield her from her own intensely painful memories. Oh, God! No matter what he had done or why, she knew she could not bear it if she were to be the unwitting instrument of his death.

Then all at once it came to her what a fool she had been. *She* was the one Channing wanted. If she were to give herself up to his men now, might not she be able to persuade them to take her at once to the baronet? And once there, would it not be a relatively simple matter to convince him that if he harmed either Myles or her brother, the content of his stolen papers would be sent to the admiralty forthwith?

It was, after all, what she had originally intended: to use the stolen documents as a lever to win Wes's release. She need only add the stipulation of Myles's safety. And if Myles must inevitably view such an act as further evidence of her guilt, indeed, as an act of betrayal, what, in the end, could it possibly matter?

The irreparable differences that had split asunder their two worlds must inevitably separate them as well. For was he not a true son of English aristocracy, born and bred to uphold the tradition of British supremacy in the New World? And was not she, in spite of her own blood, her

185

own aristocratic heritage, indeed, in spite of her feelings of ambivalence concerning all she had undertaken in order to serve her struggling country, in spite of everything—yes, even, her impossible love for Myles—was not she, in all ways that really mattered, an American? Alas, it was true she and Myles were meant to be enemies, and nothing, not even this dreadful ache in her heart, could change that bitter truth.

All at once it was painfully obvious that she *must* go through with her hastily contrived plan, for to do otherwise would in the end only bring them both greater anguish. Indeed, she must make certain that she and Myles never met again, or, failing that, that there could never again be anything between them. Giving a sudden, defiant toss of the head, Sabra started back the way they had come. No doubt, she reflected bitterly, she could console herself with the knowledge that she had at least insured the dauntless captain would be alive to detest her for what she had done.

The muffled report of a shot froze her in her tracks. Myles! she thought, her heart leaping to her throat. Sudden, stultifying fear for the man whom she loved, but who must inevitably remain her enemy, drove all else from her mind, and she bolted wildly up the ramp.

Running heedlessly, she was within a few steps of the doorway when the slender heel of her shoe caught in a crack between the bricks and her foot twisted out from under her. Encumbered by the bundle in her arms and thrown off balance, she fell hard to the floor.

As she landed, Sabra felt Tanner's pistol, rammed like a steel fist into her ribs. Then her head struck the floor. Pain was a white-hot flame lancing through her, catching at her throat and strangling her as she struggled to draw a breath into deflated lungs. Darkness began to flood her mind, and at last with a small groan, she gave in to it.

When she came to moments later, Sabra was made instantly aware of her head throbbing to the rhythm of her pulse and her cheek pressed most uncomfortably against cold, unrelenting bricks. Aching in every inch of her body and knowing herself to be more than a trifle shaken up, she lay for a moment, trying to think how she came to be in such a fix, when all at once she noticed a faint, but distinct odor of something near at hand.

Instantly she froze, her throat burning as she willed herself not to be sick. She had smelled that scent too often before not to know what it was. Filled with a sort of nameless dread, she felt along the floor until her fingers came in contact with something wet and sticky. As if burned, she drew away and shoved herself unwisely upright. A gasp was torn from her as the pain came, swift and merciless. Clutching at her side, she raised her hand to the moonlight lancing through the open door behind her.

"Merciful God," she groaned. Her fingers were stained red with blood. Myles's blood! she realized and felt a vise clamp down hard on her vitals. In her mind she saw Myles, standing in that very spot with his back against the door, the wound leaving its own tale in the dust at his feet.

Bitterly she cursed the man's stubborn pride. Such heedless disregard for his wound might yet cost him more than his arm. She had known ships' surgeons who, rather than risk the dread onset of putrefaction, would remove a limb for lesser wounds than his. The arm should have been attended to by a physician at once, just as she had wanted. And now he was somewhere out there, likely weak with the loss of blood, or worse, because of it. Because of *her,* she thought, her mind reeling with the memory of the gunshot, which had sent her blundering after him.

Thoroughly alarmed, she struggled to get up, only to fall back again, retching, as she felt the pain, like the touch of a hot iron, probe her side.

"*Damn* Myles anyway!" she gasped, her voice harsh in the weighted silence. She felt sick and weak; her head ached abominably, and Myles was driving her mad with his sud-

187

den quirks of temperament. Why the bloody hell must he be constantly stepping in and out of character: cynical and impenetrably aloof one moment and charging recklessly to her defense the next? And now this! It really was too much.

She must get up. She must! she told herself, clenching her teeth against the pain as she struggled to free herself of Myles's greatcoat. Somehow she had to find him before it was too late, if, indeed, it was not already.

She was panting when at last she found herself on her feet, her side on fire but her head remarkably clear. Her skirt was in ruins, the fabric rent in numerous places and the whalebone hoops broken and bent at grotesque angles from the fall. It took only a second for her to decide to discard it in favor of whatever was contained in the cursed bundle. Indeed, she could not imagine why she had not thought to do it sooner.

Thus it was that moments later a slight figure clad in a midshipman's uniform, complete with coat, breeches, stockings, and shoes, emerged in the alleyway at the back of the theater. Pausing to sling Myles's heavy coat around her shoulders, Sabra glanced furtively about her.

The cul-de-sac, she saw, was narrow, hedged on either side by an irregular line of garden walls, fences, and small shops. To her right stood the German Reformed Church, fronting Nassau Street. The steeple loomed darkly against a background of intermittent, moon-drenched clouds, while winter-barren elms and towering white cedars heavy with snow and ice writhed in a blustery wind sweeping off the Hudson. Sabra, instinctively hugging the greatcoat to her, was reminded that Myles was somewhere out there with naught but a cloth coat to ward off the chill. For an instant she hesitated, suddenly uncertain which way to go. Then a harsh cry shattered the stillness behind her.

"I found somethin'! Over here. It looks to be a female's

188

petticoat, or what's left of it, and there's blood on it."

Sabra shot a last, hurried glance over her shoulder, then, bent nearly double, she bolted along the alley toward the church. Coming to the chest-high wall that encircled the grounds, she tossed Tanner's pistol over and scrambled after it, gasping with the pain it cost her.

For an instant she crouched among the gravestones, panting for breath. Then behind her, she heard Channing's men burst into the open. Tucking Tanner's gun into the waistband of her breeches, she fled along the wall paralleling the theater, hoping against hope to discover some sign of Myles.

That was to come sooner than she could have imagined, for she had gone only a dozen or so yards when she stumbled over something in the darkness. Catching herself just in time to keep from falling, she cursed herself for a clumsy fool. Then the moon came out from behind a cloud, and all at once an icy hand clutched at her heart as she saw what had nearly precipitated her fall.

At her feet, sprawled facedown across the snow-covered mound of an old grave, was the body of a man, lying ominously still. A caped cloak had been flung haphazardly over the upper body, leaving a shoulder uncovered, the arm outstretched against the snow. Sabra shuddered at the sight of the sword clutched in the lifeless hand.

"Oh, God," she moaned, a hand clasping at her mouth as she made out the glimmer of a gold epaulette on that single, bared shoulder, and the pale sheen of white breeches in the moonlight. Her lips moved, soundlessly forming a single name—Myles!

Chapter 12

Striken with sudden, rending grief, Sabra sank to her knees, her arms clutched about her middle.

"*Damn* you," she choked, feeling the tears, hot and stinging, against her eyelids. "How dare you get yourself killed! Oh, God, who asked you to? Not I. I should rather die than be left with the memory that you gave your life defending me. Indeed, I *shall* die, for I cannot bear it."

"Then doubtless you will be comforted to know the wretch fell not in your defense," drawled a voice at her back. "Quite the contrary, in fact. He was obviously hand in glove with Channing's cutthroats, else I should not have seen fit to put a period to his existence, I assure, you. First officers, even bad ones, are hard enough to come by."

"*Myles*?" cried Sabra, twisting her head around. She stared at the shadowy figure leaning with an arm propped atop the grave's tall marble headstone, and for a single, aching moment, knew such an intense feeling of relief that she thought she must swoon from it. Then she read the weariness in the broad shoulders hunched against the cold, noted the way his left arm hung stiffly at his side, the coat sleeve slashed to the elbow revealing a second, hastily contrived bandage wrapped clumsily about her own.

Suddenly a lump rose to her throat.

"You look perfectly dreadful," she murmured huskily.

A wry grin twisted at his lips.

"And you look anything but a scrawny midshipman, Miss Tyree, in spite of the uniform."

Sabra assayed a tumultuous smile, but then, seeing a tremor shake the long, lithe form, she muttered an oath and reached for the dead officer's cloak.

"You crazy fool," she mumbled, flinging the cloak about him. " 'Tis a wonder you're not as stiff as he." For a moment she fumbled with the fastenings, her fingers awkward from the cold, when suddenly she froze as his hand covered both of hers. Swallowing, she looked up into the still, hard face, and all at once she felt something crumple up inside.

Uttering an anguished groan, she threw her arms around his waist and clung to him with a terrible, aching urgency.

"I thought it was *you*," she choked. "Merciful God, I thought you were dead."

For the barest instant Myles went rigid with surprise. The handsome brow furrowed grimly as he felt the slender body shudder against him. Then his arm closed about her, and he held her close, a curious glint in the steel-gray eyes as he waited for her to cease her silent weeping.

After a moment, Sabra drew in a long, shaking breath and, angry with herself for having given way to tears for the second time in less than an hour, she started self-consciously to pull away. Suddenly she heard Myles utter a curse. Startled, she lifted her head. Without warning, Myles's hand clamped hard over her mouth and dragged her, protesting, down into the shelter of the gravestone.

"Softly," he murmured close to her ear. "Someone's coming."

Sabra, yet rigid with surprise and indignation, went abruptly still. The distinct crunch of snow beneath heavy boot soles came clearly to her. Feeling her go lax against him, Myles released her, his hand reaching for the pistol at his belt.

Sabra thought of the body, lying drenched in moonlight out in the open, and drew her own, empty pistol from a pocket in her coat. She released the hidden spring along the underside of the barrel. With a small click, a two-inch blade swung up into stabbing position and locked in place. Hardly of a size to be deadly, it had yet proven useful at times in a clinch. Her nerves tingled as she heard a low

191

grunt, and the unmistakable sounds of someone hefting himself to the top of the wall. Then the moon vanished behind the thickening clouds, and the churchgrounds were filled with a dark and brooding silence.

"Inness!" rasped, harsh and gravelly, across the stillness. "Damn, it man. Show yourself."

Sabra bit her lip to keep from crying out as Myles, after only a split second's hesitation, coolly put her from him. Rising to his feet, he stood clear of the marble headstone.

"What is it, you fool?" he growled. "You're liable to wake the dead with that racket."

"Yeah? And you're mighty damned quiet, it seems to me. Didn't you hear the commotion over there? Tanner lost 'em, an' nearly got his skull creased fer his trouble. The boss thinks they'll make fer the wench's place. Have you seen anyone come this way."

"Not a soul, leastwise not a living one." Myles's chilling laugh raised goose bumps in Sabra's flesh. "They can't have got far. You go back and report to the others. I'll search the grounds and along the street as far as the woman's house, if need be. One way or the other, I shall meet the rest of you there."

"Christ, you're a nervy bastard, I'll say that fer ye," muttered the villain, apparently of a superstitious bent. "The devil hisself wouldn't find me prowlin' through a bloody graveyard in the dead of night. Belike you'll come to a bad end, Inness."

"No more than will you, my doltish friend," sneered his companion, "when your employer discovers how the lot of you have bungled things. Now begone before I mistake you for one of the spirits you're so in dread of and send a bullet chasing after you."

"The hell you say," the man grumbled, but dropped hastily to the ground nevertheless. "The devil take you, Inness, and be damned, says I!" drifted back to them.

Then Myles was dragging Sabra to her feet and propelling her deeper into the graveyard, away from the wall. He

192

did not stop until they reached the cover of two enormous white cedars, crowded together in the middle of the churchyard. There, without saying a word, he pulled her to him and kissed her with a sort of pent-up fury that sent her mind reeling. With a groan Sabra melted against him, knowing herself to be utterly and hopelessly lost.

When he released her she felt dazed, but strangely happy. With a sigh she let her head loll back against his shoulder.

"What happened to you?" she murmured huskily, a fingertip tracing the firm line of his jaw. "I heard the shot and started after you. But then my heel caught and threw me for a tumble. By the time I got myself straightened out, there was no sign of you." All at once she remembered. "I found blood near the door. Myles, your arm . . ."

"It will do for a while," he said, smiling a little at her impetuous outburst. But immediately he sobered. "At the moment we've another, more pressing problem. After I left you, I circled round to the place where two of my men were to have been waiting with a wagon and team. Unfortunately, Channing's cutthroats were before me. I found only my men, their skulls caved in, and some tracks leading into the street. I was coming back to you when Inness fired at me and made the mistake of missing his mark." Sabra shivered at the look in his eyes. Then suddenly the mask was in place again. "It would seem, *ma mie,*" he added grimly, "that not only was Channing privy to my plans ahead of time, but because of it, we find ourselves in the damnable position of being afoot."

"Then we shall find some other conveyance," rejoined Sabra impulsively. "Or barring that, my house is not far. We can go there. If you insist on leaving the city, Robert and Jubal will help us."

"And run straight into the arms of Channing's men? I think not, my impetuous love." Her skin tingled where his fingers brushed a stray lock of hair from her face. "At any rate, I'm afraid it's not that simple. With any luck, I shall

193

have managed to convince Jubal that whatever you have of Channing's should be removed without delay to a safe place. If he's smart, Wayne has already taken care to make himself scarce for a while."

Sabra stared at him, her lips parted in startled surprise that he had thought to warn Wayne of the danger. Then a sudden uncomfortable stab of conscience spurred her to lash out at him in anger.

"You take a great deal on yourself, do you not?" she uttered bitingly and drew away.

"Sabra." His tone was patient, but she could not fail to note the weariness that dragged at his voice. "Now is not the time to quarrel. I made the error tonight of underestimating the efficiency of the baronet's network of paid informants, but I was only doing what seemed necessary to protect you and your friends. If I was mistaken in that as well, I shall apologize for it later."

Sabra bit her lip, already regretting her brash words. And yet the pride that had compelled her to utter them now prevented her from taking them back. Damn Myles! Was it not enough that his interference had already nearly cost him his life? Why now must he shame her further with this new evidence of his hitherto unsuspected thoughtfulness? He was chipping away at her defenses, rendering her more and more vulnerable to this dreadful yearning to have him always close, to feel his arms about her, and his lips—No! She must not think of such things. Not now when she was still warm from his kiss.

Recklessly she plunged ahead, compelled to drive a wedge between them, now, while she yet had the will and the strength.

"Yes, of course," she said, striving for her old role of the impetuous beauty. "And in future will you also think to advise me of what you intend before blundering to my defense? Faith, captain, has it never once occurred to you that I might be quite capable of managing my own affairs?"

194

"Thus far I have seen little evidence of it," he stated flatly. "If anything, you display an appalling propensity for landing yourself in one toil after another. Had I the charge of you, I should see you wed posthaste to a man capable of beating some sense into that lovely head of yours."

Sabra came about with eyes flashing dangerously.

"And I, sir, suggest that hitherto I have rubbed along quite well without a man's interference. Indeed, it has only been since *you* obtruded yourself into my life that I find myself on the brink of one disaster after another, tonight's fiasco being only a minor case in point."

"And putting yourself in the position to be brutally assaulted and nearly raped is but another, I suppose," observed Myles caustically. "Quite frankly, my dear, I find the notion of your having incurred the enmity of one of the most powerful men in British-occupied territory rather worse than useless. It was the act of an unthinking, hotheaded fool."

Sabra could feel the blood rush to her cheeks. In normal circumstances she would have known to put a tight rein on her tongue, and with any other man, she would have done so. But this was Myles, who had the power to unleash her temper as no one else had ever been able to do. Nor did it help to know that he was in part right to accuse her of having bungled it with Channing.

"To win my brother's release, captain, I was prepared to risk a great deal more than that," she said bitterly. "I was prepared to kill for it—or die in the attempt. That much, at least, has not changed. Your attempt to thwart tonight's abduction has only postponed the inevitable. For I shall confront Channing again, and there is nothing you, or anyone, can do to stop it. Had you not interfered, at least this time I should not have faced him with an empty hand."

"No, but with an appallingly empty head," he retorted blightingly. "Do you think for one moment that Channing would hesitate to use whatever tools come to hand—your brother, for instance, or even Wayne or your intensely loyal

195

Phoebe. Or perhaps you hadn't considered what Channing might do to anyone who stood in his way. Right now he undoubtedly has men searching your house, and should he find what he is after, not even the duke's name will be enough to stop him from tying up all the loose ends."

Sabra's slender frame seemed to vibrate beneath the lash of his words. It was true. She had not considered the danger the others would face because of her. And yet Jubal and Wayne were neither stupid nor naive. Myles had thought to warn them. She must simply trust that they had taken measures to protect themselves.

"Perhaps your cousin's influence will not be enough to stop him, captain," she said, suddenly all ice, where before she had been flame, "but neither will all Channing's power and influence *save* him if he goes so far. The baronet will not find what he is seeking if he dismantles my father's house brick by brick, I promise you." She read the skepticism in his face and uttered a short, mirthless laugh. "Come now, captain, surely you cannot truly believe I should be such a fool as to keep it in my home. It is where none shall ever find it lest I alone should choose that it be found."

With that, she turned away from him and, having gone so far as to end all doubts that she did indeed possess something which rightfully belonged to Channing, she withdrew behind an impregnable barrier of icy aloofness. She refused to say anything more on the subject of Channing, and Myles, wisely, forbore to press her — at least for the moment. He knew well enough the streak of stubbornness that underlay that deceptively fragile exterior. Pushed too far, she was quite capable of striking out on her own, and into the very teeth of danger.

Besides, he reflected, they had dallied long enough. It was time to put some distance between themselves and those who would come backtracking for Lieutenant Inness when he failed to materialize. The devil of it was, he hadn't the slightest notion how best to proceed from here. He had counted on finding his way to the country house on the East River, the English manor reputed to have been Tyree's gift to his colonial bride, for he had a most particular desire to explore the grounds thereabouts. But that was before the truly incomparable Sabra had spoiled all his plans.

A wry smile tugged at his lips. He had hardly accounted for the possibility that this slip of a girl would fight off the effects of the sleeping powder with a pertinacity and strength of will that would have done credit to a British sailor. Nor was it any comfort to realize that she had managed to procure a weapon and had thus come within a hair's breadth of putting a period to his own existence. She was dauntless, was this slender woman, who seemed destined utterly to disrupt his peace of mind. Nevertheless, it was not her indomitable spirit that had made his ulterior motives seem so suddenly unpalatable, but something altogether different.

Ecod, what a fool he was not to have seen through the aloof façade of the haughty young beauty long before this. He must have been mad to believe her the heartless jade Channing's carefully planted lies had made her out to be. She baffled him with her sudden starts of temper, her swiftly changing moods. Her utter fearlessness both appalled and infuriated him, and her fierce independence, her absolute refusal either to trust him or to accept his help, was enough to drive him to the brink of wringing her neck. But she would never again be able to pull the wool over his eyes. She was Sabra Tyree, beautiful, tempestuous, and proud, but vulnerable, too, and capable of a fiery passion which set his loins afire with wanting her.

Bloody hell! What was he about to embroil himself in anything so patently impossible? Not even as a callow youth, he reminded himself in disgust, had he allowed his obviously male urges to overrule his head; and, indeed, at seven and twenty, Myles was anything but a novice in the art of love. True, since his father, despairing of Myles's

197

unruly temperament, had at last been prevailed upon to allow his only son to be commissioned as midshipman at the tender age of fourteen, his visits home had been both rare and intermittent. Still, there had been other ports, and neither in England nor in those farflung lands to which his chosen career had taken him, had he suffered a dearth of feminine companionship. He had known many women before Sabra Tyree, had even fancied himself to be in love on one or two occasions. But no other had ever so thoroughly aroused in him the male instinct to succor and protect, indeed, to fight to the death for her, if need be, as did this mettlesome female.

Had he a whit of sense, he'd have put a thousand miles of ocean between himself and this beautiful American rebel long ere this, he told himself. Not because of her loyalties, which, in the circumstances, were not to be unexpected; indeed, were only the natural outgrowth of a deep and abiding love of home and family. These he could understand. Nor was it her reckless pursuance of a cause in which she obviously believed. The truth was he would have been dishonest with himself had he not acknowledged a grudging respect for her bold ingenuity and wit—her sheer daring. No, it was because he saw clearly where in the end it must lead her that he found himself wishing her to the devil. Indeed, he knew all too well that, whatever else she might be, this single slip of a girl posed a far greater threat to him than an entire fleet of enemy ships might have done.

He knew that were there any way to preserve her from the consequences of her own dauntless courage, he would not hesitate to make use of it, and there was the rub. For he had yet to perceive how it might be accomplished without sacrifice of what he knew to be his duty, indeed, his own cursed sense of honor.

Thus burdened by weariness, attenuated by the persistent throb in his arm, and occupied with his own, exceedingly unrewarding thoughts, Myles struck out in a direction roughly north across the grounds, his intention being to distance themselves from both Nassau Street and the theater as swiftly as possible. Beyond that, he had no concrete plan, having been quick to discard the notion of heading for the brick house on Barclay. There was every possibility, after all, that it was known to Channing and consequently would be one of the first places the baronet would look for them. By avoiding the theater and Nassau Street, he hoped simply to elude their pursuers at least long enough either to discover a safe place in which to hole up or, barring that, to procure a conveyance to bear them to the outskirts of the city along the East River, which would put them within striking distance of his anchored ship. In formulating this decision, however, he failed once again to account for the utter unpredictability of his companion.

After having docilely accompanied him through a fenced yard and thence between two houses to reach the nearly deserted Fair Street, that incalculable female bolted without warning across the avenue and vanished in the shadows between two buildings. Cursing, Myles followed after her, only to find himself in a narrow passageway bounded on either side by three-story brick walls. Of the elusive Sabra there was no sign, nor of anything else, save for an impenetrable gloom permeated with an uneasy silence and with snowflakes beginning to drift heavily out of a cloud-covered sky.

Drawing his gun, Myles stole cautiously along one wall, his nerves tingling as he tried to pierce the curtain of darkness. He had known too much of danger not to sense it all around him, like a living, breathing thing waiting to pounce out of the shadows.

At the whisper of movement behind him, Myles came around, glimpsed fleetingly the gun at his back. Instinctively he swung with his left, knocking the weapon up. At the shock of the barrel, striking the wound, he doubled up, a groan seemingly ripped from his very depths. He fell back, retching, his knees threatening to buckle beneath him. Then he sensed rather than saw the man moving in to finish what he had started. Gnashing his teeth against the pain searing his arm from wrist to shoulder, he launched himself bodily against his assailant. Both men went down. Grimly Myles dragged himself to his knees, struggled to bring his gun to bear.

A woman's anguished scream slashed like a knife through the silence.

"No! Don't hurt him!"

Then a leaded weight, glancing off the base of his skull, rammed hard between his shoulder blades and slammed him to the ground. A dazzling light seemed to explode in his brain, leaving him helpless and blind. He heard footsteps hurtling toward him, then Sabra's voice, sharp with fear and anger. At last he felt her fingers, trembling and cold, against his neck. Wanting to reassure her, he tried to speak, but somehow he could not summon the strength. Going suddenly lax, he gave himself to the darkness waiting to bear him into oblivion.

Chapter 13

Sabra dragged herself free, leaving the greatcoat in the grip of the man who had been trying to restrain her. Wild with fear, she came hurtling out of the shadows at the figure hunched over Myles's inert form.

"There was no need to strike him! Faith, Rab, couldn't you see he is hurt?" she cried, thrusting the captain's assailant furiously aside. "Quick, light the lantern and pray you have not killed him."

Muttering under his breath, Rab moved to do as he was bidden, but Sabra paid him no heed. Her thoughts were all on Myles, lying so still at her feet. Breathing a prayer, she dropped to her knees and with fingers that trembled, groped for the pulse at his neck. For an interminable moment she felt nothing. Then at last she had it, a faint, but distinct, throb beneath her fingertips.

"Thank God," she groaned.

The alley leaped with a sudden flare of light, and Sabra, quickly recovering herself, threw a hurried glance up at the man towering over her, the lantern swinging from his hand.

"He's alive," she said. "Please, help me turn him over."

Together, they eased the unconscious man to his back so that his head rested in Sabra's lap.

"You crazy damned fool," she uttered hoarsely, brushing a raven lock of hair away from his brow. "You just couldn't leave well enough alone, could you. And now look at you."

"Miss Sabra, we'd better be moving," intruded her companion, glancing nervously over his shoulder toward the street. The plain, honest face revealed in the yellow glow of the lantern appeared anxious as he waited for the rest of his small party to come up to them. They were five in all, not counting herself and Myles; and, like the blacksmith, Rab Wilkins, they were all simple shopkeepers or tradesmen, who were better off at home in bed than skulking through dark alleys on a night like this.

She had counted herself fortunate when, emerging on Fair Street, she had suddenly realized where she was and how she could elude Myles at last. But had she known there was a run scheduled for that night, she would never have risked making that mad dash into the alley. It had proven to be the greatest folly.

"Rab's right, ma'am," enjoined John Tully, a saddler by trade. The light danced off the lenses of his eyeglasses as he darted a look up the alley. "The night patrol's due along here directly."

Sabra's blood went suddenly cold at the sight of the crimson stain spreading slowly over the snow beneath Myles's arm.

"Yes, quickly," she said, struggling with stiff fingers to tighten the bandage. "The captain must be carried to safety at once. *Damn* the cold! He is half frozen already."

Rab, detecting the strain in her voice, looked suddenly uneasy.

"I don't know, Miss Sabra. I've nary a wish to have this man's life on my conscience, but just where to take him would seem to pose something of a problem."

Sabra lifted incredulous eyes to the frowning blacksmith.

"Just what are you trying to say, Rab Wilkins? That you intend to leave him here?"

Wilkins flushed a dusky red and looked hastily away.

"No, not exactly. It's just that . . . well, what's to keep him from turning us in once he comes to himself? We have families, Miss Sabra — all of us. What guarantee do we have they'll not be made to suffer for it?"

"You have *my* word, my guarantee. It will only be until he has rested—a night or two, no more. I shall care for him, so that he need never see any of you or know where he has been taken. Then we shall be gone, under cover of night, I swear it."

She could see Wilkins hedge and sternly curbed her impatience.

"I reckon your word's good enough," he muttered, albeit a trifle reluctantly. "Anyway we'll have to chance it. We'll take him with us to the meeting place. It has most of what you'll need to see to him, and it's warm enough, what with the stove and all. I don't reckon we'll be using it for a spell anyway after tonight's run. It'd be too risky."

"Not half as risky as giving in to this cunning piece of baggage, I'll wager!"

Sabra's head came up, her cheeks flushed with anger, as a spare, stoop-shouldered figure thrust through the gathering into the circle of light. "You fool, can't you see 'tis a king's officer she would bring among us? Her *word*." The old man spat contemptuously. "*That* for the word of an English blue-blood. I say let him bloody well rot where he lies. It'll be one for my boy that starved to death in that stinking British hellhole yonder."

Sabra stared up into a countenance etched in bitterness. Beetle-browed and saturnine, he was like some fierce old bird of prey, she thought, the fleshless contours of his face all protruding points and angles from which the nose, hooked and sharply chiseled, stood out in bold-faced relief. The eyes beneath bristling white eyebrows smoldered with a vitriolic distemper; and suddenly her own anger subsided before an involuntary wave of pity. Jedediah Hawkes had little reason to love the English. His son had fallen in the Battle of Long Island, and only a few weeks past his grandson, hardly more than a boy, had perished in the Old North Dutch Church, the British-converted prison less than a block from where they now stood. She could not

203

blame Hawkes or condemn him for wanting to take his anger out on someone, but neither, she vowed, could she allow that someone to be Trevor Myles.

Nevertheless, her heart sank at the low rumble of agreement coming from the others, and it was only with a good deal of effort that she was able to quell the torment caused by this new delay. Somehow she must keep her wits about her. Somehow she must *make* them listen to her.

"No, wait!" she cried. "I do not deny that this man is a loyal officer in the king's navy and an enemy to our cause, but still would I beg you not to allow yourselves to be swayed by prejudice — or by another man's rancor. Captain Myles will die without your help. You must see that."

"Then let him!" snarled Hawkes, turning on her with venom in his eyes. "And you, woman, would do well to hold your tongue. There is the stink of the Loyalist about your part in this."

Ignoring the warning in those final words, Sabra looked past Hawkes to the others. She read the first stirring of mistrust in their refusal to meet her eyes and realized with a sense of pained disbelief just how far the old man's rancor had already gone in poisoning their minds against her. Silently she cursed.

"Can you turn your backs on me so easily then?" she demanded, unable to keep the hurt from her voice. "Rab? John Tully? You've known Wes and me since we were children. Indeed, all of you have come to know me since first we joined together to render what aid we could to the prisoners. Is there one among you who can say I have ever failed in faith? If there is, I charge him to speak now."

There was a nervous shuffling of feet, but none of them seemed willing either to champion or condemn her. *Damn* their provincialism, their cursed barriers of prejudice and mistrust! It was as if the past three years of shared danger meant nothing to them. She felt Myles stir ever so slightly against her and willed him to hang on just a little while longer.

"Listen to me," she said, her voice ringing in the uneasy quiet. "You know as well as I that there are those who use this war solely for the profit it will bring them. They are lawless men, without morals or conscience, who espouse *neither* cause, give loyalty to *neither* country — American or British. For reasons I cannot divulge, one of the most treacherous of these profiteers has this very night made an attempt upon my freedom, perhaps my life. You must believe me when I say that I should even now be at that man's mercy had not Captain Myles helped me to escape."

Suddenly the old man loomed over her, his lip curled and contemptuous. "And I say we will believe you only when we hear the truth," he declared. "Speak that which is plainly writ upon your face. You would do anything to save this man — perjure yourself, even sell out your countrymen, *Miss* Tyree — because you and this Myles are lovers."

"How dare you! By what right do you impugn my name, *my* honor?"

"By the right of a man who has lost everything in the cause of freeing us from the British tyrants. Come now, d'you take us for fools? A blind man could see you are in love with your precious English captain."

Sabra's face went deathly pale, but instantly her head came up, her eyes ablaze.

"Yes, I love him!" she shot back, every inch of her slender body scintillating proud defiance. "Did you think I should be ashamed of the truth? I loved him before it was treason to have done. And God help me, I love him still. But I have never lain with him or any other man. Nor, as God is my witness, have I done anything to betray my country *or* you. If you can prove otherwise, then slay me now and be done with it. But can you not, then stand aside, Mr. Hawkes, and let me be judged by men whose minds are not wormwood and gall. You, sir, have let

bitterness deprive you of reason."

The old man appeared to leap before her eyes.

"Mad am I?" he thundered, his face turning a purplish hue. Why, you impudent baggage! If 'tis mad I am, then I say 'tis a madness which gives one to see with greater clarity. In my eyes your presence here in the company of a British officer is more than suspicious. It brings into doubt your character and integrity, and most certainly your virtue. In fact, madam, it condemns you!"

"Oh, does it indeed," she retorted scathingly, her temper loosed at last. "Then you are no better than the English tyrants you claim to abhor. They who thought to deny a man like Hancock his right to fair trial by jury. Obviously you are a hypocrite, Mr. Hawkes, as well as being impossibly pigheaded and obtuse."

Instinctively Sabra froze as Hawkes, his mouth working but no sound coming forth, towered over her, his arm upraised as though he would strike her.

"Strumpet!" he choked at last. "Blue-blood! Serpent-tongued shrew! I'll teach you to slander your betters!"

Then Rab Wilkins mercifully stepped between them.

"I reckon that'll be about enough, Jedediah," he said, standing unflinching beneath that quivering hand. Something in his voice or manner must have reached through the old man's blind fury to touch a chord of reason within. Hawkes visibly wavered.

"Seems like maybe you're forgetting what this—er—'blue-blood' tried to do for young Jed," continued Wilkins in that same soft-spoken manner. "I admit it looks a mite bad, but I reckon Miss Tyree has earned the right to at least speak her piece."

Something flickered in the fierce old eyes.

"No," he muttered, shaking his head, "I'll not listen to the likes of a Loyalist sympathizer. They took my Jed. They denied him food enough to keep a rat alive, blankets to keep him warm in a winter so harsh the harbor's froze

206

from it. God rot 'em, they *starved* my boy to death. Don't you see? Someone has to pay for that!"

"And someone *will*, but not Miss Tyree, surely. Think Hawkes. She did what she could. It wasn't her fault it came too late to save the boy. And I expect there'd be a lot more of our boys dead if it wasn't for the food and blankets she's give us. She's taken her chances right along with the rest of the Naughty Pack of Ann Street lots of times, smuggling them things into the prison. I reckon as how no man here can say different."

A look of compassion softened the plain, honest face.

"Put down your hand, Jed," he said quietly. "You know you don't intend Miss Tyree harm. You're tired, man. We all are."

For an interminable moment Hawkes stood as if transfixed by the other man's steady gaze. Then suddenly his hand began to quiver and slowly he lowered it. All at once he seemed to shrink in upon himself.

"Let her speak then, if that's what you want," he growled, turning his back on them. "I'll say no more."

Slowly Sabra let out her breath. Wilkins had more than redeemed himself in her eyes, but he had still only bought her time to plead her case, she realized with a feeling of helpless frustration.

The old man's accusations had cost her more than any of them could possibly realize. Indeed, it had cost her their trust, something she had worked painstakingly to build over the past three years in the face of nearly impossible odds. For was she not Sabra Tyree, the darling of the king's loyal subjects in New York? And, worse, was she not the granddaughter of a powerful English lord? She had won grudging acceptance among these tradespeople in the beginning solely on the basis of her kinship to Wesley Locke, a man they respected as one of their own. Trust had come later, and only after she had run risks that would have made an already anxious Robert Wayne blanch had he known what she was doing. Now even that might not be enough to win them back again.

At the nervous shuffling of feet, Sabra lifted her eyes to look at them, one by one, searching her heart for the right words to undo the damage Hawkes had worked. In the end she decided naught but the simple truth would serve.

"Several months ago," she began in a low, quivering voice, "I was told that my brother Wes was taken captive. And now I have learned he is being held in the prison ship *Jersey.*"

She gave them time for the news to sink in. Then in a gesture, half defiant, she flung back her head and swept the luxurious mass of her hair up and away from her face. "The man who put him there," she said with chilling dispassion, "is the same man who put his mark on me."

In the yellow glow, the bruise shone livid against the pale transparency of her skin over the temple. Someone cursed, and for a fleeting moment she thought it was the old man's voice.

"What kind of a man uses his fists against a woman?" demanded Wilkins.

Deliberately Sabra let her hair fall back again.

"The kind of man who uses war for profit. The kind of man who would kill my brother to punish me. He found out, you see, that I have been working against him, that I have been trying to bring an end to his villainy. Oh, can you not see that what I may or may not feel for Captain Myles has no real bearing here? What does matter is that thus far he has been all that stands between Wesley and certain death. He has risked everything to that end—his name and reputation, his career—And *that,* Mr. Hawkes, is why I shall do everything in my power to save him. Perhaps I have not the right to ask you to set aside your own feelings—and yet I do, I *must* ask it of you. Please, I implore you—all of you—if not for him or for me, then for my brother, who has been your friend these many years. In God's name, I pray you will not leave this man to die a lingering death!"

There was not one among them who was impervious to her earnest entreaty, or to her haunting loveliness, which, in the end, proved far more telling. Her eyes shadowed with weariness and huge in a face gone pearly white, she shamed them with her simple eloquence.

John Tully was first to step forward.

"It seems to me we've let this man lie in the cold long enough," he said, gruff-voiced and vaguely defiant. "I'm begging your pardon, Miss Sabra, for having doubted you. I expect Jedediah would do well to remember all them times you risked your own neck just to sneak a word or two in to his grandson. In fact, there's a lot that's been forgot this night that had ought to've been remembered sooner."

"I reckon John speaks for all of us," agreed Rab Wilkins, gravely.

For an instant Sabra's shoulders slumped, the strength that had carried her through the fight deserting her now that the battle seemed won.

"Please, hurry," she managed around the lump in her throat. "He is so cold. I—I'm afraid . . ."

A shadow fell across her, and involuntarily Sabra stiffened as she looked up to find Hawkes standing over her, his head bared to the falling snow.

Without meeting her eyes, he bent to drape Myles's greatcoat over her shoulders.

"You need not fear I mean you or your captain harm," he muttered thickly, the words seemingly wrenched from him. "I was—am—a God-fearing man. But coming from the prison after seeing the suffering of those men—Merciful God, it all came back to me. My boy—" Suddenly he broke off, a spasm seeming to leap across his face. Then abruptly he straightened to his full height to stand stiff-backed before her. "You did your best to try and get my boy paroled, I know that," he admitted, staring rigidly past her into the thickening curtain of snow. "I expect I owe it to *him* to even up our account. I'd be grateful if you could bring yourself to forget an old man's folly."

Sabra was touched again with pity as she saw what it had cost him to deliver that final speech. He was proud, was Jedediah Hawkes, but somehow his harsh features seemed less daunting now. Indeed, the deep lines carved in his brow and the hollows of his cheeks made him appear merely a man, aged beyond his years, perhaps, by the hardships and sorrow that had attended them.

"I fear the times have made us all a little mad, Mr. Hawkes," she murmured, reaching up to touch his arm. "It is one of the legacies of war, is it not?"

A mist blurred Sabra's vision as wordlessly he knelt in the snow beside her and after briefly meeting her eyes, bent deliberately to grasp Myles beneath the shoulders. Indeed, she thought, the first battle had been won.

The others were not long in following Jedediah's lead. Lifting the English captain's long, lax form, they made their way along the alley till at last they came to the back of a modest house fronting Ann Street. There, an outer door opened on to wooden stairs, which in turn descended into the darkness of a cellar. It soon became apparent that the cellar served various purposes, for in addition to shelves laden with dried foods, blankets, and a sundry baskets, barrels and boxes, the room was fitted out as well with a cast-iron stove, a crude wooden table and chairs, and a hand-fashioned oak folding bed.

"Easy, lads," muttered Wilkins, who, having preceded them with the lantern, was occupied with lighting a small oil lamp, which sat on the wooden table. "Lay him on the bed and get some blankets over him. Dick, you and Kelsey light the stove. Quick, men. The sooner we get out of here and scatter, the safer we'll all be."

"If you please," Sabra interjected quietly. Her level gaze

210

met Wilkins's across the room. "I shall need help in removing his things."

Wilkins briefly nodded.

"Someone give Miss Tyree a hand with the captain. The rest of you go home and wait. I'll send word when it's safe for us to meet."

Sabra wasted little time in shrugging out of the cumbersome greatcoat. Anxiously she bent over Myles, her hand going instinctively to his forehead. Merciful God! He was so pale, his brow alarmingly cold and clammy to the touch. With a fearful heart she felt his wrist and found his pulse, rapid and weak, beneath her fingertips. Thinking only that there must be no delay in getting him stripped of his wet clothes and wrapped warmly in blankets, she fell quickly to the task of removing his cloak. After much effort she managed to undo the fastenings made stiff with snow and ice. At last, gratefully, she sensed someone draw near.

"Please," she said without looking up, "see if you can lift him that I may get his coat off."

"I wonder, Miss Tyree, if it would not be better to leave your captain to me."

Recognizing Hawkes's gravelly voice, Sabra glanced up in quick annoyance. Faith, what now? she fretted, intent only on Myles.

"Mary Wilkins will not spurn to welcome you with tea and hot victuals in the house above," Hawkes added, seeing the spark of temper in her eyes.

"Perhaps, Mr. Hawkes," retorted Sabra, returning to the task at hand, "you would do me the favor of coming directly to the point. What is it that you are trying to tell me?"

"Dammit, girl! Must you have me spell it out? You are an unmarried woman. I think I need say no more, save only that when it is meet for you to return, I promise you will be summoned."

211

Sabra's fingers never paused in their work. Deftly they traveled down the front of Myles's waistcoat, undoing the buttons one by one.

"You are very kind, but you must not think that this will be the first time I have seen a man's naked body," she stated frankly and moved to the task of removing the neckcloth of fine silk. "I have attended the needs of sick and wounded men before. I pray you will disregard that I am unmarried and a woman. I shall not be persuaded to leave him."

Little caring what Hawkes thought or did, she turned back to the problem of the tight-fitting coat, determined to cut the clothes from his body if need be rather than to let Myles perish from shock. Nevertheless, she was relieved to have a strong pair of masculine hands come almost immediately to her aid. Smiling briefly, she looked up.

"I am obliged, Mr. Hawkes. Now, if you will lift him, I shall free him of this damnable coat."

With Hawkes's disapproving, but capable, assistance, they soon had Myles divested of both coat and waistcoat. Then, deeming it fruitless to attempt working an already ruined shirt over the head of a man who lay in peril of his life, Sabra unhesitatingly drew forth a small penknife and slit the fabric down the front.

Hawkes, watching her as she worked with an almost unnerving detachment, could not but marvel at so much strength in one so frail-seeming and young. Still, no one, not even a woman made indomitable by love, could continue indefinitely on sheer willpower alone. She looked worn to the nub, she did, and it seemed inevitable that eventually she must crack beneath the strain. Otherwise, he told himself, she could not be made of flesh and blood.

Her businesslike manner had long since driven all thoughts of impropriety from his mind, and he moved automatically to assist her in easing the captain's small-clothes down over the strong, masculine limbs. Thus he was more than a little taken aback when suddenly he felt her reel and glanced up to find her white-faced and trembling.

"Merciful God!" she groaned, reaching hesitantly out to touch the scars, freshly healed and livid, high up on the outside of one muscular thigh. Abruptly she wheeled, her hand clutching at her mouth as though only thus could she contain her horror. And, indeed, it was a terrible wound, the puckered mass of recently formed tissue revealing its own tale of infection, unbearable torment and suffering.

Hawkes stood by in helpless fascination as he saw the beautiful young woman come about again. She clenched shut her eyes as though with a terrible, rending pain, and for a moment he thought surely she would swoon. Then her eyes came open, and in awe he beheld them, shimmering with indescribable love and pity, and an unbreakable inner strength. He saw her lips move, heard her whisper brokenly, "Oh, my darling. How close we came to losing you!" Then with infinite tenderness she covered Myles's nakedness with blankets and briskly turned her attention to his still untended arm.

"The water can is full, and I've made sure there is coal enough to last through the night and most of tomorrow," said Jedediah, his gaze speculative as it rested on the woman, her shoulders bowed with exhaustion. "As soon as it's safe, I'll return with more."

Sabra stood staring down at Myles's still features, white against the pillow, and listened with only half her mind. She felt numb and strangely empty, as if she had not dared to feel anything for a very long time. With an effort she shook herself out of her lethargy enough to tender Jedediah a smile, which, though more than a trifle wan, was yet full of gratitude.

"Thank you, Mr. Hawkes," she answered simply, stretching out a slim, capable hand. "You have been everything

213

that is thoughtful."

The old man noisily cleared his throat. "I, Miss Tyree, have been nothing of the kind." At last, gingerly, he clasped her fingers in his. "Indeed, I have been extremely disagreeable, but we won't cavil over that. If I know anything, and I have not lived all these years for nothing, you are going to need all your strength in the hours that lie ahead."

He felt her hand jump in his and instantly regretted his blunt manner of speech.

"Here now," he grumbled, giving that shapely member an awkward pat. "I don't mean to frighten you. From the looks of him, your captain is a strong man. Likely he'll come through this in fine fettle. Nevertheless, it were best to be prepared."

"You think he will be taken with fever, don't you. Oh, I knew it. 'Tis what I've dreaded all along. And he lay for so long in the cold!" Her voice cracking at the end, Sabra pulled free and wheeled convulsively, the side of her fist pressed to her mouth as though to stifle any further outburst.

The old man seemed suddenly to grow older.

"The blame for which may be laid at my door," he muttered harshly.

Instantly Sabra came about again.

"No, you must not say so," she protested. "Indeed, I pray you will not think such thoughts. If anyone is at fault, 'tis I, for realizing the truth too late."

Covering her face with her hands, she gave in to a ragged burst of laughter.

"Oh, God, what a muddle I've made of things!" she gasped.

Jedediah's eyebrows snapped together. Then without warning he stepped forward and, clasping her firmly by the wrists, dragged her hands down.

"Stop it, I say! Stop it at once!"

214

As if he had delivered her a physical blow, Sabra shuddered and then froze, her eyes, wide and tormented, upon the old man's face.

"D'you think to help *him* with this womanish display of temper?" demanded Hawkes. "Think, girl. He needs you now with all your wits about you."

For a moment longer Sabra stood, white-faced and staring, then suddenly the long eyelashes swept downward to cover her eyes. Taking a deep breath, she nodded her head with short, jerky little movements.

"You are right, of course," she murmured, breathing out again. "I-I'm sure I don't know what came over me."

"You're worn out, any fool can see that. But you've the iron in you to see the thing through; never doubt it for a moment. I've got to be off now. Try and see if you can get him to take some tea, or just plain water with a little honey. You'll find what you need over there in the cupboard. And get some sleep yourself whilst you can. Like as not he'll be quiet for a while yet."

Turning brusquely, Hawkes strode to the stairway.

"I'll be back tomorrow," he said, "never fear." Then, pausing at the foot of the stairs, he gave her a pointed glance over his shoulder. "When it comes to doing what he thinks right for his woman, a brave man is like to be bullheaded. See that you keep him here if you have to hog-tie him, hand and foot. That's my advice, take it or leave it," he grumbled and started up the stairway.

"Mr. Hawkes, wait!"

Hawkes stopped and looked back again.

"Eh? What is it now, woman? Faith, can't you see I'm an old man with a hankering for his bed?"

"I see a man who a very short time ago wished that officer and me to the devil. Why, Mr. Hawkes, should you put yourself to so much trouble to help us now?

The fierce old eyes flickered away from her earnest stare, and for a moment it seemed he would not favor her

215

with an answer. Then suddenly his lips twisted in a wry sort of grimace, and at last he met her look squarely.

"If you must know, 'twas the way you stood up to a bilious old fool, as if not God nor the devil could prove you wrong." Indeed, he thought to himself, he would never forget if he lived to be a hundred the way she had looked with her head flung back, her eyes burning with a fierce pride, as she revealed the mark of a villain's fist against her white skin. At last it had been driven home that she was as game as she was lovely and likely just as fine as word in the streets had said she was.

"Though I was too pigheaded to admit it, I could see that, blue-blood or not, you were a lady in the real sense of the word," he added gruffly. "It took me a while, but I finally got it through my thick skull that any man you figured was worth fighting so hard for must be a man worth saving—even if he is a bloody damned Englishman! Now good night, Miss Tyree, and remember what I told you. From the looks of him, it'll be up to you to see your captain stays abed till his strength is equal to his will. I reckon you got your work cut out for you."

Chapter 14

A cold blast of wind and snow rattled the stairs as Jedediah let himself out. Then the cellar door dropped back in place again with a dull thud. Sabra shivered and hugged her arms across her breast. Unexpectedly, the sudden quiet in the wake of the flurry left her feeling absurdly uneasy. Indeed, she took a step toward the stairs, almost succumbing to the temptation to call Hawkes back again. Then chiding herself for a silly fool, she sternly got a grip on herself.

Faith, she was no child in need of someone to hold her hand. It was only that she was tired, and now that the immediate need for action was past, she had become ruefully aware that her clothes clung, cold and damp, to her body and that her side ached abominably. Deciding a dish of tea might go a long way toward restoring her spirits, she filled a battered copper kettle with water and set it on the cast-iron stove to heat. Then hastily stripping to the buff, she rubbed herself dry and draped herself toga-fashion in the faded counterpane that earlier had adorned the bed.

As she laid her things over the backs of the chairs to dry, it came fleetingly to her that her morals must be sadly slipping. Indeed, she was acutely aware of her nakedness beneath the thin coverlet as she padded barefoot across the room to the bed in which Myles lay unmoving. She would find herself in a fine kettle of fish should *he* come to his senses and discover her bedecked like a plump goose ripe for the plucking. Immediately she felt a soft thrill permeate her body, and suddenly she realized she would like nothing more than to have Myles awaken to her with desire.

The discovery left her stunned. Was love, then, indeed so powerful? she marveled. She had thought never to sell herself to any man who did not hold her in affection, and yet she knew she would gladly give herself to Myles. How was it that suddenly she should see no wrong in a bargain which was so patently unequal? Because, whispered a small voice somewhere inside, she might never have the chance again to know what it was to lie in Myles's arms, and when everything was over and done and he knew all the truth, with what would she be left except her few, precious memories?

The thought, somehow, gave her little comfort; indeed, she realized all too well that she had allowed herself to drift into perilously dangerous shoals. Rather than indulge herself in mooning over what could never be, she would do much better to concern herself solely with attending Myles's needs. For as soon as he could be moved to a better place of safety, she would have no choice but to leave him. Sternly reminding herself that there were those whose lives depended on the successful completion of this, her final and most crucial mission, and knowing full well she would rather die herself than let them down, she studied the motionless figure on the bed with a dull ache beneath her breast.

At least Myles's breathing was easier, she noted, observing the steady rise and fall of the blanket over his chest, and there was a returning tinge of color in cheeks, which, scant moments earlier, had been ashen. Tenderly, Sabra leaned over to comb a stray lock of hair from his forehead with her fingertips.

The sparkle of diamonds and emeralds caught her painfully unawares. With a feeling of unreality, she lifted her hand and stared at the dazzling display of color glancing from the exquisite stones. Faith, it seemed an age had passed since Myles had slipped the betrothal ring on her finger. In the excitement she had forgotten it entirely. Oh, God, why had he done it? Why that ring, when any other or none at all would have done just as well? It was to have been a charade they played, a farce that would end as soon as the need for it had passed, and then the ring was to have gone back to him, and Myles was to have vanished from her life—this time forever.

How ironic, she thought, letting her hand drop, that the intertwined bands of gold set with precious gems should seem cruelly to promise more. Her heart in her eyes, she let her gaze wander once more to the face against the pillow.

The cynical lines about the mouth were relaxed in sleep, and the black hair, unbound and rumpled against the pillow, softened the stern cast of his features so that Myles appeared younger, less the forbidding captain and more the reckless youth who four years before had insinuated himself inextricably into her heart.

Damn him! she thought. Unconscious and dependent upon her strength, he was more dangerous to her now than ever he was then. She felt helpless against the emotions that seeing him like this aroused in her—nurturing instincts, primal urges of the female to succor and protect. Indeed, she experienced a sharp wrench as she gazed upon the long, lithe form, lying so still beneath the blankets. Myles had always loomed as someone who shaped his own destiny, a man whose iron resolution and dauntless will might carry him unscathed through anything. Somehow it was not right that he should now be lying, helpless and vulnerable, and unaware.

Inevitably an image sprang unbidden to her mind of Myles in the throes of another wound, one which had been a great deal more serious than a glancing bullet through the arm. The record of what had transpired then

219

had been carved in flesh and rendered indelible by the dreadful network of scars left behind. The bullet had penetrated deep into the thigh and apparently either had shattered on impact or driven remnants of some other object into the flesh along with it, a brass button being the likeliest candidate. Each piece had had to be dug out, and from the looks of it, the surgeon had missed some particle. The wound had festered and broken, and doubtless he had had to go back in again with forceps. Merciful God, Myles must have suffered agonies!

Giving in to the weakness dragging at her limbs, Sabra sank to the floor beside the sickbed, her legs curled to one side and behind her. With a sigh she laid her head against her arms folded atop the covers and stared at Myles's profile.

"Why can you never play fair?" she murmured, tracing with her eyes the strong line of cheek and jaw. "Was it not enough to make me love you? Why had you to design for me a farce that could not but put me through the very torments of hell? God, to wear the ring which is the symbol of that I should most desire, and know 'tis naught but a cruel hoax! Had your intent been to punish, you could not have hit upon anything more sure—except, having awakened me to love, you allowed yourself to perish now before my eyes." Slowly her eyelids drifted downward. "That I could not bear, my darling," she mumbled drowsily. "Nor forgive."

At last she succumbed to the heavy toll exacted that night upon her inner reserves of strength. Breathing a long sigh, she fell into exhausted slumber.

The cold seeping from the floor into her bones brought Sabra gradually to the realization that she had allowed the fire to burn down to dying embers. Sluggishly she stirred and at last forced her eyes open to be met by a daunting scene.

Myles, his cheeks unnaturally flushed and his head moving fitfully against the pillow, let out a harsh stream of invectives. Thrusting aside the bedclothes, he struggled to get up.

Sabra came hastily to her feet and tried to press him back again.

"Myles, no!" she cried. Strong fingers closed hard on her shoulders, dragged her roughly to within inches of his face.

"Dammit, can't you see?" he demanded bitterly, his vision blurred, unrecognizing. "He won't fight! They sent him to the guns *knowing* he won't. *Curse* their bastard souls, they planned it all too well. I can't do a thing to stop it. It's too late—the bloody French are on us!" With a groan he collapsed against the pillow, his eyes clenched shut as he relived the memories of his own, private nightmare. Then all at once his brow creased in a frown of concentration. "They took him while I lay wounded," he muttered fretfully. His eyes flew open, and he struggled once more to rise. "Must find out why. Must know who's behind it."

Frantically Sabra pressed her hands against his chest.

"Myles, please!" she cried. "You've been wounded, you must lie still."

Reaching out, he caught her arm below the shoulder. She gasped as his fingers dug cruelly into the tender flesh.

"Inness, the bloody bastard!" he spat at her. His eyes, aflame with fever, burned into her own. "Knows more than he's saying. Have to get out of here. Find him. Find the truth."

"Yes, yes. *Soon,* my darling. But first you must rest," she murmured soothingly.

He stilled, the fierceness in his eyes abating somewhat

221

before a vague sense of confusion. A crease etched itself between his eyebrows, and he fell to studying her face as if it were a puzzle he must somehow sort out. Thinking to take advantage of the moment, Sabra tried gently to loosen the punishing grip on her arm.

It was a mistake. With a curse he dragged her down onto the bed so that she landed on her knees beside him, her hands braced hard against his chest.

"Damn your bloody witch's eyes! It's *you!*"

As if struck, Sabra recoiled before the white blaze of passion in his face.

"But then, you're not real, are you?" he added bitterly. "You never are."

"Myles, no," she began, reading the reckless birth of intent in the half-curl of his lips. His arm lifted, and she froze in horror as he caught hold of the coverlet and yanked it from her. An indrawn gasp shuddered through her at the touch of his hand to her breast. Then, freed at last from the paralyzing grip of shock, she tried to pull away.

"Oh, no, my beautiful Lorelei. You will not get away so easily. Not this time. I shall not let you vanish."

For a moment she stared, mesmerized, into firelit eyes.

"None of this is real," he muttered thickly and dragged her down to him.

His mouth closing savagely over hers hurt her, and the hard thrust of his tongue between her lips brutally violated the sweet tenderness of her mouth. Frightened by his ruthless assault on her innocence, Sabra groaned and fought to break away, but with a strength intensified by delirium and unbridled lust, he yanked her back again. Her struggling only landed her astraddle his hips. His fingers entangled in her long hair as he forced her to submit to his cruel kiss, to his hand kneading the soft vulnerability of her breast, to his tongue probing the depths of her mouth.

Sabra writhed in his grasp, helpless against the sudden leap of desire. Uttering low, animal moans, she was swept away in the engulfing tide of arousal that surged upward through her belly from the hot moistness of her awakened desire.

Never had she known that she could burn with need so terrible she feared she must perish from it. And yet his mouth, devouring her, breathed sweet fire into her veins; his tongue, exploring the turgid promise of her nipples, aroused a conflagration in her depths. If it was indeed an unreality, a dream, then Myles was an incubus with hands and lips of flame, and she was naught but tinder to his touch.

Her hair tumbled wildly about her back and shoulders as, with a groan, she arched above him, her head thrown back and her breath coming in hard, swift pants. Then his hands, trailing liquid fire down her sides and over her belly, found the moist, molten depths between her thighs. Sigh upon sigh burst from her lips as he probed the swollen orifice, teased and tormented the turgid center of her concentrated desire. Mindlessly she murmured his name over and over as within her, her need grew to an unquenchable ache. Her fingers clutched at the powerful shoulders, then mindlessly caressed the sensuous ripple of muscle across the sinewy chest, entangled themselves in the curling mat of black hair. She felt the masculine nipples harden beneath her touch. Then she groaned and clutched his lean waist between her warm moist thighs as her swelling bud of arousal seemed transformed into a throbbing heat. Her eyes feverish through half-slitted lids, she begged him to end her unbearable anguish. In a frenzy of passion, she felt his hands on her waist, lifting her, guiding her, and at last his hard manhood pressing upward against her. Willingly she opened to his promised thrust, spreading wide her thighs, wanting him, needing him to come into her. Savagely he forced her down upon him.

There was pain, white-hot and searing, as he plunged through the virginal membrane. Sabra caught her lip between her teeth to keep from crying out, tasted the pungency of her own blood. Then she was moving with him inside of her, the pain forgotten as she rode the crest of swiftly mounting ecstasy. She cried out in delirious rapture at the sharp, explosive burst of pleasure, coupled with the shuddering expulsion of his own culminating passion. Low, moaning sighs burst from her lips with the fierce contractions that seemed to ripple upward through her depths. Left trembling and weak at last, she collapsed, shuddering, on top of him. Her face nuzzled into the strong curve of his neck.

For a long moment she lay, limp with exhaustion, and dragged in great breaths of air. In spite of her tiredness, she was conscious of a strange exhilaration only gradually giving way to a delicious languor. Never had she felt so wondrously alive, so fearlessly vulnerable, so imbued with tender feelings. Indeed, her love for Myles was so overwhelming she thought her heart must surely break from it.

Oh, God, if only that love were returned in some small measure! she thought, and suffered an unexpected pang. For she could not but be ruefully aware that he had taken her in the throes of fever, not knowing what he was doing or even who she was. Indeed, she experienced an unfamiliar stab of jealousy for that other woman, his "beautiful Lorelei."

Shivering suddenly, she became aware of the chill air of the cellar and of the sweat clinging to her body. Alarm came swift upon the realization that Myles must be in a similar state, and she pushed herself up, her gaze going to him anxiously.

── FREE ──

B O O K   C E R T I F I C A T E

ZEBRA HOME SUBSCRIPTION SERVICE, INC.

YES! Please start my subscription to Zebra Historical Romances and send me my free Zebra Novel along with my first month's Romances. I understand that I may preview these four new Zebra Historical Romances Free for 10 days. If I'm not satisfied with them I may return the four books within 10 days and owe nothing. Otherwise I will pay just $3.50 each; a total of $14.00 (a $15.80 value—I save $1.80). Then each month I will receive the 4 newest titles as soon as they come off the press for the same 10 day Free preview and low price. I may return any shipment and I may cancel this arrangement at any time. There is no minimum number of books to buy and there are no shipping, handling or postage charges. Regardless of what I do, the FREE book is mine to keep.

Name _____

                             (Please Print)

Address _____ Apt. # _____

City _____ State _____ Zip _____

Telephone (   ) _____

Signature _____

           (if under 18, parent or guardian must sign)

Terms and offer subject to change without notice.   12-88

MAIL IN THE COUPON BELOW TODAY

To get your Free **ZEBRA HISTORICAL ROMANCE** fill out the coupon below and send it in today. As soon as we receive the coupon, we'll send your first month's books to preview Free for 10 days along with your **FREE NOVEL.**

GET
FREE
FREE
GIFT

His chest and shoulders glistened with sweat. The raven hair clung damply to his forehead. She laid her hand against his brow, felt the skin, cool against her palm, and knew at once the fever had broken.

Catching her lip between her teeth, Sabra bent her head, the luxurious waves of hair sliding forward to hide her face. Now that the crisis was over, all at once she felt immensely drained, and yet somehow she must find the strength to rise and cover her nakedness and his.

She made as if to drag herself away, experienced a sudden pang of loss as she felt his now flaccid member slip out of her, then Myles's hand was in her hair, lifting the concealing red-gold mass back away from her face and curling it gently behind her ear. Startled, she glanced up to find him looking at her, the steel-gray eyes, drowsy and faintly puzzled, but clear of fever.

"Myles?" she whispered faintly.

For a moment he said nothing. Then a hint of a smile touched his lips.

"You're still here," he murmured and brushed his fingers lightly along her cheek. "You didn't vanish." His eyelids drifting down over his eyes, he lowered his hand to his chest. "Not a dream," he muttered thickly and was asleep.

Sabra huddled in a chair with her knees propped against her chest and a blanket wrapped about her shoulders as she watched Myles sleep. It was, she judged, about an hour before the sun was due to rise beyond the windowless confines of the cellar. All night she had dozed on and off in the acursed wooden armchair. Finally, unable to bear her cramped position any longer, she had risen stiffly and, after hurriedly donning her dry clothes, had helped herself at last to hot tea before returning to her post. The metal cup cradled between her hands, she sipped absently

225

at the steaming brew and brooded over the unsettling events that had taken place in the night.

With a wry twist of the lips she recalled the Herculean effort of attempting to strip the bed of its soaked linen and replace it with dry bedclothes, which had been a necessity in the circumstances. It would hardly have done, after all, to allow her patient to become chilled in the wake of his fever. The problem of how to accomplish the task with Myles still abed had taxed all her powers of ingenuity. Doing half the bed at a time had seemed a simple enough solution until it had come to moving Myles from one side to the other. Mumbling in his sleep, he had tumbled her neatly into bed beside him. Then apparently not at all put out to find her pinned, naked as a jaybird, against his equally natural state, he had enfolded her in the delicious warmth of his arm.

She smiled whimsically, remembering the firm, muscular length of him molded wondrously to her backside. Faith, she had never dreamed a hard chest and sinewy thighs could make so marvelous a cushion. It had been only with a great deal of reluctance that eventually she sought to work her way out from under the arm draped securely about her waist. To her chagrin, Myles grunted at the first hint of movement and merely snuggled closer. Still, undaunted, she had at last managed the thing by luring him a few inches at a time across the bed till at last she had him where she wanted him.

Slipping off the bed, she had made short work of completing the changing of the linens. Then had come the unexpectedly disturbing task of buffing the masculine body dry before swathing it in warm blankets. In vain had she sought for the clinical detachment which had attended her earlier ministrations, facilitated by Hawkes's able assistance. Indeed, she found she could not but be aware that, despite the disfiguring scars on his thigh, Myles,

226

with his muscular limbs and broad chest, the dark mat of hair tapering to a V over the lean torso and firm, flat belly, presented a magnificent example of the male physique.

All at once she flushed hotly, remembering the stark maleness of him, the curling mass of dark hair tinged with blood—her blood. Oh, God, how would he greet her upon awakening? she wondered with sudden, unavoidable misgivings, though in truth, she was not certain what she dreaded more: that he should recall the unbridled passion that, engulfing her like flames to tinder, had rendered her a wild and wanton creature, quite unlike anything she had ever imagined of herself—or that he should remember none of it. Clearly there was a great deal about herself that she did not know, a depth of feeling, a whole range of emotions and hitherto unsuspected needs and yearnings for which Myles was somehow the touchstone. Only Myles could spark them into being and, conversely, only Myles could have brought her to a fulfillment of all that he aroused in her. She could not but mourn for that which she had been given to glimpse but would never fully realize. For she knew with bitter certainty that for her there could never be another love like Trevor Myles.

Still, she could not regret what had happened or that he had taken her solely out of a mindless fever of desire. She knew she had no claim on that well-armored heart, nor was it likely that she ever would. In another time, another place, perhaps, when the wounds of war had long been healed, things might have been different. It would somehow have to be enough that for a brief, glorious moment in time, she had lain in his arms and known the wonder of consummated passion.

A sudden tingling of nerve endings startled her out of her reverie, and all at once she became aware of Myles staring at her from beneath drooping eyelids.

"You're awake!" she blurted foolishly and felt a slow blush invade her cheeks.

"It would seem so," he murmured, observing her confusion with apparent interest. Then with a grimace, he ran a hand gingerly through his hair till he came to the lump at the back of his head. "How long have I been out?"

"Through the night. You were out of your head with fever. How are you feeling now?"

A wry smile twisted at his lips.

"Like the aftermath of a particularly incontinent evening—and devilishly sharp-set." His gaze wandered appraisingly around the rock walls of the cellar, and Sabra, wishing to postpone the inevitable, hastily lowered her feet to the floor.

"Some black coffee should set part of that to rights," she said, rising with alacrity. "And then I'll try and discover what may be contrived for breakfast. I'm afraid even a king's ship may have more to offer in the way of cuisine than what is available here, but we shall see."

Myles, quick to discern the false note of cheerfulness in her voice, arched a quizzical eyebrow. He had beheld the provocative young beauty in many moods—charming, witty and gay, haughty, outraged, and tantalizingly mysterious—but never before nervous, even jittery, as if she were hiding something or suffering, perhaps, the throes of an uneasy conscience. Curious, he mused, for if either were the case, he would have thought her far more likely to retreat into cool impenetrability than to betray the smallest sign of discomposure. Indeed, it occurred to him suddenly that the change he sensed in her went rather deeper than an apparant aberration in her many intriguing moods.

Hooking an arm lazily behind his head, he settled back to observe the slender girl more closely.

And, indeed, she made a delectable creature with her

228

glorious hair all atumble down her back in an unruly mass of red-gold curls. Taking in the long, shapely legs and delightfully rounded posterior, undeniably set to advantage in skin-tight breeches, he felt a familiar stirring in his loins. Then Sabra turned and came toward him. For an instant her lissome form was limned against the lanternlight, the lovely outline of her breasts revealed beneath the thin, white fabric of the shirt, and suddenly his belly clenched with the first resurgence of a memory so startling he could not credit it with reality.

Something had happened while he lay in the grip of fever, something which was somehow connected to the disturbing mixture of dreams and events that had come to him, distorted and confused, in his delirium. But surely *that* had not been real! Bloody hell! Asleep, he had possessed the illusive Sabra too many times to count. And always he would awaken, drenched in sweat, his body tormented with desire and his mind with the realization that he had been visited by another of his cursed dreams of Sabra, which, like spectres of the past, came all too often to haunt him in his sleep. Still, it had never been like this, so vivid he had only to close his eyes to see her framed against a yellow halo of light, her supple beauty poised above him like a vision sent from hell to drive him mad. A frown creased his brow as he struggled to sort out fact from fantasy.

Then she was leaning over him.

"Myles?" she queried, her voice vibrant with concern. "Myles, what is it? Is it your arm? Are you in pain?"

His eyes flickered to her face, and all at once his gaze narrowed sharply at the sight of her cut and swollen lip. At last he shook his head.

"No. It's nothing." His lips stretched in a smile that felt stiff against his teeth. "I suppose I'm still a trifle muddled, that's all."

229

Not completely convinced, Sabra hesitated. Then Myles was pushing himself up, and as she quickly moved to arrange the pillows at his back, the moment passed.

As it turned out, the morning repast was at least comparable to ship's fare, if hardly better, comprised as it was of strong coffee, strips of saltpork roasted over the hot coals, and nuts and tangy cheese. Nevertheless, the meal, notwithstanding the unexciting cuisine, proved an unusually stimulating affair.

Sabra, ruefully aware that Myles was turning on the charm that had in the past proven devastating to more than one feminine heart, found herself responding to his repartee with keen enjoyment. It was not often she discovered herself with a companion who was not only both well read and intelligent, but possessed as well of a dry humor and a wit as penetrating as her own. Long before Myles, over her protestations, had downed his second cup of black coffee, she had been rendered totally at her ease. Her guard lowered, she discoursed at length with him on any number of subjects, save only those, which by tacit agreement, would inevitably have marred their easy camaraderie.

Indeed, Myles, contrary to his reputation for recklessness, was playing close and deep, and it was not until she had been led to relate a great many things of an intimate nature that she became suddenly aware of how greatly she had fallen under his spell.

She was perched unself-consciously on the foot of the bed, the remains of their picnic laid out on a tray, contrived from a wooden packing crate, between them. Having spoken freely on the subject of her father's death and her keen sense of loss, she was launched on the story of how Wes manfully had stepped in to fill the void, while

Myles rested with his back to the headboard and listened.

"I wish you could have known him," she murmured, her expression wistful as she propped her chin on top of her knees drawn to her chest. "The two of you would have got on famously. He can outsail the best, and there's no one, save maybe Skyler, who knows these waters better than he. My father used to say Wes was half Cornish sea dog and half New England coaster. But then he came by it naturally. Josiah Locke stowed away on a whaler before his eleventh birthday, and by the time he was five and twenty, he was building and outfitting his own fleet of ships. That's the one way Wes is different from his father. Wes was wild to sail, but he didn't care a whit for the shipping business. Sometimes I think he was glad the war came along, just so he could get away from all that."

She frowned and for a moment it seemed she would sink into a darker mood, but then resolutely she shook off the spell her final words had wrought.

"He taught me to sail, you know," she said, flinging up her head with a defiant little toss. "And how to fence and shoot. Even before Father died, he used to let me tag along with him. And afterward, he was everything to me—parent, friend, confidante. He is the one man in my life who has always treated me as an equal rather than some troublesome female to be married off at the earliest convenience and then consigned for the rest of her life to domesticity and household drudgery. 'Twas what my mother wished for me, what she had. But I was never cut out for it. I should rather die than be obliged never to sail my own vessel when and where I choose!"

"And should you be?" queried Myles offhandedly, watching her animated visage through half-closed eyes. "Obliged, I mean, to give up your passion for sailing?"

"And how not?" she answered with a shrug. "What man would have his wife junketing about on the high seas in

231

command of a sailing ship?"

"But I should have thought that was obvious. A man who understood and shared her need for independence. A man who, neither threatened nor intimidated by her strength of will, her backbone, if you would, would stand with her at the helm."

Something in his voice made her look up sharply. Myles, she suddenly recalled, had a way of sneaking up on one when he seemed at his most disarming.

"But of course, captain," she retorted, able to read nothing in his face. "And where, I wonder, am I to find this paragon?"

His slow smile would seem to mock her, but of the sudden glint of steel between his slitted eyelids, she could not at all be certain.

"I should think your brother sounds just such a man, and if there is *one,* would it not be reasonable to suppose there could be others?"

"Would it?" she countered bitterly. "Hitherto, I have seen scant evidence of it."

"But then, to see, one has to look." For a long moment fraught with a seeming multitude of things left unvoiced, he held her with his eyes. At last he shrugged, and the moment fled. "But then, perhaps you're right," he said, settling more comfortably against the pillows at his back. "There comes a time when even a paragon might wish for a more settled existence. A home and family—and a woman to warm his bed."

"And no less should I desire to be such a woman, a wife and mother, and yet more than that. A woman whose entirety is neither encompassed nor defined by four walls and a family. I could never be a mere extension of a husband, like some convenient appendage."

Suddenly, as if she could no longer bear to be still, she slid from the bed and paced restlessly a step or two before

232

turning to face him with flashing eyes.

"Faith, do you think I know nothing of passion or desire? I am flesh no less than you. But I would be what I choose, not what some man would make of me. Why is that so difficult to comprehend? Why should I be called willful and wrongheaded because I ask only that which a man takes for granted as his due? Yet I, who have commanded men and directed my own affairs, am thought mannish and forward. I am branded a harlot because I have seen fit to maintain my household unchaperoned. And because I look to no man for guidance, I am considered unruly and intractable, no fit woman for most men. Indeed, a woman who should have some sense 'beaten into her head'!" she ended bitterly.

Myles's wry laugh brought a flush of resentment to her cheeks. Hands on hips, she awarded him a darkling look.

"I fail to see what I have said to amuse you," she uttered pointedly.

"No doubt it was having my own words flung back in my face," he evaded and immediately sobered. "Still, I find I have even less provocation to change my mind about you. You, madam, are as hotheaded as you are beautiful, and only an utter fool would allow himself to become willingly embroiled in your intrigues. Since I apparently am just such a fool, however, it would seem only fair that for once in your life you played it straight with me. Who was the good Samaritan who came to your rescue in that cursed alley? And where the deuce are we? What happened last night, *ma mie,* that you're keeping from me?"

Sabra went suddenly as white as she had been previously flushed.

"I'm sure I haven't the least idea what you mean, captain," she stated, forcing herself to meet his eyes. "Nothing happened. As for the man who struck you in what he supposed was my defense, I have not the right to divulge

233

either his name or to what place he saw fit to have you transported. But you should be aware that he saved your life by bringing you here and as a result has placed himself in grave danger. Further than that I cannot tell you anything."

"*Will* not tell me anything. Very well then, I shall tell *you*. The man you are protecting is one of the 'Naughty Pack of Ann Street,' a small band who have made it a practice to smuggle aid into the North Dutch Church prisoners. And this, I should assume, is one of their places of rendezvous." A grim smile curved his lips at the sight of her momentary start, quickly concealed behind a stony visage. "Yes, it begins to come back to me. I seem to recall there was some hesitation as to whether I should be rescued or left to a less kind fate. I believe I have you to thank for this rather more felicitous outcome."

"You heard?" she demanded, her heart suddenly cold. "How much more did you—" She could not finish it, nor did Myles leave her to suffer long.

"Enough to put the pieces together. I seemed to have drifted in and out of consciousness."

Yes, she thought and turned away, remembering, suddenly, how she had felt him move ever so slightly against her. He could have regained his senses at short intervals. Still, perhaps he had not been privy to her impassioned avowal. God in heaven, pray he had not heard her declare her love!

"What," she said with her back to him, "do you intend doing? These men are not soldiers. Their sole concern is to relieve the suffering of the American prisoners. They are no threat to the British. Surely you must see that it would be a gross miscarriage of justice to punish them as rebels."

Something like impatience flickered in his face.

"Spare me your descent into bathos, I beg you," he

drawled cynically. "I've spent my life in the king's navy. It is not my practice, I assure you, to wage war against rank amateurs and civilians."

"You do mean that, don't you?" she said, turning at last to probe his face with troubled eyes. "You won't change your mind later?"

"Good God, why should I? You've a deuced odd notion of my character do you think I should take some sort of pleasure in punishing shopkeepers and old men for something that does not concern me in the least."

The look that came to her eyes then nearly took his breath away.

"Myles, I must tell you—" she began in a tumultuous voice.

A burst of wind flinging down at them from above cut short whatever it was she had been about to say. Sending a startled glance toward the entrance to the cellar, she stiffened, her hand reaching for Myles's gun on a shelf near the bed. Then suddenly she breathed a sigh of relief as she beheld a lank form descending the stairway, his arms filled with an awkward bundle.

"Jedediah!" she exclaimed, rushing to help him with his burden. Myles, watching her hasty retreat, silently cursed the old man for his untimely interruption.

"I see our patient is more himself," observed Hawkes dryly as he beheld the English captain regarding him from the bed with something less than enthusiasm.

"Indeed, he is much recovered this morning." Sabra grinned. "Despite the fact that he made quite a nuisance of himself a great portion of the night. Goodness, what have you brought?" With all the exuberance of a child, she knelt to undo the bundle, which she soon discovered contained, not only warm clothing of a size to fit Myles, but a boy's woolen sweater, stockings, gloves, and a pair of leather boots, all of which were meant obviously for herself. There was a small store of ammunition as well, a bar of shaving soap, a razor, and a flask of what smelled suspiciously like brandy.

Exclaiming softly, she looked up at the old man with eyes that shimmered.

"These belonged to young Jed and his father, didn't they," she queried gently. "Jedediah, are you sure?"

"Of course, I'm sure," he growled before she could finish. "Now say no more, missy. I'll not stand for any sentimental mish-mush."

"Very well. I'll not embarass you," she answered, laughing as she rose to her feet. "Come. I'll introduce you to Captain Myles, and then you must have a cup of hot coffee to chase the cold away."

As Sabra moved to help him out of his coat, however, Hawkes stopped her with a brusque wave of the hand. "Never mind that. I'll not be staying long. I'm afraid we don't have time for socializing, lass."

Sabra glanced sharply up, her heart turning over as Hawkes returned her look with telling gravity.

"Then we mustn't tarry, must we," she said at last and, taking his arm, calmly led him toward the bedside with the intention of presenting him to Myles.

Chapter 15

Acutely aware of the tension in the arm linked in hers, Sabra smiled beguilingly up into Hawkes's flinty face. Firmly she led him near the bed.

"Captain Myles, I should like to present Mr. Jedediah Hawkes. Mr. Hawkes, Capt. Trevor Myles. Jedediah's come bearing gifts, captain, which, you will no doubt be glad to learn, include shaving soap and a razor, among other things."

"Obviously a man of rare acumen," commented Myles, quizzing her with a look from beneath slightly drooping eyelids. Flushing, Sabra awarded him a darkling glance and gave a small, meaningful nod in the direction of their caller. Myles grinned ever so slightly as, obligingly, he turned his attention to the American. Extending his hand, he said, "A pleasure, Mr. Hawkes. I believe I am in your debt, however, for more than soap and a razor. It would appear I owe you my life."

Hawkes's face appeared carved out of granite as, pointedly, he ignored that strong supple hand.

"If you think that, captain," he stated baldly, "I reckon you're more of a fool than I would have figured you for."

A single eyebrow swept upward in the captain's brow. "You are, if anything, forthright, sir," he remarked, carelessly letting his hand drop to his side.

"I'm a man who likes to lay his cards on the table. My grandson had naught but fourteen years in his cup, captain, when he was cast into prison for striking a bloody Redcoat." Hawkes spat in contempt. "A drunken lout who

237

thought to lay vile hands on the boy's mother! They let him die in that stinking hellhole—for want of food or even blankets and a warm fire to stave off the cold in the dead of winter. So you see, I wouldn't give a tinker's damn if you'd breathed your last in that alley, captain. Now, if knowing that, you still want to shake my hand, out of respect for Miss Tyree I'll not choose to disoblige you."

Ye gods, groaned Sabra, her glance winging anxiously to Myles as she tried to anticipate his probable reaction to that little speech. *Why* had she not thought to warn him about Hawkes? Myles, however, appeared as maddeningly aloof as ever.

"I see," he temporized, reaching up to stroke the stubbles on his chin. "You are generous indeed. And quite fond, it would seem, of the lady." He paused, his gaze playing briefly over Sabra's taut face. "Very well," he drawled suddenly. "I accept your terms. In mutual respect of the inestimable Sabra, I am not averse to offering my hand. You see, Mr. Hawkes," he added with a singularly mirthless smile, "I am hardly a stranger to death. I've seen boys die. Some younger than your grandson. I can assure you that no matter who they are or what the circumstances, it is never an easy sight."

Feeling a trifle foolish for having feared the worst, Sabra relaxed. She should have known that in dealing with Hawkes, Myles would act according to his own, peculiar notions of honor.

Hawkes, on the other hand, was keenly aware that he had been skillfully outmaneuvered. Gruffly he cleared his throat and after only a momentary pause, met the captain in a firm, if reluctant, handshake.

"Perhaps you had better save your thanks, captain," he commented dryly, "until you've heard what I've come to say."

238

"Am I to assume that you are the bearer of ill tidings, Mr. Hawkes?" queried Myles gently as he settled back against the pillows.

Hawkes, gazing into those still, gray eyes, could not but marvel at the man's steadiness of nerve. Oh, he was a cool one, all right, was the bloody Englishman. And nobody's fool, if Jedediah Hawkes was any judge.

"The truth to tell, I reckon it couldn't be any worse," he said. "The fact of the matter is, captain, that a naval lieutenant and two seamen were found dead last night. I don't suppose you know anything about that?"

"Should I?" Myles smiled coldly.

"I'm sure I couldn't say, one way or the other." Hawkes shrugged. "But as it happens, you're the one who's been charged with their murders, captain, along with treason and desertion to the enemy."

Sabra's sharp gasp pierced the air.

"But that's preposterous!" she breathed. A hand went to her breast as though to contain the sudden pounding within. "Surely you must have got it wrong."

The old man's gaze, swinging from Myles to the girl, noticeably softened.

"I wish I could say I had, lass, but I've seen the troops searching house to house. You mustn't waste any time in making yourselves ready to leave. We've an hour at best to get you and your captain safely away."

Sabra went pearly white.

"No, we cannot possibly," she stated flatly. Gesturing with her hands, she began to pace as she pointed out the obstacles in their way. "Myles isn't ready yet. And even if he were, we've no way of going. I dare not send for my coach, which would in any case soon prove worse than useless if this snow continues." Suddenly she whirled to face Myles with accusing eyes. "Faith, captain, have you *nothing* to say to this?"

239

The sardonic lift of an eloquent eyebrow brought the blood rushing back into her face.

"Nothing," he returned with insufferable calm, "which cannot wait until we've heard this gentleman out. You do have something more to tell us, have you not, Mr. Hawkes?"

"Oh, how well you do that!" blurted Sabra contemptuously before she thought. Instantly she wished she could snatch the words back again. Faith, what was wrong with her to play the hysterical fool before Myles, of all people? And, worse, he had been right to call her down for it.

Then, to make matters worse, Hawkes blundered in, thinking, no doubt, to smooth rough waters.

"Easy, mistress. Myles is right. There's no need to work yourself into a lather. I've arranged for a sled and horses to take you whither you will. And whether the captain's up to it or not, I'm afraid you're going to have to take the risk."

Something in his manner warned her of worse news to come.

"Why, Jedediah? What haven't you told us?" she demanded. Suddenly she felt ice cold.

Hawkes shifted uncomfortably.

"I've been to your house and talked with your servants. Sir Wilfred left a message for you with your Mr. Wayne. He wanted you to know the price of your brother's life has gone up. In addition to the earlier terms and the return of certain items he claims were stolen, he wants the captain's meddling in his affairs brought to an end, and he doesn't care how you do it. Otherwise Wesley Locke won't live to see the new year. I'm sorry, lass."

"Channing!" declared Sabra bitterly. "Faith, I might have known." Clenching her hands into fists at her sides, she turned her back on the two men.

"We are in something of a coil, Mr. Hawkes," Myles

commented dryly. "And Wayne and the others of Miss Tyree's household? I trust they are well?"

Hawkes, favoring the captain with an appraising look, was surprised to discover that Myles was younger than he had first supposed. Indeed, he did not appear to be above thirty, if he was that. Probably it was the way he had of looking at a fellow, as if he could see right through to what a body was thinking, that had misled him. That, he mused, and the hint of steel in the steadiness of the gray eyes, which clearly bespoke a man of experience beyond his years. Without a doubt he had the aspect of one used to command. Nor was there any mistaking that lean look, that hardness of body, which was yet well defined with muscle. He was a fighter, all right, and from the looks of the scars he bore, one who had seen more than his share of battle.

In spite of himself, Hawkes could not but sense that here was a man worthy of the spirited Sabra. Indeed, he little doubted that in normal circumstances Myles was a man to draw to, and an extremely dangerous one to cross.

Nevertheless, the sternly chiseled features were unmistakably pale, and there was a slight tautness about the lips that told their own story. Obviously the lass was right in thinking her captain was far from being fit.

"From what I have seen they appeared well enough," he answered, choosing his words carefully, for, worthy or not, Myles was still an English officer. "Some men showed up at the house late last night, claiming they had orders to search the place. Went over every inch of it before they left, empty-handed. A few of your people were shoved around some, lass, but luckily no one was hurt. I expect they'll be safe enough for the time being."

"Thank God," breathed Sabra and shuddered.

Straightening her shoulders she came about to reveal

241

magnificent eyes shimmering with gratitude. "Dear Jedediah, how shall I ever repay you?" she murmured huskily.

Instantly Hawkes stiffened to alertness. Despite the trembling of her lips, there was a resoluteness in the proud lift of the head, which he instantly mistrusted. A frown darkened the fierce old brow.

"I told you," he rasped. "Anything I've done was to even accounts for my grandson."

Smiling mistily, Sabra nodded.

"So you did and, indeed, you have more than repaid me for what little I was able to accomplish for young Jed. But now you must involve yourself no further. If you can but tell me how to reach Jubal Henry, the captain and I shan't trouble you anymore."

"Oh, you shan't eh?" growled Hawkes. "Well, beggin' your pardon, Miss Tyree, I reckon I'll decide for myself what I will or won't do. You've hatched some darned fool notion in that stubborn head of yours, haven't you? You might just as well tell me now, for I'll not give up till you do."

Conscious of Myles watching her with gimlet eyes, Sabra silently cursed the old man's meddling. She had preferred to keep her own counsel till a more propitious time, but Hawkes obviously intended to pursue his suspicions with characteristic bullheadedness.

"I think it must be obvious there is only one thing to be done," she answered with a careless shrug of the shoulder. "I intend to make sure the captain is cleared of all blame, and in that, you cannot help me."

"I knew it! It's as plain as the nose on your face. You mean to give yourself over to the troops when they show up here looking for you! Well, you can't do it, lass. You tell her, captain. There's not a chance in hell they won't hang her for a traitor."

The captain gazed speculatively at the slightly flushed

242

features of the haughty young beauty.

"You are mistaken, Mr. Hawkes," he said deliberately. "It's not to the British army she intends to deliver herself, but to Sir Wilfred Channing."

Sabra's head came up, her eyes winging in proud defiance to Myles.

"The hell she does!" blustered Hawkes, mystified by the look that passed between the two. "Faith, lass, if that's true, you can't be thinking straight. From all you've said, it's plain the villain's not to be trusted."

"Perhaps," she replied, dragging her eyes away from Myles, "and yet that is the risk I must take. I should be grateful if you would relay a message to my man Jubal before I go. There are certain matters I must attend concerning the house and the servants."

"Hang it! You can give your man the message yourself if it's so all-fired important," Hawkes rumbled, clearly exasperated with them both. "It's Henry that's coming to fetch you with the sled, and if I have my way, he'll pack you in it, bound and gagged, all the way to Boston if need be."

"Perhaps, Mr. Hawkes, that shall not prove necessary," Myles coolly interjected. "If you could but see your way to granting me a few moments alone with Miss Tyree?"

Sabra, well aware that he meant to dissuade her from her chosen course, steeled herself to do battle. Suddenly very beautiful and very dangerous, she turned to meet Myles, glance for glance.

"On the contrary, captain," she stated coldly, "there is nothing you can say which cannot be said in front of Jedediah."

Myles's expression never altered.

"Mr. Hawkes," he murmured patiently, "if you would be so kind?"

The old man, glancing from one to the other, took

only a second to decide. A single look into the captain's grim countenance was enough to persuade him that his presence was no longer required. Growling something about being too old to play nursemaid to a couple of young hotheads intent on courting disaster, he cravenly abandoned Sabra to her fate.

As soon as they were alone again, Myles purposefully thrust aside the covers and swung his legs over the side of the bed.

"Stop!" cried Sabra in quick alarm. "What, in heaven's name, do you think you are doing?"

"I, my love, am getting up."

Indifferent to the fact that he was naked as a newborn Myles started to his feet.

"Wait!" choked Sabra, seeing the muscle leap along his jawline as he steadied himself.

Ill-humoredly she gathered up the clothing from Hawkes's pack, along with Myles's own stockings and small-clothes, and fairly flung across the room to him. Shoving him down on the bed, she knelt with the obvious intention of helping him on with his breeches.

Myles quirked a bemused eyebrow. "You surprise me, Miss Tyree," he murmured, his expression suspiciously bland. "Do you usually make it a practice to render aid of so intimate a nature?"

Blushing in spite of herself, Sabra cast him a baleful look. "Don't be stupid, captain. How do you think you came to be in the natural state? Now, do you intend to accept my help or not?"

Myles's lip curled sardonically.

"In the norm I shouldn't dream of disobliging you," he rejoined in heavily ironic tones. "But I assure you it has been some time since I was breeched. I am well able to don a pair of unmentionables without the aid either of a nursemaid or an overweaning, meddlesome female."

Stung by his sarcasm, Sabra glanced furiously up into his handsome visage. "But of course, captain," she uttered scathingly, "how very stupid of me to presume. Very well, suit yourself. Far be it from me to bruise your masculine pride."

"Quite so," he murmured smoothly. "And now, if you've no further objections, I shouldn't dream of detaining you any longer."

For an instant Sabra stared dumbfounded into insufferably sleepy gray eyes. Then suddenly her mouth clamped shut as it came to her that he was waiting with exaggerated politeness for her to present him with her back.

Unaccountably flustered at having thus been reminded of the amenities, Sabra flushed. Indeed, she almost obliged him in his request, until suddenly she glimpsed the unholy gleam of amusement in his eyes. Instantly she got hold of herself.

"Oh, but I'm afraid that is out of the question, captain," she purred, crossing her arms across her breast as she presented him with a wholly innocent mien. "I should be greatly remiss did I not stand ready to render whatever aid might prove necessary should you succumb to an unexpected wave of faintness. I feel a certain responsibility for you. You have been, after all, my patient."

"And you, *ma mie*, are making a great deal out of nothing. I've weathered worse and lived to tell of it," drawled Myles, coming suddenly to an awareness of the enormity of the task he had set for himself as he struggled to still the spinning of the room. Donning fashionably skin-tight unmentionables with naught but a single hand would be no mean feat even if he were not alarmingly light-headed. Indeed, he was ruefully aware that his bout with fever had left him weaker than he wanted to admit, even to

245

himself.

"Oh, no doubt," retorted Sabra sarcastically. "And shall you similarly weather the charge of treason, captain? Why can you not admit that Channing has won? Indeed, there can be no purpose in attempting to escape the city now."

"Odd," he mused, "I should have thought you would be the last person to cave in to Channing without a fight. But then, I suppose one should make allowances for feminine frailty. Perhaps you even fancy the notion of playing the baronet's mistress."

At her sharp intake of breath, Myles steeled himself for the inevitable outburst of fury.

For an instant Sabra went deathly still. "Yes, perhaps I do," she retorted in a muffled voice and, keeping her head down so that he could not see her face, she fairly snatched the breeches from his hand and held them out to him to don.

A dangerous glint leaped in his eyes.

"Well, I, my love, do not fancy it!"

Rapier-sharp, his words seemed to pierce through Sabra. She flinched as his hand came ungently beneath her chin and forced her to look up at him.

"You absurd little innocent," he drawled in a voice edged with steel. Idly he ran his thumb over her swollen lip. "Can you truly think I should stand blithely by while you nobly sacrificed yourself to save my good name? Good God, did I not find the notion so vastly diverting, I should be tempted to wring your foolish neck for the insult you do me. At least allow that I am man enough to fight my own battles, if you please."

For a moment she stared enthralled into eyes so light and piercing they took her breath away. Then defiantly she jerked her head aside.

"I'm afraid, captain," she managed without the slightest

246

quaver, "that you have nothing to say in the matter."

The sensuous leap of muscle across his chest should have warned her.

"Have I not?" he queried ominously. "I wonder." Too late she realized her danger and tried to pull away. His fingers, closing mercilessly in her hair at the nape of the neck, drew her to him.

"No, don't!" Tears of pain and rage blurred her vision as she strained to avert her face, and all the while his eyes, like glittery points of flame, held her, seemed to burn themselves into her brain. Slowly he bent his head. "Damn you!" she gasped. "Let go of me!" Then his mouth closed implacably over hers.

She hardly knew how she came suddenly to be lying on the bed beside him, her shirt open and her hands aiding his in working her breeches feverishly down over her hips. She knew only the delirious madness of his lips arousing her as only he knew how. Free of the confining garment at last, she entwined her legs in his and deliriously explored with wildly seeking hands the fascinating length of his bare back, the muscles, sinewy and hard beneath the firm, smooth skin.

If, before, Myles had been an incubus igniting white-hot flames with his fevered touch, this time he was her tormentor. He was merciless in his lovemaking, driving her mad as he stroked her supple body, his hands, creating paroxyms of delirious pleasure as they teased and tickled the acute susceptibility of her breasts, the nipples already peaked and hard with arousal. Then, feather-light with the sharp smoothness of his fingernails, he trailed a tormenting journey down her slender torso and over her flat belly, finding with uncanny preciseness the exquisitely sensitive nerve center at the outer corner of the silky triangle of hair. Her flesh leaped and quivered as he pressed his lips to the tantalizing spot, then lower still to the pulsating bud of her desire.

A shuddering gasp burst from her lips at the rapturous new sensations he aroused with each liquid caress of his tongue—agonizing ripples of pleasure coursing upward through her belly, a slow-burning heat building in her loins toward some wondrous final conflagration, the rising torment reaching to a feverish pitch of desire to have him finally inside her. As she felt herself peaking and knew she could not stem the bursting tide of pleasure, her hands clutched at the pillow beneath her head.

"Trevor. Trevor, hurry!" she moaned, not wanting to be alone in her ecstasy.

Quickly slipping off the bed, he maneuvered her till she lay with her buttocks resting at the very edge of the mattress, her long, slender legs folded to her chest. Spreading wide her thighs, he poised his hard manhood against her. Her single, earlier experience had taught her to expect a savage thrust, and instinctively she tensed in anticipation. Even in her frenzied state, she was yet startled at his unwonted gentleness. He entered her slowly, with seeming heedfulness. His heavy-lidded gaze, silvery with his own inner fire, was steady and somehow reassuring, on hers.

Even so, the pain came swift and unexpected, like a hot blade searing her depths. With a strangled cry, she clenched about his probing member.

Myles stilled, a curious gleam of triumph leaping in his eyes. Then he was stroking the quivering flesh of her inner thighs with long, soothing strokes.

"Softly, my love," he murmured. "It was too soon for you, but do you not fight it, the pain will not take from the pleasure."

She had difficulty grasping the sense of his words, but his low, easy tone was somehow comforting. By degrees she relaxed to the slow, pulsating rhythm of his renewed

248

movement, losing herself in the sensual arousal that dwarfed her pain. Her climax, when it came, was neither so intense nor so shattering as that other time, but was deeper, more soul-satisfying. She was drinking in long, thirsty breaths, her half-closed eyes locked on his, sustaining her, carrying her upward into new heights of ecstasy. As she felt the moist, hot tidal wave building once more inside her, she arched her head backward. He thrust deeply, his seed bursting forth, a catalyst for her own release. Myles's name breathed through her lips on a gusty sigh and, wrapping her legs around his lean waist, she shuddered with wave after wave of pleasure.

Myles shared her release, communicated in the exquisite, rippling contractions of her flesh gripping his. With their passion spent at last, he eased onto the bed at her side, her legs still clasping him to her. Suddenly Sabra bit her lip to keep from crying out in startlement as, propping himself on one elbow, he leaned over her lithe, slender body to peer into her face.

He was breathing heavily, and his eyes were dark with lingering passion—and with a strange, hard glint of triumph.

"Now . . . tell . . . me," he whispered huskily, "I have no . . . *say* . . . in the matter."

For a stunned moment she lay staring up into his face, hardly comprehending what he had said. Then the terrible significance of his words at last sank home.

"Damn you to bloody hell!" she exploded, striking out at him with her fist.

Laughing, Myles ducked his head and rolled over on top of her, pinning her to the bed with his weight. In a cold fury she writhed beneath him, fighting with all her strength to shove him off. Then uttering a sudden, sharp gasp of pain, she abruptly ceased to struggle.

"Hellsfire!" rasped Myles, throwing himself free of her

slender length. Her low groan as she clasped a hand to her ribs and curled convulsively into a tight ball on her side was like a knife twisting at his insides. "Sabra. Dammit, woman, what is it?"

"It's . . . nothing. A bruise," she panted. "Please . . . just . . . leave me alone!"

"Don't be a fool," he muttered harshly. "You're hurt."

"And if I am, 'tis . . . only what I deserve," she retorted bitterly. "I fell, rushing headlong like the veriest idiot to your rescue." Her brittle laugh ended abruptly in a groan. "Oh, God, it hurts like the devil."

"I promise it shall hurt more if you don't lie still and let me have a look at it," Myles declared grimly, yet his touch was surprisingly gentle as he tried to force her hand away from her side.

Weak with pain, Sabra could not find the strength to resist him. In a gesture, half weary, half defiant, she flung herself onto her back and lifted her arms over her head.

"Good God," he muttered, his aspect exceedingly grim at the sight of the angry discoloration the size of his fist along her ribs. "You little fool, why didn't you tell me?"

"You didn't ask. Besides, there was nothing you could have done," she countered bitterly and, covering herself with her arms, made as if to get up.

"Oh, no, you don't!" he growled, pulling her back again. "I suppose it never occurred to you I might simply have wished to know that you had hurt yourself. To prevent causing you further pain, if nothing else."

For an instant she stared up at him with wide, incredulous eyes.

"Now, why, I wonder, did I not think of that?" she marveled acidly. "Is *that* what you intended with this most recent demonstration of your solicitude—to save me greater anguish—by playing me for a fool? You will no doubt pardon me if I find it difficult to express my gratitude. Indeed, in the future, it would be better if you restrained from doing me any more such favors. I swear, captain, if you ever touch me again, I shall most assuredly shoot your eyes out!"

Myles grinned, apparently unmoved at the prospect. "Kind of you to warn me, my love. But I'm afraid I shall just have to take my chances, for I intend to lay my hands on you a great deal from now on. It is, after all, a husband's prerogative to make love to his wife."

"Your wife!" she exclaimed, hardly able to credit her ears. Faith! How *could* he be so despicable as to continue his bizarre game at her expense? "Good God, you go too far, captain!"

"Nevertheless, you will marry me just as soon as I have taken care of this troublesome affair with Channing."

"How sure you are," she choked, hating him for hurting her so. "But, indeed, I can think of nothing which could persuade me to do anything so utterly inconceivable,"

"Then allow me to refresh your memory, my love," he muttered thickly and, closing his steely fingers about her wrists crossed over her chest, bent his head to kiss her. Helplessly, Sabra felt the leap of fire in her veins. After a moment or two she ceased to struggle.

No little time later, Myles propped himself on one elbow to study the interesting pallor on her face. She lay rigidly still, her eyes like deep pools of anguish.

"You *know!*" she whispered huskily.

A smile, faintly rueful, touched his lips.

"And how not?" he drawled, winding a lock of her hair about his finger. "Even in my delirium, I could not but realize that you, my darling Sabra, are exquisite in bed."

Sabra winced and turned her head away.

251

"Damn you!" she breathed, clenching shut her eyes.

Instantly his hand stilled in her hair. "Did you truly think to keep it from me, *ma mie?*" he queried softly. "Or that I should not be interested to know what happened between us last night?"

"I thought," she said, looking up at him with flashing eyes, "that it could not possibly make a difference. We are enemies, you and I, and what happened doesn't change a thing. I'm afraid I must refuse the honor you would do me, captain. In truth, there is no need for it."

His short bark of laughter seemed to pierce through her.

"But on the contrary," he countered cynically, "after last night and today, there is every need."

Instantly Sabra bridled with angry resentment.

"Spare me your gallantry, captain," she said witheringly. "I assure you I have no intention of wedding you to save either my reputation or my name."

"Nor am I asking you to. You naive little fool, do you believe for one moment I should offer if that were my only reason? I assure you it is not my habit to ruin innocents, and you, as I recall, were no unwilling participant."

Sabra felt her cheeks flame. Good God, he made her sound the veriest whore! she fumed. Apparently he recalled everything that had happened—everything, that is, except that the woman upon whom he had vented his passion had been a virgin. But then, she had obligingly removed the evidence had she not? she bitterly reflected. And even if she were to show him the soiled bedding, an act which she vowed she would rather die than perform, he was far more likely to discredit her than take her word for what it was—the word of a woman he had already condemned as an opportunist, curse him!

"No, I was not unwilling," she said at last, the cool

green depths of her eyes unfathomable. "But then, why—"

The wry glint of humor in the look he gave her made the breath catch in her throat so that she could not go on.

"Faith, must I spell it out?" he quizzed her, and with sensuous deliberation lowered his head to kiss those haunting orbs, first one and then the other.

"*Don't!*" uttered Sabra in a strangled voice and wrenched her head aside. "Don't play with me. I cannot bear it."

"Damnit, woman, look at me!" His hand, cupping the side of her face, compelled her to meet his eyes, glittery in the dim light of the cellar. "This is no game, I promise you," he said in deadly seriousness. "Good God, I've been driven mad with wanting you. Since the first time I saw you at Almacks' and looked into those cursed lovely eyes—witch's eyes! And your lips, so cool when they smile and so damnably enticing. Awake or asleep, I cannot escape the truth. And nor can you. Not anymore. Not after last night. If there is an an ounce of honesty in you, you will admit that you belong only to me. I want you, Sabra—as my wife. And I fully intend to have you."

For an instant Sabra felt her senses reel as it came to her that she need only utter a single word to have what she most desired. To be in reality Myles's wife! It was too incredible to be true. Indeed, it was a hopeless dream, a fantasy impossible to be realized! She was a rebel spy and, worse, the mysterious privateer who had wreaked havoc on illicit shipping up and down the coast. It was preposterous to suppose even for a second that she might dare wed an English naval captain, especially this one.

Her heart bitter with despair, she forced herself to look at him.

"Do you?" she demanded passionately. "Then take me if you will! But as your mistress, nothing more. Such an

253

arrangement is better suited to us. Indeed, it is all that you and I can ever have."

The glint of steel between his slitted eyelids was like a dagger to her heart.

"But I have a mistress," he reminded her. " 'Tis a wife that I require. Make no mistake, my love, when the time comes, you will marry me. I make it a point never to be wrong."

For an instant green eyes scintillating sparks clashed with gray.

"In this instance," she flung wearily back at him, "you are far off the mark, I promise you. Too much lies between us for that time ever to arrive."

"Perhaps." His teeth flashed in a reckless grin, and Sabra's heart lurched as he lightly flicked her chin with his forefinger. "I shall, at any rate, consider the gauntlet thrown," he said, then suddenly became stone sober. "In exchange for which, I want your promise you will do nothing foolish. You must trust me in this, Sabra. Channing believes himself to be treading on very thin ice, else he would never have gone to such lengths to bring us in. To give yourself up to him now would be worse than useless. It would be playing into his hands."

A troubled furrow creased her brow, and he had little difficulty in reading the uncertainty in her face.

"Obviously," he murmured, running his fingers lightly through her hair, "we are very close to having him exactly where we want him. We must buy time enough to spring the trap, *ma mie*, and to do that, we have to elude the baronet just a little longer. *That* is the only way you can insure your brother's safety, I promise you. Believe me, Sabra, we are after the same thing, you and I. It needs only your word you will not try to go it alone."

Sabra's lips curved in a faint, ironic smile.

"Oh, no, captain. It shall need a deal more than that.

Nevertheless, for the time being, you have my promise. I shall not undertake to go after Channing—unless it becomes clear to me I have no better course before me."

Mentally he cursed. He required more than that from his mettlesome love if he hoped to keep her safe until he had the proofs on Sir Wilfred Channing. With an effort he subdued the impulse to pursue the matter further and succeeded only by assuring himself that once they reached the cottage on the East River, there would undoubtedly be time enough to win her over. Still, he could not quite subdue a vague feeling of unease as reluctantly he gave in to her.

"So be it," he drawled, his face inscrutable as he released her and sat up. "And now I suggest we both prepare ourselves for a very cold and undoubtedly less than gratifying journey."

The feeling had not left him when, some time later, Hawkes returned to find him fully dressed and stretched out on the bed, waiting. At the old man's questioning look, Myles allowed his lip to curl sardonically as he nodded toward a blanket stretched across one corner of the cellar.

"She's in there, changing. Perhaps in the meantime you would care to join me in a brandy, Mr. Hawkes. Before we undertake to elude the king's soldiers, I should be interested in hearing whatever else you might be able to relate about events going forth in the world outside."

For a moment Hawkes stared wordlessly at the relaxed figure on the bed as he absorbed the significance of that softly drawled speech. Then at last a wry grin of enlightenment tugged at the corner of his mouth.

"If I understand you correctly, captain, I suppose a drink would not be out of order," he responded, wondering how Myles had managed the thing. Obviously the bloody Englishman was a man of many talents, not the

255

least of which was a soft touch and a silver tongue with the ladies.

Splashing a generous portion of brandy into two metal cups, he handed one to Myles and lifted the other.

"To Miss Tyree's delivery from the devil's henchman, sir," rumbled Hawkes. "And may the black-hearted baronet meet a swift and bitter end."

"Quite so," murmured Myles, but did not immediately raise the cup to drink. His peculiarly compelling gaze appeared to gauge the temper of the American. "I, however, had a somewhat different toast in mind. To those who pay the price of war, Mr. Hawkes. Indeed, to you, sir, and to your grandson, who suffered unjustly, it would seem, at the hands of my countrymen. God grant that one day men will learn a better way to deal with one another."

The old man's startled glance narrowed sharply on the officer's impassive features. Then his throat working, he slowly nodded.

"Amen to that," he muttered gruffly, no longer wondering how Myles had achieved the seeming impossible with the headstrong young beauty. He supposed even among the accursed British, one must occasionally run across an Englishman who was a man.

Chapter 16

Hurriedly, Sabra exchanged her borrowed midshipman's uniform for the warm woolen clothing that Hawkes had brought. Then sweeping her hair back as best she could without the aid of either brush or comb, she hastily bound it in a queue at the nape of her neck and stepped back to view herself in the small cracked mirror she had discovered in a box of old, discarded things.

A rueful smile touched her lips at the sight of the hoydenish creature staring back at her. The piquant face framed in unruly wisps of curls was a far cry from the fashionably turned-out young woman of the night before. In that other girl there had been an air of calm composure, even hauteur, in the tilt of the stubborn chin, but that seemed gone now, replaced by a sort of reckless determination, a desperation almost, which she had never seen in herself before. But more than that, it was in her eyes. Those usually cool green pools of unfathomed depths appeared suddenly shadow-ridden and wild, as though a storm simmered somewhere just beneath the surface, ready to break forth.

Faith, was it only yesterday that she had donned the red silk dress and her mother's diamonds and descended the curved staircase to meet Myles? It seemed a lifetime ago, and all that she had known and done before that moment, only vague and distant memories, as if they had happened to some other woman in some other place in time. And in truth, the Sabra Tyree who had reigned over the drawing rooms and elegant balls of New York's fashionable élite seemed gone forever. In her place was this strange wild-eyed creature with a disquieting aura of mystery about her—and all because of Trevor Myles!

Unable to stand the sight of herself any longer, Sabra pressed her forehead against the wall and clenched shut her eyes. Oh, God, how was she to live with this terrible tumult inside her, this dreadful yearning for that which could only be fleetingly hers? As if to add to her torment, an image of piercing gray eyes and stern lips curled in a cynical smile rose up to haunt her. Myles's voice saying he wanted her as his wife, indeed, intended to have her, sounded over and over again inside her brain. And what if, she wondered suddenly, the words had been of love instead of desire? Could she then have found the strength to deny him as she had?

A muffled blow against the cellar door was followed in quick succession by two more. Sabra's head came up with a jerk. For a bare instant, she stood, poised and tensed. Then swiftly she turned and slipped past the makeshift screen into the greater part of the cellar.

Immediately her eyes sought Myles, who was sliding his legs over the side of the bed. With a finger to the lips, he motioned her to silence. Carefully Hawkes scooted his chair back from the table and climbed to his feet. Easing a pistol into the pocket of his greatcoat, he glanced from one to the other of his companions.

"Likely it's nothing—only Jubal with the sled," he suggested quietly. "Still, I reckon it never hurts to be prepared. You two wait here while I go and see who it is." Without another word, he crossed to the stairway and went up.

The cold whisper of steel brought Sabra's head around. She saw Myles standing with his sword in hand. Something in the pale glitter of his eyes sent a chill shuddering through her. Then a faint, sardonic smile curved his lip and, leaning forward, he dimmed the lantern.

As the cellar was plunged into near darkness, it suddenly came to Sabra with numbing clarity what it would mean to Myles if, instead of Jubal, the king's soldiers waited on the other side of that door. No matter that Channing had manipulated the truth to frame the one man who might have brought him down, Myles himself had done nothing as yet to tarnish either his command or his honor. All that, however, would be instantly finished, along with his career and any possibility of clearing his name of the charges already pending against him, the moment he was forced to meet king's men over drawn swords.

The realization that he would of his own, free will render up so great a sacrifice in her defense shook her to the core. To lose his ship, his name, his honor would be tantamount to destroying everything that made him what he was. Indeed, it would be kinder to end his life than to leave him with nothing, she thought and knew instantly she could not allow that to happen.

Unexpectedly her mind flashed back to the plunging decks of the *Nemesis,* to the British frigate *Black Swan* standing off the stern like a prophet of doom, and to William Skyler saying there were worse things than striking the colors when the odds were all against her. She could hear him yet, telling her how they had worked it all out, and he and "the lads." Willingly would they give up the ship without a fight, let themselves be taken and thrust up in chains so long as it meant that she would go free and her secret thus remain forever inviolate. She need only go below and exchange her breeches for one of the fancy gowns she kept stashed in

259

her cabin.

The cellar door opened and then dropped back in place as Hawkes let himself out, and behind him, Skyler's voice, like an echo from the past, seemed to whisper through the darkness. "If you was locked below when the British come aboard, it'd be natural for them to think you was here against your will. We'd say you was a prisoner that we'd took for ransom, like."

A plan having taken root in her mind, Sabra deliberately drew the captain's gun from her belt and stepped back into the shadows.

Myles, preoccupied with his own less than rewarding thoughts, had been jarred from his reverie by the sound of the cellar door dropping into place. Impatiently, he had shaken off the dark mood, occasioned by the bitter certainty that he had failed utterly to anticipate the baronet's latest strategy, and glanced over his shoulder in search of Sabra. Upon discovering that his troublesome love had apparently vanished into thin air, he experienced an unpleasant prickle of nerve endings.

Damn the chit! Surely she had not been fool enough to follow Hawkes up the stairs, he told himself, and knew immediately that that was quite possibly exactly what she had done. Indeed, how like the impetuous Tyree to fling herself recklessly into the very forefront of danger! Angry with himself for not foreseeing such a contingency, he started across the cellar for the narrow stairway.

The chill caress of a gun barrel against his ribs took Myles unpleasantly by surprise. Stiffening, he half turned before a hard voice, distinctly familiar, stopped him cold.

"I suggest you stand easy, captain. Indeed," murmured

Sabra, reaching out to relieve him of his blade, "I think you shall have little need for this."

"Sabra! What the devil—" exclaimed Myles, surprise giving way to impatient bafflement. "Dammit, woman, this is no time for games."

"Indeed, captain, it is not. Which is why I can assure you that I have seldom in my life been more deadly in earnest. Until we know who awaits us beyond that door, you, sir, may consider yourself my prisoner."

For an instant Myles struggled with a feeling of disbelief. Then the truth hit him like a hard fist to the belly. Damn the chit! he cursed, in the grips of a sudden, cold rage. How cleverly she had duped him, putting him off with an intentionally vague promise that she had never meant to keep—but, no. She had been even cleverer than that. She had kept to her word, for obviously before she had ever given it, she was already convinced her only viable course was to rid herself of his interference. And what better way than to turn him over to the troops who were sure to come looking for him? Good God, he thought furiously, surely he could not have been so mistaken in her. And yet why else should she pull such a stunt as this unless she had meant all along to fulfill the final term of Channing's offer?

Having thus come in a matter of a few seconds to certain damning conclusions, Myles experienced a sudden deadly calm. He had a score to settle with the baronet, which would not rest until he had the evidence needed to convict Channing of treason, proofs, which, he doubted not, were in Sabra Tyree's possession. It would be a cold day in hell before he allowed Channing to slip out of his fingers now simply because an impossibly headstrong, incurably designing female would rather risk losing everything than submit to the man who had sworn to tame her. The game was not finished by a long shot, would not be until the final cards were played out. And he, she would soon learn, had no intention of walking away the loser.

An exceedingly grim smile touched his lips. So far, he had commanded an amazing tolerance in dealing with the impetuous beauty, but now he found his patience was worn thin. Indeed, just how thin, Miss Tyree was about to discover.

"No doubt," he observed with flinty dispassion, "you are to be congratulated, *ma mie*. You played your part brilliantly. I confess you had me wholly convinced I was grossly mistaken ever to have believed you the heartless jade rumor made you out to be. You must pardon my curiosity. Now that you have me at something of a disadvantage, what is it, exactly, that you intend?"

Impossible not to discern the heavy irony in his tone, Sabra flushed. How easily he believed the worst of her!

"Intend, captain?" she retorted bitterly. "You know me so well, I feel sure you will have little difficulty in figuring that out for yourself. For now, I must ask you to return to your sickbed and remain quiet. Oh, and, captain, do please desist from making any sudden moves. By now you can have few illusions as to what I am capable of doing."

At the prod of his own gun in his back, Myles smiled grimly and obligingly moved toward the bed. Sabra followed, her nerves on edge as she strained to detect the faintest sound from beyond the cellar.

The groan of the door being lifted echoed down the stairs, followed by a sudden burst of sunlight. Squinting to make out the figures limned against the opening, Sabra felt her breath suddenly hard in her throat. Even in the uncertain light, there could be no mistaking those powerful shoulders, which seemed to dwarf Hawkes's

262

slighter build.

"Jubal!" she exclaimed softly, letting the gun drop limply to her side. In a flash, hard fingers clamped about her wrist and, pinning her arm painfully behind her back, disarmed and dragged her into the shadows.

"And now, Miss Tyree," murmured a velvet voice next to her ear, "if you have no wish to discover of what *I* am capable, I strongly suggest you behave yourself."

"Myles, no!" she exclaimed in a harsh whisper. "You don't understand!"

"Oh, but I'm afraid I do," he answered. "Far more than you give me credit for. Did you truly believe turning me over to the troops would be enough to satisfy the baronet? At best it was an empty gesture. Indeed, you'd have done better to put a bullet through my head. That, at least, might have been something worthy of Channing's harlot."

Sabra flushed, torn between anger and at his harshness and dismay at the sudden turn events had taken. Somehow she had to make him understand.

"No! It wasn't like that at all —" she began, twisting her head back in order to see his face. The look in his eyes froze the words, unuttered, in her mouth.

"You should have waited, *ma mie,* before tipping your hand. I was prepared to use my not inconsiderable influence to clear you of any suspicion. Fool that I was, I meant even to go so far as to try and win a parole for your brother. But now, I'm afraid, it's too late," he uttered chillingly. "It would appear Hawkes and your faithful Jubal are nearly on the point of descending."

Sabra could almost hear her own heartbeat as she felt Myles go suddenly unnaturally still. Unreasoning fear gripped her heart. Believing himself betrayed, might he not be capable of anything? Indeed, in the circumstances, he would be a fool if he did not take Jubal and

263

Hawkes out before they realized what he was about. Merciful God, she must make him listen before it was too late!

"Myles, I beg you," she uttered hoarsely, straining in his clasp. "You must believe me. Jedediah has no part in this. And Jubal will do as I say. You are in no danger from them, I swear it. I alone must be held responsible."

"Even so," murmured Myles in heartless tones. "And now it is time you paid the price of your ill-considered actions."

Sabra blanched as she stared into pitiless gray eyes, cold-seeming and utterly ruthless in their intent. A terrible pain rent her heart; indeed, for the barest instant it seemed she must give in to the bitter hurt of knowing he could condemn her without having granted her even so much as the benefit of a doubt. Then anger, swift and terrible, came to her rescue.

All at once she straightened.

"Enough, captain. Do you think I don't know you are bluffing?" she demanded, scathing in her contempt of him. "I'm the only one who can prove your innocence. Indeed, the only one who can give you what you want—all you have really wanted from the very first—Channing's head on a platter!"

Myle's grin was singularly mirthless.

"Your grasp of the situation is, as ever, flawless, my love. Rest assured, I have no intention of putting a period to your wretched existence, only of disabusing you of certain unfortunate misconceptions. If you would choose to play the harlot, *ma mie*, you should take care to be an honest one. Unlike others upon whom you have used your obvious charms, I am never, I assure you, one to be taken lightly."

Without warning he sank down on the bed and

264

yanked her hard across his knee.

Sabra, already livid with rage, could hardly summon the voice to protest his obvious intention. "You wouldn't dare!" she rasped.

"Oh, but I would," he pronounced grimly. "I cannot throttle you as you deserve, but I can, most assuredly, beat you."

Mercilessly he brought the flat of his hand down resoundingly against her backside.

Sabra uttered a strangled scream of pain and purely feminine outrage and erupted into a furious struggle. At great risk to his wounded arm, Myles managed to get in three more punishing licks before she was able to fling herself free of her tormentor, only then to land ignominiously on the floor. Instantly she scrambled to her feet and was met by the loathsome sound of Myles's laughter.

"*Damn* you!" she breathed, breasts heaving, her magnificent eyes ablaze with indignation. "*No* man can dare lay a hand on me and expect to go free."

"Quite so, *ma mie,*" drawled the captain with a curiously ironic twist of the lips. "But then, that was never your intention was it? You did say you would go to any lengths to win your brother's freedom, did you not? Therein lay my greatest error. At least in that, I should have taken you at your word."

Sabra stared speechlessly into the hard cynical features and could scarcely credit either her eyes or her ears. How dare he condemn her without giving her the least chance to defend herself! And then to raise his hand to her as if she were little better than some low-born strumpet. Good God, he should be horsewhipped for such insolence! Indeed, she'd half a mind to give the order. If not Hawkes, then most certainly Jubal would willingly oblige her.

265

As if summoned, Jubal towered suddenly over her, a long-nosed pistol in his hand trained with ominous deliberation on the English captain.

"You all right, Miss Sabra?"

The unmistakable menace in those softly spoken words seemed to hang in the air. Sabra swallowed dryly, anger and bitter resentment leaving a sour taste in her mouth.

"Miss Sabra?" Jubal repeated.

Out of the corner of her eye she saw Hawkes watching her with curious intensity and inexplicably she flushed. Then suddenly rage gave way to icy resolve.

"Indeed, I am not," she answered. Her eyes glittery and cold, she met the captain's mocking glance across the intervening distance. "Henceforth, this man is to be our prisoner. He is never for a moment to be left unguarded. Is that understood?"

"I, for one, can't say that I understand it at all," spoke up Hawkes, laconically. "Seems to me you've a mite of explaining to do."

Instantly Sabra bridled, keenly aware how incomprehensible her motives must seem in the face of all that Hawkes had been witness to in the alley and, later, in this very cellar. Let him wonder. What he, or anyone else, might think of her could no longer possibly matter.

"If it's explanations you want, I suggest you ask the captain," she uttered coldly. "He, no doubt, will be happy to oblige you. Jubal—the captain's pistol, if you please. And his sword, over there on the floor."

In glacial detachment Sabra waited for Jubal to carry out her orders. Myles, with a contemptuous curl of handsome lips, coolly flipped the gun in his hand and extended it, butt first, to the unsmiling Negro. Still, her gaze never flickered, nor did she betray by any outward sign the realization that she knowingly was destroying whatever remained of the tenuous bond that briefly had sprung up between the captain and herself. It was as if every emotion she had ever felt, along with any illusions she might once have entertained about herself and Myles, had all been frozen up inside of her, a state, which, curiously enough, had left her mind astonishingly uncluttered.

"Mr. Hawkes," she said when Myles had been duly relieved of his weapons, "I should be grateful were you to keep a close guard on the prisoner in order that I might have a few words with Jubal."

Hawkes gave a wry face and shrugged.

"Whatever you say, Miss Tyree. Only I'm a little confused by the sudden shift in the captain's status. Do you expect me to shoot the poor bastard if he takes a sudden notion or just knock him alongside the skull? The one's likely to be a whole lot more permanent than the other, and I sure wouldn't want to get it wrong."

Laughing shortly, Myles quirked a cynically amused eyebrow. "I suggest, Mr. Hawkes, that you might boil the prisoner in oil, then hang, draw and quarter him without the least fear of incurring Miss Tyree's displeasure. It would seem whatever usefulness I might once have served Channing's doxy has come to a rather swift and sudden end."

It appeared that the captain's barb had reached its mark, as Sabra suddenly checked in turning away. Slowly she came about again.

"On the contrary, Mr. Hawkes," she said, a cold gleam flickering in the depths of the sea-green eyes. "I have every wish that the captain will continue in reasonably good health. If he gives you any trouble, shoot him in the arm or a leg. It has already been demonstrated, after all, that even thus impaired he is well able to perform the one function which might prove in any way

267

useful to a 'harlot' and a 'doxy.' Now, if you will excuse me, I have more important matters to attend."

At her pointed reference to the unflattering terms with which he variously had described her, the corners of the captain's lips twitched appreciatively. Odd, but did he not know better, he would have believed the lady was offended, he mused sardonically.

Then immediately he sobered as it came briefly to him to wonder if he could possibly have misjudged her. Unwittingly, he suffered a sudden unfamiliar wrench as he recalled her sweet fire, her strength, her unaffected manner as she tended his wound, nursed him through his fever — gave herself to him! He had been utterly convinced she was as fine and as good as she was beautiful; indeed, he had already seen demonstrated with what rare courage and unswerving loyalty she would fight for one who held a place in her heart. For Wesley Locke, he appended wryly, ruefully aware that he was fast developing an intense dislike for that paragon among men.

In fact, at the thought of the half-brother, who would seem to possess the lady's affection to the exclusion of anyone else, Myles experienced a decidedly unpleasant jolt. Good God, he was demonstrating all the signs of jealousy, a state to which he had, up until now, considered himself immune. Yet there was no denying that the rage he had felt at the beautiful Sabra's betrayal had sprung more from the knowledge that he had failed utterly to win the smallest place for himself in her affections than it had from anything else. The chiseled features took on a decidedly grim aspect, for he was ruefully aware that, in spite of everything, he had not altered one whit in his determination to have her for himself.

Finally, conscious of baffled anger, both at himself and his incomprehensible love, he turned to a consideration of what his own next course of action should be.

"Jubal, I was never so glad to see anyone!" Sabra exclaimed softly, drawing him apart from Hawkes and the odious captain. Eagerly she scanned his face. "Quickly, tell me everything. Phoebe—and Wayne and the others—are they safe?"

"They was when I seen 'em last. I expect Phoebe done put the fear of God in them no-good white trash." At the quizzical lift of Sabra's brow, a faint grin tugged at the corners of his mouth. "She was waitin' up, like she always does, for you to come home, when they come bustin' in the house and started wreckin' things. Pullin' the drawers out of chests and dumpin' everything on the floor. Well, you knows Phoebe. That ole black nanny come rarin' in, swingin' the broom like she does at them stray dogs that gets in the yard. Knocked the gun out of one of 'em's hand before he knew what hit him. And had another penned in the corner squealin' like a shoat in the hand of a butcher. Then Mr. Robert come in. If he hadn't tole her to let the gentlemen see for themselves we ain't got nothin' to hide, I expect she'd drove 'em plumb out of the neighborhood."

"Faith, I might have guessed," choked Sabra, little knowing whether to laugh or cry with relief. But then all thoughts of the redoubtable Phoebe fled as she turned to the one thing that was ever uppermost in her mind.

"Jubal," she said, instantly sobering. "Wesley is alive."

"Yes, Miss Sabra."

Something in the Negro's studied impassivity caused icy fingers to clutch at Sabra's heart. Nervously she paced a couple of steps and turned.

"I think Wayne was going to tell me that last evening, but he never had the chance. And since I learned about Wes from Captain Myles, I've been plagued by the fear

269

that wasn't all Robert knew. Jubal, has he said anything to you?"

Her heart sank as something flickered behind the expressionless eyes. "Jubal, what is it? Please, you must not keep it from me."

With obvious reluctance, Jubal nodded.

"I reckon as how you got a right to hear the truth. Mr. Wesley's alive all right. But we got to hurry and get him out of that place does we want him to stay that way. You'd best brace yourself, Miss Sabra. Mr. Wesley's real bad. Mr. Robert say he can't last much longer."

Sabra's face went suddenly ashen, and for a moment it seemed she wavered on the point of swooning. Jubal's hand reached out as if to steady her. But all at once the slender shoulders straightened.

"Then we shall get him out," she said, "if we have to lay siege to the bloody ship to do it!"

"I'm sorry, Miss Sabra, but I reckon it ain't that easy. Not with the whole damn garrison out lookin' for you and the cap'n. If we does get away from this white man's town, which ain't real promisin' right now, you can be sure gettin' back in again'll be the devil's own work."

"But I haven't the least intention of leaving the city just now," she did not hesitate to inform him. "So that cannot possibly signify. Indeed, it occurs to me that I have been away from home quite long enough."

Jubal frowned. He had seen that look in those lovely orbs before. But Sabra, beginning to pace as she sorted her thoughts aloud, did not notice.

"Where is Wayne? I must see him as soon as possible."

"Mr. Robert be waitin' at the house, Miss Sabra, till you sends word where to meet."

270

"Thank goodness for that much at least. Faith, there is so much to be done," she fretted, "and so little time in which to do it. First I must talk with Robert. Then somehow I have to find out what happened to Ellsworth and Miss Barrett after they left us. Surely they will know what steps the admiralty is taking. But first we must think of a way to get the captain into the house on Nassau without being seen." Suddenly she came to a halt in front of the stolid-faced Jubal. "You must help me, Jubal. We can use the sled to transport him as far as the alley in back, but then getting him inside would seem something of a problem."

"There's the old trellis on the blind side of the house," Jubal ventured doubtfully after a moment. "Where the drive go to the stables in back. I reckon there won't nobody see a man slip from the sled and up to the balcony outside Mr. Robert's room, if he was to be real quick about it."

"Two men!" exclaimed Sabra softly, giving him a radiant look. "Or, rather, one man and what shall appear to be a boy. But that's perfect, Jubal. Don't you see, neither Channing nor the Redcoats will ever think to look for Myles right under their very own noses. He should be safe enough until I have dealt with Channing. We must get word to Skyler to have *Nemesis* ready to sail at a moment's notice. As soon as we have Wes safe, we shall turn our heels to New York once and for all, I promise you."

"If you says so, Miss Sabra," rumbled Jubal with something less than total conviction.

Sabra's eyes sparkled dangerously.

"Well, I *do* say it," she flashed back at him. Fitfully she walked a pace, then came back to confront him, her face set with bitter resolve. "Not anything or anyone shall keep me from seeing my brother free. In God's

271

name, you may take my oath on it!"

The sled, it soon developed, was of the sort used to carry freight inland from the docks during the winter months. The flatbed sat on rough-hewn wooden runners banded in steel rims and was conveniently loaded with supplies Sabra herself had, for her own private reasons, ordered shipped from England some time ago. In no little dismay, Sabra crawled through the opening beneath the tarp at the back and beheld the space that had been reserved for her next to Myles among the sundry barrels and wooden crates. Faith, there would hardly be room left to breathe when she squeezed in beside the more than six feet of insufferable masculinity that reposed with hands clasped casually behind the head and gray eyes observing her with sardonic amusement from beneath heavily drooping eyelids.

Now what the devil had *he* to look so smug about? she wondered crossly. And, indeed, the abominable captain had displayed an irritating insouciance ever since she had informed him of her intention to hold him prisoner in the house on Nassau until such time as it pleased her to turn him over to the British. Uneasily it came to her that only a man who was certain of regaining the upper hand in some, no doubt despicable, manner, could possibly view imprisonment with such marked unconcern. Firmly she wished him to the devil, telling herself that if Myles dared to try anything, she would quite happily order Jubal to put a bullet through him. Then at last, resolving to see what was delaying their departure, she turned and poked her head out through the opening at the back.

She found Hawkes, aided by Jubal, in the process of pulling the tarp in place in preparation of securing it with lines to the sled. Immediately sensing the old man's reticence, she suffered a swift stab of conscience for her earlier brusqueness. Hawkes, she realized, had deserved better from her.

When Jedediah glanced up from his task, he was met with a rueful look from troubled green eyes.

"I guess it's time to say good-bye," Sabra ventured, feeling her way. A flurry of snow sweeping beneath the tarp recalled her to an awareness of the clothing snug on her back. Her hand rose to finger the fabric of young Jed's coat. "I'll see that this and the other things are returned as soon as ever I can."

Hawkes nodded curtly then coughed to clear his throat.

"Yes, well," he growled, "never you mind about *them*. You've enough to worry about just keeping out of trouble. Now begone with you. It's too blasted cold for an old man to stand around jawing."

She had come to know him far too well in the short time they had been thrown together to be fooled by such talk. Indeed, there were times, she thought suddenly, when she felt she had known him all her life.

"Indeed it is too cold," she answered, unable to refrain from smiling. "I shall expect you to go right home, Jedediah Hawkes, and bundle up before the fire with a cup of hot cider. I should never forgive myself, after all, if you were to come down with an ague because of me."

"Nor should I forgive you," he grumbled back. "You've put me through enough trouble as it is. And if you've any feelings of gratitude, you'll oblige me by not showing your face around here again any time soon. Leastwise, not until we've driven the bloody English back across the Atlantic where they belong, d'you hear?"

"Yes, I hear," she murmured. "And I understand perfectly, I promise." Leaning forward all at once, she

273

kissed him lightly on the cheek before drawing back again. "Good-bye, Jedediah. And God bless you."

Hawkes was granted a final glimpse of cheeks, made rosy from the cold, and of eyes, luminous with tender affection. Then she had vanished from sight, and Jubal moved quickly to secure the tarp.

For a long moment Hawkes stood, oblivious to the cold, as he watched the sled pull out of the alley into Ann Street and head west, eventually to turn into Kip Street and vanish from sight.

"God keep you, lass," he muttered beneath his breath. Then his mouth twisted in a curiously wry grin. "And the bloody damned Englishman, too, I expect!" He spat a stream of tobacco juice into the snow before turning to trudge home.

Chapter 17

Beneath the tarp it was pitch black, and the air, in spite of the chill, was uncomfortably close. Sabra huddled at the very edge of the blanket spread beneath her and tried to ignore the misery of cramped limbs, growing increasingly numb from the bitter cold. She lay rigidly still, held there by stubborn pride and by the certainty that the slightest move would bring her unavoidably into contact with the thoroughly infuriating Myles.

At last, unable to bear her torment longer, she raised herself up on one elbow in the hopes of finding an opening, no matter how small, which might reveal at least a glimpse of the street outside. Just then the sled sharply swerved.

"Damn!" she muttered as, with a sickening thud, her forehead came up hard against the corner of a wooden crate. Her eyes swimming, she sank down onto the blanket and bit her lip to keep from giving vent to her sorely tried temper. The low murmur of a masculine voice heavily tinged with amusement did little to improve her disposition.

"In the circumstances, Miss Tyree, you would do well to dispense with both pride and the proprieties. I give you my solemn word not to eat you."

"No doubt I should be both gratified and comforted by such an assurance," retorted Sabra waspishly, "if I had the least notion what you are talking about."

"Odd," Myles whimsically reflected, "I was sure I had expressed myself perfectly clearly. Perhaps a small demonstration then. Purely to get the point across."

Sabra stifled a startled cry as a muscular arm circled her about the waist and dragged her relentlessly against the captain's lean, disturbing length.

"Now do you understand my meaning?"

"Your meaning, captain," Sabra assured him in accents of utter loathing, "has ever been as transparent as glass. Unhappily, 'tis your motives that escape me. Now, unless you would have me order Jubal to tie and gag you, I suggest you unhand me at once."

"I'm afraid you should have thought of that before we set out on the crowded thoroughfare, Miss Tyree," replied Myles imperturbably. "As to my motives, I assure you they are perfectly plain. I was merely trying to persuade you to adopt a commonsensical approach to our ordeal. It hardly seems practicable, you must agree, to insist on maintaining a proper distance, even between confirmed enemies, when confined in a space little larger than a pauper's casket."

"Agree? But of course, captain," she bitterly rejoined. "Indeed a hardened doxy such as I should have as little use for the proprieties as would a practiced rogue with devilry on his mind."

"Quite so," he applauded, apparently pleased at the quickness with which she had grasped the entirety of the situation. Furious, Sabra gritted her teeth.

"Which brings to mind certain other practical considerations," he had the gall to continue. "Two people nestled together to stay warm, for example. You cannot deny that it is more comfortable like this, now can you."

Feeling his hand begin to journey tantalizingly up her hip to tary fondly at her breast, presumably to explore the fascinating ramifications of his proposed theory, she rammed her elbow eloquently into his ribs.

"No, quite obviously I cannot," she said, smiling with distinct satisfaction at his involuntary "oomph." "But I fear you may wish to revise your opinion."

"Hornet!" he uttered.

"Unconscionable bully!" she countered without the least remorse.

For the space of a heartbeat or two there was total silence. Then unexpectedly Myles threw back his head and laughed, a low, infectious rumble, which sorely tried Sabra's mettle. Indeed, only by deliberately calling forth every iniquitous deed he had ever perpetrated against her was she at last able to recall that her present situation was anything but a cause for mirth. By that, and by the fact that a harsh shout abruptly split the air.

"Halt, in the name of the king!" penetrated the suddenly charged silence with forceful eloquence.

Sabra's heart gave a convulsive leap as Myles's arm tightened significantly about her waist. Then his lips came near her ear.

"I trust, my love," he murmured infuriatingly, "that you have a *convincing* explanation as to why you should be discovered lying in the arms of a known fugitive from justice while concealed beneath a tarp?"

"I shall claim, no doubt, to have been taken by a fit of madness!" she shot back at him. "It should be as convincing as the truth, which, after all is said and done, amounts practically to the same thing."

Then the pound of hooves filled her ears, and the sled, lurching, came swiftly to a halt.

"Er—you, there!" called out a rather uncertain tenor, which, oddly enough, seemed to jog a chord of memory in Sabra. "I—I'm afraid I shall have to ask you to stand down while the sergeant here searches your sledge."

"No need to be apologetic, lieutenant," came with an air of resigned tolerance as one of the men dismounted.

"You've the king's authority to back you up."

"Y-yes, of course. Thank you, sergeant. I'll try to remember that in future."

"You do that, sir," was the sergeant's dry response. Then, as if to obliterate any manifestations of appreciative mirth among the ranks, he bellowed the order, "Eyes front and center! That's better. Now then—McCleary and Jones—let us see what we have here."

The sounds of harness and creaking leather followed by the crunch of boot soles in the snow came to Sabra like a bad dream. In spite of the cold, she could feel the sweat begin to trickle over her ribs beneath her shirt. Grimly she resisted the urge to reach for the pistol tucked in her belt. If they were discovered, a gun would hardly be of use against armed dragoons. Involuntarily, she winced as someone experimentally jogged one of the crates only inches from her face. Then Jubal's voice, deceptively quiet and unobtrusive, carried thrillingly to her ears.

"Beggin' your pardon, Lieutenant Parker. But was there somethin' in particular you was lookin' for? Maybe was I to know what it was, I might could facilitate matters some."

Lieutenant Parker! The name hit Sabra like a revelation. But of course! She should have recognized that voice at once. Mentally she summoned up an image of a young, eager face, notable for round, blue, worshipful eyes that had a tendency to follow her every movement with unnerving perseverance whenever their owner was around. And he had been around quite often in the past six months or so. Indeed, he had been a regular member of her cortége from the moment Sabra had observed him at a governor's reception, ill at ease and so incredibly young that she had made a point to draw him out.

"I say, I know you. It's Jubal Henry, isn't it, though

278

I'd hardly recognize you in those clothes. Faith, man, don't tell me you're hauling freight? I mean, one would hardly expect to see Miss Tyree's man driving a rig like that."

"No, sir. I expect it does seem a mite strange, but Miss Sabra wouldn't trust no one else with this job. I expect she'd have my hide if the word was to get out what she be doin'. She was powerful riled when the colonel done tole her there be men fightin' that don't be gettin' enough food and such to keep a growed man alive. Right then was when Jubal Henry got into the freight-haulin' line. But then, you done tole me not to tell you that."

There was a moment or two in silence, during which the young lieutenant pondered the obvious implications in what Jubal had related and his men began to undo the ropes that secured the tarp in back.

"But then, am I to understand that this—this shipment is intended for—well, for our men on the lines? That Miss Tyree herself purchased them out of the goodness of her own heart?"

"I done already talked too much, you being sort of a special friend of Miss Sabra's 'n' all. But I reckon as how it can't matter much now. Them things was meant to go to the colonel soon's a ship was found that'd carry 'em. Now they'll most likely go the way of them other supplies that nobody knows what happens to. The word jest seem to have a way of getting in the wrong ears oncet it get out. But I reckon it can't be helped. An' you doesn't need to worry none that Miss Sabra'll hold it against you. Likely she be knowin' you be just doin' your duty."

Sabra felt suddenly queasy as the tarp fluttered loose in the back to let in a pale shaft of light from outside. Unexpectedly, Myles's face seemed to leap out of the gloom scant inches from her own. Taken unawares, she stared, unblinking, up at him out of huge, unguarded eyes. It seemed an eternity passed in that single moment, then Parker's voice suddenly rang out.

"Sergeant! Belay that. This man has a—er—a special writ of—of clearance from the general himself."

"Begging the lieutenant's pardon, sir, but are you real certain about that?" inquired the sergeant with an exaggerated air of stoic patience.

"Maybe the lieutenant's jest tired o' playin' soldier in the snow, sarge," speculated Jones, propping chin on elbow atop one of the wooden crates.

"Nah, ye got it all wrong, me boy. 'Tis time the sergeant were about changin' the poor laddie's nappies for 'im."

"That's enough, McCleary," snapped the sergeant. "Unless you've a mind to spend the duration walking the picket line. Now lieutenant. About this 'writ.' Meaning no disrespect, sir, but it *was* my understanding our orders were to spare no one. Might I suggest you consider most carefully wherein your duty lies before allowing *any* vehicle to go unsearched?

"You are impertinent, sergeant," replied the lieutenant coldly. "I've no need to be reminded of my duty, I assure you." Myles's eyebrow shot up in sardonic amusement, and Sabra nearly choked. Faith, but Lieutenant Parker, it seemed, had suddenly taken on a whole new stature. In fact, his voice resounded with the assurance of an army colonel as he continued to instruct his subordinate in his proper place. "Indeed," he said, "if you would spare us both a certain general's displeasure, might *I* suggest, sergeant, that you give the order to mount up. At *once,* sergeant! I shall join you directly."

Sabra could almost feel the sergeant's stupefaction in the instant or two before he suddenly snapped to attention.

"Yes, *sir!*" he answered smartly, then, no doubt with a

certain grim satisfaction, turned to carry out his orders. "All right, you bloody goldbricks. You heard the lieutenant. Mount up!"

Sabra had hardly come to realize their miraculous good fortune when Parker's voice sounded again in a confidential undertone to Jubal.

"I shall probably be courtmartialed for making false implications concerning a superior officer," he said, seemingly a trifle dazed at his own temerity.

"I wouldn't worry too much, lieutenant," Jubal offered in the way of comfort. "I expect you got what it take to keep them boys in line."

"You do?" Parker queried, apparently thunderstricken at such a possibility. But then the idea seemed suddenly to take on merit. "Yes. Yes, I believe you may be right. Er—thanks. And—and good luck. I hope you get those supplies through to Colonel—er—Colonel—"

"Ridgley, sir, that be sent down to Charleston a while back."

"Not Colonel Ridgley of the Fifty-second?" demanded Parker in a manner that sent a sudden chill down Sabra's back.

"Yes, sir, that very one."

"But, good God, man. Surely you must have heard? Ridgley caught a bullet. Some sort of accident on board the ship. One of the men cleaning a rifle or some such thing. Killed him almost instantly. . . . I—I say, did you hear something?"

Beneath the tarp Sabra stared fixedly at Myles over his hand clamped to her mouth while Jubal solemnly shook his head in the negative. "No, sir. I be too struck with the news about the colonel to hear nothin'. Miss Sabra goin' to take it real hard."

"Yes, I remember now. The colonel was used to call quite often in Nassau Street. But then, from all accounts he was a good officer—er—well liked by his

281

men, you know."

"Yes, sir, lieutenant," Jubal murmured sadly. "By all accounts, he was."

"Yes, well, I—I don't suppose I should keep the sergeant waiting." There was a small silence, then Parker could be heard mounting his horse. "Be pleased to give my respects to your mistress, if you would."

"Yes, sir. I surely will." The trample of horses' hooves filled the air, then Jubal spoke quietly. "They be gone, Miss Sabra." The two beneath the tarp could almost feel his hesitation. But at last he seemed to find the words to go on. "I reckon you heard everythin'. I'm really sorry, Miss Sabra."

Myles, his expression unreadable in the dim light, lifted his hand off Sabra's mouth. For a moment longer she stared with frozen blankness into his face. Then unable to speak around the ache in her throat, she closed her eyes and turned her head away.

"I suggest you secure the tarp, Jubal," Myles said at length. His gaze thoughtful on Sabra's averted profile, he settled back on one elbow. "And then get us out of here straightaway. Our luck cannot hold forever."

Happily, the rest of the way passed without mishap. Sabra, more stricken by the news of Ridgley's death than she would have thought possible, lay in brooding silence, and Myles, for once, seemed content to leave her alone to work out her grief in her own way. Thus the first sharp edge of anguish receded gradually to a bearable ache, leaving Sabra filled with a sort of dull lassitude.

It was inevitable, perhaps, that, mulling over her last encounter with the colonel, she should be visited with uneasy feelings of guilt. Indeed, when she recalled the manner in which she had maneuvered Ridgley into

282

helping her learn what had happened to Wes, she was overcome with shame. Just so had she used the young Lieutenant Parker, she thought, and so many others, who, dazzled by her gracious charm and beauty, had freely given of their trust. Oh, God, she had never known she could feel so unclean, so small and despicable! How could she ever have thought noble-seeming sentiments and fine abstractions enough to give her the right to betray that trust?

The sled checked and swerved in a wide arc as Jubal maneuvered a sharp corner. Taken unawares, Sabra started out of her somber reflections.

"We must be almost there," she said. Her blood quickened involuntarily, and all at once she was overtaken with an unbearable impatience to be free of the loathsome darkness. Indeed, she thought she must go mad if she could not soon draw a breath of fresh air, unfettered by the cursed tarp. Heedless of the crates and the swaying sled, she made her way to the back.

"Myles, help me loosen the lines. We must be ready to slip out when the sled passes between the stables and the house. We shall have only a second or two to reach the trellis unseen."

Her fingers were all thumbs as she fumbled impatiently with knots, which should have slipped easily free. Wet and half frozen, they resisted her every effort, until at last she called out to Myles in utter exasperation.

"Dammit, captain. Are you going to help me or not?"

"I'm afraid you greatly misjudge the matter if you think I should," Myles answered in grim amusement. "As a prisoner of war, I should be shot, and rightfully so, for aiding and abetting in my captivity. It is, on the other hand, my sworn duty to make every effort to escape. So, there it is. Unless you can show me good cause why I should help you, it would seem my hands are tied in the matter."

Weary from an almost sleepless night and weighted down yet with the oppression of a sorely stricken conscience, the captain's refusal seemed only the final culmination of events. Indeed, Sabra experienced an almost overwhelming urge to break out in laughter.

Good God, how neatly Myles had trapped her! she thought, on the verge of hysteria. For a great deal had been made suddenly quite odiously clear: the abominable captain's total lack of concern when she informed him that he was presently to take up residence in a cold and barren attic, for instance. And his smugness as he allowed himself to be ushered by gunpoint to the sled. Faith, she had been so intent on reaching the house on Nassau that it never once had occurred to her to wonder what she would do should Myles refuse to cooperate. He must have known all along that, indeed, there was nothing she could do without giving herself away. Good God, the absurdity of it all!

A giggle burst from her lips. Faith, what a fool she was, an utterly insane, idiotic fool! she thought and suddenly could not keep from laughing. Weakly she sagged against one of the crates at her back.

"It is . . . too . . . funny," she gasped, a hand clasped to her forehead. "A . . . plague on you . . . captain. Has . . . no one . . . ever . . . got the better of you?"

Finding Myles with startling suddenness at her side, Sabra gave a convulsive little hiccup.

"Not until you dropped into my life, Miss Tyree," he drawled in singularly dry tones. Leaning forward then, he loosened the ropes with a few quick tugs before settling broad shoulders against the crate across from her. "From that moment on, however, you seem to have been destined to best me at every turn."

Sabra lifted startled eyes, her laughter drying up at something she seemed to sense in him. In the pale streaks of light admitted by the fluttering tarp, she could just make out the probing intensity of his gaze. Feeling a vague sense of confusion steal over her, she glanced nervously away.

"I'm sure I don't know what you mean, captain," she retorted. "Indeed, on the contrary, you always seem to catch me out on the wrong foot. In any case, we are only moments from our destination, and while it is quite true that I can neither carry nor force you to come willingly, I can most assuredly betray you to the soldiers who are searching for you. I need only scream, and they, no doubt, will come riding *ventre à terre* to my rescue."

"You could," agreed the captain coolly, "but you won't."

"How abominably cocksure of yourself you are!" Sabra snapped irritably. "Indeed, that is the one thing I have always detested most in you. But that is neither here nor there. I believe I have already demonstrated that I am quite willing to let the king's men have you. It is, you recall, one of the stipulations of my brother's release."

"I recall it and a great deal more with the utmost clarity, I assure you."

"Well, then, you must also recall that I have sworn to go to any lengths to win my brother's freedom," she took pains to point out. "You yourself said, after all, that that was the one thing in which you should have taken me at my word, did you not?"

"I did," he replied, smiling oddly. Inexplicably, Sabra's heart gave a little flutter of fear.

"Yes, you did," she repeated firmly. "And you would do well to believe it."

"Oh, but I do believe it. In fact, I am quite sure of it, which is what makes it the most difficult piece to fit in the puzzle."

"I-I beg your pardon?" stammered Sabra, little trusting that look in his eye.

Without warning, he leaned forward and imprisoned the back of her head in his hand. For a long moment the gray hooded eyes peered intently into hers. Then, before she could protest, he drew her near and kissed her, his lips moving over hers with a sensuous deliberation that seemed somehow to draw upon her very soul. When at last he lifted his head, she was left feeling breathless and weak, her defenses in an utter shambles around her.

"Now tell me," he murmured, holding her with eyes that seemed somehow able to paralyze. "If you'd never any intention of turning me in, *why*, my love, did you see fit to pull a gun on me?"

"Wha-at?" Sabra stammered, her heart lurching in quick alarm. "I-I'm afraid I don't understand you, captain."

"I should simply like to know the purpose behind your latest game of pretense. Surely you must see the absurdity, after all, in this elaborate plan of yours to transport and then conceal me in an attic? Had you truly meant to give me over to the law, all of this would seem patently unnecessary, would you not agree?"

In a last ditch effort to stave off the inevitable, Sabra tried to pull away.

"Indeed I'm afraid I should not, captain," she managed with a semblance of her old hauteur. "You yourself have already explained both my motive and intent with your usual keen insight into my dubious character. I cannot see that I can have anything more to add—"

"Enough," he growled, yanking her back again. "No doubt I deserved that. I was, I fear, overly quick to judge you. And for that I suppose I should apologize. However, if you still think to lock me in your attic room, my love, I suggest you start talking. Otherwise you may rest assured that neither of us shall step down from this sled, for I shall have the truth from you, no matter how long it takes."

A single glance into the flint-eyed countenance told Sabra that, indeed, he would not be put off, and finally her temper flared.

"The truth, captain?" she said, flinging up her head in bitter defiance. "The truth is that I am everything you have said I am. Deceitful and conniving, a heartless jade, who thinks nothing of using men for my own purposes. Just as I have used you and that young lieutenant. Just as I used Colonel Ridgley."

Here, her voice broke and, turning her head sharply away, she swallowed hard.

Mercilessly Myles forced her chin around. Sabra's eyes flared in defiance as she found herself face to face with him once more. His lips curled in a humorless smile.

"I'm afraid that's not good enough, Miss Tyree," he stated baldly and covered her mouth with his in a bruising kiss.

Sabra broke into a furious struggle. Straining her supple length against his pitiless embrace, she rained her fists against his back in frantic blows rendered largely ineffectual in the close confines of the sledge. A strangled scream of rage sounded deep in her throat as she felt his hand undoing the buttons at the front of her jacket. In a cold fury, she bit his tongue as he forced it between her lips. Myles cursed and with a savage yank, ripped her shirt open to the waist. His hand punished her breast, chafing the nipple to a hard rigidity, kneading the soft flesh with fingers that hurt. Choking on tears of pain and fury, she raked her fingernails across the back of his hand. He caught her wrist in a steely grip and forced her arm into the small of her back. His mouth bruised her throat and sent unwitting shivers down her length, igniting sparks of desire within her.

Horrified at her body's betrayal, she braced her foot against the gate at the back of the sledge and shoved with all her might.

They toppled sideways to the floor. Myles grunted as he landed on his injured arm. His other still clasped her wrist at her back, and with his weight half on top of her and one muscular leg clamped around her slim hips, she was helpless to do more than stare her defiance at him. She lay still, her breasts rising and falling with each panted breath.

Myles straddled her, his breathing heavy as he peered into the white blur of her face. At the sight of the telltale gleam of wetness on her cheeks, his lips thinned to a grim line.

"Curse your stubborn pride!" he muttered harshly, as, with savage deliberation, he covered her mouth with his.

There was, nevertheless, a subtle difference in the way he kissed her this time, a difference that Sabra could not define. But nor could she stop herself from responding to it. In spite of herself, her lips softened to his and at last parted in a tremulous sigh. As his tongue sought out the warm moistness of her mouth, she did not retaliate as she had before, but opened to him, thrilling to the sensations of pleasure he aroused. Her blood flowed hot in her veins, and she hardly knew when she arched her slim hips into the sinewy embrace of his muscular thighs. As Myles released his grip on her wrist to frame the side of her face with his hand, she tugged impatiently at the waistband of his breeches, her fingers longing for the touch of his bare skin.

An unwitting cry of disappointment escaped her lips as he pulled abruptly away, his hand closing like a vise about her wrist.

"Not this time, my love," he breathed, his eyes glittery with a passion hardly restrained. "Not until I can come into you without causing you pain." At the soft pleading in her eyes, he uttered a groan and kissed her again, his mouth open and drawing sensuous moans of pleasure from deep within her as he savored her fiery response like rich, potent wine to his senses. Still, his eyes, when he released her, glinted with hard resoluteness, and once more he demanded the truth from her.

"Why the gun, Sabra?" he murmured, his thumb running lightly over her swollen lips, driving her to distraction. At last she gave in to him.

"Because," she flung bitterly back at him, "when I saw you in that abominable cellar—with your sword drawn, waiting—it suddenly came to me what it would mean if you raised arms against men loyal to the crown. Your life would have been ruined, and for what? No doubt I should still have been taken." Her short laugh sounded harsh even in her own ears. "'Tis most ironic, would you not agree? I found the debt of such a sacrifice too great, captain, even for me."

"And so you decided to make it look as if I had been an unwilling participant in all of this—your prisoner, in fact," he finished for her. "Good God. You astound me, Miss Tyree. Not only would you save me from my own brash self-destruction, but you would also, in one bold stroke, make sure I should be cleared of the charges of treason and desertion to the enemy. Is there no length to which you would not go to protect me from myself? *Dammit*, Sabra. Did it not once occur to you that you might simply have trusted me to know what I was about?"

"No! I—" she uttered passionately, then seemed immediately to recollect herself. Drawing a deep breath, she continued in frosty, even tones. "It *seemed* that you had no choice but to wreck everything with your stupid heroics. Faith, captain, what *did* you intend to do? Had you your sword in hand in order to present it to the Redcoats, haft first? You will pardon me if I say that

289

somehow you had not the look of a man ready to submit peacefully to manacles. But perhaps it would not have mattered to you to wait in prison while your precious baronet made ready to . . ."

Realizing where her unruly tongue had led her, she bit off what she had been about to say.

"To *what, ma mie?*" Myles demanded, his voice, soft and yet stinging as a whiplash. "To flee? To betray another ship and crew to the enemy as he did mine?" She winced as his fingers bit into her arm. "To *what*, Sabra? What treachery is Sir Wilfred planning next? Answer me!"

"I can't tell you!" she gasped. "Not yet. Not until I know my brother is safe. Myles, stop it! You're hurting me."

She nearly sagged with relief when abruptly he released her. Then she saw his eyes, and suddenly her blood ran cold.

"You must see that I have no choice in this," she uttered, her voice flat and expressionless. "It's the only weapon I have against Channing."

"Yes, no doubt," he answered coldly and, disentangling himself from her, shoved himself up into a sitting position with his back once more against the wooden crate. "And now 'twould seem I, too, am fast running out of alternatives."

She was spared from having to give reply to that enigmatic utterance by Jubal, signaling that they were coming up to the drive. Immediately the sled began to slow down to make the turn, and as Myles peered impatiently through the gap at the edge of the tarp, Sabra hastily covered herself with her ruined shirt, then buttoned her coat over her heaving bosom with fingers that shook.

"We are approaching the stables," he said grimly, without turning around. "If you are still set on this harebrained scheme, I suggest you ready yourself to make the leap. Once you are on the ground, don't stop for anything. I shall be right on your heels."

Sabra had barely enough time to pull herself up into a crouch at the edge before Myles turned and caught hold of her hand.

"Now!" he uttered in a harsh whisper.

Clinging to his hand, Sabra dropped off the back, running as she hit the snow-packed drive. Then Myles released her. Her limbs numb from the cramped quarters of the sled, she stumbled to her knees and, cursing, scrambled to get up again. Then Myles was beside her, half dragging and half carrying her the few steps to the house.

"There," she panted, pulling him toward the structure of wrought-iron clinging to the brick wall. Without waiting for Myles, she began climbing and in a few moments was pulling herself over the balustrade onto a small balcony some twenty feet above the ground. Exhilarated from her exertions, she turned eagerly to look for Myles.

She saw him, still standing at the bottom of the trellis, his uninjured arm braced against the wall as he gazed up at her, and all at once she felt icy fingers touch her heart.

"Myles, don't be a fool. You must know you haven't a chance on your own."

"Just tell me one thing," he called back. "How much time have we before sir Wilfred makes his move?"

Sabra bit her lip. If he knew the date, might not it be enough for him to figure out the rest of it for himself? How empty how would be her only lever against Channing then! she thought grimly. And yet, had he not a right to know?

"Perhaps a week," she answered finally. "Certainly no more than that. Myles? Where will you go? The troops are everywhere, scouring the city for you."

Even from the balcony, she could see the flash of white teeth against the tanned face.

"I regret I must turn down the offer of your hospitality," he said, flourishing a bow. "To be your prisoner, even in an attic, has its temptations, my love. Unfortunately, there are matters to which I must attend. You will have the pleasure of my company one day soon, I promise you. Then, my beautiful Sabra, be warned. I shan't be put off again. I shall have come to claim everything that is mine."

Stunned into speechlessness at his cool effrontery, Sabra watched the captain turn and stride leisurely across the drive toward the alley. Not until Myles was nearly to the stables did she gather her wits about her enough to try to stop him.

"Myles, wait!" she cried, leaning perilously over the balustrade as she sought to keep the tall figure in view. Involuntarily her hand went out, as if by that she might draw him back to her. Then he had vanished round the corner, and she let it fall slowly back again.

For an instant her shoulders drew together, and she clung tightly to the balustrade as though her limbs could not sustain her.

"Damn you, Trevor Myles!" she gasped, bitter with the knowledge that she could do nothing to stop him from whatever reckless course he had determined on. Then in spite of herself, she felt a thrill course through her as the significance of his final words at last sank home.

All at once her head came up, and tossing caution to the wind, she leaned far out over the balustrade.

"The devil fly away with you, Trevor Myles!" she shouted, heedless of everything but a wild compulsion to fling her defiance after him. "Do you hear me? Sabra Tyree is *no* man's simply for the taking!"

292

Her ears filled with the fury of the blood pulsing through her veins, she never heard the soft click of the latch behind her or the windows swinging outward. As from a distance Wayne's voice carried to her, sharp with warning.

"Who are you? What are you doing out there, boy? Come away from the edge at once."

Sabra shuddered, suddenly cold. With an effort, she schooled her features to a semblance of calm and slowly turned to face Wayne.

He was watching her warily from the open window, a gun in his hand, and she had a fleeting impression of a rumpled shirt, open at the throat, and of brown hair, rather disheveled, as if he had thrust his fingers through it more than once. Then she gave him a quizzing look and nodded at the loaded pistol.

"You won't need that, I think," she said, her lovely smile slightly awry.

"Sabra?" he exclaimed, as if he could not believe the evidence of his own eyes.

Wearily she walked across the balcony toward him.

"Oh, Robert," she murmured, coming to a halt directly in front of him, "it *is* good to see you!"

Chapter 18

Hastily, Wayne pulled Sabra into the room, then closed and latched the windows before turning to sweep her with a look from head to toe.

"Sabra. Good God, is it really you?" Setting the gun aside, he grasped her by the shoulders. Anxiously, he scanned her face. "You mad, foolish girl. Are you all right? What the devil are you doing here? You should have been halfway to Thornhaven by now."

Sabra favored him with a fond glance. He looked tousled and worn, as if he had only managed to snatch moments of sleep during the night and, even then, he must have been fully dressed and slumped, no doubt, in a chair here in his sitting room. Apparently he had not even taken time to shave that morning, she thought, wondering when she had ever seen him before with his chin bristling with a day-old beard. Instantly she suffered a swift pang of remorse for having caused him to worry.

"I am sorry, dearest Robert," she murmured, reaching up to lay the palm of her hand against the side of his face. "I fear I've been a sad trial to you. But now I am home and quite sound in every limb, I promise you. As for Thornhaven, I have decided to put that off for a while—now that I know Wes is here."

Wayne, taking in the lovely face, the stubborn tilt of the firm chin and the eyes, shadowed with weariness and yet steady as they returned his look, felt swept with an utter sense of helplessness. Faith, what a fool he had been ever to have believed she was safely on her way to Thornhaven, away from Channing and the mess he had made of things.

As she cocked her head to one side, quizzing him for his lengthy stare, a wry grin tugged reluctantly at the corners of his mouth.

"The same old Sabra," he said gruffly. "I might have known you'd turn up here."

Laughing, Sabra slipped easily from beneath his grasp and went to stretch her hands out to the small fire crackling in the fireplace. To all intents and purposes, she appeared relaxed, relieved to be home. Only someone who knew her very well indeed would have guessed that she was troubled by the faint tinge of bitterness in Wayne's last remark. Uneasily, it came to her that all was not well, for she could not be mistaken in thinking that Wayne was anything but pleased at seeing her there.

Then resolutely she dismissed the notion. No doubt he was only a little put out with her for causing him an anxious night. And, indeed, who could blame him?

"Here, take this," said Wayne, coming up behind her. "You look as if you could use a drink."

Startled from her thoughts, Sabra turned. Wayne stood at her shoulder, a glass of something in his hand. Madeira, she thought, a faint whimsical expression flitting over her face at the memory of Myles, elaborately sampling Lily Barrett's prized bottle of the stuff.

"Faith, I shouldn't be at all surprised if I shall need more than a drink to bring me back up to snuff." Grimacing, she took the crystal goblet and sipped experimentally. "H-m-m, good," she murmured. "Thank you, dear friend. You always seem to know exactly what is best for me."

"I've had a lot of practice at it," he answered, watch-

295

ing her settle on a rug before the fire, her knees tucked up under her chin in the manner of a contented child. "When are you going to tell me what happened last night?"

Sabra shrugged and took a sip of wine.

"I should have thought Mr. Hawkes filled you in on all of that. But, no, I guess he couldn't have known Myles dosed me with a sleeping draught and abducted me so that Channing couldn't. In fact, come to think of it, he never even asked how 'the bloody English captain' came to be wounded," she mused, smiling a little strangely. "I shot Myles in the arm, you see, when he tried to take my pocket gun away from me. I had a time stanching the bleeding, let me tell you. Then, no sooner had I managed to get it bandaged than an extremely disagreeable man named Tucker got the drop on us. That's how we ended up fleeing backstage through the theater. We might have got away, too, if Channing's ruffians hadn't stolen the wagon and left us stranded in the churchyards with Lieutenant Inness's dead body. Lord, I shall never forget how I felt, stumbling across him and thinking it was Myles stretched, lifeless, over the grave." She gave a small shudder. "It was simply dreadful. Anyway, you know practically everything else, for it was just after that that we ran into Rab and Jedediah and the others. They carried Myles to the cellar, where I looked after him, till Jubal came to fetch us, and I guess that's pretty much all there is to tell . . . Except that—"

Suddenly she stopped. Wayne, who had become hopelessly lost in this highly expurgated account of her adventures, frowned as he saw her eyes close as if in pain.

"Except for what, Sabra?" he prodded, his voice edged in concern.

"Oh, Robert," she breathed, looking up at him with huge, shadowed eyes. "Except that I have learned that

Ridgley has been killed."

"Good God, I am sorry. In spite of his being a British officer, I respected and liked Ridgley."

"But that's not all. It's *how* he died. Robert, he never made it to Charleston. He was killed in some sort of accident on shipboard."

For a moment their eyes met and held. Then Wayne turned and with marked deliberation set his glass on a grog tray near the fireplace.

"What sort of accident?" he said, staring down at the half-empty glass as if it held the solution to some dark and deadly riddle.

"He was shot. Some sort of nonsense about one of the men cleaning a rifle. I don't believe it for a minute."

"Nor do I," murmured Wayne. "The thing would have had to be primed and loaded. Only an idiot could have been unaware that the gun was dangerous."

"That was my thought exactly," Sabra said. "It seems all just a trifle too convenient somehow."

Suddenly she shuddered and looked away.

"It's my fault he's dead. If I hadn't—"

"Don't," Wayne interrupted. "That sort of thinking won't get us anywhere. Ridgley knew what he was up against when he wrote you that letter. I wonder how much else he knew."

He said this so grimly that Sabra glanced up at him, surprised.

"Why? What do you mean?" she asked, quizzing him with her eyes. Then immediately she felt a sharp stab of fear. "It's not something to do with Wes, is it? Robert, Wes is still alive, isn't he?"

Wayne, jarred from his brooding thoughts by the keen edge of anxiety in her voice, looked at her a trifle blankly.

"What? Wes?" he uttered distractedly, then seemed to recall himself. "No," he said. A wry glint darkened the blue eyes. His hand lifted to run haphazardly through his hair. "No, I wasn't thinking of Wes. So far as I know, nothing has changed. He's still hanging on."

"Somehow you don't make that sound very encouraging," Sabra accused with a wry twist of the lips. Wayne appeared to wince.

"Well, what do you expect?" he demanded savagely and began to pace the room in fitful starts. "The place is a bloody nightmare."

"You talk as if you'd actually been there," Sabra murmured, taken aback by his violent outburst. Her heart almost stopped when he turned to impale her with a look, which was both haunted and somehow accusing.

"Oh, but I have," he said mockingly. "Shall I tell you what it is like?" Once again he began his fitful pacing, as if he could not bear to be still lest whatever was haunting him should suddenly pounce on him from out of the shadows. "Did you know that they've crammed eleven hundred prisoners in the hold so that they dare not even lie down for fear of being trampled to death? Or that most of their clothes, not to mention whatever valuables they might have had upon descending into hell, have been stripped—*stolen*—from them. To keep from dying of exposure, they have to keep moving continuously. And the food the bloody bastards give 'em— God rot their black souls—comes from stores condemned aboard their men-of-war as unfit for human consumption. Putrid beef and pork, and vermin-infested bread! But even that isn't enough to satisfy their insatiable cruelty. In plain sight of the ship flow clear streams of clean water to be had for the taking. Yet the bloody British go to the expense of having a lighter bring water from the city. Faith! Can you believe it? No one in his right mind would drink so much as a swallow of that stinking belly-rot! And you can imagine what effect it has on the prisoners. They're all suffering from dysen-

298

tery, and not a few from consumption and heaven only knows what else."

He had come blindly to a halt and stood weaving on his feet, his eyes fixed on some terrible scene out of hell that only he could see. Suddenly his face convulsed and he staggered.

"Oh, God, Sabra!" he groaned, sinking down onto a chair, the heels of his hands jammed into his eye sockets as though to block everything out. "It made me sick to see what it's done to Wes!"

Sabra, alarmed, had already come to her feet, her gaze anxious as she watched him hacking away at something deep inside. Now she crossed swiftly to his side and, dropping to her knees before him, reached out to comfort him.

"Robert, it's not your fault. You must not blame yourself."

As if burned at her touch, Wayne thrust her almost brutally from him and lurched drunkenly to his feet.

"You don't know!" he uttered savagely. "You didn't see. *I* saw. And Channing — *curse* his bastard soul! — *knew* how it would be. That's why he came to me. That's why he was so obliging. God, how he must have savored the look on my face, the smell of my horror when it was over and I was allowed topside again. That's when he made me his offer — my life for my soul. Oh, God, how I wish I had driven a knife through his heart, then, when I had the chance and, afterwards, turned it on me. But I had not even the courage for that."

White-faced and shaking, Sabra dragged herself up off the floor. She could not believe it. This could not be happening to her — to Wayne, good noble Robert, who had always stood her friend. And yet she could not deny the terrible anguish in his face; merciful God, the self-loathing in his final utterance!

"What offer, Robert?" she said. "What did Channing

demand in exchange for your life?" In sudden, terrible fear, she clutched the front of his shirt with icy fingers. "What did you give him, Robert?" she queried, her heart slowly freezing to death inside her. "Damn you, what was worth Wes's trust and mine?"

As if mesmerized, he stared into the cold fear in her eyes, the stunned disbelief giving way to slow-mounting horror. His words, when they came, seemed dragged from his very depths.

"I gave — him — everything. The truth — about you and the *Nemesis*. Where and how we managed to keep her hidden from everyone all these years. Even our contacts, where and when we meet, the passwords — everything."

Dropping his head, he shuddered convulsively.

"And did you also tell him that he failed to sink the *Nemesis*? Are Skyler and the others even now rotting in some vile prison somewhere here in the city? Did you sell them out, too, Robert?" she demanded, yanking fiercely at his shirt as though to emphasize each word with her growing anger. "Did you? Did you?"

Unable to bear the bitter loathing in her voice, the accusations like a knife slashing at him again and again, Wayne wrenched his head up and looked at her out of eyes, wild with suffering.

"*No!* Never! I swear it. He thinks you made it to shore with a few of your men. I told him, that with the ship gone, those who survived scattered and made their way north. All, except you and Jubal, which meant there wasn't any reason to give Skyler away. Channing already thought he was dead, and I saw no need to tell him anything different. You must believe me, Sabra. Skyler used to make me feel as if I were like the other boys. He taught me how to fish and sail. Let me stow away when he put out for short runs up the coast. Surely you must see that I could never have betrayed Will?"

"No, of course you couldn't," Sabra replied in a flat, unemotional voice. "You could only betray Wes and Jubal and all those who trusted you to keep their identities a secret. You betrayed *me*, Robert," she said, utterly scathing in her condemnation of him. Letting go of his shirt, she backed a step. "Damn you to hell, Robert Wayne! I hope to God never to lay eyes on you in this world again!"

Wayne winced as if he had been struck. Then Sabra had spun on her heel and was striding rapidly for the door.

"No, Sabra, wait!" he called after her, his voice breaking. "I *couldn't* face the thought of being thrown in there with the others. I'm a bloody cripple. What chance would I have had? Damnit, Sabra, you must see that I could not have borne it!"

His anguish pierced her like a blade to the heart, and she faltered, her hand on the door handle. It was true, and she knew it. With his weak leg and his ever uncertain health, he would never have stood a chance of surviving conditions in the prison ship. She could understand his fear. In time she might even come to forgive him for having given in to it. But whether she understood and forgave him or not could not possibly signify in the least. Not now. Wayne had betrayed her and, consequently, was not to be trusted. Henceforth, he could only be a danger to her and to everyone around him.

With grim deliberation, she pressed down on the handle and walked through the doorway into the hall. As she turned to pull the door to, she saw Wayne, broken and in torment, sink slowly into a chair, saw him clutch his face in his hands and double up over his knees. Noiselessly, she drew the door closed, then, retching, clasped her hand to her mouth and fled down the hall as if pursued; and, indeed, she was—by her last glimpse of Wayne, sitting with shoulders hunched and wracked with bitter sobs.

Sabra lay on her back staring at the rose pattern on the canopy above her and listening absently to Phoebe tiptoe about the room, inventing things to keep her busy and near while her mistress supposedly slept.

Poor Phoebe, she thought dully. She had been beside herself with relief to have her charge back again, safe under her wing, relief which had changed quickly to concern at the sight of the wildness in Sabra's eyes—the anguish and the grief. Wisely she had forborne asking the questions that undoubtedly had crowded her mind and, instead, had made short work of seeing her mistress undressed and swathed in a warm robe while she ran a brush soothingly through the long, tangled mass of red-gold hair. Indeed, she had allowed herself only a single, glad exclamation upon discovering Sabra's diamonds tucked safely away in a coat pocket. Then, when at last the wildness had gone and Sabra's eyelids began to drift down over her eyes, Phoebe had made certain her mistress lay down in her bed.

Nevertheless, Sabra had not fallen into the sweet oblivion of sleep as Phoebe had expected her to do, but instead had lain gripped in the lingering aftermath of her living nightmare. Oh, God, how she longed to go to Robert and tell him she had not meant her last hateful words, uttered out of anger and terrible hurt. And yet she knew she could not, not so long as there remained so much to be done, so much that must be carried out in secret; indeed, not ever. Faith, why could the nightmare not end and everything go back to the way it had used to be between her and Robert? How, indeed, was she to go on without his wisdom to guide her? *Damn him!* How could he have betrayed her, himself, everything they had worked to achieve? She did not see how she could bear ever to look at him again, see the pain in his eyes, the terrible shame, and know she could do nothing. He was breaking her heart—and his. It would have been better if Channing had simply killed him.

Rent by the memory of that last, painful glimpse of him, she came near to giving herself away with a low groan, but she caught herself in time and, rolling over, buried her face in the pillows. When at last the spasm passed, she curled up on her side, a pillow clasped to her stomach. Vaguely she wondered how long it had been since she had burst into her room and flung herself, weeping, into Phoebe's arms. An hour—two, perhaps? Longer? She couldn't tell from the light filtering in through the drawn curtains around the bed. It seemed like an eternity. If only she *could* sleep, she thought, feeling her weariness, like a weight, dragging her down. And then she thought of Myles.

Fleetingly, a small, uncertain smile curved her lips at the wondrous memory of that last, lingering kiss beneath the tarp when the captain had found her out. Faith, what was this power that he had over her, to make her blood burn and her will to evaporate with naught but a kiss? When they were apart, she could see all too plainly how impossible was such a love, but when he touched her, she knew only the sweet madness of an all-engulfing passion.

Faith, where was he? Where could he go with the whole city roused against him? Her heart grew suddenly chill as it came to her to wonder if even then he was in the power of his deadliest enemy.

Channing, curse him! Her eyes glinted green sparks as she thought of all to which the baronet must one day answer. His poison had touched the three men she loved most in the world. He had already all but destroyed Robert Wayne, and Wes was only just clinging to life in

303

the hellish prison into which Channing had ordered him confined. If Myles, too, paid the price of having a place in her heart, she would not rest until the baronet had suffered some terrible, lingering torment.

Suddenly she thought she could not bear the dreadful anguish of not knowing where Myles was or how he fared. If only there were someone who could give her some clue as to where he might have gone after leaving her. And then it came to her—the one person, other than herself, who might be willing to help him—Miss Lily Barrett, his mistress!

Good God, she mused ironically, she had changed indeed if she could truly contemplate begging Lily Barrett's help in finding the man they both loved. Aside from being Myles's mistress, after all, the woman *had* been a party to dosing Sabra with a sleeping draught, stripping her of her clothing, and leaving her to the tender mercies of a would-be abductor. No matter that that abductor had been Myles and that he had been acting in Sabra's defense, she had still, she vowed, a score to settle with Miss Lily Barrett. A score, however, she was forced to acknowledge, that would have to wait at least until after she knew Myles was safe.

She would somehow swallow her pride and go to Lily, of that much she was quite certain. She had only to decide where and how. Not in the backstage dressing room, she vowed. She wished never to have to set eyes on that again. And aside from its being fraught with disturbing memories, there was the added disadvantage of being far too public. With so many people milling about, achieving an interview with the actress, private and unremarked, would be risky in the extreme. Obviously, she would have to seek out Miss Barrett at her lodgings—number thirty-four Barclay, no doubt, the house to which Myles had ordered to go the previous night did he fail to return for her. But what if, she thought suddenly, instead of Lily, she found Ellsworth there? Could the man be trusted? Who, in heaven's name, was he? And what part had he to play in this deadly game?

For a moment she hesitated, wondering if she were playing the fool. After all, Lily might know nothing of Myles, or she might simply refuse to tell Sabra anything. Indeed, why should she help? She could hardly feel generous toward the woman Myles had presented to her as his intended. Then fatalistically Sabra shrugged. Fool or not, she knew she would risk anything for the merest chance of discovering some word of her beloved.

Never one to dally once her mind was made up on a thing, Sabra could barely restrain herself from rushing out of her bed. There were other matters to consider before she went off half-cocked to enlist the aid of her rival. First and foremost was her reluctance to give herself away just yet, for she needed time to plan and make ready for her final confrontation with Sir Wilfred. When Channing learned of her presence, she fully intended that the time and the place would be of her own choosing. Until then, she must be very careful to remain incognito, and thus far the only ones who knew of her return were Jubal, Phoebe, and—God help her—Wayne!

Thus returned to the bitter cause of her sleeplessness, Sabra writhed in her bed. In her heart, she still could not accept that her friend from earliest childhood had, in truth, sold her out, and yet reason dictated that he could no longer be trusted. No matter how much she might wish to have done, she knew she could not put it off indefinitely. Something would have to be done about Robert. But what?

Then, in a sudden, rending moment of truth, the final implication of what Robert had done at last struck her with horrible significance. God help her, Wayne was a traitor, and traitors were shot!

Gripped in the awful throes of bitter reality, she lay deathly still, staring into the sudden abyss of hell. How did one go about killing a man as dear to her as her own brother? Of course, she might order Skyler or Jubal to do it, place the gun next to his temple and fire. But that would be the coward's way, would it not? No, she reflected with a sort of insane and utterly chilling dispassion. If she were to do the thing right, she herself must pull the trigger.

Then at last did she give in to bitter despair. She might as well shoot Wes as kill Wayne. Or pull the trigger on herself. It would all be the same. God help her, she could not do it. Never in a million years. Indeed, by what right should she set herself up as judge and executioner? No. It would be enough to put a guard over him, to confine him to the house until Wes was safe and they could all escape the madness of this place, this time, this war.

Yes, that was it. Robert and Wes had always talked about sailing to the Great South Sea. Well, together they would do it — go far away, the three of them, and together heal their wounds. But first she must know that Myles was safe, see him, perhaps — feel his arms about her, one last time. She would rouse herself from her lethargy and summon Jubal. He must be told about Robert, and then, in the guise of a serving wench, she would seek out Lily. With Phoebe to accompany her, she might well pull it off without risking any undue unpleasantness, for it would take a brazen rogue indeed to accost her with the formidable nanny at her side.

In grim determination, Sabra thrust open the bedcurtains and started to get up.

"Now jest you holds on a second!" exclaimed Phoebe, glancing up from a gown, a rent in the hem of which she was in the process of mending. "Where does you think you be goin'? Why, I can see by your face that you ain't hardly closed your eyes in all the time you been layin' there." Suddenly the keen old eyes softened. "What's the matter, honey? What be troublin' you so that it won't let you sleep?"

Such sympathy proved almost too much for her. Biting her lip, she hastily turned her head away.

"Miss Sabra," cried Phoebe softly, setting her mending aside in quick alarm. "Honey, what is it?"

"Oh, Phoebe. If I were to tell you, you doubtless wouldn't believe me and, even if you did, it's better that you don't know what it is." Sabra sighed and glanced ruefully up. "I'm afraid you will just have to trust that I know what I'm doing."

"Oh, I trusts *you* knows what you be doing, all right," retorted the shrewd old nanny. "It's *me* not knowin' that I finds troublesome. An' chile, you done got that look in your eye that don't spell no good for nobody."

"How well you know me, dearest nanny." Sabra laughed and, flinging herself out of bed, impulsively threw her arms about the older woman's neck. "I do love you, you know," she whispered, "but sometimes, Phoebe, you are the awfullest nag."

Phoebe sniffed and noisily cleared her throat.

"If I is a nag, it's because someone gots to be, Miss Sabra," she said with sudden determination. "I swear, sometimes you acts like you ain't got the sense you was born with. Your mama most likely be rollin' over in her grave right this minute does she know you done stayed gone all night with that no-good cap'n. An' I ain't even ask yet how come you to show up to home dressed like some pore street urchin when you done left here wearin' a queen's ransom in silk and jewels. An' I ain't goin' to neither, 'cause I knows more'n likely I just be wastin' my breath."

"Would you indeed?" retorted Sabra, filled with a sudden recklessness. "And what if I were to tell you that I had been rendered unconscious then nearly abducted, not by one party, but by two different ones? And, furthermore, that that no-good captain, at great risk to himself, rescued me, that we were forced to hide out in a cellar overnight and that a friend provided me with the street urchin's attire to replace my silk dress, which was quite ruined in our harrowing flight? What, my know-it-all nanny, would you say to that?"

"Humph!" answered Phoebe, emphatically.

"But it is true, all of it," Sabra answered her. "May I be boiled in oil if it is not."

"I wouldn't tempt fate, was I you, Miss Sabra," Phoebe retorted, eyeing her young charge askance. "An' why you done tell me all this? Whenever you talks like butter won't melt in your mouth, I knows you be after somethin'!"

"What I want," said Sabra, suddenly dropping her playful manner, "is for you to summon Jubal to me at once. Then, my dearest Phoebe, you will fetch me a skullery maid's dress, complete with mobcap, shoulder scarf, apron, and shoes. Oh, yes, I shall also require the use of Mrs. Kirkpatrick's kerry cloak for the afternoon, if you please. You and I are going calling just as soon as everything is made ready. No doubt it will please you to accompany me on one of my nefarious excursions, will it not?"

"That depend on where we be goin', don't it? And what for you wants me to go with you, I expects," Phoebe wisely pointed out. "But I don't asks nothin', I jest does what I be told. An' right now, I reckons I be goin' to fetch Jubal and them things you wants."

"Thank you, Phoebe," murmured Sabra, smiling a little at her maid servant's air of martyrdom.

No sooner had the door closed behind Phoebe, however, than all traces of mirth vanished from Sabra's face, leaving behind a haunting sort of sadness. Sighing, she crossed to the window seat and, curling up in it, stared somberly down upon the small walled garden below her.

The garden, embraced in pristine loveliness, had been her father's favorite place to think. He had had it laid out as like as possible to his memory of another one, far away in England, save for the sundial mounted on a stone dais at its center. That, and another one exactly like it that stood similarly arranged in the garden at Thornhaven, he had ordered constructed shortly after the trouble with the customs inspectors began, and for a very good reason. She had been no more than eight or nine the first time he had taken her by the hand and led her into the garden to show her the secret of the twin dials, and though the image of her tall, aristocratic father had grown blurred with the passing of the years, that single memory of her hand, warm in his, was as vivid now as if it had been only yesterday.

Suddenly she bent her forehead to her knees. Oh, God, not since his death had she missed her father so much. He would have known how best to deal with Robert. He had always known what to do.

The brief rap on the door brought her head up with a jerk, her heart pounding. Swallowing the ache in her throat, she called out.

"Yes, who is it?"

"Jubal, Miss Sabra. Phoebe say you wants to see me."

Quickly, Sabra swung her legs down and stood up.

"Yes, Jubal, come in please."

When the door opened, she appeared cool and composed, her lovely face betraying nothing of the havoc within.

"Thank you for coming so quickly," she said, searching for the words. "Was there any trouble with the sled? I trust you were able to get it safely stowed in the stables?"

"Yes, Miss Sabra. It wasn't no trouble."

"Good." She knew that he had to be puzzled by the small talk, when, from the urgency of her summons, he must have expected something quite different. And, indeed, there could be little purpose in skirting the real reason she had called him here. Better to jump right in. Jubal, she would say, her voice coldly unemotional, as though she weren't talking about a man with whom they had shared nearly four years of continuous danger, a man upon whom they had always been able to count for counsel and advice or just plain moral support. Jubal, the man slowly breaking up into a million pieces in the room downstairs, is a bloody traitor.

Dammit! She couldn't do it. Not if it meant Channing bloody well won. If Wes were here, he'd understand; she knew it. Robert was like a brother to him.

"Jubal, I have to go out in a little while," she said, turning to gaze out the window. "I'll be taking Phoebe. We won't be gone long—an hour, perhaps, surely no more."

"Yes, Miss Sabra," he said, his voice betraying nothing. "If you was needin' the carriage, I done already made sure it was put on the runners."

"No. It's only a short way, hardly worth getting the cattle out. That isn't why I called you here. It's Wayne. I'm afraid he's feeling under the weather and, well, you know how he is." She came easily about, her smile a trifle awry. "I want you to keep an eye out for him. Just in case. I don't think it wise to leave him alone just now."

She could see him taking it in and turning it over in his mind. And then he looked at her with studied blankness.

"I expects I be around, Miss Sabra, does Mr. Wayne need somethin'. I ain't got no pressin' engagements nowhere."

He knew, she thought, turning away. Not all of it, not that Wayne had sold out, but enough not to turn his back on him.

"Thank you, Jubal. It will greatly relieve my mind, knowing he shan't be alone. Oh, and Jubal. No callers, if you please, and if you could contrive some way to keep Mr. Robert from going out, I should be most grateful. Business can wait, and he does, after all, need his rest."

She could feel his eyes on her and detested herself for what she was doing to Wayne; and, indeed, to Jubal. Robert would soon be made aware that he was henceforth a prisoner in this house, and now Jubal was aware of it, too. It would wear on them both, she knew, and yet she could see no other choice in the matter. She would do her best to keep Wayne's secret to herself for as long as possible. With any luck at all, perhaps no one had ever any need to know. Other than that, she did not see how she could help him. The rest was up to Robert himself.

Resolutely, she dismissed Wayne from her mind, as Jubal left and Phoebe, her arms full, came in almost immediately thereafter.

"Here you is, Miss Sabra," she panted, breathless from her climb up four flights of stairs. "I done jest as you say. I expects them that loaned you these things'll keep mum as church-mice with a hunk of cheese. It ain't often they gets tole they is to have two whole days off with the promise of full wages. I never even give 'em a chance to ask any questions before I done sprung that on 'em, an' afterwards, they never thought to question no gift horse in the mouth, I can promise you that."

The prospect of doing something besides lying, sleepless and brooding, in her bed, brought a sudden sparkle to Sabra's eyes.

"Then 'tis well done." She laughed, feeling her excitement, almost as heady as wine, as she took the borrowed gown and held it up to her in front of the mirror. "What think you, Phoebe? Shall I not make an excellent scullery maid?"

Phoebe glanced doubtfully at the flushed cheeks and sparkling eyes above the plain bed gown of brown drab.

"Maybe," she answered dourly, "if you was to wear a sack over your head and keep them lily white hands covered. But even then, I'd say it was doubtful. You is a lady, honey—and not jest 'cause you was born and bred to it. It's what you got inside you, an' ain't nothin' goin' to keep that from shinin' out."

Chapter 19

Phoebe and Sabra, bundled in plain woolen cloaks, made their way down the steep, snow-covered incline of Little Green Street, past the old Quaker Meeting House and cemetery on the left and on toward Maiden Lane, crouched below them. It had stopped snowing, and uncertain shafts of late afternoon sunlight filtered through occasional rifts in the clouds to explore the red and black-tiled roofs of the houses and shops crowded together at the bottom of the hill.

In short order they emerged into the lane itself and went on to follow the narrow curve flanked by three and four-story buildings. The narrow fronts, made of multicolored bricks in checkered patterns, housed shop windows of every sort of trade and, as usual, there was a goodly number of people plying the street. Indeed, the small shops appeared to be doing a fair amount of business in spite of the inclement weather.

From the depths of her hood, pulled well forward to conceal her face in shadows, Sabra darted swift glances along the thoroughfare, hoping against hope to spot Myles among those hardy enough to have ventured outdoors. Then, as they approached the end of the curve, where Maiden Lane widened to embrace the "Old Swago" Market, she was made unpleasantly aware of the boisterous sound of voices raised in drunken song and, coming toward them, arms linked and strolling three abreast so as to take up the entire width of the narrow walk, a party of Hessian soldiers, obviously under the influence.

"Honey, this be where we gets off," muttered Phoebe in a dire undertone to her mistress and, grabbing her by the arm, directed her forcibly across the street toward the arched portico of Oswego Market. There, in the shadow of one of the columns, they waited for the soldiers to pass by. Not until King George's foreign mercenaries were well out of sight did Phoebe venture to release her grip on Sabra, and then she did so only with apparent reluctance.

"Whew! I must've been plumb out'n my head to let you talk me into this, Miss Sabra," she panted, a plump hand clutched at her heaving bosom. "The streets ain't safe for no woman no time. An' they sure ain't no fit place for the likes of you. Your mama be rollin' over in her grave right this minute."

Sabra, catching sight of a rough-hewn face having an unsavory cast and regarding them with undue interest from one of the wooden benches scattered here and there, jabbed an elbow none too gently in the distracted nanny's side.

"Hush, Phoebe!" she whispered sharply. "Do you want the whole world to hear?"

"The whole world don't be blind, Miss Sabra. Ain't no way you gonna get away with this," Phoebe pronounced in no uncertain terms, but dropped her voice, nonetheless. Mumbling to herself, she turned reluctantly to follow her mistress, who was making for the far end of the nearly deserted gallery. Thus she failed to observe a stealthy figure detach itself from the shadows and follow after them at a discreet distance.

Phoebe was still muttering under her breath when, some moments later, they emerged from the market at the junction of Maiden Lane with Broadway, nor did she cease to do so before they had traversed the few remaining blocks to Barclay and stood at last on the threshold of number thirty-four. Then, however, catching a glimpse of the expression on her mistress's face as Sabra took in the trim brick two-story with its charming Italian front, she judiciously clamped her jaws shut.

And, undeniably, Sabra was rather more than a little perturbed at discovering Myles's mistress cozily ensconced in what gave every indication of being a quaint little love-nest. No doubt when in the spring the roses bloomed on the trellis in front and the blossoms burst forth on the cherry trees, it would be a charming cottage indeed, she reflected grimly as she stepped forward to rap an emphatic summons on the brass knocker whimsically wrought to resemble a cherubic Cupid.

And then Mayella opened the door. Granting the grim-faced Phoebe naught but a cursory glance, she let her sloe black eyes trail over the other, considerably more intriguing, figure, swathed funereally from head to toe in black.

"Was you all wantin' somethin'?" she inquired with a lofty arch of a single, finely plucked eyebrow. "Maybe you ain't aware the servants' entrance be at the back. 'Course, it won't do you no good," she added, gazing significantly at the glowering nanny. "Miz Lily don't take kindly to no sour pusses—nowheres, no time, I promises you that. Besides, we don't need no more hired help. Cap'n Ellsworth like to keep things real simple round here."

Sabra, sensing Phoebe start to swell, stepped hastily to the fore.

"You're Mayella, aren't you," she said pleasantly, and judiciously reached up to pull the hood a little ways back on her head. "Miss Barrett has mentioned you often; and, indeed, now I understand why. You are everything I should have expected from the manner in which she described you."

Anything but a fool, Mayella was not so easily taken in.

"Is you sayin' you knows Miss Lily, honey?" she queried, affecting magnificent surprise. "Maybe you and her done all this exchangin' of confidences over tea and biscuits, is that it? Or maybe you was jest eavesdroppin' where you ain't had no business to."

"Actually, I suppose you could say it was a little of both," reflected Sabra with a rather wry, if whimsical, twist of the lips. "Only it was over wine, which had been drugged, and Miss Barrett mistakenly assumed I was oblivious at the time. But no matter. It is extremely important that I speak with your mistress. I should be very grateful if you would inform her of our presence here."

"And jest maybe I might even oblige you—*if* you can account for why you be git up like somethin' you ain't. For if you is a servin' wench, honey, then I must be the Queen of Sheba. You's a lady, ain't you, and this here black-faced mama be your gooseberry. Now, ain't I right."

"But how clever of you to have seen through me so quickly," applauded Sabra. "I was ever so certain my disguise was quite foolproof."

"Humph!" Phoebe snorted.

"Actually, Mayella," continued Sabra, pointedly ignoring the interruption, "I fear my movements are being watched by men who mean me no good. Which is why the necessity of this masquerade. I wonder, would you mind awfully if we stepped inside?"

Mayella, who had been leaning forward, her interest caught, suddenly drew back to eye Sabra askance.

"What kinda story you be tryin' to hand me now? You shore is keen to get past this door. Maybe you jest gives me your name and then I see is Miss Lily in."

"I'm sorry, but I really cannot do that," Sabra replied

316

with as much patience as she could muster. "You see, I must remain incognito, and I really haven't all that much time. I assure you, however, that Miss Barrett will not be sorry to learn I have called."

"In fact, you brazen-faced hussy," uttered Phoebe, provoked beyond the limit, "she be like to take a stick to your skinny little behind does you not get a move on. An' if she don't, I will!"

A spark ignited in Mayella's eyes.

"Well! Maybe you'd jest like to *try*. Your ugly ole scowly face don't scare me none," she retorted, elaborately placing hands on hips and swinging her "skinny little behind" in a manner most assured to convey contempt.

Sabra, shutting her eyes in the manner of one suffering the sudden onset of a splitting headache, steeled herself to leap between the two, should they be moved to out and out violence. Fortunately, however, it was at that precise moment that Miss Lily Barrett herself chose tellingly to announce her presence.

"Mayella!" resounded from the entry hall. "You will be pleased to cease making a goose of yourself and allow our visitors in at once!"

Thus effectively routed, Mayella had no choice but to open wide the door with as good a grace as was possible.

"Won't you please come in, miss. It seem my mistress be receivin' after all," demurely announced the wench, irrepressible to the end. With a sublime air of imperturbability, she moved to help them off with their cloaks.

"Oh," uttered Miss Lily Barrett in something of distraction and came forward to greet her visitors, "it *is* you. I thought I recognized that voice, but then I assured myself it could not possibly be yours. I was ever so certain you would be—er—away for a considerably

317

longer time. Please, won't you join me in the parlor? And perhaps your maid servant would be pleased to take some refreshment in the servants' quarters while we—er—have our little visit? Mayella, see to it at once," she added, without giving Sabra the opportunity to reply, and urged her guest toward the doorway at the far end of the entryhall.

"Yes, Miz Lily," said Mayella, her gaze speculative on her retreating mistress. Then, turning, she favored Phoebe with a saucy glance. "Does you care to follow me, *Miz* Phoebe," she informed her with exaggerated deference, "the *kitchen* be this way."

"And, now, Miss Tyree," said Lily when she had seated her guest and herself in the parlor, "to what do I owe the pleasure of this visit?"

Sabra, apparently occupied in admiring the gilt-framed replica of Titian's *Nude Venus and the Lute Player* above the mantelpiece, took a moment before replying.

"I came, Miss Barrett, to discover if Captain Myles had sought refuge here with you," she uttered point-blank, when at last she did assay an answer. Turning from the portrait to survey Myles's mistress, breathtaking in a burgundy taffeta gown over a pale rose-pink silk petticoat embroidered in sprig, Sabra tilted her own delightful chin with an unconscious air of defiance. "For if you must know, I cannot be other than concerned. He is being sought all over the city, so that I cannot imagine where he might find sanctuary if indeed he has not come to you. And if that were not worrisome enough, there is his wound to be considered."

"Wound? What wound?" gasped Lily, growing alarmingly pale. "Pray do not say 'tis mortal serious?"

"Not if he has a care for himself, which is highly doubtful, considering his insufferably obstinate nature," pronounced Sabra. Seemingly unable to sit still for a moment longer, she got up and started pacing round the garish display of red-velvet furnishings, pausing here and there to finger a porcelain oddity as she discoursed on the captain who no doubt pocketed the bills for such tasteless extravagance. "Curse the man! I have never before known anyone so abominably undependable. I should never have climbed to the balcony, I assure you, had I the least little inkling he had never any intention of following after me. As my prisoner, after all, he would have been perfectly safe locked up in my attic. And then to simply walk away without deigning to supply the smallest hint where he might be going! Oh, he makes me wish I had not jerked the gun aside at the very last moment. 'Twould have served him right had I shot him dead center!"

"Er—quite so. Indeed, I shouldn't doubt it for a moment," agreed Miss Barrett, torn between relief at discovering Miss Tyree evidently had not come to wreak vengeance on herself for aiding in Myles's odious abduction scheme and conjecture as to just exactly what the fiery young beauty was so furious about. She could not tell if she was upset because she had failed to incarcerate him in her attic for his own safety or because she had not murdered him when she had the chance. It was all very confusing, but of one thing she was quite certain. And that was that Miss Tyree was displaying every manifestation of a woman head over heels in love.

"I am sorry, Miss Tyree," she ventured judiciously after this brief moment of reflection, "but I confess I find myself somewhat at a standstill as to the nature of your difficulty. I do assure you, however, that, to my knowledge, Captain Myles is not presently in this house and has not been in the past several hours. Perhaps if you were to sit down and tell me everything from the beginning, I should better understand how I might be

319

of service to you."

Momentarily caught off balance by the other woman's attitude of calm, good sense, Sabra gave her a darkling glance.

"Yes, well, perhaps I have been rather raving off the top of my head," she admitted. "However, I have had an extremely trying time these past twenty-four hours or more. For which, I might add," she appended significantly, "you yourself have played no inconsiderable part, Miss Barrett. No doubt you will pardon me if I seem a little curious, but I cannot help but wonder what happened to you after you drugged and abandoned me to Captain Myles's tender mercies? And *what*, by the way, have you done with my red silk dress and ermine pelisse?"

"Now, now, my dear," Lily gently chided, "I thought we were going to discuss things calmly. But if you must know, I have already sent your pelisse round to your house. As for the red silk, well, I'm just afraid you will have to wait a little longer to have that back again. It is presently at the seamstress undergoing just a few repairs, along with, *I* might add, certain linen petticoats of my own, which unaccountably appeared to have suffered a mauling by an enraged Bengal tiger. I don't suppose you can supply any suggestion as to how they might have come into such a condition, can you, Miss Tyree?"

"But of course I can, as you must very well know," retorted Sabra shortly. "After all, I had to use *something* to stanch the bleeding and, afterward bandage the wound, and I'm afraid your linen petticoats were the only things that suggested themselves as in any way useful. Naturally, I knew you could not object, for I assure you our dear captain would already be stone dead without them."

"I see," rejoined Lily, with annoying unruffability.

"You were quite right, of course. I should have been most distressed had dearest Trevor succumbed for lack of a simple bandage. Still, I cannot but wonder that *one* skirt in its entirety might not have served just as well as *five* deprived solely of a strip or two. But that's neither here nor there. After all, one is apt to do any manner of odd things when one finds one's self in a particularly stressful situation, would you not agree? The important thing is that I still have not discovered *why* Captain Myles would seem to find himself in something of a coil."

Sabra, blushing unaccountably in the face of as masterfully delivered a set down as it had been her privilege to hear, was caught with her defenses down.

"You, Miss Barrett," she said with an involuntary spark of humor, "are undoubtedly a complete and utter hand. I begin to understand why Captain Myles would seem to be well pleased to enjoy your company."

Lily, who had missed neither the wry glint of amusement in the younger woman's look nor the undertone of bitterness in her final remark, could not but relent somewhat.

"Yes, well, that may be as may be, my dear," she quietly pointed out, "but 'twould seem that 'tis *you* who wear the Myles betrothal ring, would it not? Now, if you please, *sit down*, Miss Tyree, and tell me all that happened from the time I left you. And I, in turn, shall relate the details of my own adventures."

"Fair enough, Miss Barrett. I shall be all ears to hear them, that I promise you."

As it turned out, Lily proved a no less attentive listener to the account of all that had befallen Sabra and the captain—all, that is, save for a few pertinent details of a private nature, which Sabra understandably chose to keep to herself. And if a faint blush would have appeared to tinge her cheeks as she skipped lightly over

321

the hours encompassing Myles's bout with fever, Lily was far too discreet to make public note of it. She did, however, have little difficulty surmising that *something* had happened between the two and, further, that either in spite of or because of it, Miss Tyree was inexplicably determined that nothing further should be allowed to come of it.

Suddenly Lily knew a dreadful feeling of foreboding for her dearest Trevor's future happiness. The girl was obviously every bit as proud and headstrong as the dauntless captain. If there was some valid reason for Sabra's apparent conviction that insurmountable obstacles must of necessity keep them apart, she was very much afraid that not even Myles would be able to convince her otherwise. And what if those obstacles had their foundation in treason, what hope then could either of them have? Their ill-fated love would become more deadly than a curse to one of Trevor's sort, one of those rare breed who had seemed born and bred to command a king's ship. It could very likely prove the unmaking of him.

"Yes, well, no doubt you have every reason to be put out with me," admitted Lily when Sabra had reached the end of her tale no little time later. "But I assure you I suffered more than what could be considered just punishment. Being made to endure for three hours a corset laced fully four inches too small is both cruel and monstrously inhuman. Add to that the ignominy of being forcibly ejected from one's carriage and having one's clothes practically ripped off one, and I'm sure you must agree I have been punished quite enough."

"Perhaps," hedged Sabra, sardonically amused at the actress's profound air of martyrdom. "But where, might I ask, was Captain Ellsworth while all of this was going on?"

Sabra's interest was caught by the faint, but unmistakable, hardening of the china-blue eyes. Then Lily was smiling, a kitten's smile that revealed small white pointed teeth.

"You needn't say that, Miss Tyree," she reproved, rather too gently, thought Sabra, "as though poor, dear Ellsworth had remained naught but a mildly interested observer. For if you must know, we had decided to descend by way of John Street to Queen and at a leisurely pace circle back here by way of Frankfort and Chatham. We had got no further than Cows-foot Hill, however, when we were set upon by an entire band of cutthroats. I assure you, my dear, Ellsworth and Leeks were very hard-pressed. It was only at the greatest risk to himself that Will managed to fight off three of the villains in time to prevent a fourth from riding off with me across his saddle. Facedown, you understand, which is how it was that your red silk suffered the most grievous damage. I'm afraid the truth is that I quite literally burst my stays. Indeed, I was close to resembling a modernday Lady Godiva when the gallant captain was at last able to rescue me from that wretched animal. So you see, I quite owe my life to William Ellsworth."

Perfectly aware that this latter was directed pointedly at her, Sabra arched delicate eyebrows.

"I do beg your pardon, Miss Barrett, if I have in some manner offended you," she uttered ironically. "I was far from meaning any aspersion on the captain's courage — or his character either, for that matter. Truly I had no idea he meant so much to you."

Impossible not to realize Sabra was fishing for something, Lily favored her with a limpid look.

"Oh, but, my dear," she smiled, "Ellsworth and I have been intimate friends for ever so long. This is, after all, his house. Indeed, he has been most kind to offer me

323

his hospitality for as long as my engagement at the theater lasts."

Sabra was understandably taken aback at this revelation. "The captain must be possessed of a very generous nature," she blurted before she thought. "I should think he would have certain objections to—to, well, to—"

"To having Myles underfoot?" Lily obliged understandingly as, elaborately, she shook out the *engageantes* of fine lace which appeared to flow from her pagoda sleeves. "But why should he object when they are quite as close as brothers? Perhaps you are unaware that Trevor served with Will some years ago—on the *Antioch*, as it were. As a matter of fact, it was Trevor who introduced me to Will. I assure you there is never a dull moment when those two are together."

"I shouldn't doubt it for a moment," Sabra reflected in very dry accents. "Especially if last night was any example. As I recall the *Antioch*, too, came very near to suffering total disaster."

"Why, yes, as a matter of fact," agreed Lily without the bat of an eyelash. "She was beset by Barbary pirates and nearly blown out of the water. Sadly, Will was grievously wounded. The *Antioch's* captain was relieved of his command for negligence. For his valiant effort in saving the ship, however, Myles was given his own command, and deservedly so. I'm surprised you did not know any of this. I can assure you he was quite the hero at home."

"Yes, I remember," Sabra murmured, her fine eyes suddenly distant. "But that is neither here nor there, is it," she added, seeming impatiently to shake herself. Deliberately she rose from her seat preparatory to leaving. "If you cannot tell me where Captain Myles might have got himself off to, Miss Barrett, I shall not impose on your hospitality any longer."

It would have been impossible not to see that fleeting

shadow in Sabra's eyes and the determined manner in which she straightened weary shoulders, and Lily was anything but oblivious to the cause of her dejection. All at once she felt her pique at the girl's unfortunate reference to her dearest Ellsworth suddenly dissipate. Miss Tyree, after all, she reminded herself, had every reason to be displeased with the three of them—herself, Ellsworth—and Myles, of course. They had treated her quite shabbily. And she *had* risked a great deal, coming here as she had, purely in the hopes of learning that Myles was safe and well. It had taken courage and a depth of caring that Lily could not but admire. Indeed, she felt suddenly compelled to try in some way to relieve the child's mind of worry.

"I am sorry I could not be of better help to you," she said in all sincerity. "But, you know, my dear, I find it very difficulty to credit that this Sir Wilfred Channing has dared to bring charges against Myles. He may tout a loud horn here in New York, but, after all, he must still answer to London. And I fear he will find himself very quickly at loose ends once word of this fiasco reaches there. He is either exceedingly hard-pressed or the veriest fool, I promise you."

"Indeed? But surely you exaggerate, Miss Barrett," Sabra replied with scant forebearance for what seemed the wildest conjecture on Lily's part. "I hardly think Myles's consequence can be accounted so very great as all that."

A peculiar expression of astonishment widened Lily's eyes.

"I, on the other hand," she roundly asserted, "should hesitate to presume so much. A duke is nothing to be sneezed at, Miss Tyree, and Waincourt even less than most."

"Yes, well, no doubt you are in the right of it." Sabra shrugged, weary of the whole pointless discussion. "I

325

suppose I am too much an American. I never met His Grace, but Ferdinand Roderick James Myles never seemed to me other than a very long name for a rather nice boy who had been mollycoddled and kept in white linen all his life, till sometimes I feared he would be quite smothered to death by it all. No doubt his grandfather presents quite a different picture, but even so, he is in London, and Trevor Myles, in the final analysis, is only a naval captain."

"I beg your pardon, but am to understand that—"

"My dearest Lily, you should have informed me we had a visitor." The deep voice from the doorway startled them both. Indeed, Lily quite jumped before turning with a hand at her breast to favor the intruder with a darkling glance.

"William Ellsworth, how dare you sneak up on a body like that!" she gasped. "Faith, you near took my breath away."

"Then I must apologize for it, m'dear," grinned Ellsworth, crossing the room to take up her dainty white hand in his own bearish paw. Gallantly, he saluted her knuckles. "Am I forgiven, Miss Barrett?" he queried, a twinkle in the eyes lifted meaningfully to hers.

With a sense of having missed something somewhere along the line, Sabra beheld Lily Barrett blush with almost girlish confusion. All at once she was overwhelmed with the oddest sensation that nothing was as it was made out to seem. Not this house, with all its vulgar opulence, nor Lily Barrett, with her china-blue eyes and easy, voluptuous charm—and certainly not William Ellsworth.

"Sir, 'tis gracefully done," gurgled Lily, laughing up at him, "for all you are a sad scapegrace indeed. But then, I've ever had a softness for a rogue with a gentle manner and a devil in his eye. I suppose I shall have to find it in my heart to forgive you just this once, Captain

Ellsworth."

"You are all generosity, ma'am. And, now, perhaps you would present me to your visitor. Strange as it may seem, Miss Tyree and I have never been properly introduced."

"Why 'strange,' captain?" Sabra asked coolly, distrusting his genial manner. "Should we be somehow acquainted?"

Ellsworth's resonant chuckle perfectly fitted his big frame and wide, pleasantly joweled face, she mused cynically. Even the bushy eyebrows bristling upward in his forehead like great jovial caterpillars as he laughed, and the slight paunch, jiggling beneath his waistcoat, suited the image of bluff amiability. It was something in his eyes that gave him away. A steadiness framed in laugh-wrinkles, a stillness amid motion, as if he missed nothing and yet had seen more at some time or other than he had ever wanted to see. She had beheld that look before — in Skyler, sometimes, and in Myles.

"No, not exactly, ma'am," he was saying. " 'Tis more like 'two ships forever passing in the night,' as the saying goes."

"I see," murmured Sabra in extremely dry tones. "Captain Myles, in other words, has kept you informed of me."

"You are a needle-witted one, ain't you," he beamed, apparently delighted with her quick apprehension. "But then Trev told me you was, what?"

His laughter this time brought a reluctant half-smile to her lips, and suddenly their glances locked with a strange sort of understanding. Then the moment was gone as Lily came to her feet and moved toward them with a soft rustle of taffeta and silk.

Ellsworth's arm, Sabra noted with interest, appeared to lift and encircle Lily's shoulders unguided by any conscious thought on the captain's part. It was like instinct. Or habit, maybe, so long established that neither Ellsworth nor Lily was very much aware of it any longer. And yet, somehow she doubted not that the absence of that easy, unconscious gesture would have been instantly noted by either one or both of them.

Sabra's glance narrowed sharply. It was the way her father had used to embrace her mother as they stood together on the terrace at Thornhaven and gazed out over the East River bathed in moonlight.

"Well," she said, in that unmistakable tone of finality that signaled it was time she was leaving. "It was a pleasure meeting you, captain. Perhaps you will do me the favor of giving my regards to Captain Myles the next time you see him."

"You may count on it, Miss Tyree." The blue eyes set in smile-wrinkles seemed to look right into her, so that she had almost to force herself to turn away. Then Lily's hand slipped confidingly beneath her arm.

"You will call on us again sometime," she uttered, more in the manner of one divulging an inescapable truth than in that of a hostess going through the formalities. "I promise I shall be looking forward to it. And try not to worry overmuch about Captain Myles. Even if he does give the appearance of utter disregard, I think you will find he is actually quite good at taking care of himself. Besides, he has — er — something that gives him a sort of protective edge over a mere Sir Wilfred Channing, Baronet."

" 'Something'?" chided Ellsworth, chucking Lily playfully under the chin. "A lucky charm perhaps? A rabbit's foot, no doubt, or maybe one of these Indian medicine bags I've heard tell of. Come now, Lily, be sensible. You'll have Miss Tyree believing you are just a trifle eccentric."

"Shall I indeed," Lily retorted with a flash of blue eyes. "And yet 'twas not I who brought up the subject of magic charms. Nor do I care to be made light of, William Ellsworth, as you know very well. I was simply trying to reassure Miss Tyree. Trevor has the advantage of something a deal more substantial than any silly rabbit's foot. Of that she may be sure."

"But of course, m'dear. He has you to speak up for him, has he not? What more could a man ask?"

Of this extremely odd exchange, Sabra was able to make out very little, nor did she feel overly moved to try at the moment. She had far too many other things on her mind, chief of which was the certainty that, whether or not Lily and Ellsworth actually knew where he was, they knew *something* that made them reasonably confident Myles was not in any immediate peril. At least not from the charges that had been brought against him by Channing, she amended, thinking of what Lily had confided.

Sabra, however, was not so sure. They, after all, were not privy to Channing's secret papers and thus could not possibly know just how treacherous the baronet actually was, or how desperate. Indeed, she doubted not that he was capable of anything, even of murdering Waincourt himself had the duke been available in the flesh and had it behooved Channing to do it.

Still, she could not feel her visit had been entirely wasted, she mused as she waited for Lily to summon Phoebe and for Ellsworth to help her on with her cloak. She had, after all, learned a great deal about Lily Barrett of an entirely unexpected nature, and about Ellsworth, too, whose part in all of this was suddenly quite odiously clear. Had Myles miraculously appeared at that very moment, she thought she would very likely have scratched his deceitful eyes out!

"Are you sure you will not have Ellsworth accompany you and your maidservant home?" queried Lily for the third time as her two callers stepped out onto the stoop.

"I cannot think it is at all safe, my dear, for two women alone. If you are not set upon by cutthroats and thieves, you still run the risk of insult, or worse, from the riff-raff that roam the streets."

"Lily is quite right," Ellsworth put in. "In fact, I'm very sure I should insist on seeing you home."

"It is very kind of you to be concerned," Sabra replied, firmly ignoring her maidservant's eyes burning holes between her shoulder blades, "but truly there are very good reasons why it is better that you do not. Besides, I am quite used to looking after myself."

"Oh, what a nuisance it is not to have use of the carriage!" burst out Lily irritably. "Indeed, had I known one could simply set the body of one's coach on runners, I should have seen to it before this. No doubt you would be a great deal safer in a 'booby-hatch' than roaming the streets afoot, no matter how adept at looking out for yourself you think you are."

"No doubt," Sabra rejoined, her lips twitching appreciatively. "Only I should prefer to think I am not quite yet a candidate for Bedlam." At Lily's blank stare, she could not suppress a small gurgle of laughter. "Forgive me, Miss Barrett, I should not poke fun when you are so obviously concerned about Phoebe and me. The type of vehicle you have described, however, is called a 'booby-*hack*,' though I haven't the foggiest notion why it should be. Good-bye now, and don't worry. We shall be fine, I promise you."

" 'We shall be fine,' " mimicked Phoebe sourly, as they retraced their steps down Barclay and, turning on to Broadway, headed for Vesey Street and St. Paul's Chapel, its square tower glinting in the last faint rays of day. "If we's be fine, then a guardian angel must be lookin' after us."

"Oh, hush, Phoebe!" Sabra retorted, in no mood for a harangue from her maidservant. "Had I allowed Captain Ellsworth to walk us home, I might just as well have sent out announcements that I was still in town. Doubtless we would have Channing's men beating down our door again before we had time to sit down to dinner. So let that be an end to it!"

Phoebe gave a loud sniff.

"Why, sure, Miss Sabra," she said with an air of long-suffering. "Anythin' you says. Only in case you hadn't noticed, the sun be goin' down. An' *nobody* but a fool be goin' to find himself walkin' down Maiden Lane in the dark."

"Oh, come now, Phoebe, I shouldn't have expected you, of all people, to be frightened by a story meant to scare children. And that is all the Screaming Woman of Maiden Lane is. If that is the worst that we have to worry about, then our journey promises most certainly to be an uneventful one."

"I surely does hope you is right, Miss Sabra," muttered Phoebe, rolling her eyes up as if in supplication to the statue of St. Paul, looking down at them from its nook over the chapel door. "I surely does hope you is right."

"But of course I am right," Sabra said, as she waited impatiently for a horse-drawn sleigh to pass. Then, picking up her skirts, she made a dash across Partition Street in a most unladylike manner, Phoebe lumbering to keep up with her as best she could.

The phantom in the shape of a woman robed in white, which for some years had been reputed to roam Maiden Lane after nightfall, had very little to do, however, with Sabra's hurry. Aside from the bitter cold and the obvious, very real dangers attendant with being out on the streets at night, she had, since leaving the house on Barclay, experienced the uncanny feeling of being watched, a feeling which grew stronger as they left St. Paul's behind and made short work of the two remaining blocks to Maiden Lane. Little wishing to alarm whoever might be following them, she had by dint of sheer willpower restrained from looking back. Now, with night fast coming on and the gloomy environs of Maiden Lane immediately before them, her fingers tightened instinctively on the gun she carried, concealed beneath her cloak.

She was hardly surprised to find Maiden Lane deserted. As the businesses in the area were mostly concerned either with the silver trade or with the selling of dry goods and food stuffs, it would have been odd, indeed, had the proprietors not already locked their doors and withdrawn upstairs, for the most part, to living quarters above the shops. The street seemed to brood in the thickening shadows, made even more uninviting by the marked absence of street lamps. Shivering a little, Sabra toyed briefly with the idea of continuing on to Crown Street, thus avoiding Maiden Lane altogether, but, all things considered, she disliked the notion of going even so little as half a block out of their way. In the end, she shrugged fatalistically and, ignoring Phoebe's grim prophecies of utter doom, made with a firm step down the narrow alley running alongside the "Old Swago" Market.

The high-pitched shriek, when it came, took Sabra unpleasantly by surprise.

"The Lawd have mercy!" muttered Phoebe, gazing wild-eyed behind her.

"Sh-sh!" Sabra felt her nerves stretch as the cry sounded again. "It's coming from over there!" she whispered, gesturing toward the mouth of Little Green Street, which was directly across the way from them.

"Phoebe, wait here."

"Oh, no you doesn't," Phoebe answered, grabbing for her mistress, but Sabra was too quick for her. "Dad drat it, Sabra Tyree!" sputtered Phoebe, finding herself left standing with naught but a fist full of air. "You comes back here. Right now, does you hear me?"

She might just as well have saved her breath, since Sabra had already reached the mouth of the alley and, running heedlessly, was quickly out of sight.

Talking to herself, the old Negress waited, undecided. Then a muffled scream rent the air, followed less than the space of three heartbeats later by Sabra's voice, low and piercing in the chill night air.

"Stop it! Stop it at once, or I swear I shall shoot!"

"Hellsfire and damnation!" Phoebe muttered and without wasting another moment, took off as fast as she could manage straight for the alley. She had not gone ten yards up the steep grade before her breath was whistling in her throat, and only the dreadful certainty that her mistress had blundered into whatever thing had uttered those bloodcurdling screams kept her puffing up the hill. At last, unable to plod another step, she lumbered to a halt and, gasping for air, leaned an arm against the low wall surrounding the Quaker Meeting House and cemetery.

Then the crack of a gunshot split the air, and with a gasp, Phoebe lifted up her head to see her mistress grappling with a figure draped in flowing white. Without waiting to see more, Phoebe started for the gate and moments later was searching among the gravestones for her mistress, who seemed to have vanished.

"Miss Sabra? Miss Sabra? Dad drat it, girl, where you at?"

"Phoebe, over here," whispered back at her, and at last she saw her, kneeling over a still figure on the ground.

333

"Miss Sabra, what in the world—"

"Not now, Phoebe." Sabra was quick to cut her off. "The poor woman has been beaten and is nearly half frozen to death. Quickly, we must get her up."

"Yes, Miss Sabra," retorted Phoebe irritably. "I can see that. But who in blazes is she?"

"She said her name is Kitty Quinby," Sabra answered with scant patience. "Now, go and see if you can find her cloak. I think she dropped it somewhere over there. And hurry, Phoebe. I'm very much afraid we may already be too late to save her."

Chapter 20

Feeling like a caged animal, Sabra prowled endlessly about the library. It was four days since she and Phoebe had made the trek to see Lily Barrett, and in all that time she had yet to hear anything about Myles, good, bad, or indifferent. It was as if he had simply dropped off the face of the earth, she thought irritably. And for all she knew he had taken Ellsworth and Lily along with him. She had heard nothing from them either.

When there had been no word of Myles's arrest after the first forty-eight hours, she had felt a measure of relief. But when two more days had passed and he had made no attempt to contact her or let her know how he fared, she began to fear that Channing had made sure that he couldn't. How difficult could it be, after all, to dispose of one more dead body, when each day the death carts were to be seen leaving the prisons with their grisly loads? Faith, she could not even be sure Wes's body was not among them.

"You must not let yourself think that way, Sabra Tyree," she said out loud to the empty room. "Wes is alive. He has to be!" And no doubt Myles was, too, she tried to tell herself, but somehow the muscles, clenched like a fist inside her stomach, simply would not let go. "Oh, *why* isn't Jubal back yet?" she exploded, wanting to scream, smash a glass figurine against the wall, *do* something—*anything* to relieve the terrible suspense of waiting.

Petulantly she flopped down on the sofa before the fire and glared at the inoffensive leap of flames. She could not bear the waiting. It wore at her so that she could neither sleep nor eat. But worst of all, it left her too much time alone with her thoughts. If only she had someone to talk to, she fretted, then frowned. No, not someone. It was Robert she needed, Robert she missed. Indeed, she had never realized before how much she depended on him, not only to act as a sounding board for her ideas, but to fill these endless voids of waiting before a thing could finally be acted upon. Damn him and this whole impossible situation he had got them in!

Instantly she was driven to her feet again, to roam the stultifying familiarity of the book-lined room, till at last she found herself at the window staring out at the street enshrouded in fog. No doubt that was what was holding Jubal up. He had left for Thornhaven at dawn the day before, and should have been back in plenty of time. Well, no matter. She would go tonight without him if need be. Indeed, she would not lose this chance to gain a slight advantage over Channing. She was the granddaughter of the earl of Dearing, after all. Why should she not curry the favor of a royal prince, if it could be done?

She started to go over it all again in her mind, step by step, detail by detail. She must look stunning when she made her entrance at General Riedesel's reception, for which the emerald velour Robe a l'Anglais worn over a ruffed petticoat of ivory satin should do admirably. In spite of the guest of honor, she would wear her hair unpowdered so that she would be sure to stand out among all the bewigged New York fashionables. And at her throat and ears would reside the emeralds given her by her grandfather, the earl. She would arrive late, just moments before the receiving line had reached the point of dispersing for the evening. The timing must be perfect if she were to command the notice of a certain newly appointed midshipman in His Majesty's navy — young Prince William.

Here her thoughts were interrupted by a subdued rap on the library door. Turning impatiently from the window, she called out permission to enter. Then the door opened, and her brief pique at being disturbed suddenly vanished.

"Kitty," she exclaimed softly, espying the young woman standing hesitantly on the threshold. "What are you doing out of bed? Come in out of that draft at once and sit by the fire. We cannot risk a relapse now, when you are just beginning to get your strength back, now can we?"

The girl fluttered embarrassed eyelashes before lifting frank brown eyes to the other woman's face.

" 'Tis good in you to be concerned, miss," she said with simple candor, "but you doesn't need to worry none about the likes of me. I been stove up worse before an' got up to work the next day. These bruises don't mean nothin'."

Sabra experienced a sharp pang at the implications inherent in that little speech, made doubly eloquent by the fatalistic shrug that had accompanied it. Despite a certain boldness in the tilt of the chin, Kitty Quinby could not have been more than eighteen or nineteen, if she was a day, and with those great brown eyes accentuated by tawny hair, parted simply in the middle of the forehead and drawn into a single braid down her back, she looked even younger. Yet the fair skin, sprinkled lightly with freckles, bore the livid marks of a man's brutal fists, even as her back and torso beneath the fabric of her borrowed gown gave mute evidence of other, repeated beatings. The lout who had done this to her should be publicly reviled and forcibly restrained from ever raising his hand against any woman again, thought

Sabra darkly, recalling the cloaked figure of the man who had fled the Quaker cemetery with her bullet singing past his ear. And yet how many Kitty Quinby's there were in the world, women and young girls who unhappily would know nothing but brutality from the men in their lives!

"Yes, well, suppose you let me be the judge of that," replied Sabra, going to her visitor and drawing her firmly into the room. Then closing the door, she led her to a wing chair near the fire and bade her to be seated. "There, that's better," she said lightly as she tucked a crocheted shawl around the girl's legs and stood back to survey her with pretended disapproval. "You know, there was no need for you to come all the way down here. I was planning to pop in to see you just as soon as Phoebe informed me you were awake. However, as long as you are here, perhaps it would not be amiss to touch on your plans for the immediate future."

Kitty flushed and glanced painfully away. Then the bold little chin came up with a sort of desperation born of pride.

"I know all you done for me, Miss Tyree, an' I reckon I haven't the words to thank you. If it wasn't for you, I'd most likely be dead now, instead of sittin' here in these fine clothes in front of a warm fire. But now I'm on me feet again, I expect it's time I was leavin'."

"It is no such thing, Kitty Quinby," Sabra replied sternly. "Indeed, I shall not hear of it. You are far from ready to brave the streets on your own. However, I must admit that your presence here presents me with something of a problem. You see, I shall be leaving New York very soon, and I'm afraid it is unlikely that I shall be coming back again. Which is why I am forced to have this interview, painful as it may be for you. Is there no one, Kitty, to whom you might apply for protection? A relative, perhaps. Or an acquaintance. Have

338

you any friends who might be willing to help?"

A shadow, like pain, passed fleetingly across the girl's brow.

"I did have—a—a friend for a while," she said, looking past Sabra into the fire as though she had forgotten the other woman's presence. Then suddenly the brown eyes hardened. "I expect he was the fair-weather kind, though. For he left without nary no word nearly a se'ennight past, and I ain't seen nor heard from him since. I expect he's found himself another woman in some other port by now, and I got no one. But that's just the way of it in this world." She shrugged again with that same toughness she had used before to mask her bitterness. " 'Course, me mum an' dad'd take me back, though they've hardly enough to keep themselves and the little ones what still be to home. Only I been sendin' 'em every penny what Quinby hasn't took from me, so's there ain't none left for passage to England. Likely *he'*d find me anyway and stop me from gettin' on the boat. He's got spyin' eyes everywhere, *he* does. Ain't nothin' he doesn't know."

"Who, Kitty?" queried Sabra, wondering at the flash of fear and bitter loathing that darkened the brown eyes to a dusky hue. "Mr. Quinby, your husband?"

"Oh, no, miss. Not 'im. Quinby's just plain small and mean, but he don't scare me none. If it wasn't for his master, I'd done left Quinby ere this."

"I see. And will you not tell me his name—this man who employs your husband?"

"But I thought as how you knew, Miss Tyree," Kitty said, obviously puzzled. "Quinby is gentleman's gentleman to Sir Wilfred Channing . . . Miss? Be you all right? Did I say something wrong?"

Sabra, who had been understandably stricken with surprise at the announcement that she was harboring the wife of Channing's valet beneath her roof, managed a somewhat crooked smile.

"No, of course not," she said, recalled to an awareness of the girl gazing up at her in alarm. "Indeed, how could you? I was just a trifle startled is all. I'm afraid that the baronet has done little to endear me to him in the years I have had the misfortune to be in his acquaintance."

"Yes, miss, I know. It was because of him you had to leave London, wasn't it. An' long before that, he done near ruint your father. I know all about what Sir Wilfred tried to do. It was me what overheard him plottin' to have you snatched and brung to him. I hope I done right, Miss Tyree, tellin' me friend'n all. He swore he wouldn't let nothing bad happen, an' I believed him. But then Quinby found out I'd bribed the upstairs maid to get the message out, and he beat me somethin' awful. He said Sir Wilfred would have me neck for it, and his, too. And when I bragged me friend wouldn't let 'im, he just laughed, real spitefullike. Said there wasn't nobody goin' to do nothin', for where I was goin' there wasn't nobody goin' to find me, not ever."

"And that's when he locked you in the wardrobe?"

The girl nodded.

"Left me in me nightdress, he did, so that when *they* come for me, I wasn't even decent dressed."

" 'They'? You mean the baronet and your husband?"

"No, or I'd not be here today." The brown eyes that looked up at Sabra were hard and cynical beyond their years. "They was slavers, Miss Tyree," Kitty told her. "Sir Wilfred done sold me to slavers, bound for the West Indies."

Shocked, Sabra could not conceal her horror.

"But he wouldn't dare!" she exclaimed and knew at once that she was being naive indeed. There had always been stories told among sailors about the white slave trade. It was just that she had always supposed it hap-

340

pened only in the Far East.

Kitty was suffering under no such illusions.

"White women bring a good price, if they be young and healthy," she said in a hard little voice. "I seen it before. That's why I'd 've done anything to get away. I was just lucky they was already three-quarters pickled in rum, for they was real careless 'bout not tyin' me hands. Only flung me cloak about me shoulders, they did, and led me out bold as you please. When we come to the Vly, I just pulled loose an' run for all I was worth. That first night I slept in a stable or I expect I'd frozen to death. Come mornin' I tried to sell me weddin' ring, which Quinby somehow forgot, an' that's how *he* found me out. I was hidin' in the Old Swago when I seen you and your woman. 'Course I didn't know it was you, but I knowed her. Quinby pointed her out to me a couple of times in the Vly. So I followed her, hopin' maybe she'd take me to you."

"*You* followed her!" exclaimed Sabra. "But then, all along it must have been you I sensed behind us. And I thought it was Channing, or one of his henchmen."

"I don't know nothin' 'bout that. I didn't see Sir Wilfred till we was headed back through Oswego. He come out'n the shop where I parted with me ring just as you come near the alley."

Suddenly Sabra's eyes narrowed on the girl's face. So it had been Sir Wilfred in the cemetery, she thought, realizing suddenly how desperate he must be indeed to risk trying to murder the girl with his own hands—the girl who was an indisputable witness to his own calumny.

"That first scream," she said, ponderingly. "You meant that as a warning to me. You deliberately drew him off, Kitty, didn't you."

Kitty's hands twisted nervously in the folds of the shawl across her lap.

341

"I heard all that was said before you went into that house on Barclay. It wasn't hard to guess who you was, nor it didn't take much to know Sir Wilfred would figure it out, too, soon's he saw your woman." She shrugged. "Anyway, you know the rest. I didn't get no farther than that bury patch behind the Old Quaker Meetin' House when he caught up to me." Suddenly a shiver shook the slight frame. "He meant to kill me, Miss Tyree, right then and there. I could see it in his face. An' when his fingers closed about me neck, I couldn't do nothin'."

Seeing the girl's brittle composure suddenly crack, Sabra knelt instinctively and drew Kitty's head to her shoulder.

"Yes, that's it," she murmured, oddly touched at the sudden flood of vulnerability in one who had seemed inured to so much of horror. "You have a good cry. And then we shall see what can be done about reaching your friend—er—Mr. Leeks, is it not?"

The girl hiccupped and sat up with a start.

"But—but—how did you—" she managed somewhat convulsively between shuddering gasps.

"It wasn't difficult to guess. Your friend told a friend of mine, who saved me from Sir Wilfred's wicked plot. So you see, 'tis I who am in your debt, at least twice over." Smiling, Sabra ran her hand soothingly over the girl's hair. "But never mind that now. For the time being, I want to concentrate on getting back your strength. I promise you've nothing to worry about. If I cannot find your Mr. Leeks for you, you will just come away with Phoebe and me when we leave. But you must promise me you will not try to leave this house. If you are to remain safe, no one outside of the household must know you are here. Will you give me your word?"

"Ezra said you had the look about you of an angel of mercy, Miss Tyree, an' I expect he was right. I give you me word, an' gladly."

"Good," Sabra murmured approvingly. "Now, I think it's time you went back upstairs to rest for a while. No doubt Phoebe will be wondering where you've got yourself off to, and when she finds out, I shall be all in the suds with her for keeping you so long. No, no need to say anything more. Just be off with you."

Smiling and sniffing, Kitty Quinby got up and obediently went toward the door. Just as she was about to slip out of the library, however, Sabra stopped her.

"Kitty?"

"Yes, miss?" replied the girl, looking back at her.

"Why did you hope Phoebe would lead you to me? Was it because you thought I might be able to tell you something of your friend Mr. Leeks?"

"No, miss, it was because of the captain," she answered matter-of-factly.

Sabra's eyebrows lifted in startled surprise. "Captain?" she echoed, her heart skipping a beat.

"Captain Myles. He come to see Sir Wilfred the day I bribed the girl to take me message out. It was me what took his hat and coat, and when no one wasn't lookin', he whispered real low that Leeks had told him everything. Pressed me hand, he did, and said he was a friend, did I ever need one. And so when I seen Phoebe, I thought as how maybe you, bein' the captain's lady 'n' all—well, that you maybe could . . ."

"Could help you reach your newest friend, Captain Myles."

"Yes, miss." Kitty swallowed. "Is he in some kind of trouble, Miss Tyree? Is that why Ezra Leeks couldn't come for me?"

"Yes, Kitty, I'm afraid that he is." She smiled then, deliberately breaking the mood. "But never you mind. I have it on good authority that the captain is well able to look after himself. No doubt the same can be said for your Mr. Leeks. Now go and rest. We shall talk again later, I promise."

Nodding, the girl reluctantly turned and, pulling the door to, left her benefactress once again to the private torment of her own doubts and anxieties.

Later that evening, Sabra slipped the loop of her ivory-handled folding fan over her wrist and paused for one last critical look at her reflection in the ormolu looking glass. The green Robe a l'Anglais with its ivory underskirt was everything she might have wished, as was the delicately wrought necklace of gold filigree of leaves set with emeralds, which graced her neck. Nor was she disappointed with her daringly simple coiffure, which, foregoing the accepted fashion of pads and rigidly styled horizontal curls, was drawn high up on her head beneath a small jeweled cap and allowed to fall in charming disarray down her back, a single red-gold curl having the distinction of resting on her bosom. Everything from the top of her head to her embroidered silk shoes with the diamond buckles and Italian heels was just as she had envisioned it would be. And if there was a pearly translucence to her skin, the result of sleepless nights and lack of appetite, it was, after all, the vogue to appear as white as Dresden china. Nor was it all that disadvantageous that her eyes, in contrast to the pale oval of her face, seemed enormous gems glinting emerald sparks.

She would do, she decided, conscious of the strangeness of not having Phoebe fussing over her. In fact, it gave her a rather uneasy feeling, as if Phoebe were some sort of good luck charm whose absence boded ill somehow for the evening. Tonight it had been Kitty who fixed her hair and helped her on with her dress, while Phoebe kept watch over Robert, driving him to

344

distraction, no doubt, with her persistent mothering.

A pang wrenched at her heart.

She had seen Wayne only once since that fateful confrontation in his room four days past, and he had looked like the very devil. Unshaven and dirty, his hair matted and his clothes rumpled from having been slept in, he hardly resembled the Wayne she knew. Obviously he had been drinking heavily, and from the looks of him had not touched solid food in days. That was yesterday, after Jubal had had to leave so that there had been only herself to stand watch over him. When he had failed to answer her summons on the door, she had let herself in and found him stretched, insensible, across the bed, an empty decanter on the lowboy nearby. Even as she had suffered an agonizing wrench at the sight of him, however, it had suddenly come to her what must be done.

What better way to keep an eye on Robert and at the same time see to it that he did not drive himself to the brink of destruction than to set Phoebe to watch over him? Wayne himself had been enough to convince the old nanny that indeed he was very ill and must be kept to his room. Sight of him had aroused every formidable motherly instinct in that generous bosom and, soundly reprimanding Sabra for having ever entrusted a man in Wayne's condition to Jubal's ineffectual care, she had in very short order had Wayne cleaned up and laid properly in his bed. Hard upon that had come chicken broth for his stomach and a tongue-lashing for his soul. By late afternoon the next day, Sabra was informed by an inordinately pleased Phoebe Henry that Mr. Robert had already come a long way toward bearing resemblance to a human being on the road to recovery.

At least she could be grateful for that much, she told herself. Gathering up her ermine pelisse, she doused the lamps and let herself out of the room, only to find herself face-to-face with the object of her recent reflections.

Wayne, fully dressed and neatly groomed, stood over her, his aspect pale in the uncertain light of the hallway.

"Robert," she gasped, caught unawares. "Faith, you startled me half to death!"

A grimace crossed the thin features.

"Forgive me," he muttered. "I've been waiting, hoping to catch you before you left. Please, Sabra, I have to talk to you."

"What are you doing here?" she blurted, alarmed by something she sensed in him, a reckless sort of desperation, she thought. "Where's Phoebe?"

The wry twist of his lips went to her heart like a blade.

"You needn't worry that I've strangled our good-hearted nanny," he answered cynically. "I left her dozing in her chair. Sabra, I know you intend moving against Channing tonight. Let me help you, I beg you."

For an instant she stood, undecided, her heart torn by the torment in his eyes.

"At least tell me how you intend to pull it off," he uttered harshly, grasping her by the arms in his desperation. "Surely you must see that nothing Channing might do to me could possibly be worse than what I have already suffered. Please, you must give me the chance to make things up to you."

"There is nothing you *can* do," she said, forced to it, "except stay here and wait. If I am successful, I shall be back tonight with Wes. If I am not, then I shall be depending on you to get Phoebe and the others to safety. One way or the other, you must be ready to leave here at a moment's notice."

"Yes, yes, all right. You can count on me for that, but what are you going to do?" he insisted. "Dammit, Sabra, you can't face Channing alone. You, of all people, should know what he's capable of. You must

346

take me with you."

"Robert, I can't!" She thought she could not bear the look on his face as slowly he released his grip on her arms and stood staring down at her as if she had pronounced his sentence of death. Impulsively she lifted her hand toward him.

"Robert, try and understand," she said.

"Oh, I understand," he cut in bitterly. Turning away, he slammed the side of his fist against the wall and held it there. "God knows, I can't even blame you. Indeed, you've been more than generous in the circumstances, have you not. Anyone else would mercifully have had me shot by now."

"Yes, no doubt they would," she answered coldly, suddenly out of patience with him. "However, that has nothing to do with this. I cannot take you with me, because there would be no purpose to it. Whatever happens with Channing is between him and me. No one else. On the other hand, I really do need you here to look after things. If worse comes to worse, you're the only one who could see Phoebe and Kitty Quinby safely across the lines. If you will stop and think, Robert Wayne, instead of wallowing in self-pity, you'll see that I am right."

For a moment longer he stood rigid and unmoving. Then suddenly his shoulders sagged.

"Forgive me, Sabra," he uttered on a shuddering breath. "I didn't mean to take it out on you. You will have Jubal somewhere close by at least, won't you?"

"Yes, of course," she lied glibly. "Jubal's driving me to General Riedesel's. He'll be sure to keep me in sight, whatever happens after that."

Wayne nodded. "Good," he said and, letting his hand slide down the wall, turned back to her. Somehow he managed his old, sweet smile, which hurt her worse than anything else he could have said or done. "Be careful tonight, will you? And don't worry, I'll have everything ready here for you and Wes when you get back. If, that is, that old harridan in my room doesn't have me strapped down in my bed."

Sabra gave a watery laugh.

"That old harridan is very fond of you, Robert. And so am I."

"Yes, I know," he said, but something in his look frightened her.

"Robert, it's going to be all right, I know it. As soon as we have Wes, we'll be out of here, and then everything will be as it was before."

"Sure," he answered. The corner of his mouth curled wryly. Suddenly he looked away. "You'd better go now, hadn't you? You wouldn't want to be too late to meet the guest of honor, after all."

"No, I don't suppose I should," she murmured, little liking to leave him in his present mood, but unable to see what else she could do. "Very well," she added bracingly, "I'll see you later then."

"Yes, no doubt," he replied, low-voiced. Biting her lip, Sabra brushed past him and hurried along the hall and down the stairs to the footman, waiting to escort her out to the sled-converted carriage.

Some fifteen minutes later, Sabra, having timed her arrival to perfection, found herself the cynosure of all eyes as she made her curtsey to her hostess, who was striking in a Watteau gown of yellow silk embroidered in arabesque, her powdered wig adorned with ostrich plumes dyed to match her dress. "Frietschen" Riedesel, as she was fondly known by the officers, whose darling she was, greeted Sabra with a decided twinkle of amusement.

"I confess, my dear, that I always look forward to

your entrances with a deal of anticipation," she observed, giving a gentle wave of her fan, "and I must say you have never once disappointed me."

Sabra smiled. "One tries one's humble best," she replied, in perfect accord with her hostess. She had always gotten along well with the general's lively young wife.

"Oh, indubitably," agreed Frietschen, laughing. "But since you have hardly gone to all the trouble to arrive last purely for my entertainment, allow me to apologize for the general's failure to be here to extend his welcome personally. He was called away earlier on some military matter, which quite naturally could not wait a more opportune time. It has thus been delegated to me in his absence to make everyone acquainted with this young gentleman at my left. Your Royal Highness, may I present to you Miss Sabra Tyree, granddaughter of the earl of Dearing."

"Your Royal Highness," murmured Sabra, dropping into a deep curtsey before the fourteen-year-old prince, arrayed in the uniform of a midshipman in the navy.

Knock-kneed and already too stout for his age, Prince William was yet possessed of a not altogether displeasing countenance. Bidding her rise, he paid her a pretty compliment on her appearance, replied to her inquiry that he found the life of a midshipman under Admiral Digby stimulating and that New York, while provincial, was not uninteresting. He then proceeded to regale her with the account of a recent excursion to Vly Market, which, owing to his midshipman's uniform, had been accomplished most satisfactorily incognito. All of which netted her a total of some twenty minutes in intimate conversation with the third-born of King George's sons.

All in all, she was not displeased with the outcome of this, the first phase of her planned strategy, as, waving her fan gently to and fro, she allowed her gaze to roam with apparent casualness over the sea of faces in search of one gentleman in particular. That Sir Wilfred Channing was somewhere among the multitude, she did not doubt for a moment. A man in his position could hardly afford, after all, to slight a prince of the royal blood, even one the tender age of a mere schoolboy. As to whether or not he was actually witness to her noteworthy success with the guest of honor mattered not at all. It was enough that he would hear about it and wonder what His Royal Highness had seen fit to discuss for a full twenty minutes with the dazzling Miss Tyree.

Prince William, perceiving that he was about to be relieved of the duty of receiving further guests, invited her at that moment to partake of some refreshment. Smiling, Sabra parted her lips to accept of his kind invitation, when a grin of boyish pleasure suddenly broke through the formal mask of royalty on display. As of its own accord, Sabra's glance followed that of the young prince.

All at once her heart nearly stopped as she caught sight of the tall masculine figure approaching the receiving line with slow, supple grace.

Across the distance gray, cynical eyes found hers, and for an instant the world seemed to waver and recede, leaving only her and Myles and a roaring in her ears. A mocking gleam of amusement flickered between the slitted eyelids, then Myles looked away to make his bow to his hostess.

As she watched him salute the soft, white hand of the general's lady, it was all Sabra could do to keep from screaming out at him. The reckless fool, she thought, expecting at any moment to behold him placed in manacles and dragged away to the stockade. But, unbelievably, no one seemed at all perturbed at his presence. Indeed, if anything, Frietschen Riedesel gave every indication of a woman exceedingly pleased to have him there, she noted.

350

"It would seem, Captain Myles, that you are indeed everything that your reputation has made you out to be," murmured the general's wife, taking in with an appreciative glance the sensuous leap of a dimple in either masculine cheek as graciously the captain returned her smile. "I understand," she added, "you and His Highness are already acquainted."

"Indeed, ma'am," spoke up His Royal Highness with greater enthusiasm than he had thus far shown anyone, "Captain Myles and I are old acquaintances. May I say, sir, that I have seldom heard a more thrilling tale than the account of your recent encounter with a French ship of the line. Indeed, I should have given a great deal just to be there to see it for m'self."

"I trust, Your Highness," Myles replied in dry tones, "that as midshipman under Admiral Digby you will soon have your own tales to tell. With d'Estaing on the loose in the Caribbean, there promises to be more than enough action for every British ship in the Atlantic."

"Or at least for those fortunate enough to run across him. I've heard that one might go for months on blockade duty without spotting more than an occasional coaster. And you, sir, on a single cruise were able not only to net five prizes, but to disable a French two-decker. But then, that is the advantage of serving aboard a frigate as opposed to a seventy-four — the freedom, the very mobility which is yours."

He said this with a fervor that brought a faint smile to Myles's lips. No doubt, thought Sabra acerbically, the captain was recalling his own days aboard the cumbersome three-decker, *Antioch*. Then Frietschen Riedesel, ever the accomplished hostess, moved to turn the conversation away from purely masculine subjects to one which was certain to include her female guest.

" 'Tis true the captain has made a proud record for himself in the service of His Majesty, Your Highness,"

351

she smoothly interjected, "but now I understand congratulations are in order on quite a different head. Indeed, I assure you the question in everyone's mind at present is whether the captain and Miss Tyree will be taking their vows here or in England. Have you decided when the happy occasion is to be, my dear?"

"I must confess that I have not yet given the matter much thought," replied Sabra. Her glance flicked to Myles's, sardonically amused, then back to her hostess. "The day-to-day existence of a naval captain is so filled with uncertainties that I find I hardly know what to expect from one moment to the next. As a matter of fact, since Captain Myles has been kept unavoidably from my presence for some few days, I wonder if you would be so kind as to excuse us. I find I have a great deal to discuss with him."

"But of course," murmured Frietschen. "I perfectly understand. Feel free to take the captain to the general's study if you wish for privacy. In the meantime, perhaps Your Highness would not be averse to taking some refreshment? I myself am positively famished."

"What the devil are you doing here?" Sabra whispered fiercely moments later, as she led Myles along the nearly empty gallery.

"But I should think that was obvious," drawled the captain, insufferably smiling. "I came to be with the woman who is to be my wife. It would hardly serve, after all, to allow you to appear neglected so soon after our betrothal. Imagine what the tattlemongers would have made of it."

"They could have made of it what they wished, I'm sure," retorted Sabra waspishly, "and still you have not answered my question. Why are you not trussed up in irons and languishing in some prison for murder and treason?"

Myles grinned ironically.

"I am sorry to disappoint you, *ma mie*. However, it seems Sir Wilfred has graciously admitted the whole thing was all just an unfortunate misunderstanding on his part. Evidently Mr. Inness was the guilty scoundrel all along, and I, the innocent object of a well-wrought frame. The baronet was touchingly apologetic."

"Was he indeed," muttered Sabra, unamused. "And how, I am moved to ask, did this come about?"

They had arrived, as they talked, at General Riedesel's study, which they discovered to be a modest-sized room containing a contemporary mahogany writing table with three matching chairs, a few shelves of books, and a magnificent paneled firescreen set across one corner of the room. No sooner had they entered and closed the door behind them than Myles, without warning, cornered her with her back to the carved wooden barrier.

"Let us just say," he murmured, leaning a hand against the oaken panel on a level with her head, "that Waincourt is not without its influence, especially for one who was used to take a younger Prince William on occasional outings."

"You?" she queried in accents of disbelief.

"No, Ferdy, actually. However, I was present on two of these memorable occasions. Or at least they were memorable, fortunately, to William. It seems he has made it a point ever since to follow my career with great interest."

"Are you saying it was the prince who cleared you of the charges?"

"Not exactly. As a matter of fact, I believe it was the admiral, at his midshipman's respectful request."

"You rogue!" exclaimed Sabra, suddenly furious as it came to her how foolish she had been to lose even a single moment's sleep over the odious captain's safety, when Lily Barrett had told her exactly how it would be. "How dare you leave me to wonder for four days and as many nights if Channing had had you locked up or murdered!"

Twin devils of laughter appeared in the sleepy gray eyes.

"You say that, my love, as if it might have caused you some grief had the baronet done so."

"On the contrary, captain," she retorted, lifting her chin, "I should no doubt have been delighted to learn you had at last met with your just desserts."

"That's one of the things I have always loved most in you — your tender concern for my welfare. My arm, by the way, is well on the way to recovery, due, no doubt, to your unusual methods of treatment. My ship's surgeon was greatly impressed, I assure you."

"Your ship's surgeon? Good God, you've been on your ship all this time?"

"It does seem the most logical place for a ship's captain, don't you agree?" he rejoined, watching the dazzling display of lights in her eyes.

"I agree only that I was a fool ever to have troubled myself over you. Now, release me if you please. I came to mingle with the guests."

"On the contrary, my love," murmured Myles, with a lazy smile. "You came to work a deal with Channing. And when I am ready, we shall proceed to the bargaining. Until then, Channing can wait. I have yet to avail myself of a proper welcome from my bride-to-be. A man comes to expect a little warmth from his woman, after all."

Sabra's breasts heaved in indignation.

"I am *not* your woman, sir," she flashed back at him in magnificent scorn. "Furthermore, I do not recall inviting you to join me in the 'bargaining,' as you call it.

354

I shall deal with Channing alone and on my own terms."

Myles's slow grin was anything but comforting. Indeed, Sabra's mouth went suddenly dry.

"Not if you want your brother back, I'm afraid. In so far as Locke is concerned, Channing is out of the game. You'll deal with me now, Miss Tyree. You have no other choice in the matter. For I assure you I am the only one who can deliver your brother."

Chapter 21

At first Sabra was too startled to do more than stare at
Myles. But then, as the stunning implications of what he
had said began to dawn on her, she went suddenly pearly
white.

"You—have him?" she faltered. "Myles, are you telling
me Wes is safe?"

A curiously rueful expression flickered in the gray eyes,
quickly to be masked behind drooping eyelids. This was
not how he had meant to play it. The last thing he had
wanted was to set himself up as some sort of hero. That
could only complicate matters. Besides, it was not her
gratitude that he wanted.

"I have him," he drawled, somewhat evasively. "And,
for the time being at least, he is safe enough."

"Safe where?" she cried, trying to grapple with the
startling news. "Oh, God, how is he?"

"I am afraid I cannot tell you where he is—at least not
yet. As to how he is, with any luck you will be able to
see that for yourself very shortly."

"But I don't understand," she persisted, sensing a reticence in Myles that could not but make her uneasy.
"Why can I not see him now?"

A look of ennui descended over the stern features.
"Suffice it to say that for the present you are better off
knowing as little as possible concerning events surrounding your brother's release. Your brother may be safe, but
so long as Channing is free, you, my dear, are not."

All at once she grew pale as one startling possibility occurred to her.

"You're afraid if I know too much, Channing will try to use me against you," she accused, her eyes huge on his face. "That's it, isn't it. You've put your career—your life—in danger for my sake—for my brother's!"

He almost cursed aloud as without warning she threw her arms about his neck. "Faith, how I have misjudged you!" she exclaimed softly.

Myles stiffened, his hands going up to grasp her wrists with the intention of stopping things before they went any farther.

Sabra never noticed. Loosening her hold about his neck, she tipped her head back to gaze earnestly up into his face.

"I should have trusted you," she murmured, a smile trembling on her lips. "Myles, can you ever forgive me?"

It was on his tongue to set her straight, now, before things got out of hand. But as luck would have it, he made the fatal error of looking into those eyes, enormous and lustrous with unshed tears.

Bloody hell, he thought, why had she to be so cursed beautiful! Then she was reaching up on tiptoes to pull his head down, and as her lips found his, Myles stifled a groan and tossed caution to the wind. Muttering an oath, he caught the slender body to him.

The air seemed crushed from Sabra's lungs as Myles kissed her with a fierce, demanding passion that seemed meant to draw fire from her very soul. Feeling caught in a tempest, she clung to him, responded to the fury of his embrace with all her woman's love. And when at last he released her, panting and dazed, her heart hammering beneath her breast, she let her head loll back to reveal eyes like dusky pools, deep, alluring, mysterious.

Myles, more shaken than he could have thought possible, cupped Sabra's cheek in his hand. A rueful smile curved his lips as he studied the soft play of emotion in the face turned up to his.

357

"Damn your witch's eyes," he muttered strangely. "I fear they have all but ruined everything."

Sabra blinked.

"Ruined everything?" she echoed, her smile uncertain.

For an instant his thumb played lightly over her lips. Then the muscle leaped along his jawline, and his expression hardened, like a shutter dropping into place.

"You must forgive me, my love," he drawled. His lip curled sardonically. "I fear your beauty quite overwhelmed me for a moment."

Sabra drew back. A heated blush invaded her cheeks as she stared at Myles and beheld the cynical mask of the man who had betrayed her trust once before. Good God, what had she done? With terrible certainty it came to her that she had allowed herself to be played for the worst kind of fool! Humiliated and stricken with the belief that she had misread the abominable captain, she curled her hands into fists at her sides till her nails bit into the palms and the pain had steadied her somewhat. Damn Myles to bloody hell! she thought. She was not someone to be toyed with and then discarded until the next time it might strike his fancy to play with her again.

Vowing to show him that his kiss had meant as little to her as it had to him, she snapped open her fan and gazed at him over the top of it with dangerous green eyes.

"Forgive you, captain? But there is nothing *to* forgive, surely. It was only a kiss, was it not? A trifle to be quickly forgot, nothing more."

She had the dubious satisfaction of seeing the cold leap of steel in his heavy-lidded gaze. Then it was gone. Insufferably, the captain inclined his head.

"At least tell me, captain, how my brother fares. Surely that is not too much to ask?"

Her heart caught in her throat as she watched him turn and saunter wordlessly to the window overlooking the street. Parting the drapes, he gazed out for a long moment before answering.

"He's alive, just barely," he said at last. Dropping the curtain, he turned to look at her. Suddenly the gimlet eyes seemed to pierce through her. "I shan't lie to you. It's a bloody miracle that Locke has lasted this long." His mouth twisted in a wry smile. "Apparently he is as stubborn as at least one other of his family. Perhaps such tenaciousness of life will even be enough to tip the scales in his favor."

"But you don't really think he has a chance, do you," she declared bitterly. Dragging in a shuddering breath, she leaned her head back against the door. "God, but this is the final irony. To see him die now, after all he's been through. It would hardly seem fair, would it."

The captain's glance narrowed sharply.

"Life has a peculiar habit of hitting below the belt," he observed dispassionately. "Rather than bemoan that indisputable reality, I suggest you concentrate your time and energy on something worth the effort. Locke refused to give in, no matter what they threw at him. Surely he deserves at least that much from you."

Stung by his harshness, even as he had meant for her to be, Sabra lifted magnificent flashing eyes.

"How dare you speak of what my brother deserves! Did he *deserve* to suffer what should not be done even to the lowest of creatures, let alone to a man? The indignities of nakedness, hunger, and exposure are not even the worst of these. Good God, captain, have you British not the least sense of humanity? We were all one people once. Think you it is any wonder we would be free of you now?"

Myles's lip curled sardonically.

"I think, Miss Tyree, that this is neither the time nor the place to debate the issues that have separated our two countries."

Sabra glared resentfully back at him, but in truth she was furious with herself. Faith, what a fool she was ever to have lowered her guard with him — Myles, of all people! And how even more insufferable that he should be forced now to remind her of the priorities. Quite obviously it would avail them nothing to rake over the wrongs perpetrated by either side against the other.

"You are right, of course," she said, unconsciously lifting her chin with all her old hauteur. "This is not the time for that. When, then, shall I be allowed to see my brother?"

"That depends entirely on you."

Sabra's eyes followed him, as, leisurely, he crossed to the general's desk and helped himself to a decanter set conveniently on a silver tray.

"Rest assured that he is being well cared for," he said, pouring brandy into a crystal goblet. At his brief, questioning glance, Sabra impatiently shook her head in refusal. It was not a drink she needed from him now, but something far different. Replacing the stopper, he picked up the goblet and stared down into the amber liquid for a moment with an odd sort of irony before lifting the glass to drink. When at last he turned to look at her, she could read nothing in his face. "Meantime, I'm afraid there are certain conditions that must be met before you will be allowed to see him."

"Faith, I might have known," declared Sabra bitterly. "What 'conditions,' captain?"

Myles sat on the edge of the table and gently swirled the brandy around the sides of the glass.

"It's quite simple really," he reflected. "We have known for some time that we had a traitor in our midst. A man in a position of prominence who was using his office for his own ends. I've managed to convince certain parties that you have the evidence we've been looking for to expose him for what he is—a turncoat who sells information to the French and American forces and quite possibly double-crosses them as well."

"Channing," Sabra pronounced in a hard voice.

"Exactly," he applauded.

Upon which she ventured cynically to guess the rest of

it. "You want the papers I took from Sir Wilfred. But in exchange for what? I want my brother's freedom, nothing less," she warned.

"Naturally," he drawled. "If my superiors find the documents are all that you have led me to believe they are, there should be no problem. If not—" Myles shrugged.

Angrily, Sabra paced a step and turned.

"In other words, you expect me to turn over the papers *before* my brother is released to me. Faith, captain, 'twould seem a one-sided bargain you offer," she stated flatly. "What possible guarantee can you give that your *superiors* will not simply take the papers and toss Wes back in that damnable pit? I can't say I care much for your bloody 'conditions.'"

"No?" Myles rejoined, strangely mocking. "And yet it is, I assure you, the best offer you are likely to receive."

"Well, I'm sorry," retorted Sabra, "but it isn't good enough. It leaves far too much to chance. Can't you understand? It's my brother's life we're talking about!"

"Oh, no, *ma mie*," Myles drawled, his voice suddenly edged with steel, "it's far more than that. It's the only hope you have that you and your brother will not both spend the rest of your lives in a British prison."

Perhaps Sabra's cheeks went a trifle pale at the implied message in these words, but by no other sign did she betray the sudden clench of fear in her stomach.

"I'm afraid I haven't the least notion what you are talking about, captain," she uttered in cold disdain. "Surely you cannot mean I should be sentenced for shooting the man who was trying to rape me?"

A faint smile, wholly lacking in humor, touched the stern lips.

"It's a trifle late to pretend innocence. You're far too experienced a player not to know your activities have incurred more than Channing's suspicions."

Instantly Sabra's head came up, her eyes scorching in their bitter condemnation. Faith, how naïve she had been to think Myles had effected Wes's release from prison for

361

her sake. Good God, for a single, wildly insane moment as he kissed her, she had even allowed herself to believe he might love her just a little. But all along it was Channing he had wanted. Channing and the proofs that would see him hang.

"Of what are you accusing me now, captain?" she demanded, feeling cold inside. "Something more serious this time, it would seem, than preying on innocent, love-sick boys. Seduction of a naval captain, perhaps, while he lay helplessly in the grips of delirium? That would be in keeping with my reputation as a self-seeking harlot, would it not?"

She nearly winced at the sound of his sharply indrawn breath. Indeed, she saw the cold leap of anger in his eyes and for a wild moment thought that he meant to strike her. Then he laughed, a harsh sound in the quiet of the room.

"Oh, but you play the game so well," he murmured, raking her with his glance. "It seems almost a shame to bring an end to the charade at last. And yet you force me to lay my cards on the table. Very well, my love. Fact: You are an American agent. Fact: You have for the past several years entertained British officers in your home for the sole purpose of collecting information concerning military operations, troop movements, anything, in short, which might be of the slightest interest to your compatriots. Fact: You have organized and maintained an entire network of spies within British-occupied territory. Fact: You have collaborated with an extremely successful American privateer in order to prey on British merchant ships."

Flinging back his head, he tossed off the rest of his drink and set the empty glass on the desk with a sort of weary finality.

"Shall I go on?" he queried coldly.

"Oh, by all means, captain. I'm sure I cannot recall when I have been better entertained," she replied, though she felt ill with the bitter certainty that he had, from the

362

very first, known everything. Indeed, she little doubted that all he had said and done up to that dreadful moment had been nothing more than an elaborate tissue of lies. Good God, what a fool she had been ever to fall in love with him!

For an instant she thought she beheld a flicker of something like wry admiration behind the piercing intensity of those cursed eyes. Then his lips curved in a smile that chilled her to the bone, and she was quite certain that she had only imagined it.

"There seems little point in delving into your connection with the 'Naughty Pack of Ann Street,'" he continued ironically.

"Oh, but I insist," Sabra flung recklessly back at him. "It would hardly do to leave anything out, and I have, after all, already admitted to smuggling the bare necessities into the poor wretches in the Old North Dutch Church, have I not? But perhaps you were unaware that I have performed similar feats for those whose plight is even more reprehensible. Those condemned to suffer the atrocities of the Livingston Sugar House! Now there is a prison which should gladden the heart of its British masters. I myself can attest to the fact that in its daily pilgrimage, the death cart bears no fewer than six corpses each trip from that abomination of horrors."

She had begun to pace as she went over the list of her infamies perpetrated against the crown, but now she halted to impale Myles with glittering eyes.

"But please do not stop there, captain," she challenged. "Of what else am I guilty in the eyes of the British tyrant? Perhaps you would care to add attempting to smuggle supplies to your own troops, who more often than not are forced to forage off the land in order to survive. But then, that is only one of my more recent endeavors, and unfortunately the man for whom they were intended has paid the price of collaborating, unwittingly, I might add, with the enemy. I'm afraid that Colonel Ridgley's men will be deprived of the food and blankets I had intended for them. 'Tis a shame I shall not be given the opportunity to see they reach General Washington. No doubt *he* could have found some use for them."

"I should take care, captain, to school your lady's tongue," commented an amused voice from behind them. "Those sound peculiarly treasonous sentiments for the future wife of one of His Majesty's naval officers."

A steely glint leaped in the captain's eyes. Then slowly he turned to survey the indolent figure arrayed in pale rose silk brocade who stood limned in the open doorway.

"Sir Wilfred," he observed, ironically inclining his head, "we've been expecting you. Pray, let us not stand on formality. Since you have already seen fit to let yourself in, perhaps you would be good enough to close the door behind you."

The baronet's face, powdered and adorned with a beauty patch at the corner of rouged lips, displayed naught but a slightly bored amusement at Myles's well-polished put-down.

"By all means, captain," he purred, performing the task with gracile ease. "After all, we should not wish Miss Tyree's remarks to fall on the wrong ears, now should we. Others of the assembled company might not be so sympathetic as am I, who have long enjoyed an intimate acquaintance with the lady's charming impetuosity."

Myles smiled slightly.

"I felt sure you would understand," he gently murmured. "Might I suggest, however, that Miss Tyree's sentiments are entirely her own and hardly subject to your concern, one way or the other?"

"Really?" queried the exquisite, dabbing at his lips with a scented lace handkerchief. With elaborate insouciance, he strolled to within a foot of the haughty beauty eyeing him with undisguised loathing. For a moment he held Sabra's gaze. "And yet," he murmured, "as a king's trusted servant, I should think it my duty to concern

364

myself."

The thin lips curled in cold amusement at the contemptuous flash of sea-green eyes, then, fluttering the delicate froth of fine lace, he turned his attention back to the captain.

"But then, you, no doubt, would know better than I what is due one's king. I understand a Baron Myles fought at the side of William the Conqueror, or so I have quite recently been informed. Your esteemed family's acceptance into the peerage dates from that glorious period in history, does it not? To be followed by the rank of earl, bestowed by King Richard the Lionhearted. There were, I believe, one or two other titles attached to the illustrious name, until finally it seemed naught but a dukedom would do, for which Lovely Queen Bess was kind enough to oblige you."

"No doubt this recital of my family history has some purpose?" Myles queried in a bored tone.

"Oh, come now, captain. Surely the need for pretense is long past. We both know how you were able to slip out of the noose, which, I assure you, I prepared with the most infinite care just for you. I cannot but wonder, however, if even your credit shall be enough to carry Miss Tyree—especially when certain of her—shall we say—less than acceptable activities are brought to light?"

All at once Myles's aspect of advanced ennui seemed utterly to vanish.

"If you have any accusations against my future wife, Sir Wilfred," he drawled in a voice, dangerously soft, "be pleased to state them unequivocally. For your sake, however, I strongly recommend they be accompanied by incontrovertible evidence."

"Ah, but therein lies the rub, does it not?" chuckled the baronet, apparently not at all put out at having the captain call his bluff. "Miss Tyree, it would seem, has been far too clever for me. Since Mr. Wayne has been markedly absent from his usual haunts for some few days now, I must assume that my 'proof' has unfortunately to remain in the realm of hearsay. A pity, really. I had placed a deal of faith in the gentleman's highly developed sense of self-preservation. But then, I find one's fellow man disappointingly unreliable, don't you, my dear?" he queried gently of Sabra.

"One is never disappointed in *you*, Sir Wilfred. Only occasionally surprised that you have found new levels to which to sink in your iniquity. I should gladly have killed you with my own hand for what you have done to me and to the members of my household. But for what you sought to do to Kitty Quinby, I should rather see you rot in prison the rest of your miserable existence."

For the first time since he had insinuated himself into their presence, she saw a flicker of uncertainty in the soulless blue eyes. All at once she laughed.

"What if I were to tell you, captain," she said, conscious of a heady sense of triumph, "that there is a witness to the baronet's treachery? As a matter of fact, I believe you and she are acquainted. Or at least she has told me that you once offered to stand her friend. But that was before this honorable representative of His Majesty's government decided to rid himself of Kitty Quinby by selling her to white slavers."

"I should say that there are more than I who would find that very interesting indeed," drawled the captain, settling once again on the edge of the desk, his legs, crossed casually at the ankles, stretched out before him. "If you could supply such a witness, along with certain pertinent documents, I doubt even the king himself could deny you have met the conditions of Mr. Locke's release. What say you, Sir Wilfred? As a 'loyal king's agent' and former vice admiralty judge, you are well versed in such matters."

Sabra's skin crawled as she watched Channing gently wave the scented handkerchief beneath his nose. Any trace of discomposure he might have felt was artfully concealed behind the painted mask of his face. Any, that is, save for the look of cold calculation in the metallic eyes.

"Ah, but to answer that, my dear captain, I should have to know the terms of release. Just as a matter of curiosity, you understand—what are you demanding of the lovely Sabra?"

"Your head on a platter, I'm afraid, Sir Wilfred," replied the lady, with a frosty smile.

The baronet's laugh was singularly unpleasant.

"Which you, I judge, are not only perfectly willing to deliver, but foolish enough to think you can."

"Oh, but you know I can," she rejoined without the least hesitation. "Indeed, I cannot tell you how greatly I shall enjoy handing your private journal over to the captain, along with the dispatch from a certain French liaison officer attached to le Comte d'Estaing. I believe Admiral Howe will find them most interesting reading, do not you? As a matter of fact, I should think d'Estaing himself will have discovered the written account of your activities in the Caribbean enlightening in the extreme."

She had the uncanny feeling that beneath the powder and rouge Sir Wilfred blanched to a sickly hue. Most certainly his eyes bore into hers with a chilling coldness.

"You're lying," he stated emphatically. "D'Estaing sailed weeks before you availed yourself of my private correspondence."

"Yes, he did. Fortunately, however, *Nemisis*, was able to overtake a French corvette, which was to rendezvous with the fleet somewhere off Martinique. You see, I'm afraid Mr. Wayne did not, after all, tell you the whole truth. Not only did your British frigate fail to sink my schooner, but with any luck, d'Estaing should already have received a copy of your journal. Or certainly shall before many more days have passed. Your usefulness either to the French or the British is finished, Sir Wilfred, and your smuggling operations, I should judge, are, at the very least, in serious jeopardy."

Channing muttered a harsh obscenity, and for the barest instant Sabra glimpsed beneath the painted mask to the man's murderous hate. He was like some twisted thing, poisoned by his own venomous dislike, and suddenly it came to her that so great an antipathy could only have built up over a very long period of time.

Realizing that Myles's presence was all that kept the baronet from murdering her on the spot, Sabra stubbornly refused to back an inch. Head high and eyes glittering with proud disdain, she stood unflinching before him. Indeed, she vowed she would die first before she allowed the detestable creature to see her quail before him. Nevertheless, she was relieved when a tall, commanding figure stepped casually between them.

"It occurs to me that you must have more pressing matters to attend, Sir Wilfred," observed Myles pointedly. "Do not allow us to detain you any longer. I trust you will be *available* should a court of inquiry desire your presence?"

"Were anything quite so unlikely to arise, captain," he responded with chilling self-assurance, "I shall no doubt be located easily enough."

"Oh, no doubt," agreed Myles affably. Sabra was quick to note, however, that the captain's smile failed utterly to reach his eyes. "In any case, I should tell you I- have arranged for an armed guard to escort you to your lodgings, where they will remain until further orders. My coxswain, with whom you are already acquainted, is even now waiting outside the door to take you to them."

The rouged lips were no longer smiling, and yet it seemed obvious to Sabra that Channing was not the least concerned over the possibility that he might hang as a traitor. No, the malevolence emanating from the slim, elegant figure stemmed not from any sense of desperation or defeat, but rather from that something she had glimpsed earlier in his eyes: his hatred, his obsession to destroy those whom he conceived either as enemies or stumbling blocks to his lust for power, that thing, whatever it was, that drove him.

Out of the corner of her eye she glimpsed a furtive movement and turned to see Channing reach a hand into the ruffles flowing from his coat sleeve. Her lips parted to utter a warning. But it was Myles who spoke.

"I shouldn't, Sir Wilfred, if I were you."

Channing froze, and for the briefest moment the two men locked glances. Then deliberately Myles reached down to retrieve the small pistol cleverly strapped to the baronet's forearm.

"You disappoint me, Sir Wilfred," mused the captain, balancing the weapon in his hand. "Somehow I expected something rather more subtle from a man of your accomplishments. Did you truly think to bluff your way out with a single-shot pistol?"

The baronet's hand clenched on the scented handkerchief. Then suddenly he laughed.

"You are quite right, captain," he admitted, bringing the delicate fluff of lace to his nose and inhaling its fragrance. "No doubt I should apologize for my momentary lapse."

"Not at all," Myles drawled negligently. "One cannot always be clever, it would seem."

The rouged lips curved in a singularly mirthless smile as he surveyed the officer and the slender girl.

"But how very generous you are," he commented with undisguised venom. "And so amusing, too. A republican and the heir to a dukedom. Somehow I doubt either of you will enjoy very much satisfaction in so unlikely an alliance. But then, one could have said the same of your father, married to my brother's wife, would you not agree, my dearest Sabra?"

Sabra's senses reeled as she grappled with the enormity of those maliciously uttered words.

"I'm afraid your meaning escapes me," she said at last, feigning a cold hauteur she was far from feeling. "I promise I should have known were you any kin to me."

"No, not to you," Channing agreed. "But rather to the unfortunate young man whom the captain has so gallantly removed from my—er—'protection.' "

Sabra felt sickened by the vile implications of the barnet's claim, and still he was not finished.

"A shame, really," Sir Wilfred reflected. "From all accounts he would have been dead in another few days. Indeed, he lasted far longer than anyone could possibly have predicted."

"I don't believe you," she breathed. "Not even you could be so monstrous as to condemn your own nephew to the atrocities of a British prison."

Channing's amused laugh grated on her already taut nerves.

"Such innocence. But how delightful," he applauded. "Indeed, you quite surprise me. However, I assure you I could be much more despicable than that. Your beloved Wesley is far from being my nephew, my dear. To put it frankly, he is my son."

"You're lying!"

"Not at all. It is, in fact, naught but the simple truth. Shall I tell you how it was?" he queried. "Yes, I can see you are all impatience to know everything—how I, a youth of eighteen, should have found my way into your mother's bed."

"You are mistaken, Sir Wilfred," Myles cut in, his soft voice edged in steel. "And you've overstayed your welcome. *Ma mie,* go to the door and admit Leeks, if you will. I believe it is time this 'gentleman' was leaving."

"No!" Sabra uttered harshly. "He is right. I do wish to hear what he has to say."

"You, my girl, will do as you are told," returned Myles in a flinty voice.

Sabra's eyes blazed in a face gone deathly white. "No, I will not. Indeed, I beg you will not interfere, captain!" she snapped. Then, recognizing the grim set of the lean stubborn jaw, she suddenly relented. "Myles, please," she said, turning the full force of her eloquent gaze on him. "Can you not see that I must?"

For a long moment their glances met and held. Then at last Myles's lips curved in a thin smile.

"Very well," he drawled, coldly dispassionate. "I shall

370

not stand in your way. You have ten minutes, Channing. No more."

"You are the soul of generosity, captain," sneered the baronet, making an elegant leg. "Ten minutes is more than enough, I assure you."

"Now, let me see, where shall I begin?" he mused, striking a pose as he elaborately paused to consider. "Ah, yes. Elizabeth, whose beauty is rivaled only by that of her daughter. Picture her, if you will, at the age of sixteen—fresh, charmingly innocent, a delectable piece even had she not been the offspring of a wealthy Boston merchant. I vow not even you could have resisted such a morsel, my dear captain. Imagine how much less could I."

"You, sir," murmured Sabra in a voice that would have chilled the heart of a lesser knave, "will kindly address your remarks to me. And do not think to push your luck too far. You will either get on with your story or keep your silence, but you will not belabor my mother's part in this. Is that understood?"

"Oh, perfectly, I assure you. Very well, I shall cut straight to the heart of the matter. I was a lad of thirteen when Josiah Locke returned to Cornwall in search of the family he had deserted some eleven years before in order to seek his fortune in the New World. And of course he had been enormously successful, as you already know—thanks to the generosity of your aristocratic father. Alas! Poor Josiah found only me, his orphaned younger brother and, more disappointing still, I was a convicted felon on the point of being transported.

"Strangely enough, he blamed himself for my unfortunate circumstances. But then, he always was a softhearted fool. Or perhaps I should have said softheaded," sneered Channing. "But what would you? He purchased my freedom and took me to his bosom, a young viper, who despised him for his generosity. And, indeed, he was generous." The baronet laughed, a cynical chortle that grated harshly on Sabra's nerves. "He saw that I was given the same advantages as were normally granted only to the sons of gentility—money, clothes, admittance to the finest schools in England—everything, in short, but the one thing he could never give me: an aristocratic bloodline, a noble name, and a heritage to make me one of them."

The pale sheen of his eyes against the white, painted face scintillated spite.

"How I hated him for that, just as I learned to loathe those self-serving aristocrats. But not as much as I despised those few who condescended to tolerate me out of some misplaced sense of pity! Then came the crowning touch. When at last I was deemed a properly turned-out young gentleman, what did my dear brother do but bring me here to the provinces to learn the shipping business!"

Channing flung his arm in the air in a gesture of contempt.

"Ecod! What a cruel jest was that! I, who had rubbed shoulders with lords and the sons of lords, was expected to earn my living at trade. Luckily, however, I had ever an eye for opportunity when it presented itself, and the lovely young Elizabeth fell into my lap like a ripe plum. In fact, it was almost disappointingly easy. Fairly stifled by her father, who was by nature an overbearing prig, Elizabeth, I suspect, was ready to fall in love with anyone who might deliver her from the bleak existence of church sermons and self-righteous maunderings on the nature of sin. Faith! One almost felt sorry for the miserable wretch!

"Unfortunately, no sooner had I got her with child and informed her of my intent to broach her father for funds sufficient to support wedding her, than the absurd little fool balked at marrying so detestable a creature as I. Indeed, rather than wed me, she preferred to try and do away with herself in order to save her family from my greedy manipulations. It fell my brother's lot to discover the self-sacrificing Elizabeth on the point of flinging her-

372

self into the sea. The rest is history. My brother bought my silence with a goodly sum and sent me packing to England, while he nobly wed the mother of my son. And had that been the end of it, I should have been content to leave things as they were."

Sickened, Sabra clenched her fingers on the ivory sticks of her fan. Merciful God, he could not truly be talking about her mother. Not Elizabeth Tyree, who had seemed embued with a gentleness of soul, which could not but touch all who came into her sphere. To speak in such terms of her was a vile desecration.

"And what happened, I cannot but wonder, to change your mind?" queried Sabra in tones of utter loathing. "Why go to such lengths to try and ruin my father and myself? Indeed, what could possibly have determined you to use your own son in so cruel a manner?"

The malignant glint of cold blue eyes sent a chill down her spine.

"Ah, yes, what indeed?" he uttered cynically. "To answer that, I shall have to take up my narrative at a point several weeks after my arrival in London. Never one to waste a golden opportunity, I used my acquaintanceship with my brother's partner as a pretext to gain an introduction with the earl of Dearing. It was meant purely as a means of entering the lofty circles of the privileged class. Indeed, that I should meet and fall in love with Lady Caroline Tyree, alas, was never part of my plans, I assure you. But there it was. In a matter of a few months I was granted permission from the earl to approach his eldest daughter with an offer for her hand in marriage and happily was accepted."

"You were betrothed to my Aunt Caroline? Good God, if 'tis true, you were not lacking in gall! Did it not once occur to you that when my father learned of your infamy, he would move to block so untenable an alliance?"

"Oh, I feel sure the thought must have crossed my mind at one time or another, but the possibility that we should ever meet again seemed so wholly unlikely that I quite dismissed it. He, after all, was in the West Indies at the time, working to expand his shipping interests. Who could have foreseen that Elizabeth, learning of my coming nuptials from her father's agent in London, should take it upon herself to send word of it to her husband's partner? I vow I was quite taken aback to encounter an outraged Phillip Tyree literally on the church steps, as it were."

"As no doubt was he," murmured Sabra, seeing it all in her mind's eye. "Indeed, I imagine he called you out for it."

"You are a provincial indeed do you think that," Channing answered with an ugly laugh. "Come now, my dear, surely you must be aware that a gentleman never crosses swords with a commoner. No. The earl's son took a horsewhip to me, Miss Tyree. No doubt had they not wished to wrap the whole incident in white linen, he would have driven me out of England. As it was, he returned to America, and I, shortly thereafter, managed to purchase the office of a vice admiralty judge in his own beloved New England.

"I think that a capital jest, don't you? Not only did I have the power that would enable me nearly to ruin the three I detested most in this world, but it was given me to grow wealthy off them while I worked my little scheme. It was a shame, really, when that business with Hancock, brought an end to so lucrative an arrangement. And an even greater disappointment that my brother Josiah should have perished in a hurricane at sea, thus robbing me of the pleasure of rendering your mother a widow. But at least the war provided me with the opportunity to take up where I had left off, and your father had even obliged me by succumbing to a morbid fever only scant years after wedding his secret lover, thus sweetening the pot. Come now, my dear, you needn't look so shocked. It was quite obvious, no doubt even to my besotted brother, how the wind lay in that quarter. But as I was saying, my revenge was at last nearly com-

374

plete—I had Elizabeth's son in my power, and I should soon have had you, along with your father's fortune and my brother's."

Sabra's blood ran cold as the baronet sauntered close.

"Breaking you, my lovely, was to have been the *piece de resistance*." Deliberately he raked her with his eyes. "But then, the world is a chancy place, is it not?" he murmured, smiling. "And one can never be absolutely sure of anything till the game is truly played out."

As the soulless eyes locked with hers, Sabra knew a moment of bitter realization. Channing had kept one last card to himself, and it was his to play whenever he chose. He knew she was the master of the *Nemesis*, while Myles and his superiors did not. How intolerable that she could do nothing to stop Channing from revealing it!

"Get out," she said scathingly. "Get out now, while you still can."

His sweeping bow deliberately mocked her.

"But of course," he grinned in perfect understanding, "I should not dream of imposing further on your generous nature. I bid you au revoir, mademoiselle. For I vow something tells me you have not yet seen the last of me."

Chapter 22

As soon as the door closed behind Sir Wilfred, Sabra whirled with an angry rustle of silk skirts and began furiously to pace.

"He knew!" she exclaimed. "He knew he was walking into a trap, and he cared not a whit. Why? I ask you."

"Perhaps he was feeling us out, or merely fishing for information." Myles's careless shrug was curiously at odds with the hard, speculative gleam in his eyes. "Whatever his reasons for coming, however, you may be sure of one thing. When he left, he was inordinately cocksure for one facing possible charges of treason. Obviously he has something up his sleeve."

"Yes, but what?" Abruptly she halted in her tracks, her glance fixing on Myles. "Wes!" she exclaimed. "Channing came because he had found out about Wes."

"Then he came for nothing. Your brother is quite safe, *ma mie*. I promise you that."

Sabra shook her head. "No, don't you see? It makes no sense to suppose Channing would dare so much to gain so little. What could he possibly have needed to find out that he did not already know? He knew about Wes and the papers. He must have realized how near you were to exposing him for what he is. No doubt he has had his escape planned and made ready for weeks. Which leaves me to believe he came for one reason only—to finish what he started with my father those many years ago."

Once again she began to pace. Only this time she seemed driven to it, compelled by a nervous excitement.

"Channing is obsessed with his vengeance," she said with the utter certainty of one who had seen it in his eyes, been made to suffer the consequences of it at his hands. Her lips curved in a cold little smile. "Thanks to you, however, Wes is alive and I am about to be made your bride—or so you would have him to believe. At the very moment when he should have seen all his plans come to fruition, you stepped in and spoiled everything. And that is why, captain, I think his purpose was to kill you. Had he succeeded, everything he has worked to achieve all these years might very easily have been within his grasp again. But then, having failed in that, too," she ended with a brittle laugh, "he struck out at my father's daughter in the only way left to him."

"He made sure you learned the truth about himself and your mother."

Sabra winced.

"Yes," she said in a husky voice.

A hard glint came to Myles's eyes as he watched her turn away.

"Everything you have said seems to make sense up to a point," he remarked thoughtfully, when she had had a moment or two to compose herself.

The slim shoulders straightened. "And what point is that, captain?"

"It occurs to me that Channing is not the sort of man to accept defeat so easily," Myles drawled in such a way as to bring Sabra around, a queasy sensation in the pit of her stomach. "Which is what he would have done had his purpose been to put me out of the way. The possibility that he should have escaped undetected is far too negligible, especially with you as a witness. He would in the end have found it necessary to kill us both, and somehow I think he has other plans for you, my love."

Sabra, remembering the baronet's final words to her, could not deny Myles's logic.

"Then what is your explanation, captain?" Weariness lent an edge to her voice. "Surely you must have some theory for everything that happened here tonight."

Myles shrugged.

"I think Channing achieved exactly what he intended all along. He wanted us to believe we had won, probably hoping to lull us into a false sense of security, the purpose for which remains to be seen. But, more than that, he had to be sure you knew why he had gone to such trouble to do you and your family injury. Without that, his revenge would be meaningless. And consider how much sweeter that revenge, should he yet manage to lay his hands on the evidence that damns him."

"He would walk free," Sabra said in a stunned voice.

"Exactly so."

Something in the pale glitter of his eyes made her blood run cold.

"You think he knows where the papers are, don't you. You think he means to come after them. But he is under guard. You said he would remain under guard until a court of inquiry should be convened!"

"Those were the orders I gave. Unfortunately, Sir Wilfred's apparent lack of concern suggests that he has already foreseen and thus provided for such a contingency. It is not impossible that he will be free in a matter of hours . . . Which is why it is crucial to move quickly. If we fail to act, we may lose the only chance we have of putting him where he belongs."

"I see," murmured Sabra, staring at Myles. Abruptly she turned away, wishing she could be by herself for just a few moments, wishing she could have time to think.

Myles was deliberately goading her. She knew it, and she knew why he was doing it. He wanted the papers now, this very night, and she had yet to agree to his precious conditions. And, indeed, why should she when they were so patently unfair? Channing could not possibly know where the documents were, she told herself. Or could he?

378

Uneasily it came to her to wonder if someone had seen her slip out of the house that night after dark. She had already discovered one spy in her household. Why could there not be others? But whether there were or not, obviously she would be risking a great deal if she tried to hold out for a better bargain. Indeed, she might forfeit her freedom and her brother's life if she failed now to give Myles her trust.

In helpless anger, she saw how cleverly she had been maneuvered. Damn Myles! Obviously she never had any choice but to meet his demands. In which case, she decided, the sooner she relinquished the documents to him, the better. In sudden impatience to be done with the business, she turned to find Myles watching her with a faint, sardonic gleam in his eyes.

"What is it? Why are you looking at me like that?" she challenged, bitterly aware that he must have known all along how it would end. Myles, to her annoyance, merely arched quizzical eyebrows.

"You win, captain. Unless you have some objection, I should like to retrieve the papers at once and give them over to you. I am anxious to see my brother as soon as possible. I'm sure you understand."

"I understand perfectly. For once we are in complete accord." Sweeping her a bow, no less graceful for its irony, he smiled. "I am, as ever, at your service, ma'am."

"I am obliged, captain." Even so, his indifference hurt her. A defiant sparkle smoldering in the depths of sea-green eyes, she made her curtsey. Then wordlessly she rose and, wishing him without remorse to the devil, stepped coolly past him to the door.

Some few moments later Sabra watched from the gallery as Myles made their excuses to the general's wife. A wry glint came to her eyes as she observed the gentle undulations of their hostess's fan eloquently cease, followed soon after by a decidedly scandalized ripple of laughter. Indeed, she was still wondering, when Myles rejoined her, what he could have said to earn either a playful thwack of the fan across the back of his wrist, or that provocative sidelong glance, which followed his leisurely retreat through the crowded hall. Faith, the man was impossible. What was it about Myles that made him so devastatingly attractive to members of her sex? Feeling restless and vaguely dissatisfied, she allowed him to escort her to the entrance of the cloak room, then waited for him to bring her wrap.

A peculiar ache tightened her throat as she watched him walk toward her with that controlled, supple strength that was so much a part of the man. Resolutely she sought to ignore the involuntary tingling of nerve endings as, slipping the fur mantle over her shoulders, his hands brushed against bare skin. Then foolishly she glanced up into the gimlet eyes regarding her with bemused interest. A blush suffused her cheeks and, furious at herself, she hastily averted her face. Fortunately for her peace of mind, Ezra Leeks chose just then to appear striding toward them.

Recalling the look that had come to Kitty Quinby's eyes as she admitted to having had at least one friend, Sabra studied Leeks curiously as the two men, drawing a little away from her, exchanged low-voiced words.

Not handsome in the strictest sense, he was yet possessed of strong, honest features, pleasingly bronzed from exposure to sun, wind, and sea. He had a generous mouth, one to which good-natured, rollicking laughter would come readily, she judged, a theory which was soon borne out by the evidence of laugh-wrinkles at the corners of keen blue eyes. He likewise was blessed with a large nose, hooked at the bridge, a cleft chin, and a wide brow topped by nut-brown, sun-bleached hair swept back from the forehead and bound at the nape of the neck in a queue. Broad-shouldered and barrel-chested, he looked a brawny seaman somewhere in his middle to late twenties.

Instinctively Sabra liked him and was all at once glad for Kitty Quinby. Indeed, it was apparent that she must devise some sort of plan which would allow the girl to remain safely behind when she herself departed.

"I'm happy to see that you did not fare badly in your recent encounter with cutthroats, Mr. Leeks," she said when the two men, having finished their brief exchange, came near. Smiling, she extended a slim, white hand toward the burly coxswain. "Miss Barret informs me 'twas a prodigious battle, with you and Captain Ellsworth perilously outnumbered."

"It were a bit of nip 'n' tuck a time or two," admitted Leeks, with no apparent discomposure at being thus addressed by his captain's lady. "But we've seen worse an' lived to tell of it. Them buggers never knew what they was up against."

"I don't doubt it for a moment." Smiling a little, she turned toward Myles. "I wonder, captain. Would it be asking too much to allow Mr. Leeks to accompany us? I believe there is someone where we are going who would like very much to see him. I promise you would be doing a very great kindness."

A wry glint flickered in the gray eyes as Myles observed his coxswain stare straight before him with an air of sublime detachment. It would seem, he mused ironically, that Leeks had managed to glean a great deal through the study door—enough that he apparently had a fair notion who that 'someone' might be.

"You haven't the least idea what you are letting yourself in for," he murmured, taking a measure of satisfaction in seeing the big coxswain squirm. "Given half a chance, Leeks has a way of rendering himself peculiarly indispensable."

"Perhaps, captain," Sabra rejoined with only a slight

trace of irony, "you have only yourself to blame. Inexplicably, you seem to have a gift for inspiring unswerving loyalty and esteem, even in some for whom it might be the last thing they might wish to have happen—indeed, even should it entail grave risk to themselves. No matter what, they would choose never to be parted from you, if they but could. Apparently they simply cannot help themselves, is that not so, Mr. Leeks?"

Though she addressed her final comment to the coxswain, she had kept her eyes on Myles the entire time, had beheld the sardonic gleam of humor change to a puzzled frown. Suddenly, as if she could no longer bear to meet his scrutiny, she turned and, without waiting for the sorely tried coxswain to give an answer, fled at a brisk walk toward the exit.

As the carriage bore her and the captain from the general's reception, Sabra stared blindly out the window, her thoughts far removed from the snow-packed streets or the old Dutch houses camouflaged behind their newer, more fashionable Italian fronts. No doubt she should have been bidding them a last fond farewell, for, in spite of everything, she loved New York and would in time come to miss its crooked streets and crowded buildings, made quaint with the almost ubiquitous small garden plots shaded by fruit trees and bordered by flowers. But even the inescapable fact of her imminent departure failed to occupy her mind, except in the manner it concerned the silent officer seated next to her.

In truth she was puzzling over those few moments in the general's study when she had looked into Myles's face and beheld the strong, compelling features apparently stripped of their habitual, impregnable mask. Faith, she could still feel his eyes probing hers with a melting intensity that had left her vulnerable and weak. And his hand upon her cheek! The gesture had seemed to communicate a tenderness of feeling she had not thought possible in the unassailable captain! In that moment she had seemed to sense the man beneath the ever-present mantle of command, a man who might have loved her.

Why, then, the sudden change? Had she imagined that moment of tenderness or had it all been an act, a simple matter of strategy in a brilliantly conducted campaign?

Silently she cursed. Damn Myles! There was no possible way to reconcile subsequent events with that incredible feeling that he had been on the point of declaring his love. No one who entertained the least affection for her would try to bargain with her for her brother's life! To exploit such a thing for his own ends was worse than unthinkable. It was utterly despicable, she told herself. And yet, a small voice whispered insidiously back, was it so very different from what she herself had done? In seeking to keep Channing's papers as a lever to gain her brother's release—indeed, in refusing to give Myles her trust—had she not forced him to employ the only other avenue open to him?

Merciful God, she did not know what to believe!

She was relieved when at last they arrived before the house on Nassau. With cool disdain she allowed Myles to help her down from the carriage, then, without pausing, she proceeded briskly up the short walk to the door. Not wishing to alert the other members of the household to her presence until after her business with the captain was finished, she let herself and the two men in with her latchkey.

"Mr. Leeks, if you would be so kind as to come with me," she smiled, flinging off her pelisse and draping it across a walnut corner chair, "I should like you to meet a houseguest of mine." Then, apparently bethinking herself of her other guest, she turned with a cool glint of lovely green eyes to Myles. "Oh, captain. No doubt you would prefer to make yourself comfortable in the front parlor— just through the door. This should not take more than a few moments, I promise you."

Not deigning to give Myles opportunity either to object or acquiesce, Sabra turned and made regally for the curved stairway, while behind her, Leeks visibly vacillated, his gaze fixed on a point somewhere beyond the epaulet on his captain's shoulder.

Myles watched her go, an appreciative gleam in his eye. Then, taking pity at last on his coxswain, he arched an inquisitive eyebrow.

"Well, Leeks?" he inquired dryly. "You heard Miss Tyree. There is someone abovestairs who is apparently anxious to see you. Surely you do not intend to keep the lady waiting?"

Leeks allowed a grin to spread across his homely face.

"Not a bit of it, cap'n," he declared feelingly. "If it's who I think it is, I'll have a lot to thank you and the lady for an' that's no lie."

"Yes, no doubt," observed Myles to himself as he watched his coxswain bound up the stairs two at a time.

Some ten minutes later found Sabra peering vexatiously through the open doorway into the darkened interior of the front parlor. She had been dismayed upon returning from her mission of charity above to discover the lamps extinguished and the fire burned down to little more than a few glowing embers. Normally a cheerful blaze was kept going in case the mistress of the house should arrive home accompanied by guests. Vaguely uneasy at such an unusual lapse in discipline among the staff, she stepped through the door into a soft swath of moonlight slanting through the front window.

"I trust," murmured a voice with cool detachment, "that Leeks's reunion with the mettlesome Mrs. Quinby was a happy one?"

Sabra's heart gave a little leap. Then she saw Myles,

384

standing near the window, his back to her as he gazed out on the street.

"From what I witnessed, extremely so," she answered, smiling a little at the thought of the slender girl clasped, laughing and weeping, against the burly coxswain's chest.

At last Myles turned to look at her.

"You have not told me yet how Mrs. Titus Quinby comes to be a guest beneath this roof. No doubt you will pardon my natural curiosity, but I cannot but find the circumstance singular in the extreme."

"No less could I," acknowledged Sabra, giving a wry little laugh, "when I discovered that instead of the Shrieking Woman of Maiden Lane, I had rescued the wife of my worst enemy's valet from strangulation. In the Quaker burial grounds off Little Green Street, if you can believe it."

"Where you are concerned, Miss Tyree, I believe almost anything," returned the captain in a wry voice. "Indeed, I have often wondered how you have managed to survive to womanhood."

"Yes, well, no doubt I am blessed with a guardian angel," she retorted dryly. "At any rate, you can imagine my surprise when this very afternoon I learned the man I sent fleeing before a bullet was none other than Sir Wilfred Channing himself. It seems the baronet had determined to rid himself of the one person who might prove willing to bear witness against him." A small frown etched itself in her brow. "Should she indeed be of importance to the crown's case, captain, shall you be able to insure her protection? Is there anyplace you can take her where Channing cannot find her?"

"No doubt my cox'n shall have something to say to that," observed the captain. "But, yes. You may rest assured of it. Possibly Miss Barrett will know of someone willing to take her in, should it prove necessary."

"Ah, yes — Miss Barrett. Now, why, I wonder, did I not

think of that probable solution. Especially since she indirectly had a part in all of this. It was on my return from a visit to her quaint little nest on Barclay, you see, that I had my encounter with Kitty Quinby and her disaffected employer. A visit, which, I might add, I found enlightening in the extreme. As a matter of fact, Captain Ellsworth and his *wife* were most obliging."

Had she expected a marked reaction to her pointed revelation, she was doomed to disappointment.

"They would be, of course," Myles replied, as though a wholly unconscionable deception had never been perpetrated against her, she thought incredulously.

She could almost feel his eyes on her and knew he must be trying to surmise how much more she either knew or guessed. Suddenly recalled to the fact that they had been standing for some time conversing in an absurdly dark and gloomy room, she crossed irritably to the fireplace.

"You don't seem surprised," she said flatly, groping along the mantle top for a taper to light the lamps.

"I should have been surprised had you *not* guessed the truth as soon as you saw them together. Why did you go there?"

"Odd as it may seem, captain, I was worried about you. I was even fool enough to think you might need my help. Lily, however, was quite adamant that that was not the case." Having found what she was looking for, she knelt down by the fire. "A pity I did not listen to her," she said, holding the slender wick out to the glowing embers until it caught. Then, rising, she shielded the flame with her hand and turned.

She almost gasped as Myles loomed suddenly over her.

"That won't be necessary," he said and, reaching out, snuffed the wick between his fingertips.

Sabra drew up indignantly. "What do you think you are doing?" she demanded, flaying him with her eyes.

386

"Surely I may judge whether a light is either necessary or desirable within the confines of my own home?"

"Indubitably, Miss Tyree," returned the captain in accents of boredom. "However, since we shall be leaving directly, candlelight would seem somewhat superfluous, would it not?"

"Leaving?" Sabra echoed blankly, having forgotten in the heat of the moment their purpose in coming there.

"It was my belief our objective was to retrieve certain documents," Myles acerbically reminded her. "Documents, I feel compelled to add, which you have assured me you do *not* keep at your father's house."

"Oh, but of course, how very stupid of me," she flung sarcastically back at him. "However, I believe what I said was that should Channing tear my father's house down brick by brick, he would not find what he was looking for."

"I see. Apparently I am suffering a misunderstanding of semantics."

"Actually, it could be considered more in the nature of a riddle in need of a solution," she retorted with a challenging flash of the eyes. "Perhaps, captain, you would care to join me in an evening stroll. A breath of fresh air does wonders in clearing the mind of confusion. At least I have often found it to be so."

She did not have to see his face to know a single dark eyebrow arched in his forehead. She could hear it in his voice.

"Have you indeed, Miss Tyree?" he murmured. "Very well, I am yours to command. No doubt I shall find the experience, if not enlightening, then invigorating at the very least."

"This way, then, captain, if you please." Turning, she led him through the foyer, pausing only long enough to gather up her pelisse and fling it around her shoulders, before continuing along a short hall that ended before a closed door.

Sabra felt along the top of the door frame till her fingers found the key. Then acutely conscious of Myles, standing close behind her, she fitted the key to the lock and turned it.

The room beyond the locked door had always seemed a special place, and that night, as she stepped across the threshold into the muted beauty of moonlight seeping through frost-covered window glass, it was even more so. Her father's conservatory triggered a flood of half-forgotten memories all mingled with sunlight and damp, fecund, earthy smells. The great oviform planters, empty now, had used to house her father's exotic plants, collected in his travels all over the world, and the wicker furniture — high-backed chairs, oval tables, the settee, and child-sized elephant — all of it looming vaguely in holland covers silvered with moonlight, he had brought for her mother from India. There was a marble fountain from Greece, as well, a leaping dolphin, which was quiet now, waiting. Indeed, as she wandered among the silent things, she felt like an intruder in a place, which, suspended in time, lay slumbering till someone should choose to bring it to life again.

"This was where my father used to come when he needed to be alone," murmured Sabra, throwing open french doors that overlooked the walled garden shimmering with moonlight and snow. "It has the virtue of almost total privacy, since it can only be seen from here and the window directly overhead."

Leaning out beyond the overhang, she pointed out the protruding shadow of the bay window, which projected from her own bedroom. "In my father's day, that was my mother's room. I remember, when I was a little girl, seeing her curled up in the windowseat watching us romp with Father in the garden."

It seemed to Myles, observing the play of moonlight

388

on her face, that she had forgotten him as she dwelt on that distant memory from her past. Consequently, her low, husky voice took him by surprise.

"Do you think Channing was telling the truth about her?" she asked, her eyes huge and shadowed in the delicate oval of her face. "Is Wes truly his son?"

"What *I* think, one way or the other, can hardly signify," he answered, choosing his words carefully. "However, it explains a great deal that would seem otherwise to make little sense."

The heavily lashed eyelids swept down over her eyes.

"Oh, yes," she rejoined bitterly. Opening them again, she gazed, unseeing out over the garden. "It would explain a great many things. Why, for example, my mother's father left Wes out of his will. I could never understand why I should be the one to inherit everything when Grandfather passes on. Though he denies it, I know it hurts Wes. Not because of the money. He doesn't care a whit about that. It's knowing that should he dare to try and cross his grandfather's threshold, he would most certainly be turned away. Do you realize my mother died without having spoken to her own father in over two and twenty years? Faith, to waste what can never be reclaimed! It is, beyond anything, absurd, is it not?"

Myles frowned, detecting a resonance of meaning in that final remark that somehow struck a chord of foreboding in his heart.

"That part about my mother and father was only a half-truth," she sighed after a moment, gazing once more about the haunting environs of the sunroom. "Concerning that much, at least, I can have no doubt. Oh, they were deeply in love almost from the first moment Josiah Locke introduced them to one another. My mother confessed as much when I was old enough to understand the rumors and sly snickers directed at me by those who thought they knew the truth. But the child my mother lost, only weeks after her husband perished at sea, was Josiah's, not my father's. And I was not delivered into the world until almost a year after Elizabeth and Phillip Tyree were wed, although there are some who profess not to believe it. They departed for the West Indies to oversee my father's shipping interests there not a week after they were wed. And they did not return until I was three. It was easy for those with small minds to fabricate and believe the lies, for I was always considered tall for my age and just a trifle too precocious." She gave a wry smile. "No doubt I have my stubborn streak of independence to blame for that," she said. "From the first it has always landed me in hot water of one kind or another."

A sudden chill swept her then, and Myles, grim-faced, silently cursed Channing's malice.

"Unless you are determined on contracting a fatal inflammation of the lungs, Miss Tyree, I think it is time you took me to Channing's papers," he observed pointedly.

"Rubbish!" declared Sabra. "I promise you I am not such a poor creature. Indeed, I am seldom, if ever, ill. The papers, furthermore, are here. Or, more accurately, over there," she amended, giving a sweeping gesture in the general direction of the sundial at the center of the garden.

Myles's eyebrow shot up.

"The papers are hidden in a secret compartment within the stone dais. I should assume they are quite safe," she added just the smallest bit doubtfully. "I am, so far as I know, the only one who is aware of its existence, let alone how to open it."

"There is one way to find out for certain. Tell me how to open it, and I shall have a look at them."

"I fear you presume too much, sir," Sabra declared, drawing back in sudden suspicion. "That is not something I am privileged to tell you. Besides, I—I don't think I could."

"Then we are at an impasse. Or had you planned to do the thing yourself? You are hardly dressed for it."

"Dressed for it?" exclaimed Sabra. "Pray tell what has my attire to say to the matter?"

"Apparently nothing at all," Myles observed acerbically. "You, no doubt, are accustomed to wading through snow in silk slippers with diamond buckles."

"Oh!" exclaimed Sabra, her cheeks suddenly warm. "I had forgot."

Chiding herself for not having thought to slip on her pattens before venturing out, Sabra eyed the white blanket of snow askance. While she shuddered to think what the stuff would do to her silk brocade shoes, she was even less enamored of the idea of taking time to rectify the omission. In the end it was Myles's patronizing air tinged with sardonic amusement that decided her simply to brazen the thing through.

"Yes, well, never you mind, captain," she said with magnificent disdain. "If I have been remiss, I am fully prepared to pay the consequences. You, sir, need not concern yourself."

Willing to sacrifice any number of silk brocade slippers rather than concede Myles a moral victory, she gathered up her skirts and strode recklessly to the open French windows. Before she could take that first ruinous step, a strong arm swept ruthlessly about her waist and, clasping her breathlessly to a hard chest, held her there. Startled into uttering a strangled cry, Sabra threw her arms about Myles's neck.

"Myles, your wound!" she blurted before she thought. "For heaven's sake, put me down at once."

"If it is my wound that concerns you, I suggest you hold tight and cease at once to struggle," he admonished, a gleam of devilry in the sudden flash of strong white teeth. "For I promise I have no intention of setting you

391

on your feet short of our objective."

Suddenly aware that she did not find it all distasteful where she was, Sabra relaxed. Even so, pride precluded allowing him to see how readily she would give in to him.

"But this is not at all necessary," she insisted, tilting her chin at a beguilingly stubborn angle. "I promise you I am not the least afraid of getting my feet wet."

"Having been convinced for some time that you are appallingly lacking in common sense, Miss Tyree, I shouldn't doubt it for a moment," he unhesitatingly informed her.

As Myles had by this time reached her father's sundial, she saw little point in carrying the argument further. With what little dignity she could muster, she allowed him to set her on her feet atop the low stone bench built around the dais. Then, conscious of a sharp stab of regret at having his arm removed from her waist, she made a great show of turning away.

"No doubt I am obliged to you for your unsolicited gallantry," she conceded stiffly. Whereupon Myles openly grinned.

"Not at all, Miss Tyree. I assure you I was acting purely in the line of duty."

"Indeed," Sabra replied frostily. "Then, as I, too, have a duty to perform, you no doubt will excuse me?"

Giving a small toss of her curls, she resolved simply to ignore him.

With the sleeve of her pelisse she swept the snow from the face of the dial plane made of bronze. Then, bending near in order to make out the numbers of the hours, she worked diligently to loosen one end of the style from its moorings. After several moments without success, she glanced up in exasperation at Myles.

"Have you a penknife, captain!" she demanded crossly. "The wretched thing refuses to budge."

"Perhaps," drawled Myles, shrugging purposefully out of his greatcoat, "you would not object to letting me have a go at it."

"On the contrary, I believe I should be eternally grateful!" she admitted with rueful candor. "You will be careful, will you not? The stile is the key to the mechanism that operates the sealed door. Did anything happen to it, we should require a sledgehammer to break in."

Myles, quirking an amused eyebrow at her, propped a foot on the bench.

"I shall do my best to keep that in mind," he solemnly promised and reached down to draw forth a dagger from his boot top.

"Is it your usual practice to go heavily armed when attending formal receptions, captain?" inquired Sabra, eyeing him curiously.

"*Only* when attending formal receptions, Miss Tyree," Myles answered dryly. "Now, if you could bring yourself to move aside."

Taking instant umbrage at his ironic tone, Sabra lifted disdainful eyebrows.

"Oh, by all means," she retorted. Clasping her arms across her bosom, she settled with her back to him on the far edge of the dais.

It was not long, however, before her eyes strayed, as of their own accord, back to his face. Forgetting herself, she let her gaze play over the strong contours like a caress that memorized everything it touched. At last a whimsical smile came to her lips as she saw him brush impatiently at the raven lock of hair that had a wholly captivating manner of falling stubbornly across his forehead. The simple familiarity of the gesture made him seem fallible somehow, more human, and suddenly she felt a lump rise to her throat.

She did not know how long she remained thus, stricken with the painful awareness that she wanted nothing more than to have him turn and take her in his arms, before suddenly she realized he had spoken her name.

"I—I beg your pardon," she stammered. "What did you say?"

"Only that you may try now and see if it works," he answered with an amused tolerance that brought an unwitting blush to her cheeks.

She was acutely aware of his eyes on her as she leaned over to brush at the wisps of snow yet clinging to the dial plane and concentrated on moving the stile, like a clockhand, from number to number in the correct, patterned sequence.

"No doubt you are aware, captain," she said to break the unbearable silence, "that sundials are not normally equipped with movable stiles. My father had this one specially designed and for a purpose other than telling the time. The stile, you see, is attached by a cylindrical shaft to a series of cogged wheels and pinions inside the column. When I rotate it to the prescribed sequence of numbers, the wheels release a succession of springs inside—" She paused in her recital as she brought the stile around to the final number. A soft, metallic click sounded from inside the column. "Which in turn," she finished triumphantly, "springs the catch."

There was a rumble of stone sliding over stone, then Sabra stepped back to reveal the gaping maw of her father's secret compartment. Inexplicably she was trembling a little as she crouched in the snow and reached inside for the leather pouch. Rising, she probed Myles's face with suddenly troubled eyes.

"Here, captain," she said at last. "I believe this is what you have been looking for."

A loud report punctuated the end of her speech, and as a corner of the dais shattered, Sabra fell back, stung by the flying particles. Dazed, she touched her cheek and stared stupidly as her hand came away stained with blood.

"Sabra, get down!" Myles shouted. She looked up to see him standing over her, his sword drawn, then his hand shot out to thrust her sprawling, facedown, in the snow.

As Sabra struggled to shove herself up amid the tangle of her skirts, it seemed that the garden had erupted into a fierce battleground. Dashing her hair from her eyes, she was in time to behold Myles catch the thrust of a cutlass on his dagger hilt. In dread, she saw him clench his teeth against the strain to his wounded arm. Then lunging, he thrust straight with the sword to the unprotected torso. Even as the other man's harsh features registered a horrified disbelief, Myles dragged the blade free and bounded forward to meet the slashing onslaught of yet another assailant.

Sabra was left staring in horrid fascination at the wounded man, a hand clutched to his belly that was spouting blood. As if performing a grotesque parody of a courtly bow, he slowly doubled over, until at last he toppled forward to land in a lifeless heap beside her. Gagging, she scrambled hastily to her feet and, snatching up the leather pouch and the slain man's cutlass, gazed wildly about her for Myles.

She saw him near the house. Two men circled warily before him, while a third crouched in the shadows, waiting for an opening. Oblivious of her skirts and high Italian heels, Sabra bolted heedlessly across the grounds in their direction.

Myles must have glimpsed her coming. Yelling at her to stand away, he pressed forward with the *coupe de temps*. In the face of that relentless, slashing attack, the two men were driven back, until, finding themselves trapped against the high wall surrounding the garden, one of the villains suddenly threw down his weapon and begged for mercy. Without warning, the other cursed and struck him a savage blow in the back with a long-bladed dagger. Then, thrusting him in Myles's way, he turned and bolted over the wall.

His chest heaving from his exertions, Myles wearily lowered his guard and watched him go.

Only then did Sabra realize he was unaware of the existence of that third man. Having lain in wait for this very moment when he should have the captain, standing with his back to him, the brigand rose noiselessly and stole with murderous intent toward the unsuspecting Myles.

What came next happened so quickly that Sabra was never able to recall the exact details with clarity. As in a dream she heard herself scream, "Myles, behind you!" and in horror watched the sword descend toward Myles's unprotected back, saw him twist around, bring the dagger up. A grimace of pain lanced across his face as the assassin's blade struck the dagger hilt with resounding force and, holding, bore him down to one knee. It had come to her then that his arm, not yet fully healed, was giving way, and suddenly she knew with terrible certainty that she was about to see Myles murdered before her very eyes. She remembered launching herself desperately toward the two men, when all at once someone had come out of nowhere and hurtled into her, knocking her to the ground. As she fell, she caught a glimpse of a pale, set face and in a terrible, rending flash, had recognized it as Robert Wayne's.

Shaken, she shoved herself up in time to see Wayne fling himself at Myles's assailant. There had been a wildness about him, a recklessness, that filled her with fear as she watched him strike the other man and send him spinning away. In horror she saw his weak leg buckle beneath him, saw him gamely catch himself, then, at the sudden caress of steel against his cheek, saw him go

396

deathly still.

"You disappoint me, Wayne. You should know better than to interfere in matters concerning men." The voice, sounding coldly amused, taunted and demeaned.

Heedless of the touch of steel against his chest, Wayne straightened his back. "Should I?" he murmured. "But then, we both know there is only *one* man here this night. The man *you* would have struck from behind!"

A harsh breath hissed between the other man's teeth. Fearlessly Wayne stared into the face of death and smiled. "Damn you to bloody hell," he said.

"You fool," rasped the villain.

An anguished scream seemed torn from Sabra's throat as savagely he ran Wayne through, then, yanking the blade free, watched contemptuously as the stricken man crumpled slowly to his knees. Sabra, racked with bitter sobs, began to drag herself toward Wayne, when Myles's voice lashed across the dreadful stillness.

"Channing!"

With awful certainty, the baronet turned. His gaze flickered to Myles's injured arm held stiffly at his side then back again to the gimlet eyes. A cold smile touched his lips.

"Whenever you are ready, my dear Myles," he taunted.

Myles dropped with chilling deliberation into the fighting stance. *"En garde, monsieur le baronet,"* he flung coldly back at him.

Warily the two blades circled one another, feinting and parrying, as each man tested the other.

"No doubt I should congratulate you, captain," observed Channing conversationally, feinting left, then, passing neatly under Myles's blade, thrusting right. "You have caused me a deal of trouble."

Myles, countering *en quarte,* swept the baronet's blade aside and, disengaging with an overhand twist of the wrist, replied immediately *en riposte* with a straight thrust

397

to the chest.

"It was my pleasure, Sir Wilfred, I assure you."

Channing leaped back, denying Myles the coup by a scant fraction of an inch. A bead of sweat broke out on his upper lip, as warily he sidestepped.

"Yes, of course," he murmured, his smile rather more strained now than mocking. "I feel obligated, however, to lodge a complaint against you."

Without warning he lunged forward, struck Myles's blade, and lunged again and again, and yet again. Myles, driven back across the grounds, came up hard against the stone bench encircling the dais, and Channing, quick to pursue the advantage, straightened his arm and thrust. As Myles dodged and Channing missed, the two men lurched together, chest to chest, and grappled, Myles's sword between them a hair's breadth from Channing's cheek.

"I am . . . compelled . . . to ask," Myles ground out between clenched teeth, as, bracing his back against the stone dais, he brought the heel of his hand up against Channing's chest and thrust with all his strength. "*What* complaint?"

Channing staggered several steps and caught himself. Never taking his eyes off Myles, he deliberately wiped the sweat from his brow with the back of his sword hand.

"Your orders, captain. Have you forgot why you were brought here?" Channing's laughter grated in the chill air. "You have failed abysmally to live up to your reputation, my dear Myles. But then, the master of *Nemesis* has played us all for fools, has she not?"

Myles's blade came up, quivered, and held.

" 'She,' Sir Wilfred?" he queried softly.

"But of course, captain." An ugly smile crossed his lips. "The most seductively beautiful rebel privateer ever to outwit the British navy—the incomparable Sabra, your

398

bride-to-be. But surely you must have guessed?"

Abruptly Channing froze as a shout carried clearly from the interior of the house, along with the loud clatter of approaching footsteps. Involuntarily he glanced toward the french door. Then, just as quickly, he looked back again at the captain.

"She will hang if you turn those papers over to your superiors. I shall make sure of it."

"*You* will be dead, Channing," Myles answered and stepped deliberately toward him.

Without warning, Channing flung his sword at Myles's head. "Another time, perhaps, captain," he called mockingly and bolted across the garden. Knocking the projectile aside, Myles started after him, while, behind him, Leeks burst through the French windows into the open, followed seconds later by Jubal, who faltered at the sight of his mistress on her knees next to Wayne. Channing reached the stone barrier, pulled himself to the top. As he dropped off on the other side, Myles halted, panting, and waited for the other two men to come up to him.

The big coxswain reached him first, his eyes anxious as he noted the finely drawn lines of strain and fatigue in his captain's face.

"I heard a shot, cap'n, an' come runnin'. But I couldn't find where you an' the lady had got to. I expect I'd still be beatin' my head against the wall if this man Jubal hadn't come along."

Myles shoved the sword into its scabbard with a sort of weary finality. "Go after him," he said to Leeks. Then grimacing, he clasped a hand to his wounded arm.

The coxswain required no further urging.

"Aye, cap'n. With pleasure."

As he sprang forward, Myles reached out and caught his shoulder in a steely grip.

"Take care, my friend," he murmured quietly. "The baronet is full of tricks." Releasing him, he stepped back and watched as Leeks heaved himself over the wall. Then coming about, he gave Jubal an appraising glance.

"Your mistress witnessed Channing cut Wayne down in cold blood," he stated bluntly. "It was not an easy sight."

"No, sir. I reckon Miss Sabra be takin' it real hard," observed the Negro, his eyes steady on the other man's. "Might be you could talk her inside, captain, so's I can be about cleanin' things up a bit."

Slowly Myles nodded, satisfied. "I should be grateful," he said and turned at last to look at the woman huddled in the snow beside Wayne's ominously still form. A sardonic smile curled his lip. There was little about her now of the privateer whose daring and sheer cold-blooded nerve had carried both ship and crew to safety over the sandbars off Fire Island. And little wonder. Wayne had set himself up for execution before the one person most likely to hug all the blame for it to herself.

Myles uttered a blistering oath. Then, with long, purposeful steps, he strode toward Sabra.

Chapter 23

Sabra huddled in the snow, Wayne's lifeless body cradled against her, and felt nothing but the cold seeping into her bones. Somewhere, in some small part of her mind, she was aware that her limbs had grown numb, like her heart and her brain. Yet she dared not move, for to do so might be to release a horde of punishing thoughts to come screaming at her from out of her numbness—thoughts of Wayne, his eyes open and staring up at her—sightless, cold, without life. And memories she sensed, like things, hovering in the dark, waiting— remembered words bearing claws that would rip at her, images with teeth to torture and rend. She wanted none of it. She wanted to sleep, to drift in darkness, unmoved, untouched, unfeeling.

From somewhere outside the dullness, like a cocoon insulating her from her surroundings, she heard footsteps coming toward her across the barren garden. Detached, she listened to them draw near, stop, fill the silence with waiting. When at last a voice said her name, she let it pass over her like an insignificant ripple of noise, only to have it come again—arrogant, this time, and demanding—impossible to be denied.

"Sabra. *Look* at me!"

The ruthless clasp of a hand on her arm, shaking her, shattered everything, and her eyes flew open to Myles, standing over her. She saw his glance narrow sharply on her face and grow suddenly hard.

"So, you are determined to play the martyr, are you," he murmured softly, gazing into the blank vulnerability of her wounded orbs. "Odd, but I should have thought you were made of sterner stuff. Or is it all a lie, what Channing told me? I find it hard to believe the notorious privateer would turn suddenly womanish."

His deliberate contempt struck a faint spark from the sea-green depths of her eyes, but as they came to bear on him at last, they were opaque again, concealing whatever thoughts lay behind them.

"Pray go away, captain," she pronounced in flat tones. "Please, just leave . . . me . . . *alone.*"

A forbidding smile touched his lips.

"I am sorry I cannot oblige you. Indeed, you are about to discover how little prepared I am to tolerate you in your present mood. Get to your feet, Miss Tyree. It's time we were going in.

"Now!" he said, when she made no move to comply and, reaching down, clasped her ungently by the arm and started to drag her up.

If his purpose had been to rouse her fighting spirit, he succeeded all too well. As if a floodgate had burst, releasing in a single instant all her pent-up rage and grief, she erupted into a furious struggle.

"Stop it!" she cried, twisting and turning, clawing at the hand that held her. "I won't leave him. Let . . . me . . . go!"

Cursing, Myles caught both her wrists and yanked her to him.

"Sabra, enough!" he rasped, impaling her with his eyes. "Wayne's dead. His torment is ended. Dammit, let him bloody well go!"

Something in his voice broke through her frenzy, and abruptly she stilled, her eyes frozen on his with some terrible realization.

"Yes," she whispered, the word seemingly torn from her. "His torment. Oh, God, why could it not have been me?" All at once she collapsed, weeping, to her knees, her wrists yet imprisoned in his merciless grip all that

402

held her upright.

She did not know how tenderly Myles knelt to take her in his arms and hold her, his face grim, as she clung to him and wept tears all the more appalling for their terrible silence. Or how at last he felt her tremble and, fearing he had put it off for too long, forced her to turn loose of him till he had got them both to their feet. She knew only that she was swept suddenly up high into his arms and borne, still weeping weakly, from the garden.

Vaguely she was aware of the house all around her, of the shadowed halls and the silence broken only by the echo of Myles's footsteps. Later she was to wonder why it had not struck her as odd that they encountered no one on the stairs or along the hall that led to her room, but somehow it did not even come to her to miss Phoebe, who normally should have been waiting up to scold and hover over her. She seemed strangely suspended in a world whose only reality was pain and a crushing sense of loss.

She was shivering badly when at last Myles set her on her feet and ordered her to stay where she was. In moments he had a fire leaping in the fireplace, then, moving quickly to the bed, flung back the down comforters and silk sheets. At last he turned and came toward her, his eyes like piercing pinpoints of flame, and suddenly, unreasonably, he seemed to loom as the cause of everything that had happened.

"Stop! Don't come any closer, I warn you," she uttered, freezing him with a look. "You have what you came for. I pray you will leave my house at once."

For a moment Myles appeared to hesitate. His gaze sweeping her face was appraising.

"As you appear in no condition to be left alone, Miss Tyree," he said at last, measuringly, "I fear I must insist that you tolerate my presence a while longer."

"And *I* think you have already done quite enough!" she retorted witheringly, unable to stop herself. "Robert Wayne is dead, and Channing is free. That is hardly the way it was supposed to turn out when you asked me to

403

trust you, is it."

She almost quailed before the terrible leap of his eyes. Then he was himself again—dispassionate, cool, unreadable.

"Perhaps you think Wayne would be gratified by this maudlin display, Miss Tyree," he drawled, "but I assure you I am not."

"What can you possibly know of it?" she flung passionately back at him.

"Enough to know how pointless it is to blame me—or yourself—for what happened."

Wincing as if struck, Sabra stared blindly back at him. Then all at once she groaned. The back of a hand pressed convulsively to her mouth, she turned away.

"It *is* my fault," she said, her voice muffled. "Oh, God, when he went to Channing, how could I not have known what that cold-blooded viper would do to him! And when it was too late, and Channing had already broken him, how could I have refused him my simple compassion?" Suddenly she came back around to face Myles with tormented eyes. "Don't you understand? Robert was there for me, *always,* but not I. I turned away when he needed me most." She laughed hysterically. "Merciful God, I said I hoped never again to see him alive. In the end, I might just as well have killed him myself."

"Don't be a fool!" Sabra recoiled as if stung by his voice lashing out at her. Then Myles was standing over her, his eyes boring into her. "Wayne made his own choices. At least give him that. He defeated Channing and everything he stands for in the only way he knew. He conquered his fear. If you cannot bring yourself to accept that, then you wrong him and cheapen his memory!"

Stricken by the ring of truth in his words, Sabra stared at Myles as if seeing him for the first time. But in her mind it was Robert she saw—lying in the snow, his face peaceful at last as he raised a hand to touch the tiny cut on her cheek.

"Never meant for you to be hurt," he had whispered as

404

with his thumb he wiped away a dab of blood dampened with tears. "Never you."

"Don't!" she had blurted, wishing desperately for some way to halt the flow of time. "It doesn't matter. None of it does." Suddenly she sniffed noisily and forced a smile to her lips. "It's going to be all right, Robert. You'll see. Wes is safe. Myles got him out. We'll go somewhere — the South Sea Islands. It's what you and Wes always wanted."

She had thought she could not bear to see the pity in the look he gave her as slowly he shook his head.

"No, not me. *You.* You and Wes. Forget Channing. War. Everything. Make Myles go with you. Easy for you. Loves you." His sweet smile had rent her heart. "Can't help loving beautiful, fiery-eyed Sabra." Feeling his strength flowing out of him, she had grasped his hand in both of hers and held it to her cheek, wet with tears. "Promise me, Sabra," he said, grimacing with the effort it cost him. "Promise you'll do it. The three of you. For me. One . . . good . . . to come out of . . . this."

"Yes. Yes, I promise!" Seeing his eyes grow dim had wrenched the words from her. Yet from somewhere he had found the strength to rally one last time, to bare his soul of its final burden.

Feeling the tears press against her throat, Sabra swallowed and averted her head from Myles's all-too discerning eyes. A dark object lying on the floor caught her glance, and with something akin to hatred, she knelt and reached out a trembling hand to retrieve it.

"He saw me put them in the dais," she said, straightening and handing to Myles the pouch that held the baronet's loathsome papers. "That's how Channing knew." There was that in his silence that made her look up at him, and all at once something clicked into place. "In the parlor — the window. You were checking to see if anyone was watching the house. That's why you wouldn't allow the candles to be lit. You *knew* Robert had told Channing."

Myles's face remained impassive. Carelessly he shrugged.

"It was not difficult to figure out. It was obvious Channing knew where the papers were. He was too sure of himself for it to have been otherwise. Which meant someone had to have told him. Wayne, unfortunately, was the likeliest candidate. The one thing I could not figure was why Channing had not already gone after them."

"He couldn't get to them," Sabra supplied, seeing it all as Myles must have done. "I was the only one who knew the secret of the dial."

"Exactly so, which is why inevitably he had to be sure you would go after them when he would be on hand to take them away from you. That, in the final analysis, had to be his real purpose in confronting us in the study—to lay the bait."

"But if you knew the danger, why did you not summon help? Good God, you might have been . . ."

"Because," he answered before she could finish, "I could not be sure how deeply you were involved. If I had told anyone, or enlisted the aid of troops, there was the chance you would be implicated along with the rest." A wry smile twisted at his lips. "I'm afraid it simply was not something I was prepared to risk."

Myles's face suddenly blurred in her sight as the real significance of his words bore into her—all that he had dared for her that night; indeed, had dared for Wes and even Wayne.

"Why?" she said, her voice strained and hardly above a whisper. "Once you were assured of Channing's papers, why should it have mattered to you what happened to me, one way or the other?"

A disturbing light flared in his eyes. "I told you, did I not," he murmured, his smile mocking, "when next I came, it would be to claim everything that was mine. To have to do so in a jail cell, I should have found infinitely galling." When still she said nothing, his smile turned strangely quizzical. "Surely you must *know* why," he said.

Her throat working, Sabra could only stare at him out of huge, tormented eyes. In the wake of everything that had happened, she felt stunned, bewildered. Indeed, she no longer knew what to think—who or what to believe. At last Myles gave a sigh. Then, in a gesture, infinitely weary, he reached out and gathered her to him. "Sabra," he muttered huskily against her hair. "You are impossibly naive if you think for one moment I should go to all this trouble if I weren't hopelessly in love with you."

For a stunned moment she stared up at him with disbelieving eyes. Then suddenly her vision blurred as she felt her already tenuous defenses crumbling within. The revelation of Myles's love coupled with the terrible anguish of Wayne's death was simply too much for her to bear all at once. Collapsing against Myles's chest, she gave in at last to great, shuddering sobs.

Myles, running his hand over her hair in long steady strokes, let her cry it out. After a time her weeping gradually subsided and he felt her go lax against him with a tremulous sigh. Then gently he put her from him.

Deliberately the gray eyes probed hers, until at last a faint, somewhat rueful smile played about the corners of his mouth.

"Yes, that's more like," he murmured. Gently he pulled her to him and rubbed his cheek against her hair.

"Did you mean it?" queried Sabra, her voice muffled against the folds of his neckcloth.

For the barest instant he went still.

"Yes." With a sigh, she leaned her cheek against his chest and felt the strong beat of his heart.

"Sabra," he whispered against her hair. He lifted his head to look at her. "I want you. This time not only with my eyes open and my wits about me, but more importantly, because you *want* me to make love to you."

Sabra's heart skipped a beat. For a seeming eternity she looked into his gray, smoldering gaze, her blood quickening at what she saw there. Still, something held her back, a remnant of all the hurt and misunderstanding that still lay between them.

"Is it *so* important—what I want?" she queried, masking her thoughts behind an indifference she was far from feeling. "I mean, it is usually enough for a whore to play the part convincingly, is it not? What can it possibly matter what lies truly in her heart?"

Sabra's heart nearly failed her at the sudden leap of steel in his eyes.

"You are mistaken, *ma mie*," he murmured, impaling her with those eyes. "A woman who sells her favors for whatever price plays the whore, but a whore who gives her heart out of love is no different from any other woman in love. I've known from the moment I saw your face that morning in Rab Wilkins's cellar that you had never lain with a man before you gave yourself to me with such exquisite abandon. It was not until you swore you meant to incarcerate me in your attic that I learned you were no whore."

Sabra's lips parted in surprise. "But how could you possibly have guessed I was a virgin?" she blurted, eyeing him doubtfully. "You were out of your head with fever."

"My head was clear enough, I assure you, when I saw the marks of your teeth on your lip. Your maidenhead must have been as obdurate as your stubborn pride, my love. Nor is it any wonder that you should have been tender at its loss. It was, at any rate, only what I expected when I took you again so soon after. My poor darling, as careful as I tried to be, I could not but hurt you. And that is why this time I must be certain you want it for yourself."

At last she smiled, everything made suddenly crystal clear to her. A soft rapturous light sprang to her eyes.

"But, my dearest captain," she said simply, reaching up to entwine her arms about his neck. "It is what I have always wanted—to have you love me as I have loved you, almost from the very first moment I saw you."

Sabra's lips parted on a sigh as Myles clasped her to him and kissed her then, hard at first, then unhurriedly and with an exquisite tenderness quite unlike anything she had ever known before. She felt a slow heat kindle deep within and spread outward to her limbs till she was filled with a wondrous warmth that left her dazed. When at last his lips left hers, she drew in a long, tremulous breath. Slowly she let her eyelids drift open to find Myles watching her.

Her heart gave a little flutter at the meaningful warmth of his smile.

"Softly, *ma mie*," he murmured and, turning her toward the fire, began quickly to disrobe her.

Acutely aware of his hands undoing the fastenings of her gown in back, Sabra stared straight before her, her skin tingling at his touch. A blush invaded her cheeks as he slipped the gown off her shoulders and down her slender length, and though somehow she managed to quell the absurd impulse to cover herself with her arms, she could not stop herself from trembling.

In moments her clothing lay in a pile at her feet. She felt a tremor shake the captain's lean hands as he turned her and beheld her silken loveliness. Lifting her in his arms, he carried her to the bed. Gently he lowered her to its feathery softness and covered her with the sheet. Then kneeling beside her, he caressed the side of her face with the back of his hand in a gesture that seemed meant to stop her heart. His eyes mesmerized her, held her for a seeming eternity as if searching her very depths for something. Then, deliberately, they released her to move slowly over her face, until at last they came to rest on her lips, which quivered. Suddenly his hand stilled and, murmuring her name, he bent over her.

A low groan seemed wrung from his depths, as, covering her mouth with his, he kissed her deeply, his tongue exploring the delicious sweetness between her parted lips. Sabra moaned softly, clinging to him, her love for Myles a fiercely burning flame within her.

His strong hands roused her as only he knew how, so that she was already afire with need when he left her to quickly undress himself. And when he came back to her again, to tease and tantalize her with his hands, his lips, his softly murmured words of love, she thought surely she must die of it.

He took her slowly, with tenderness, his mouth savoring the enticing rigidity of her nipples, his hands wandering over the delectable planes and hidden valleys of her body until at last they found the moist warmth between her thighs. She shuddered and clung to him, thrilled to the hard ripple of muscles along the powerful shoulders. His name burst from her lips, a feverish litany to be repeated over and over as her head moved aimlessly from side to side on the pillow. Her fingers entangled themselves in the curling mat of hair on his chest, sought out and teased the masculine nipples till they stood out as rigid as her own. Then feverishly her hands wandered a path down over the rippled firmness of his ribs beneath his arms and gloried in the supple strength of the narrow waist, till at last they found and molded themselves to the muscular curve of his buttocks.

"Myles," she pleaded, lifting to him, willing him to end her sweet agony.

Quickly he parted her thighs and pressed his lean body into the warm cradle of her desire. She groaned and arched upward against his swollen member, her breath coming in hard, gusty sighs. Still he held off, savoring the lithe, supple movements of her sleek body, the moist, musky scent of her arousal, her small throaty cries as he tantalized and teased her with slow, shallow forays into the moist, swollen lips of her body. She was all silk and fire, was his sweet Sabra, the fine texture of her skin satiny smooth, her glorious hair, a luxurious, sericeous mass splayed against the pillow. Her gracile length molded with lovely, tantalizing curves—the wide hips and slender thighs, the willowy smallness of her waist, the soft pliancy of perfect breasts—infused him with a feverish excitement, an aching need to plunge savagely into her molten depths, to fill her with himself and feel her supple flesh close about him.

He felt the sweat, damp against his skin, as, controlling with an iron will the excruciating torment of his need, he arched his powerful back over her to explore with mouth and tongue the turgid promise of her breasts, first one and then the other. His delicious torture

410

drove her to utter an explosive gasp and, writhing, she sank her teeth into his shoulder. Then at last, drawing up and back, he thrust deep within her, again and again in the crescendoing rhythm of mounting ecstasy.

Sabra, moving with him, was borne upward on a cresting wave of passion, like liquid fire driven before a tempest, until at last she arched, reaching for the scintillating heights of rapture. Her name a groan emitted from his depths, Myles drove deep, his seed spilling forth in a glorious explosion of release. Never had Sabra known such pleasure as the one that burst forth inside her then. Her blissful shudder, her flesh constricting in exquisite ripples about his member, her deep-throated sighs, complemented and intensified Myles's rapturous culmination.

As one, they collapsed in a tangle of arms and legs, Myles's face pressed into the delectable curve of her neck and his lips murmuring words of endearment.

"My sweet love. So soft and silken." Gently he nuzzled her neck, pressed his lips to the throb of her pulse at the base of her throat.

After a while he lifted his head to look at her. A faint smile curved his lips at the sight of her eyes yet dusky with the lingering aftermath of their lovemaking. Tenderly he brushed a red-gold curl from her forehead.

"What a fool I was ever to let you escape me," he said, a faint steeliness edging his voice.

A wry gleam of humor lurked behind her suddenly demure smile.

"Indeed, captain, I might have told you as much—had you but given me the chance. You, however, seemed inexplicably determined to have me ridden out of town on a rail."

"Actually, I believe it was more in the nature of having you tied to the back of a horsecart and whipped," Myles reflected, giving in to the compulsion to place a kiss on the tip of her wholly delightful nose.

Immediately, however, a frown darkened his brow. "Which is something else for which we have our friend

Channing to thank."

"I don't understand," murmured Sabra, startled at the cold glint in his eyes. "What could Channing possibly have had to do with what happened in London?"

Myles did not answer at once, but instead eased his weight off her, and settling next to her, pulled her into the cradle of his shoulder.

"Myles?" she prodded.

"No doubt you were unaware," he drawled finally in a voice curiously devoid of emotion, "that some weeks after a certain fateful night at Almacks', I was summoned to Waincourt to see my grandfather, the duke. It seemed His Grace was deeply concerned that rumor linked his heir to an American adventuress out to wed a fortune and a title. Indeed, he ordered me to see that nothing came of the affair. Perhaps you can imagine my feelings when I discovered the fortune hunter to whom my grandfather was referring was none other than an utterly bewitching termagant who had at first sight enamored me of red-gold hair and green eyes the color of a stormy sea."

"But there was no truth to it!" exclaimed Sabra, torn between pique and incredulity. "I stood to inherit sizeable fortunes from my father and my maternal grandfather. And so far as a title is concerned, I believe I made my views of the privileged aristocracy plain on more than one occasion. I certainly never pretended to be other than a republican."

"Quite so," conceded Myles with an appreciative gleam of humor, "as can be attested to by at least two earls and a marquess, whose suits, as I recall, you heartlessly spurned. Not to mention those of certain barons and viscounts too numerous to mention. Unfortunately, however, you failed to demonstrate a like reticence for my cousin, who was heir to an even greater title and fortune. You were, I fear, judged guilty by omission."

"Was I indeed," murmured Sabra with a flash of green eyes. "And what was I to do? Had your precious duke loosened his reins sufficiently to allow his heir the chance

412

to acquire a measure of town bronze like other boys his age, there had been no need to worry. As it was, only a female without an ounce of feeling could have dashed his hopes out of hand. It would have been like kicking a helpless puppy for licking your hand."

"No doubt," he drawled. A fleeting shadow of something curiously like pain flickered in his lean face, then vanished. "I fear the world is not prone to be generous in its judgments. And I, unfortunately, was no less guilty. I believed the rumors that were being circulated. Rumors that painted you as a penniless opportunist, a rebel desirous of snaring a fortune for the use of her disgruntled American compatriots. We were, you remember, on the verge of open hostilities, an empire about to be split asunder. And Channing, it seemed, was adept at promulgating the image of a rebellious, ungrateful America."

A low hiss escaped Sabra's lips.

"It was Channing who started the rumors," she stated with sudden conviction. "Faith, I might have known."

"As should have I," Myles rejoined chillingly. "However, I never even surmised as much until quite recently, and then not before Leeks had gleaned the truth of it from his loquacious Mrs. Quinby."

The unpropitious mention of Kitty Quinby brought Sabra suddenly bolt upright.

"Merciful God," she choked, her eyes huge and searching on his face. "How could I have forgot? My brother! Where is he? Myles, you must take me to him. Now—at once! I beg you!"

The captain silenced her with a look.

"Softly, my love, I ordered your brother transferred to my ship three days ago and from thence by boat to your father's estate on Long Island. He is there under the protection of an old coaster by the name of Skyler."

"Wes is at Thornhaven?" she exclaimed, torn between sudden overwhelming relief and something else, only just beginning to dawn on her. "But—but the bargain you made with your superiors—the 'conditions' for his release." All at once her eyes widened in total comprehen-

413

sion. "A plague on you, captain. You tricked me! There never were any conditions. They were only a ruse to persuade me to take you to where the papers were hid."

"It seemed the only way to pry you loose from them" he admitted, smiling unrepentantly as he pulled her down to him. "It was, I judged, time to put an end to Channing's manipulations."

"And still it is not finished," she countered bitterly, thinking of Wes and all that he had been made to suffer, remembering Wayne, lying dead. "It never shall be so long as the baronet draws breath."

The captain's glance narrowed sharply at the sight of the glittery hardness of her eyes.

"Channing's power is broken," he said. "Even he hasn't enough wealth or influence to buy his way out of this. He will be found guilty of treason, my love, I promise you."

Sabra blinked and let her gaze slip away from his too-pointed scrutiny.

"Yes. Yes, of course he will," she murmured and. laying her cheek against the broad, muscular chest, ran her fingers slowly through the raven mat of hair. But in truth she did not believe it for a moment. She had known the baronet far too long to take anything that concerned him for granted. His attempt to destroy the evidence that would ruin him on both sides of the Atlantic had failed, but he was far from being finished. Indeed, everything would seem to point to the fact that he had been making ready for some time to pull up roots. Why else should he have been so anxious to bring his final acts of revenge to a climax? But, even more importantly, had not his journal, in addition to containing detailed accounts of his extensive spying and smuggling operations, made clear as well that the greatest portion of his wealth had been recently converted into gold bullion?

Far from standing trial for his crimes, Channing at this very moment was more likely to be on a ship bound away from New York, a fortune in gold stashed away in the hold. Indeed, in her heart she was sure of it.

414

Suddenly that organ seemed rent in two as the terrible significance of his probable escape hit home. Channing, alive and free, was a threat, not only to Wes and herself, but to her country as well, but what was more, she was sworn to see his network of influence broken, his lucrative business of peddling information brought to an end. That, indeed, was to have been her final mission. And yet how much more greatly was she tempted to remain where she was, at the very threshold of a far greater happiness than any she had ever before dreamed for herself!

Once Wes was out of danger and on the mend, what was there to prevent her from simply putting her past behind her and slipping away in pursuit of that dream of proffered happiness? She could buy passage on a ship bound for England, there to wait for her beloved captain. She was half English and kindred to a proud line of English lords. She need not fear that she would not be accepted, even made welcome, especially when it was learned she was to wed Trevor Phillip Delaney Myles!

All at once she bit her lip in anger at where her unruly fancies had carried her. Indeed, even as the thought had taken form in her mind, she had known she could not in truth go through with it. Half English or not, her loyalties were with her struggling young country, with Wes and Skyler and all those others—Rab and John Tully, and, faith, Jedediah Hawkes! To betray everything in which she believed, everything for which she had fought and dared so much, would be to betray them and herself—and more. To go to him on such terms would have reeked of the whore, who would steal to his bed at the cost of dignity and self-esteem, that fierce pride which made her what she was and which, in turn, demanded that she ever be free to choose her own way, determine her own destiny, captain her own ship. Not until such time as she could meet him on equal ground, her head high and her conscience free; indeed, not until the differences that set them apart were resolved and her country a free, sovereign nation in its own right, could she be joined with him in a true marriage of heart and mind. To do otherwise would be to destroy utterly the fragile bond of love that had yet somehow managed to survive the years of misunderstanding and mistrust, of tumult and strife, of upheaval and dissolution.

Myles's hand moving lightly over her hair brought her out of her somber reverie with a start.

"You seem uncommonly distracted," he said quietly.

"Do I?" she evaded. "I'm sorry. I don't mean to be."

Suddenly his hand stilled in her hair, and beneath the surface of his calm, she could feel the tension in him, the gathering of the storm.

"Sabra, if something is bothering you, I should like to believe you would confide in me."

"I pray you will not be absurd," she countered lightly, though her heart ached to bare itself of its burden. "What could possibly be bothering me?"

"Indeed, what?" he rejoined, frowning. Curling his arm about her in a sudden embrace, he turned on his side so that her head came to rest on the pillow beside him. Sabra's heart nearly stopped as he impaled her with a piercing glance. "That, my love," he said in a soft, steely voice, "is precisely what I have been asking myself these past ten minutes or more."

From somewhere she found the spirit to answer him in kind.

"Then perhaps," she declared, "you should tell me what you have concluded. For I assure you *I* haven't the least notion what you are talking about."

"It has occurred to me, my impetuous love, that you have been toying with the notion of resurrecting a ghost, the ghost of your beloved *Nemesis*." Observing her sudden pallor, he smiled mirthlessly. "Oh, yes. Channing told me. And I confess he took me completely by surprise. Though in retrospect I shouldn't wonder that the only reason I had not guessed it myself long ago was a reluctance to believe I had been outmaneuvered at my own game by a woman. I congratulate you, *ma mie*, on a boldly simple plan, brilliantly executed. I promise you were well and gone long before I recalled having noticed the portholes above the gun ports and realized you must have used sweeps to carry you back through the shoals."

For a stunned moment Sabra could not summon wit enough to speak. Her mind reeling with the terrible implications of what he had said and all that he had left unsaid, she stared at him in dreadful, dawning realization. Then at last a single utterance burst on an explosive breath from her lips.

"You!" she gasped.

Chapter 24

Sabra, staring into the hard glint of steely eyes, could only marvel that, at first sight of that tall, arrogant figure on the quarterdeck of the British frigate, she had not known who he was. Or maybe she had known, somewhere deep inside of herself. Known all along that the English captain, who relentlessly had pursued her the length of the New England coast, had pitted his skill and cunning against hers, and had outguessed her at every turn, matching her maneuver for maneuver with an uncanny precision that had, in the end, left her no choice but to dare an escape over the treacherous shoals off Fire Island, was in truth Capt. Trevor Myles.

Then, indeed, did she taste bitter gall, for it had of necessity to have been Myles, too, who had sent the Quaker, Pattison, with word of Wesley's capture and subsequent impressment into service aboard His Majesty's Frigate *Black Swan*. All along it had been Myles whom Channing had summoned to end the maraudings of an American privateer, Myles who had stalked her and Myles who had lurked in the background, a dark and mysterious figure of foreboding. And he had used her brother as bait to lure her into his snare!

"You knew that day that *Nemesis* would come," she stated flatly. "I felt it. You were waiting for us—for me. You and Channing set it up." Just as they had set up those others in the Caribbean. A dozen or more, Wayne had told her, and only she had escaped the trap.

"The *Meridian* was to serve as a decoy to draw the *Nemesis* out, it's true. But then—and until this very night—I never once suspected the privateer I had been ordered to capture and bring in was you. You, my love, had us all properly fooled."

"No, I don't believe you!" she said. The anguished glitter of her eyes accused him. "You sent Pattison to tell me about my brother. *Why*, if not because you knew I should then do all in my power to discover who that English captain was? You must have known it would lead me eventually to think of Channing and from thence to swallow the baronet's carefully laid bait."

Myles let go a weary sigh. "Did it never once occur to you that I might simply have acted thus out of concern for you? Sabra—" he murmured, reaching out to brush a stray lock of hair from her cheek. His hand froze as she jerked her head away. His lips thinned to a hard line. "Sabra, no matter what you believe, I have been convinced almost from the moment you fell swooning, half naked into my arms, that without you, my life would not be worth the living. Can you say in all honesty that you do not feel the same about me?"

"No, I cannot!" she uttered passionately. "God help me, I cannot stop myself from loving you." She looked up at him then with eyes that could neither conceal her terrible doubt nor banish from their depths a softly pleading light. "But once before, I believed in you, trusted you. This time I must be sure. I have to know why you came to me, why you wanted the world to believe we were betrothed to be married. Was it not because you wished an excuse to be close to me—to use me? Can you deny you did not believe I should eventually lead you to your precious traitor, or, indeed, that that traitor you sought was, in truth, myself?"

"It was a possibility that I could not dismiss out of hand," he admitted grimly. "Nor should I have granted you an ounce of mercy had you proven guilty. But it was

419

Channing I suspected almost from the moment of my arrival. He had been too keen to have your brother removed from my protection some three months earlier. Indeed, as it turned out, his greatest blunder was in paying my first officer to do his dirty work for him."

"That night in the stairwell," exclaimed Sabra, staring at him out of startled eyes. "You and Inness. My God, it was Wes you were arguing about. Wes who refused to man the guns—because it would have meant firing on an ally. Channing bribed Inness to set him up."

Myles's smile was singularly cold.

"It was all so very well planned," he murmured, his eyes steel-flecked and distant. "A ship's captain could hardly choose to overlook an overt act of mutiny. Not without running the risk of undermining discipline. I should have had no choice but to turn Locke over to the admiralty for trial. The fact that I fell to a marksman seconds after the Frenchman broke off the action only made it that much easier for Inness. I was, unfortunately, in no case to know Locke had been taken from the ship, let alone to do anything about it. Indeed, it was better than two months later before I was able to learn he had been confined here in the *Jersey* under Channing's orders."

"You're saying you looked for him?" marveled Sabra. "Why?"

"Because someone had made sure a French man-of-war would be waiting when the *Swan* anchored off Saint Martin's Island." Sabra felt a chill at the look in Myles's eyes. "It was to have been a closely guarded mission. None but a handful of men knew of the *Swan*'s presence in these waters, and the identity of those in command of her was a closely guarded secret. Everything depended on no one knowing that Waincourt had arranged a meeting between his representative and the Dutch governor in the hopes of working out a private agreement of mutual cooperation in the Caribbean. The fact that someone should also have had enough influence to cause an impressed seaman to apparently vanish without a trace during that same mis-

420

sion seemed a trifle too coincidental. It was, at any rate, curious enough to persuade me to try and discover if one event was somehow connected to the other. Which is what I suggested to the admiralty in my written report. Fortunately, an official with more influence at court had made repeated demands for a ship to rid the coast of a particularly successful rebel privateer. It provided the admiralty opportunity not only to investigate the possibility there was someone leaking information to the enemy, but to relieve themselves of an intolerable nuisance."

"And who suggested that traitor might be me?" queried Sabra bitterly.

She could see Myles hesitate, and instantly her stomach tightened with foreboding.

"No doubt I am sorry to disappoint you," he drawled smoothly enough, his tone ironic. "I am afraid, however, that it was done anonymously. By means of an unsigned missive delivered to the admiralty."

Sabra frowned suspiciously. He was keeping something from her. She was sure of it.

"A missive alleging what?" she prodded. "Myles, tell me!"

"Let it go, Sabra. It is nothing that you cannot go on better without knowing."

"Dammit, Myles. If you are trying to spare me, don't," she countered heatedly. "I have been looking out for myself for a long time now. I don't need you or any other man to decide what is best for me. I want to know."

A spark of anger flickered in his eyes.

"But certainly, my dear," he answered, deliberately brutal. "What is it you would have me tell you? That information was given to the effect that a Colonel Ridgley of the Fifty-second had been seduced by a probable rebel sympathizer? That the implications were that the colonel had made inquiries on behalf of this female into matters which he knew to be under a ban of secrecy? And that, further, he chose to communicate that information in spite of it? That, indeed, a badly charred letter was included,

421

bearing the lady's name and Ridgley's and enough of the written message to give some credence to the accusations? No doubt you will pardon me if I fail to see how this information can in any way profit you."

In stunned silence she stared at him, her face deathly pale. Then closing her eyes, she drew in a shuddering breath.

Myles, bitterly cursing himself for a fool, was startled by her low, husky voice.

"I burned Ridgley's letter," she said, opening her eyes to look at him. "I remember putting it in the fire and shortly afterward, a log falling to the hearth. Robert knelt with the poker to put it back again."

She fell silent then. Indeed, there was no reason to say more. There could be little doubt who had saved the half-burned letter from the fire and given it to Channing. And yet how sad, she thought, that dear Ridgley should have been made to pay so dreadful a price for her carelessness and Robert's weakness.

"What will you do if Channing makes good his escape?" she asked unexpectedly. "Will you go after him?"

"My orders are to uncover the man responsible for numerous acts of treason and see him brought to justice. Yes, my love, I shall go after him."

Suddenly his eyebrows snapped together at the sight of the curious gleam that had sprung to her eyes.

"How odd," she murmured, her gaze limpid as it met his. "Those are my orders, too, captain."

"Are they indeed?" he queried in ominous tones. "Somehow that does not surprise me in the least, Miss Tyree. I feel I should warn you, however, that even though you managed to outwit me once on the high seas, I shall not be depended upon to make the same mistake twice. You, my love, will leave Channing to me."

"And if I do not?" she rejoined carelessly, her heart frozen within her breast.

Myles gave her a long look.

"Then," he answered, the muscle leaping along his jaw—

line, "you would force me to deal with you as though yours were any other enemy vessel. I command an English frigate. I should have no choice but to blow your ship out of the water."

"I see," she uttered shortly, and turned her head away.

Myles watched her, his expression exceedingly grim. Then at last the mask slid in place.

"That, however, will not happen, will it, my love," he drawled in a voice no less dangerous for its velvet softness.

From somewhere Sabra found the courage to look up at him, to even summon a guileless smile.

"Surely not, captain. Indeed, how could it? I have my brother to think of now," she answered, drinking in Myles's beloved features. "Though I cannot but point out," she added with a spark of her old, sweet fire, "that in forbidding me to pursue the loathsome baronet in my own *Nemesis,* you have already violated the first tenet of a perfect husband. How did you put it? 'A man who understands and shares her need for independence. A man who, neither threatened nor intimidated by her strength of will, would stand with her at the helm'?"

A wry grin twitched at his lips. "You, Miss Tyree, have an unhappy knack for throwing my words back in my face," he observed, only then to assume an aspect of deadly seriousness. "Having failed you this once in that first and foremost precept, my love, I do most sincerely pray you will forgive me. But can you not, I warn you it will make no difference. No matter if I have to starve and beat you into submission, I *shall have* you as my wife."

"Shall you indeed," she retorted, awarding him a darkling glance. " 'Pon my faith, captain, you, like your proud King George, grow more tyrannical by the second. Belike you have forgot I am no knee-bender, content to be ruled. I am master of my own ship, no less than are you."

"The difference being that your vengeful lady, *Nemesis,* is, in the end, no match for the *Swan,*" he pointed out, leaning over her with a significance which was not lost on the sparkling-eyed beauty. "In so uneven a confrontation, can there be any doubt as to the final outcome?" Deliberately he lowered his head, pausing just long enough to take stock of the expression on her face, half anticipatory, half defiant. A smile touched his lips. "I would inevitably win, my beautiful Sabra. You must know that."

Sabra stared back into those marvelous, piercing eyes, and suddenly her pique and defiance vanished before a swift and bitter anguish. How dare she tell him that sometimes it is better to die than to lose that which one values most?

"Oh, Myles, I do love you," she whispered poignantly. Entwining her arms about his neck, she clung to him, wishing never to let go. "Always, Trevor. From the very first, and no matter what came between us. Indeed, I shall never cease to love you."

Startled, Myles instinctively returned her embrace, but his aspect was peculiarly grim as it came to him to note a certain hopelessness, a desperation almost, in the way she held him that would seem to augur ill for their future happiness. Then Sabra's lips sought his with a fierce longing that wiped all other considerations from his mind, and molding her supple beauty to the muscular contours of his lean body, she made love to him with all the boundless generosity of a woman who has at last learned her own heart.

No novice in the art of Eros, Myles had experienced the heady delights of passion in the arms of many women, but none previously had borne him to such heights of ecstasy as had his maddeningly elusive and yet bewitchingly responsive Sabra. All fire encased in ice, she had ever aroused in him the male instinct to conquer and possess, and with each succeeding battle of wills, he had gloried in the final capitulation, the bittersweet triumph of awakening her, body and spirit, to an ardor that had nearly consumed them both. Only gradually had it come to him that he desired far more from her than the fleeting satisfaction of successive faits accomplis. Indeed, it had been no small revelation that, in truth, he loved her and could not bring himself to try and imagine a life without her. Thus he had thought to put his newfound feelings to the touch—he had declared his love and Sabra had responded to his tenderness with a breathtaking passion that had both humbled and exalted him. And yet nothing could have prepared him for this—a Sabra wholly and unreservedly in love.

It was as if the other times he had lain with his beloved, been transported into intoxicating realms of sensual arousal and transcending completion, he had been granted only fleeting glimpses into the profound depths of the fiery passion waiting to be released within them both. Sabra, unencumbered by doubts and thus free at last of the bitter conflict between heart and mind, gave of herself uninhibitedly, initiating the free flow of passions between them with unself-conscious fervor.

A man less sure of his own masculinity might have been daunted by what Myles had awakened in her and what love had unbound, for she was sensual fluidity, her body moving over his with supple, feminine strength. She was molten tenderness, her mouth and lips learning the secret wellsprings of his need and administering to them with the female instinct for compassion. Her hands did not cleave to him as they had before, allowing him to bear her to the crescendoing heights of passion, but instead they guided his to those parts of her body in which resided her greatest sensitivity, the touchstones to her greatest arousal. Hers was a total act of love, a seeming unlimited desire to arouse and give pleasure and, in turn, to be aroused and receive like pleasure, so that together they were transported into ever greater and more rapturous planes of awareness. And when at last she mounted the fiery pinnacle of his desire, embraced his manhood within her woman's fleshy sheath, they moved as one in the all-encompassing union of shared transcendency. As one they peaked, their separate ecstasies of pleasure feeding and intensifying their joined consummation until at last they collapsed in one another's arms, the needs of their bodies fulfilled and their hearts and minds replete with an awed awareness of what together they had achieved.

Knowing that words could only sully the moment, Myles gathered his beloved to him, her head resting in the hollow of his shoulder, and held her close. Sighing deeply, Sabra closed her eyes, but neither succumbed to the soporific languor that weighted their limbs. In the aftermath of their lovemaking, each fell prey to the separateness of their thoughts, Myles, troubled at something he sensed in her but could not define, and Sabra, grief-stricken and yet resolved, fiercely hugging to her heart the memory of the blissful moment they had shared.

It was a great deal later that the captain lay awake in the bed, Sabra snuggled at his side, her quiet breathing deep and regular as though in sleep. At the soft, hesitant scratching at the door, he roused himself. Slipping noiselessly from beneath the comforter, he rose and quickly donned breeches and shirt before quietly letting himself out into the hall.

Behind him Sabra opened her eyes and watched him go. From beyond the door, left slightly ajar, a hurried, low-voiced exchange carried indistinctly to her ears. Then Myles came in again, closing the door softly behind him. A silent ache deep inside, she watched him finish dressing.

When at last he came to stand over her, she lay with her eyes open, staring up at him.

"I'm sorry, if I awakened you," he murmured. Reaching down, he curled a bright lock of her hair about his finger.

Smiling, Sabra shook her head, "You're leaving?"

"Leeks lost him," he said, as if that explained everything. "I'm not certain when I shall be back. I expect I shall have to see Ellsworth before I have myself rowed out to the ship."

Sabra's heart beat painfully as, settling on the edge of the bed, he gravely studied her face.

"There is something you have yet to know," he ventured at last. "While we were below, engaged in fighting off Channing and his men, it seems that Quinby erred in trying to make off with his wife. Having managed to lock Phoebe in a linen closet and then waited until Leeks had bolted to come to our assistance, he had the misfortune to encounter Jubal on the point of arriving."

Sabra uttered a startled gasp.

"Jubal—here? And Phoebe—Are they all right?"

"Can you doubt it?" queried the captain, with a whimsical smile. "Needless to say, Quinby shan't be troubling your friend Kitty anymore. During the ensuing fight, however, the child broke loose and fled the house. She's outside, in the hall. A trifle frozen and bedraggled after her misadventure, but well enough otherwise."

"Thank heavens!" murmured Sabra, sincerely glad for the girl. Somehow it was fitting that it had not fallen to Leeks to dispatch the mean-hearted gentleman's gentleman, she reflected. And now with Quinby gone, there would be little to stand in the way of their happiness.

Then all thoughts of Kitty and her lucky swain fled as she lifted her gaze to Myles.

"Promise you will be here when I get back?" he said, watching the emotions play across her face.

For the barest instant Sabra's glance wavered. Then she lifted shimmering eyes to his face.

"I promise, my darling," she whispered, reaching up to touch a hand to his lean cheek, "that I shall be waiting for you, praying always in my heart for the day that we may be reunited."

A frown flickered in the steel-gray depths of his eyes, and it seemed that he would say something. Then instead he caught her hand in his and pressed the palm to his lips.

"I have to go now." Rising from the bed, he leaned over to drop a kiss on her forehead, then, turning, he strode to

427

the door and left her.

Sabra gave forth a shuddering gasp. Staring blindly at the door through which Myles had vanished, she closed her fingers tightly over the palm of her hand.

Ellsworth's effusive greeting suffered a sudden check as he got a good look into his visitor's stern, set features.

"Good God, lad. What is it? You've the appearance of a man who has just learned the French are upon us."

Myles, smiling grimly, dropped a leather pouch on the desk.

"Channing's papers," he said without preamble. "I read enough on the carriage ride here to know he's on his way to Saint Thomas by way of the Summer Islands. I shall be leaving within the hour to go after him, Will, whether I have the admiral's permission or not."

"I see, and the devil be damned, is that it?" queried Ellsworth, observing his friend's lean, determined look with a jaundiced eye. He had seen that look before. "Sit down, captain, and we shall discuss what is best to be done."

"Sir Wilfred weighed anchor with the evening tide. I'm afraid I really haven't time for a lecture," Myles uttered coldly.

With ominous deliberation Ellsworth settled his knuckles on the desktop and leaned his bulk forward.

"You may indeed be the best man to command a ship I've ever known, and heir to a bloody dukedom in the bargain, but as of this moment I still outrank you. You will sit *down,* Captain Myles, and give me your report, if you please. Or I swear I shall have you hauled up before a board of inquiry. Is that understood?"

The two men clashed glances across the room, and for a moment it seemed that Ellsworth had lost the battle. Then unexpectedly the younger man relented, a wry glint tempering the hard cast of steel in his eye.

"You'd bloody well do it, too, would you not," he remarked, allowing himself just a trace of one of his rare affectionate smiles. "The same old Will. Always out to save me from my impetuous inclinations. But this time I really must insist on brevity. When you have had time to peruse those documents, you will see there is more at stake than any one man's desire for vengeance. Channing is in a fair way to establishing control of the Caribbean trade lanes. All the time he was working one side against the other, he has been in the process of setting up his own fleet of ships, with fortified strongholds on several of the key islands. In just a matter of four weeks, he was able to take better than a dozen American prizes and at least three English that I have heard of. I had the privilege of witnessing two of his armed vessels in action on my way to Saint Martin's. It was obvious he has use for neither hostages nor prisoners."

Ellsworth was hard put to meet the sudden, swift thrust of the other man's glance.

"The man is a cold-blooded butcher. And while you and I sit here talking, he is already well on his way to joining his fleet of murdering pirates. Are you prepared, my old friend, to have that on your conscience?"

Ellsworth, fortunately perhaps, was spared a retort by an importunate knock at the door, followed almost immediately by Lily Barrett's dramatic appearance in the private enclaves of her husband's study.

"Will, I beg you will forgive me for bursting in on you like this. However, there is someone here who simply must speak with Trevor without the least delay." Without waiting to give either man opportunity for a response, she turned and gestured to someone on the other side of the door. "Come, my dear," coaxed Lily. "I promise they will not eat you."

Myles, having risen to his feet along with Ellsworth, suddenly froze as a slight figure with huge, staring eyes, stepped hesitantly into the room.

"Captain Myles," burst from trembling lips. "Thank God I have found you."

In a single, swift stride, Myles reached the frightened girl. His hands gripping her shoulders, he steadied her.

"Kitty, what is it?" he queried sharply. "You needn't be afraid to speak up. You are in the presence of friends, I promise you."

Kitty Quinby visibly got a hold of herself.

"Beggin' your pardon, sir, but I've come about Miss Sabra. She's gone, captain. Not ten minutes after you left."

"Gone? Gone where? Kitty, you must tell me everything you know."

"Y-yes, sir," Kitty stammered. "But I doesn't know all that much, truly I doesn't. Save only that when she sent for me to come to her, she'd been crying. An' she talked real strange. It give me the shivers to listen to her, like maybe she didn't have no thought of comin' back alive. Put a roll of the flimsies in me hand, she did, what fair took me breath away. 'For your wedding, dearest Kitty,' says she, smiling real sad like." The brown eyes grew suddenly round. "No one ain't never give me nothin' before. I expect Miss Sabra has the heart of an angel. Then she tells me to wait until morning when I was to send a boy to Captain Ellsworth in Barclay with a note to come fetch me."

Nervously the girl glanced from one to the other of the tautly expectant faces.

"I don't know if I be doin' the right thing. But I couldn't wait, not with knowin' in me 'eart Miss Sabra were in some kind of trouble. Beggin' your pardon, captain, but it seemed to me maybe you should have this a mite sooner than late. Miss Sabra asked me to see it put into your hand when next I seen you."

Gravely the girl handed him the missive from Sabra.

It seemed to Lily, watching with suspended breath, that the strong, slender fingers hesitated ever so slightly before breaking the seal. And certainly there could be no denying that the lines about the stern mouth deepened as, unfolding the delicate sheets of fine linen paper, a ring tumbled out into the palm of his hand. The muscle leaping along the lean line of his jaw, he began silently to read. At his harshly uttered oath, her heart nearly stopped.

Staring at the others without seeing them, he slowly crumpled the paper in his fist. "The insane little fool!" he muttered softly to himself.

"Trevor, for God's sake —" thundered Ellsworth, his eyes worried. He watched, fascinated, the tall officer going from stricken silence to cool intensity of purpose.

"I fear you will have to convene your board of inquiry after all, Captain Ellsworth." The gray eyes, cold-flecked and unreadable, Myles looked at him. "Miss Tyree, it would seem, has taken it upon herself to go after Channing."

"Myles, come back here!" bellowed Ellsworth.

Halting, his hand on the door, the captain kept his eyes straight before him.

"I shall place myself at your disposal upon my return, captain," he stated coldly and opened the door. "Till that time, I bid you good-eve."

"Will, *do* something," Lily blurted, wincing at the sound of the door pushed firmly shut.

"I am, my dear," Ellsworth grimly rejoined. Drawing a sheet of paper toward him, he sank heavily into his chair. "I am informing the admiral in my judgment Miss Tyree has fulfilled the terms of her brother's release and should, in consequence, be granted the immunity requested by His Grace of Waincourt for her covert acts. What's more, my dear, I am taking it upon myself to sail the *Marbelle* in pursuit of that damned, hotheaded young fool. Pray God I shall not be too late to prevent him doing something he will regret for all the rest of his days!"

Old Matthias Bolt, the sailing master, was heard to say the captain was in a rare taking; and, indeed, the frigate *Black Swan* seemed destined to be dismasted as more can-

431

vas was laid on in the fury of the prevailing westerlies. With the hurricane season just behind them, they had been fortunate that thus far the weather seemed holding, the winds steady out of the southwest, and Myles was apparently determined to wring as much headway from existing conditions as the pitching frigate could be made to bear.

Myles, pacing the weather deck, seemed as driven as his ship. For nearly three days running, he had gone with little more than brief snatches of sleep. Prowling his beat along the taffrail during the endless days of clawing to windward and appearing on the quarterdeck for brief periods at each sounding of the bell throughout the nights, he gave the appearance of one possessed. Only Leeks, hovering in the background, could have told what compelled Myles to work himself toward what promised inevitably to be a state of utter exhaustion, but grim-faced and unapproachable as his captain, none dared to ask.

Bolt, standing at the helm, was the first openly to remark the distant sound of thunder.

"Not thunder, I fear, Mr. Bolt," said the captain, staring fixedly off the forward bow.

As the cry of "Deck there! Two sail to the starboard bow!" rang out crisp from overhead, he could feel the others look at him, wondering to themselves. Clasping a hand in the netting, he flung back his head to peer aloft at the lookout.

"Can you make them out, Steadway?" he called above the crash and boom of the ship plunging through the waves.

"A brigantine, sir, twenty-four guns. I know 'er, captain. It's the *Cyrus*, newly commissioned out of Bristol. T'other's a schooner of sixteen guns, flying the Stars and Stripes. An' less I be dreamin', captain, she's the *Nemesis* what be returned from the deep!"

Crawford, the first lieutenant, who had been promoted one rung in the ladder with Inness's untimely demise, gave a low whistle. "The American's either a very brave man or a fool," he commented, half to himself.

"Unless you've something constructive to offer, Mr. Crawford," remarked his superior in chilling accents, I suggest you pipe up the hands and order the galley fires doused. We'll come up with them within the hour, if the wind holds."

Leeks grinned humorlessly. There was no way the red-faced second-in-command could know that they were about to fire on the captain's lady. But *he* knew. And it'd be a sad day for the captain when the smoke finally cleared.

As the frigate made under full sail toward the distant scene of battle, her captain kept the glass fixed on the two vessels. At first, hardly daring to breathe, he watched the foolhardy schooner harass and flee the larger ship with a reckless daring that should have earned his admiration—should have, that is, had the maneuvers not been performed under the command of an impossible green-eyed vixen. Then it came to him that there was a pattern to the schooner's madness. On a sudden hunch, he raised the glass to view beyond the embattled vessels. All at once he froze. A grim smile thinned his lips as he glimpsed the ruffle of white against the blue ocean swells in the distance. He did not need Steadway's cry of "Land off the starboard bow" to know they were approaching the Summer Islands or to realize exactly how deadly was the game his fearless love was playing.

She was goading the other ship's captain, daring him to come after her, like a fox luring the hound from the den. Only in this case, Myles was tinglingly aware that the fox was coaxing the unsuspecting *Cyrus* toward something— the broad coral reef embracing the islands just below the water's surface on the north, west, and south, and in some places reaching out into the sea for as far as ten miles or more. His lips drawn to a thin line, he watched, spellbound, as the little schooner dashed into the range of the bow chaser, then jibed and bound for the open water on a broad reach away from her snarling pursuer. Clawing about to the windward, she dashed ahead, spewing her defiance with the puny nine-pounder set to the stern. Then again she paid off, wearing ship till, running free, she shot off broad on the starboard bow, skimming the waves like some breathtakingly graceful creature of flight, while the *Cyrus*, no mean sailor, appeared by comparison to lumber and wallow after her in dogged determination, apparently unaware of the danger lurking beneath the waves dead ahead.

Matthias Bolt's voice, edged with concern, broke across Myles's concentration, a warning that they must either shorten sails directly or wear ship themselves. The rest was lost in the sudden roar from the lower deck as the excited cry rang out that the brigantine had struck.

In a matter of seconds the trim vessel was a shambles of toppled masts and falling rigging. Even across the distance Myles imagined he heard the shrieks of men pinned beneath the fallen rubble and the terrible groan of the ship, mortally stricken, her bilges filling with the roar of rushing water as she listed drunkenly to the starboard.

The explosion of her magazine made any attempts at rescue fruitless. Broken in two and engulfed in flames, she would be gone in a matter of seconds, taking all on board to the bottom with her.

"Captain, sir! Shall we shorten sail?" penetrated the din of his own vessel flying dangerously close to a similar fate.

Barking the order to shorten sail and prepare to come about, he raised the glass to his eye, found the *Nemesis*, standing off at a discreet distance, apparently to observe its victim suffer the final death throes. His heart pounding in his chest he swept the schooner from stem to stern, till at last he came to the poop deck. The glass froze, and his breath lanced through his throat like a white-hot blade, as he saw her amidst the jubilant figures of her crew, staring not at the final death throes of the *Cyrus*, but at the *Swan*.

His face, seemingly chiseled from marble, he lowered the glass and snapped it shut.

"Mr. Crawford," he uttered in a voice, all the more

chilling for its utter lack of emotion. "Beat to quarters and prepare for action!"

Even as he gave the order to alter course, he saw the privateer spread her sails and put about close-hauled to the windward. The fool, he thought, conscious of the pressure building beneath his breastbone as he watched the trim little schooner set her prow for the open sea. Had she chosen to make for one of the countless narrow channels that wound through the welter of islands and barren rocky crags, she might have stood a chance of escape. In a chase in open water, however, the advantage must lie inevitably with the larger, fleeter *Swan*. And once in range, a single shot alone from one of the twelve-pounders would be enough to cave in her sides!

As he shouted the order for the gun crew manning the bow-chaser to load and prepare to fire on his signal, he kept asking himself why? Why this way, when almost certain escape awaited her to the leeward?

No more than two cable-lengths away, Myles drew his sword and with a feeling of having entered a nightmare from which there could be no awakening, raised it with cold calculation over his head. The muscles in his arm tensed, and the blade quivered in the air as if impatient to descend.

The topman's excited cry of "Deck there! Sail astern!" rang like a cruel hoax in his ears. "She's British, captain. The *Marbelle*. Captain Ellsworth."

"She's signaling, captain," came Crawford's voice hard upon the topman's. "Cease action!"

Myles could feel the sweat break out in rivulets beneath his shirt as carefully he lowered the sword and, sheathing it, gave the order for the gun crews to stand down. Dashing the sweat from his eyes with his sleeve, he lifted the glass to his eye with hands that shook and brought it to bear on the fleeing *Nemesis*.

Bitterly he cursed the fate that decreed his last view of

the beautiful Sabra should be that of a trim figure standing proudly erect, her glorious hair loose and streaming like a red-gold banner on the wind. As though carved from stone, she stared aft at the *Swan*, bearing down on her like a vengeful god. The image would haunt him through the aching eternity of his life and always with the same, tormenting question — *Why?*

Epilogue

It was October in the year 1782, a year since Cornwallis's surrender to Washington at Yorktown and six months since Sir George Rodney's decisive defeat of de Grasse in the Battle of the Saintes. To Myles the three days of terrible carnage which had taken place off Dominica seemed much farther removed in time than that. Marked down by a sharpshooter in the final hours of battle, he had yet somehow managed to keep his wits about him long enough to see a powerful French seventy-four strike to his colors. The weeks which had followed were like one endless nightmare of pain and suffering, from which he had finally emerged, victorious, but battered in body and soul. Against the protests of the numerous physicians employed by his grandsire, the duke, to oversee his recovery, he had booked passage for himself, and for Leeks and Kitty, who would not be separated from him, in a packet bound from London for the West Indies, for Saint Vincent and the cotton and sugarcane plantations left him by his father, and perhaps for a measure of solace for his embittered spirit.

Standing in the doorway overlooking the verandah of the caretaker's house, he let his gaze wander out over the long sweep of sugarcane, weaving in the wind, to the narrow streets and the houses of Kingstown, and finally, beyond, to the glint of sunlight playing on the masts of a schooner moored in the bay. A sharp pang knifed unexpectedly through him as something about the trim new-

437

comer struck a painful chord of memory. Taken unawares by the sudden rending of old, never-healed wounds, he tore his eyes away. He had been a fool to believe that somehow amidst the tranquil beauty of the Caribbean he might find surcease to the gnawing within, the restlessness as boundless as the endlessly moving sea itself, which filled him with discontent, made him yearn for something always beyond his reach. He had been better to remain on the doorsteps of the admiralty until at last they had seen fit to give him a ship, than to suffer the long hours with little more than his thoughts for company—his memories of the seductively beautiful Sabra!

As if her image, perfect in every detail, had been burned into his brain, he had still, after nearly two years, only to close his eyes to see her. Sabra, her ivory skin like fine silk to the touch and her hair, a glorious mass of burnished gold falling in a riot of waves down her slender back. Sabra, gazing up at him out of green, bewitching eyes, promising to wait, a prayer in her heart for the day when they might be reunited.

"Damn her to bloody hell!" he cursed aloud, his voice harsh in his own ears. She had been as false as her promise. How ironic, that, even knowing that, he had yet been prepared to give up everything for her! No doubt he should be grateful Ellsworth's arrival off the coral reefs of the Summer Islands had come in time to spare him that final sacrifice of duty and honor, he reflected cynically. And, indeed, in that split second before the *Marbelle* was sighted, as he had stood with the blade, quivering at the ready in his hand, he had known he would not bring it slashing down, had known with bitter certainty it was not in him to give the command that had inevitably to bring destruction down on the cursed *Nemesis*.

Furious with himself for allowing his thoughts to dwell on the woman whose daring and enticing beauty had irretrievably taken possession of his heart, he wrenched his

438

eyes away from the blue shimmer of water to the land, which held no appeal for him. Then bitterly he cursed again.

God help him, it would have been better had the French marksman possessed a surer aim. Better to be dead than to be so haunted by Sabra Tyree's memory that he imagined he saw her coming toward him now across the down — a slender girl dressed in flowing white, her glorious red-gold hair streaming, unfettered, like a banner in the wind. He must be mad, he thought, bewildered that this spectre come to torment him should be accompanied this time by a tall man with an easy, supple strength about him, a man vaguely familiar to him.

The sweet peal of her voice calling out to him only served to enhance the belief that, indeed, he was grown mad from dreaming of her. And, still, he stood as if paralyzed by this tormentingly real facsimile, beheld her in her eagerness, break into a run, saw her lips pronounce his name, until at last she drew near enough for him to make out the shimmer of eyes as green as the still, mysterious depths of the sea itself.

Coming to the bottom of the three stone steps ascending to the verandah, she faltered to a halt and stared up at him.

"Myles?" she queried breathlessly. When still he said nothing, but only stared at her, his face seemingly carved from stone, the lovely light in her eyes dimmed ever so slightly. "My darling, I beg you will not look at me as if you did not know me. Or, worse, as if you did not truly see me at all. It is I, Sabra, and I have brought my brother Wes to see you."

As if he could not bear the sight of her, he swung sharply away. Bitterly he cursed as his shattered body betrayed him and he staggered, his hand clutching at the door frame.

Instantly she was at his side, her face as white as his as she sought to draw his arm over her shoulder to help steady him. He stiffened, the blood leaping in his veins with the realization that here was no phantom, but Sabra Tyree in reality, as spirited and lovely as ever he remembered her. Unwilling to trust himself in her sweet, bewildering presence, he shook off her hand and crossed stiffly to the balustrade to stand with his face turned toward the sea, his vision strangely blurred.

"Why?" The single, hoarse utterance seemed forced from him. Then carefully he turned to look at her, managing somehow to summon the old, faintly mocking smile. "You must pardon me if I seem more than a trifle discomposed at discovering the master of the *Nemesis* on my doorstep. Indeed, I cannot but wonder why, now, after all this time, you should suddenly choose to materialize."

He experienced a measure of grim satisfaction, yet tempered with a heady sense of having drunk a potent wine, as he beheld a slim hand, like a frightened bird, flutter uncertainly to her breast.

"But I-I told you. In the letter. The girl, Kitty—she did give it to you?"

"Yes, she gave it to me. It was that which sent me flying after you."

"Then—then I don't understand." Unable to bear the shuttered coldness of his eyes, she stifled a small cry and took a halting step toward him. "Myles, it is over. Or will be as soon as the terms of peace are agreed upon and my country stands at last, an independent and sovereign nation on an equal footing with yours. Don't you see, my darling? It was the only way I could come to you—free!" she uttered passionately. "The things that must inevitably have kept us separate swept away. The wounds of misunderstanding and mistrust healed and made whole again. We need no longer be enemies, you and I, one or the other forced to compromise loyalties or beliefs, honor or integrity. We may be joined as equals, with neither shame nor remorse. Faith, *why* do you not say something?"

"It would appear you have said it all," he answered cynically, his eyes between slitted eyelids enough to make her blood run cold. "What, exactly, would you have me add, my love? That your letter was full of half-truths and cleverly distorted promises?"

"What half-truths? What promises?" she demanded, a spark of the old fiery tempter flickering at last in the gaze flying up to meet his in stark incredulity.

A hard glimmer of a smile curled his lip.

"Come now. Would you have me, in truth, believe you have forgotten? Words of trust, unshakable faith—love—from a woman who no sooner than my back was turned, ran out on me. Had you truly loved me, does it not seem odd that you could not bring yourself to tell me what troubled you? But then, you never could quite find it in your heart to place your trust in me, could you, Sabra? Had you done, you might have believed that together we could discover a more equitable solution to the dilemma you foresaw. Have you any notion of the damnable position in which you and your noble sentiments *landed* me?"

Suddenly no longer able to endure the fierce pressure in his chest, he grasped her savagely by the arms and dragged her to him.

"Have you the least idea how close I came to blasting you out of the water? Where was your noble-sounding sentiment then, *ma mie?* Did it not once occur to you that I must be forced to choose between love and duty as you hove to within range of my guns?"

He was shaking her so hard that her face was a blur and she could not have answered had she wanted to. Then all at once he stopped, his eyes devouring her with a hunger that made her knees turn to water.

"You headstrong, impossible little fool!" he muttered thickly. "If ever you put me through anything remotely approaching the agony of that terrible moment, I shall

441

gladly wring your stubborn neck. *Is* that understood?"

"Y-yes, Myles," she quavered, her head yet swimming from the fierce shaking she had undergone. "But you must see that I *could* not have done otherwise. I-I had my orders, *my* duty, no less than did you."

"And if I am fool enough to grant you that, still it changes nothing," he retorted, hard-pressed not to give in to her melting look and crush her to his chest. "*Why* did you not choose to escape me in any one of the narrow channels in the reef? Surely you knew you stood not a chance against the *Swan* in the open sea?"

All at once her head came up, her delightfully pointed chin jutting at a defiant angle.

"And what chance should I have stood as a prisoner in a British prison, captain?" she uttered frostily. "For that must inevitably have been the fate of an American privateer trapped in the coral lagoons of the Summer Islands. Or had you forgot they belonged to the British crown?"

"No, I had not forgot. I assumed you must find refuge amidst the numerous uninhabited islands."

"Oh, indeed, and for how long were we to wait till you finally gave us up? Till our water was gone, our food depleted? And where, captain, were we to replenish our supplies sufficiently to make the voyage back? Perhaps you intended us to petition the governor for permission to use his wells for that purpose?"

At last a wry smile flickered behind the steely glint of his eyes. For, in truth, the only fresh water to be got on the islands, devoid either of lake or stream, was from the wells sunk by the British into the soft bed of coral.

"I expect, my love, I should have had you do just as you did, had I thought of that particular."

Taking heart from the almost imperceptible leavening of his mood, she leaned provocatively against his hard chest and gazed demurely up at him through the thick veil of her eyelashes.

"And do you not think further, captain, that you might

442

find it in your heart to forgive me for being a privateer and a hopeless rebel, if I can find it in mine to forgive *you* for being a marquess, an earl, and a baron three times over, as well as heir apparent to a powerful dukedom?" Suddenly she looked at him, as sober as before she had been gently teasing. "Trevor, I am so deeply sorry about Ferdy," she murmured. "Wes told me how he died, at your back as you fought to repel boarders from your decks. Indeed, everyone on shipboard knew. Why, Myles? Why, after all those years of shielding him from the rest of the world, did the duke send his heir as envoy on so perilous a mission? Indeed 'twould seem he came close to losing both of you at Saint Martin.

A faint whimsical smile softened the stern cast of his mouth, and Sabra's heart almost skipped a beat as she drank in his beloved features. And yet how pale he looked, she thought, and how thin! But then, Lily's letter had said he had suffered terribly from the wound that had come so near to taking him from her forever. With a pang she noted the silver at his temples and had to bite her lip to keep from betraying the sudden ache in her heart that she had not been at his side during his weeks of torment. With an effort she hid her pity, which he would have found insupportable, and attended to his words.

"You've a great deal to learn about your future in-law," he was saying, "do you believe for one moment he would shield any prospective heir to the title. There was never any choice but that Ferdy should go—not with so much of importance for the realm riding on success or failure. The heirs of Waincourt are expected to take risks if the possible end should justify it, but *not*, my dear, as regards the as yet, unborn, generations. In that respect, you loomed as a danger far greater than the French. Indeed, my grandsire would have moved heaven and earth rather than let Ferdy fall to the machinations of a grasping female out to snare his fortune for the benefit of an unruly mob of rebellious Americans."

"Oh, indeed?" uttered Sabra in awful tones. "Then perhaps you will inform your grandsire for me that *this* unruly American cares not a whit for his fortune and, further, that were it not that I am quite sure my happiness depends on it, I should choose to marry the meanest beggar, the most common of commoners, than to wed the heir to Waincourt. *He,* no doubt, would prefer your beautiful Lorelei as brood mare for his precious future dukes!" she ended bitterly.

A quizzical glint came to the suspiciously sleepy gray eyes.

"I shall, of course, do as you ask, my love," he drawled obligingly. "However, I think I should point out that it was at my grandfather's request that I was able to remove your brother from the confines of the *Jersey.* Indeed, he was not released sooner only because I was powerless to rescind Channing's orders until the duke's written instructions finally arrived from England on the night of our memorable stay in Rab Wilkins's cellar. As to the beautiful Lorelei, you will pardon me, no doubt, do I confess that I haven't the slightest notion what you are talking about."

Sabra's startled "Oh!" at the middle of that lengthy speech was succeeded by a feeling of chagrin at having been caught out again on the wrong foot, which, in turn, gave way to a hard glitter of suspicion at the completion of his final words.

"Haven't the slightest notion of what I am talking about?" she echoed, attempting unsuccessfully to pull away. "And yet I assure you it was no figment of my imagination that you pronounced her name in your delirium that night in Rab Wilkins's cellar, *and,* I might add, with a great deal of feeling."

"And what, might I ask, was the context of this puzzling outburst?"

Aware of the blood rising hotly to her cheeks, Sabra

wished she had thought to keep her tongue judiciously between her teeth.

"Well, I am not entirely sure I remember exactly," she hedged. "Something about her not being real and that she should not be allowed to escape you this time as she had in the past."

All at once his dark head went back and the vibrant sound of his laugher rang out across the down. Then, sobering, he drew her firmly into his arms.

"And nor shall she — ever again," he promised, paralyzing her with his fiercely tender look. "The Lorelei, my little gudgeon, is a mythical siren reputed to perch atop a great rock on the Rhine for the sole purpose of luring unsuspecting mariners to a dreadful fate. Just so did you seduce me with a single look into impossibly sea-green eyes. *You* are my inescapable siren, my indescribably beautiful Lorelei."

His mouth covering hers in a kiss that gave vent to all the terrible longing in his heart, the anguish of two years of believing she was forever lost to him, silenced whatever answer she might have made to this startling revelation. With a groan she gave in to the sweep of fire spreading through her veins and, clinging to him, returned his passionate embrace with all her fierce young strength.

When at last he released her, she was weak and trembling, and yet imbued with a wondrous warmth, a happiness so intense she was almost afraid to believe she was not simply dreaming it. Still, she could not deny the strong beat of his heart beneath her cheek or the sweet marvel of his arms wrapped securely about her. In truth she had at last found her safe harbor, her one and only love. And if there lay troubled waters before them, as indeed there must in a marriage between English nobility and staunch American individualism, then together they would find a way to weather the storm. For, indeed, had not Myles himself said that the man who won her heart

445

would be neither threatened nor intimidated by her need for independence, but would stand with her at the helm?

She would hold him to that pledge, and somehow they would find an equitable solution to the problems that confronted them, she thought, as together they left the verandah to meet her brother, Wesley, coming toward them at a judiciously leisurely gait.

<u>FREE</u> Preview Each Month and $ave

Zebra has made arrangements for you to preview 4 brand new HEARTFIRE novels each month...FREE for 10 days. You'll get them as soon as they are published. If you are not delighted with any of them, just return them with no questions asked. But if you decide these are everything we said they are, you'll pay just $3.25 each—a total of $13.00 (a $15.00 value). **That's a $2.00 saving each month off the regular price.** Plus there is NO shipping or handling charge. These are delivered right to your door absolutely free! There is no obligation and there is no minimum number of books to buy.

TO GET YOUR FIRST MONTH'S PREVIEW... Mail the Coupon Below!